FATED FRENZY

PLANETARY PAIRING PROGRAM AQUA 01

GIGI ZARBI

AUTHOR'S NOTE

Firstly, this book discusses themes some may find disturbing. For an exhaustive list, please check: gigizarbi.com/warnings

This multicultural romance was sensitivity read by the many ethnicities represented (the author is Greek and Persian), but that does not mean it's perfect. There are mentions of inequity and societal issues because Black, transgender, and all systematically excluded lives matter. Even while mentally vacationing far, far away from Earth.

Lastly, Nala, the FMC, intentionally lacks a thorough description. Her surname, Williams, was chosen because it is equally distributed between Black and white people in the Southern US. This was chosen for inclusivity and NOT intended to minimize BIPOC or varied-sizing experiences.

Nala's only physical characteristics mentioned are: brown eyes, curly hair, curves, & stretch marks.

Happy reading!
<3 Gigi

NEPTUNE CHEAT SHEETS

AMOROSO: FATED BONDS/TETHERS
KONTROLÜ: DOMINANT IN MATING RING
RIFT: TELEPORT
PRESTIGE: POWER LEVEL

TITANS: MOST POWERFUL IMMORTALS, ETERNAL
ARE ONE OF THE EIGHT CLASSIFICATIONS BELOW
GODS: CHILDREN OF TITANS
SUPREMA + SUPREME: RULERS OF GALAXY, SUPREMAE

CLASSIFICATIONS: DEMON, DRAGON, FAE, MAGE, SERAPH, TURNU, VAMPIRE, ZOATALA

SUBSPECIES: VARYING SUBGROUPS OF THE ABOVE CLASSIFICATIONS

TURN PAGE FOR SPECIFICS >

CLASSIFICATION GUIDE

common

♡ ZOATALA

200-500 YEARS
SHIFT: FULLY + EITHER HALF
25% MAINTAIN ^ FEATURES 24-7

[SOME] SUBSPECIES:
AGNATHA, ARTHROPODA, AVES,
CEPHALOPOD, EPONA, GRIFF, HYDRA, ILLÏ,
LEONE, MANATEER, PHIBA, REPTILIA,
SELKIE, SIARC, SPHINX, WHALEN+

♡ FAE

1-2 MILLENNIA
CANNOT SHIFT
WINGED SUBSPECIES:
ASWANG, PIXIE, QUIG, WALLOP

WINGLESS SUBSPECIES:
AURA, BANSHEE, ELF, GOBLIN,
NYMPH, OGRE

♡ DEMON

LIFESPAN VARIES
SHIFT: UPPER HALVES

SUBSPECIES:
INCUBUS, GASHADOKURO,
GHOUL, GORGON, MINOTAUR,
SUCCUBUS, TANDUK, ZOMBIE

♡ MAGE

1-2 MILLENNIA
SHIFT: 25% CAN

SUBSPECIES:
PHOENIX, ROOK, SOURCE,
UNICORN, VODÚ, WARDLE,
WITCH, WOLVEN

scarcer

TURNU ♡

ETERNAL
SHIFT: INTO ANYTHING

SUBSPECIES:
BAAKO, NU

*ONLY CARRY MENSAH FAMILY NAME

DRAGON ♡

ETERNAL
SHIFT: FULLY + EITHER HALF +
SPIRIT

NO SUBSPECIES

*ONLY CARRY DRAGO FAMILY NAME

SERAPH ♡

ETERNAL
SHIFT: LOWER HALVES
*COMMON ON NEPTUNE

SUBSPECIES:
AQRABUAMELU, CENTAUR,
KULULLU, SATYR, SIREN, ZIM

VAMPIRE ♡

LIFESPAN VARIES
SHIFT: 5% CAN

SUBSPECIES:
CHIROPTERA, REVENANT,
VOOK, WRAITH, ADZE,
DÓLGR, URSUS

Pronunciation Guide

Character Names:

- Athanatos | "ah-tha-nah-tos"
- Avexeidros | "ah-vex-ie-dro-s"
- Olorun | "O-low-rune"
- Ryloh | "ry-low"
- Seong | "sung"
- Simargl | "si-mar-guhl"
- Timoset | "team-oh-set"
- Yemaya | "ye-my-ah"
- Yu-Jin | "you-gin"
- Zusicia | "zoo-is-sia"

Places:

- Bahasa | "bah-ha-sah"
- Ookea | "oo-key-ah"
- Thalla | "tha-lah"
- Uru | "uu-roo"

Titles:

- Amoroso | "amor-roo-so"
- Kontrolü | "control-loo"
- Uktena | "ook-tehn'-ah"
- Supremae | "sup-re-may"
- Turnu | "turn-oo"
- Zoatala | "zo-ah-tall-ah"

WEEK ONE

My Tuesday morning waitressing shift at Shuckers' Diner kicked-off the same as every other: a copy-and-paste of the last decade I'd been trapped in my hometown of Bluffton, South Carolina. I felt like a puppet in my own forced show. My limbs and mouth were following along, but my heart and head were no longer here. Which was fitting since I spouted lies constantly. At least my nose didn't elongate each time I said, "I'm good."

Greeting my first and only table at 7:37am with a steaming pot of beans, I knew the woman wasn't local, but there wasn't anything out of the ordinary about her. She was likely in her mid-to-late twenties based on her pink hair, tattoos, and teensy denim shorts. Miss was abnormally tall, but I was too. So, I didn't give her a second glance.

That was my fatal mistake.

I should've noticed the marks on her neck weren't tattoos, but gills.

I should've noticed it wasn't just a case, her phone actually was an oyster shell.

I should've noticed the teal sparkle in those eyes of hers was unnatural.

However, I hadn't. None of those details registered until we weren't in South Carolina anymore. My shift lasted seven minutes before she palmed my bum when I passed her table. And *poof*. I was abducted.

Who knew an ass grab could teleport?

The typical chorus of cicadas and antique fans was interchanged with an indie beat and the low hum of central air-conditioning. One blink and the moss decorated trees were gone, replaced with a pink room of sorts. A space I hardly had the chance to take in because I was too busy losing my forking noodles.

Aliens.

Alien abduction.

I knew that immediately.

However, everything I knew of extraterrestrials was a lie. From Steven Spielberg to the US Government, they hadn't prepared me properly. There was no flying saucer with flashing lights. No creepy bug-eyed creatures. Not even blue barbarians with "cooties."

It was just me and Pinky, my unassuming harasser, stuck in a horrified staring contest as she ripped her milky hand from my asscheek. Dread seeped through every ounce of my being as my heart attempted to flee its cage. I was discombobulated, it was difficult to string together a coherent reaction as her human-seeming face shifted into a pained, queasy smile.

Are you dying? Is it the reason behind her assuaging look?

Hmm…

Difficult to say for sure.

My vision remained rosy, trapped behind a filter. Each flutter of my lashes felt like an eternity. As though I was suspended in this awful moment. Trapped in my panic. Even my staccato breaths dragged on. *And on.*

The twitching of her burgundy gills ripped me back to the present. At least, it *felt* like the present. Maybe this was just another wine induced nightmare.

It's just a dream, yeah. Wake up!

Suddenly, Pinky stabbed a needle into my neck. My last thought as I face planted against a magenta cushion was a dated memory of my ex-best friend's voice saying, *"I told you it was time to leave that dusty diner, bitch!"*

Jolting awake, the realization I wasn't in bed collided with my consciousness.

From sheer panic, I forced my ears to adjust to reality first. There was a raucous Australian voice overwhelming soft background music. The tambourine-heavy beat jogged my memory. Ass grab, kidnapping, drugging… *Right, right, right.*

Then came sensations. Overall, my organs seemed intact. There weren't any restraints, no gag. Not even the needle left a mark from what I could tell with my fingertip's exploration. The only soreness was from how I'd collapsed like a pretzel.

When my eyes joined the party and cracked open, it looked as though I was in a millennial pink waiting room of sorts. It reminded me of a modern doctor's office. *Did Cupid work here?*

As if the peony walls and 3-D heart decorations weren't enough, there was an opaque hibiscus film stuck to the oversized windows. Unfortunately, the tint only allowed some treetops through, making it impossible to discern the view beyond. The reception desk, although a glossy cream, was also plastered in hearts. Behind it, a receptionist in a three-piece suit with blonde hair was talking into an oversized shell.

I repeat, a conch shell. A shell-phone, if you will.

Blondie, the Aussie, and I locked eyes quite a few times. We were the only two present and I anticipated some reaction to my awoken state. But he just continued on with his idle chit-chat about grapes. I know, *grapes*?! Each time our gazes met; he flicked his baby blues away. Yeah, it was mighty rude, but my Southern manners wouldn't allow me to interrupt his conversation. No matter how badly I needed to know what in the name of almighty Gandalf was going on here.

It was infuriating he resembled a human, 100% normal, homo sapien. You could drop him into Australia, and no one would know he was an extraterrestrial.

Scanning the space, my eyes caught on a water dispenser in the far corner, and I flung myself toward it. Blondie shared the most, 'bless your heart' look while I chugged and glugged. My mouth was drier than a week at Burning Man, so who knew how long I'd been out. While guzzling my tenth or eleventh infuriatingly tiny paper cone, the door behind the reception desk creaked open.

To reveal my captor.

Pinky's ivory suit matched Blondie's, a stark contrast to her teensy shorts from before. I was questioning how the pair looked *so* ordinary when she finally spoke. "Welcome, Nightingale Williams." Her lilt was firm, nonplus, without any accent in her American English.

"Why am I here?" My voice was little more than a rasp, so I didn't push it. Although my noggin urged my lips to spout ten more questions.

"I promise to explain. Please, come in," she replied nonchalantly, as if she hadn't just harassed, abducted, then sedated me.

Proceeding with caution, I ambled into the dimly lit, grey walled office. There were no visible threats, it resembled any regular shmegular workroom. Unlike the lobby, it lacked the Valentine's theme, except for the opaque film blocking the view. Taking one of the two ivory barrel chairs facing her executive setup, I heard Pinky say to the receptionist, "Burt, could you please raise the wards until we are finished?" *Aliens have Sesame Street names?* How bizarre.

Wait, wards? As in magical shield wotsits?

When Pinky closed the door, the lamp on her desk brightened, granting me a clearer view of the three slash-like gills on each side of her neck. "Nice to meet you, Nightingale. My name is Aphrodite," she said with an inscrutable expression. *As in the Greek Goddess of Love?* Even odder.

Despite sitting opposite my alien abductor, I wasn't frightened. My Spidey-senses weren't sensing any danger. She'd had the ideal opportunity to loot my organs when I was down and didn't. Maybe it was crazy to lower my haunches, but she wasn't giving killer vibes.

"Nala," I corrected, idly tapping on my bare knees from nerves. "I prefer my middle name." Aphrodite didn't need to know it was the name I rebranded myself with at the age of four, back when I was obsessed with *The Lion King*. The only people who used my birthname were my parents and six siblings. There were no cutesy nicknames for Nightingale. Just Gale, and you couldn't get more country bumpkin than *Gale*.

A forced grin slashed through her pale face. "Although you managed to somehow alter your driver's license and credit cards without the properly filed paperwork, you and I both know your lone legal name is 'Nightingale.'" My jaw unhinged from surprise as she continued, "Your childhood friend, Isaiah Taylor, calls you, 'Gale the snail,' if I am not mistaken. Correct?" Instead of replying, a frown teased my lips. The mention of my ex-bestie, despite the horrific nickname he bestowed, left an ache in my chest. Although we weren't on the greatest of terms, it was disheartening to question if I'd see him again.

"You will see your friends and family again, I assure you. Since you are keen to know why you were brought here, I will cut to it. I have a once in a lifetime opportunity to offer, Nala. First things first, you are no longer on Earth. We are currently on Neptune."

"The planet?" I yelled, because *what*? Burt's chuckle permeated through the door, so I lowered my volume. "How did you pinch my ass and tote me across the galaxy, exactly?"

"We will cover that, there are a few items I must confirm with you first," Aphrodite replied. I couldn't keep my frustration contained, nodding with a frown. "So, just to ensure I have the correct person. You are thirty-two-years, single, and never married. Although in the prime of your fertility—"

"Pardon?" I couldn't help but interrupt, she went from zero to one thousand.

"Mortal femmes are in their prime child rearing years between the ages of thirty-two and thirty-five. Although pregnancies during this period can sometimes cause physical complications, it is the ideal timeline psychologically. That is a statement of fact." When I narrowed my eyes, she added, "You have never birthed any children, correct?"

I canted my head, refusing to affirm nor deny. However, my gut insisted Aphrodite knew my childless truth from how her seafoam eyes narrowed. She then said, "You also have never successfully been in a happy long-term relationship." *Woah, more than a bit harsh there.* The 'successfully' and 'happy' from her lips were missiles which obliterated the last of my patience. As I scowled, things worsened significantly when she tacked on, "You can't count Joseph. He was in hospice during that three-month stint. In case you were unaware, he catfished you."

Tinder sucked, okay?

"What does that have to do with why I'm on Neptune?!"

"You have been selected to partake in a matchmaking Program which our Queen began over a century ago. Each year, six mortal humans with no romantic prospects are offered the opportunity to participate, three men and three women. If you find your match, a mate, then you are granted their immortality to live the rest of your lives together." I loudly gasped, then recoiled, before heavily scrutinizing her primly features.

"Is that why you grabbed my ass? You're trying to *mate* with me?" I croaked. Her beauty was undeniable. *You haven't dated a woman seriously before, though.* To be fair, I hadn't been legit with *anyone* in years.

Aphrodite's appalled expression blasted right through my gay thoughts, as distaste curdled her dainty features. "That was entirely by accident, I apologize." Her words were clipped. Forced.

"You don't have to look disturbed, you know," I muttered, cheeks burning. Deflating, and settling into my self-loathing's familiar embrace. *To be fair, you deserved it for assuming her bisexuality, Nala. Mating signifies hetero, duh.*

Aphrodite remained aloof, pushing forward, "As I was saying, you will inherit your potential lover's lifespan. Not all immortals live infinitely, however, the majority of Neptunians live for at least three centuries. Your age is not only ideal for procreation, but our bodies do not ripen past the same period, most are frozen in their thirty-third year. Essentially, Nala, if you fall in love, your life will be doubled in your current form. Our Planetary Pairing Program is highly successful. We have maintained an 80% success rate for the last three decades."

Think of all the books you could read with two more centuries!

"Matchmaking?" I rasped, and she nodded her curls out of place. Clearing my throat, I asked, "So, it's like a dating show where you win eternal life?"

Aphrodite confirmed with an, "*Uh-huh*," as she momentarily checked her oyster phone. This was a rollercoaster. I didn't know whether to laugh or cry. I'd always wanted to go on a dating show. But now? I was past the expiration date.

"It is a five-week long Program. Housing, meals, and anything you might need will be provided for at no cost to you. Although Neptune is more technologically advanced than Earth, you will find that, overall, our lifestyles are quite similar. As you have also noticed, we speak what you refer to as modern English."

The minuscule logical part of my brain was signaling none of this could be real, so naturally, I began spouting vehement denial. "I'm not convinced this isn't a dream. I take sleeping pills and dangerously combine them with alcohol, and have had some wild—"

"Give me your hand please," she interrupted in a commanding voice, one I strangely couldn't refuse. Which was the lone reason I placed my hand in hers.

Suddenly, Aphrodite stabbed me with a pen.

The heart of my palm gushed like a fire hydrant as I gawked. From the force of her strike, my DNA inundated her pristine desk within seconds. It took more than a few stunned blinks to process the strange turn before yelping and attempting to withdraw. But her grip was unrelenting.

"Do you see, Nala? This is no dream," Aphrodite stated calmly before snapping her fingers and clearing all evidence from the scene. An abrupt rosy beam spread from my wrist to my fingers, bringing instantaneous relief from the pain. I couldn't help but bark an uncomfortable laugh. There wasn't a drop of blood left. Not even on my hand. No mark or scab, zero chance of catching tetanus. Nothing. Just like…

Magic.

Mating Program. Immortals. Centuries in lieu of decades. A possible happily ever after. You're desperate enough to believe. You've been begging the universe to rescue you from your parent's basement.

It didn't mean I could believe. It wasn't a dream though, that much I could admit.

Aphrodite stared, waiting for me to settle. My face likely reflected every possible emotion until I mustered the ability to whisper, "Magic is real?"

"Yes. Sorry for the brief pain; however, our Program has found it necessary. Now, where were we? *Ah*, yes. Five weeks is plenty of time to fall in love, I assure you. The majority of our successful matches are solidified prior to the end of a participant's third week. Extensive research was conducted before you were selected. The six Neptunian males in your roster are compatible based on lifestyle, personality, and similar preferences."

So, they were stalking *me*? Out of the eight-billion people on my home planet?! "Why would you choose me for this? I'm no one special. Average on my best days." She needed to understand I was no better than Shrek before he found Donkey, that I should be promptly returned to my solitary swamp. Traveling was the only time I socialized, and even then, my interactions were sparse.

"You are six-foot-two, abnormally tall for a human woman, would you not agree?"

I started, "Sure, but—"

"You are supplementally attractive, in perfect health, and most would describe you as hilarious. I apologize if reviewing your background seemed harsh, it was not my intent to humiliate you, Nala."

"What does my freakish height have to do with anything?" I demanded, knowing there had to be a catch. There always was.

"You are petite by immortal standards. Most femmes are four-inches taller on average. The males even more so." That little revelation slapped me stunned. My height made me a spectacle, even among my own family. I was an anomaly, a genetic fluke, and never the shortest in any setting.

So, this was… This was suddenly less dating show and more Basketball Wives. Had I already caught Stockholm syndrome, *ten minutes in*? Because Neptune had *gigantic* alien men?

Maybe.

"Besides the existence of magic, there is typically one facet of our Program which daunts other participants," Aphrodite interrupted my internalizing. "You will be matched with what you might consider to be aliens or monsters, more accurately, shifters. Nearly all classifications possess the ability to shift. If you find your true love, your family will inherit your partner's magic. That is the primary reason humans are ideal;

the Neptunian's gifts are solely inherited by your offspring. Whereas when an immortal male and femme procreate, their children are typically born with a blend of their abilities, which can either lessen or encourage them. Only the exceptionally privileged participate in the Planetary Pairing Program, those who embody the rarest genealogies."

Her nonchalant use of *privilege* left my skin crawling.

However, and I'm embarrassed to admit, the repulsion didn't last long.

I couldn't deny I was on Neptune. I couldn't deny magic was real. Most importantly though, I couldn't deny this sounded *perfect*. Monsters? They couldn't be any worse than humans. I recently finished a beastly romance with a man-spider as the lead and was wetter than a fountain throughout all *three* books. *Yeah, that's far more alarming than this.*

"Shift into what, exactly?" I crossed my fingers she wouldn't mention possums or roaches.

"Neptune is the lone planet in our galaxy mostly comprised of water, only 2% of our world is landmass. Subsequently, most of our population requires it to breathe while in shifted form." She pointed to the burgundy slits waving on her neck.

"So, like, mermaids and mermen?"

"Yes. The technical term is Siren, many find 'mer*maid*' offensive. There are two who can take Siren form in your potential matches, actually." Aphrodite cleared her throat while I attempted to compute.

"If you are uninterested in participating, I can promptly return you to Earth, without any memory of this." Miss Goddess of Love was fishing for my confirmation, I knew that, and loathed it. But she'd hooked me. I desired a partner, who didn't? It just wasn't plausible or realistic back in Bluffton. Maybe I'd read too many fantasies, but 'mate' was far more enticing than 'spouse' or 'partner.' Even if the person in question was an alien. The mere thought was thrilling, I couldn't recall the last time I'd felt such intense eagerness. For. Any. Thing.

"Is there a way to call my parents? They're gonna flip when I don't show for weeks on end." Thank my lucky horse feathers I didn't have a 'real' career. Despite ghosting, Shuckers' Diner would hire me back without any proper begging.

"I will handle the details. They will believe you went on *Love is Blind* in Jacksonville. Netflix does not air each couple, which is why it has become a favored cover story for our Program in recent years," she explained. A snort escaped because it was totally believable. I was that desperate, plus it would give my family enough hope to placate their nosiness.

"Here is the contract you must review before we finalize your participation. I have also attached photos of the males from your roster on the third page. We found many participants wish to see photographic evidence prior to acceptance."

Shamelessly, I turned to said page the first instant the thick parchment landed in my greedy paws. They all looked human! *No. Way.* "Am I dead?" I didn't mean to voice it aloud, but these hunks were — *Wowza.* Especially the one with the glasses, he was... A shiver crept down my spine, the swoony kind, the kind urging I sign my soul away this very second.

Which was weird. Nearly the most unsettling factor thus far because I hardly ever went for looks alone. So, why now? *Are you really this desperate?*

My gaze flicked back to the page, and I no longer cared.

Aphrodite winked once I managed to rip my eyes from the six specialty sausages. "You are not dead, Nala. There are merely two caveats. If you do not uncover your match in five-weeks, you shall be returned home without your memories. If you do find your match, then your life is tethered to his, and the pair of you are contractually obligated to give birth to at least one child in the first century of your relationship. I should also mention the list of prohibitions on page two."

1 - No sexual intercourse.
If so, the selection timeline is expedited to only include violating parties.
2 - No sabotaging of the two co-participants.
3 - No more than three are to be tethered to each participant.

No exceptions. Not even if agreed upon between involved parties.

**If no candidates from the participant's roster select them in return, they are promptly returned to Earth without their memories. **

I was essentially in a relationship with a vibrator so celibacy wouldn't be a problem. And what did I care about the other women involved? I didn't.

Most importantly, *three* for the price of one? *Your womb is the sacrifice for entry, though.*

It didn't feel great to acknowledge.

However, there had to be a catch… *It could be worse, Nala.*

My eyes scanned the remaining pages to discover nothing atypical, just a contract. The verbiage did heavily focus on the baby making and admittedly, that spooked me. I'd never pictured myself as a mom, not even in childhood. When the other little girls swooned over newborns and dolls, I was play-fighting with the boys.

But who knew if I'd even be desirable to these six, and it was *distant* future Nala's problem. I'd have *decades* to let the idea simmer. When finished reviewing in entirety, I took another gander at the headshots. *You're absolutely doing this.* I'd gladly sacrifice my who-ha and pop one out to get a few *centuries* for five out of the six. The odds were in my favor.

"This is it?" I asked, lifting my gaze to find Aphrodite nodding. "And there's no Rumpelstiltskin-like clause where you'll steal our child from us in the future?" She shook her head with a deepening frown. "What happens if we don't pop one out in the first hundred years?" The repercussions for failing to adhere weren't listed.

"That is best left unsaid. The Queen herself will intervene. It has only happened once in the past," she replied.

Ominous, but again, I wasn't opposed. Not if it meant I got to pick one of these six men —er, *males. You're not in Bluffton anymore!*

Grabbing the stabbing implement, I went to sign the papers. Aphrodite interrupted, *tutting,* and passing a tablet and stylus she'd collected from nothingness. It was so much lighter than my iPad mini despite being quadruple the size. After flourishing my S, I noticed my autograph transferred to the paper contract.

Magic, obviously. There would be no getting used to that. I lifted my gaze to find an unnervingly delighted Aphrodite. "Congratulations and welcome to the Neptunian mating games, Nala. Lastly, what is your favorite color?"

"Purple."

Aphrodite '*rifted*' us to my Neptunian accommodations. She didn't pinch my ass this time around, only gripped my elbow, but it was equally shocking to teleport from one breath to the next. No jetlag, or stomach tug, or anything. Just a shift in the air and *poof*.

I quickly discovered the reason she asked my favorite color since it decorated every inch of this stunningly modern loft apartment. It was at least double the size of my current digs, and I hadn't yet explored the spiral staircase leading upstairs. The kitchen and its appliances were familiar, with an open floor plan and island extending into the living room. Well, except for the countertops, they were significantly taller, high enough they came up to my ribs. Actually, every piece of furniture was larger than what I was used to.

"The time here is one hour behind Eastern Standard, so you should have no issue adjusting. It is Tuesday afternoon. You slept through half the day, apologies for that, sedation upon arrival is required. The ether on Neptune is denser than Earth, it would have been uncomfortable to lucidly experience your calibration." My brows hid in my hairline from surprise, the atmosphere didn't feel any different.

As I readied myself to question why she called the air, '*ether*,' she interrupted. "I am quite shocked you believed me so quickly, Nala. It is undoubtedly the fastest a participant has ever signed," Aphrodite said as she darted around, flipping light switches. "As you can see, we have electricity too. Everything is solar, we only utilize renewable energy. There are no cars or gasoline or fossil fuels. No pollution either."

"Cool?" What did she really expect in response?

Aphrodite shared a perturbed look, one I returned with a shrug. "Your pre-programmed smartphone is on its charger beside your bed. You will find it contains your access and key to this building. It also has your monies, all is digitized on Neptune, we do not have credit cards nor physical forms of identification."

"Who's paying my tab? The Queen?"

"No. Your roster funds your candidacy." Like I needed another reason to drool. Tall, hot, magical, *rich* males. Vain of me, but I gave myself a free pass. I'd just been abducted, and all.

"What if there's an emergency? Do I ring you?"

The femme shook her curls, inching towards the entry. "There is an application on your phone titled, 'SOS.' The pink button will alert both myself and Burt, who you may have met. Neptune is crime free, there should not be any safety concerns. However, Burt and I are only accessible during work hours which are between 10:00am and 6:00pm, from Monday to Friday. If there is a medical emergency, or similar, beyond those hours, click the red button. It alerts the nearest healer. They will rift to your exact location within minutes."

"That's neat," I replied, shifting from foot to foot uncomfortably. The offhanded mention of lacking crime sparked a jolt of unease. I chided myself for being too dick-stracted, for not even *considering* safety before signing my life away.

"A variety of options for dinner will be delivered around 6:30pm, you only need to open your door when they arrive. Although these are your sole items of clothing," she said, eyeing my worn Shuckers' Diner t-shirt and Crocs with disgust, "I recommend spending tonight here. It is critical you grant yourself the opportunity to digest the differences between our worlds. Depending on your preference, there is informational programming on channel one and literature on that shelf there. Gabriela, your guide who participated in last season's Program, will arrive tomorrow morning at 9:00am to take you shopping. Your schedule for the remainder of the week is in your phone's calendar. I'm also leaving a copy of the contract you signed on the counter. I know this must be a lot. Do you have any additional questions for me, Nala?"

Too overwhelmed to think of anything, I gave a singular nervy shake of my head, and Aphrodite disappeared. Or rifted. *Look at you, already calibrating linguistics, champ.*

The first thing I always did in a rental was check the fridge. It was boring though: just two oversized, but otherwise normal, bananas. A case of glass bottled water was resting on the counter, so I shoved it into the ice box. When closing the door, noticing a magnetized map of Neptune's island stuck to its surface, where there was a star on 'Mov Street.' Which I assumed to be my apartment.

Thalla was the largest city in the center of the island, with the other two smaller cities, Ookea and Bahasa, sandwiching its borders. The remaining land to the East was a mountainous jungle called Gro, possibly farmland. I extended a finger to trace the distance between my starred loft and Thalla's pier, realizing it was a smart tablet not a map. Like an iPad, as the screen zoomed into street view. When I plucked its magnetized back from the fridge's face, it spoke. "Good afternoon, Nightingale. Do you require directional guidance?"

"No," I replied, and the surface abandoned the map for a three-dimensional shadow droid wearing a toga. They were minutely swaying, like an idle Sims game character against a blank background. "What are you?" I muttered, mostly to myself.

"My name is Homie. I can understand complete sentences. How may I be of assistance?" How polite, they even shared a little wave.

So, I decided to strike up a conversation, "What can you do exactly, Homie?" Since Neptune was supposedly more tech forward, taking on, "I prefer Nala to Nightingale, by the way."

"Noted, Nala. I'm your home command center. My platform is connected to local devices and appliances. No matter how slight or mighty the task, I'm here to assist. Think of me as a more advanced phone that cannot leave these walls. Ask me anything, and I'll do my best to answer."

"How large is Neptune, Homie?"

"That depends on whether you're questioning the circumference of our planet or its landmass?" They replied with a shrug.

"Landmass."

"Thirty square miles."

"That's it?" I exclaimed, strolling towards the sofa as Homie confirmed with a thumbs up. "How large is the population on land?"

"It is estimated the population currently fluctuates around one-million grounded residents. However, Neptune's total surpasses twenty-million due to its undersea cities."

"How many undersea cities are there?"

Homie's background became an ocean as they changed into a wetsuit. "There are twelve which we refer to as 'Reefs,' located below. Would you like me to list them?"

"No." It was far more interesting to learn about the places I could actually visit. "How does one get around on land?"

The ocean disappeared for a black bicycle to appear underneath my shadow friend as they said, "Most cycle around the tri-city area if they aren't rifting. However, if you would like to explore Gro, a boat is required. There are no constructed streets or sidewalks."

"Could you please show me the map again, Homie?"

⋙ ⋙ ⋙ ⋙ ⋆ ˚

After far too much time spent conversing with Homie, I was itching to get outside and explore. However, I wasn't about to squander this opportunity and go against the Program's recommendation. So, begrudgingly, I sauntered to the lone bookshelf and picked it clean before resituating on the couch.

There were only a handful of facts I found helpful after skimming through the first dozen books. The majority of the volumes were written for humans who struggled with the idea of dating a magical species, something I had no issue with. Call me coo-coo for Cocoa Puffs, but I'd wished for fantasy to be reality for my entire stinking life.

There were no juicy details to quench my thirst, just cold icy facts. Like how Neptune's Queen had reigned since its founding, her singular title was 'Her Royal Highness, Queen of Neptune.' No first or last name, or photos. She also had to be over 13,000 years old, which was bonkers.

The singularly enlightening volume explained the differences between 'classification' and 'subspecies' of what was referred to as immortal kind, since none lived for less than three centuries. Earth was, interestingly, the lone planet in our galaxy with a mortal majority. The eight classifications of immortals were demon, dragon, fae, mage, seraph, turnu, vampire, and zoatala. Dragons excited me the most, for obvious reasons, but they were the second rarest.

Most immortals in our galaxy were zoatala, consisting of full-bodied shifters, who each possessed differing subspecies. For example, the most common Neptunian zoatala subspecies were Reptilia, Phiba, and Selkies. Although most resembled homo sapiens in what they called 'prima forma,' 25% of zoatalans couldn't possess an entirely humanoid shape no matter what. A DNA chromosome determined whether they maintained some of their animalistic, or 'dua forma,' features 24/7.

Since the literature was visually lacking, I decided to switch on the 'Holotube' by pressing the lone button at its center. When the convex sphere whizzed to life, it was on channel one, showing an ochre scale covered host walking through a heavily crowded street.

I was glad to ogle in private because Aphrodite's gills and the humanly headshots didn't prepare me for Mister lizard head. *Reptilia male, technically.* Strangely, most of the surrounding crowd looked human, the host was the lone iguana face atop a normal black t-shirt wearing body. But there was something off about Neptune's Anthony Bourdain as he interviewed the passersby… It took me five minutes to realize it was this male's black forked tongue and matching gums. Iguanas back home had pink mouths.

When more varied immortal heads and wings started filling the street, I rose from the sofa to get a closer look. Those I'd previously assumed were in prima forma, actually had pointy ears or unnaturally colored eyes and hair. Since the books only shared the minimum, I tried a different route, "Homie, what are the physical identifiers of the fae classification?"

"Fae possesses spiked ear lobes. They also cannot shift their form," they replied.

"What about red eyes? Is that a trait of another classification?" I questioned as a group of smoking hot males with laser beams for peepers strolled by.

"Yes. Only demonic or vampiric blood enables red or pinkish eye coloring."

"Can demons shift? Are they evil?" They might've been the most attractive males I'd seen beyond my roster.

"Demons possess the ability to shift their upper halves in dua forma.

They are not inherently evil. However, this topic is highly contested since 30% of demons feed on the souls of other classifications." *Huh.* I still found them enticing despite the devouring souls bit.

"Since Sirens shift their lower halves, what's their class?"

"Seraph. Seraphs possess the ability to shift their lower halves in dua forma."

"Are there any classifications who *don't* reside on Neptune?" I questioned since I'd spotted so many from fifteen minutes with Reptilia Anthony Bourdain.

"Vampires. Their classification is only permitted to live on Chiron or Mercury. Although the Mercurian subspecies are granted passage to visit other planets, Chironias are not. They are considered the second most dangerous classification."

"Is it because they're bloodsuckers?"

"Yes, Nala, vampires feed on lifeblood and struggle with self-control in the presence of other classifications. More so than demons."

Since I'd forgotten which classification wasn't discussed, I picked up the paperback once more. Then dropped it, shouting, "What about dragons, Homie? You said every other class lives on Neptune?" My absolute favorite creatures were dragons, and I didn't know how I could've forgotten them already.

"There is one dragon on Neptune, yes. He is considered our most dangerous resident." *Dagnabbit. One in a million?* I'd probably never have the chance to meet him.

Now accustomed to immortal shells, I homed in on the streets. The similarities between Neptune and human cities were unmistakable, restaurants and shops lined the sidewalks. As Reptilia dude strolled through a busy strip of Ookea, it reminded me of Los Angeles with its swaying palm trees, while the brick buildings were giving DC. The hundreds of channels stole my curiosity, and I clicked around until the good stuff appeared: reality.

⋙ ⋙ ⋙ ✦.˚

Sated by half-a-season of a Selkie version of the Bachelor, where I discovered seals were far more vicious than I ever knew, the excitement of the day caught up to me. It was the information overload coupled with my food coma from the four dinners I inhaled. Even while watching trash TV, I learned aplenty, like how Selkies were various shades of neon coral in their shifted enormous dua forma. *Peachy!* Without a speck of grey in sight.

After a yawning fit, I skulked upstairs to my bedroom. There were far too many potted plants to take care of, I wouldn't even attempt to try. *No green thumb here.* I'd never possessed the patience for nurturing. It was a gorgeously decorated room, although far too lavender in spite of the offsetting greenery.

I threw myself onto the plush, larger than king-sized, mattress. I was immediately impressed by the silky pillowcases but would need more than that to keep my coils in check. I could regret the lack of hair- and skin-care in the morning. *They better have retinol.*

As my weary eyes started drifting, my peripheral caught a gold flashing fan on my nightstand. Unlike Aphrodite's oyster and Burt's conch, my phone was an oversized scallop. Reawakening me with a fresh wind of intrigue.

There were already five messages waiting. Two from Gabriela, informing that we would stop for breakfast before shopping. Two from Aphrodite, checking in. Lastly, and most thrilling, one welcome message from Her Highness the Queen of Neptune. I nearly crapped my pants at that, although the message lacked my name and seemed copy-and-pasted. The touch screen's keyboard was at a rounded angle and alphabetized instead of QWERTY, but I quickly adapted after shooting replies.

It took me less than a minute to find the browser, which was an icon of a cephalopod, called 'Cuttles.' Or Neptune's Google. It had the same search bar and everything, the most noticeable difference was how each button was a bubble in shape.

'Cuttlefishing.' Searching. *Hmm.*

'Emojis' returned no results. I chuckled when the 'No Results Found' page was replaced with 'No Pearls Found' flashing over an image of an empty oyster shell. Then I did what anyone would do, I cuttlefished the local news. Surprisingly, there was an article about the Planetary Pairing Program on the front page of *The Salt*, their largest provider.

"MATING GAMES LAUNCH TO HOOK NEPTUNE'S MOST
PRIZED BACHELORS!"

I clicked the link. But unfortunately, the page went totally blank. Each time I reversed to the homepage and tried again, the same happened. However, when I clicked on *any* other stinking article, it loaded in less than a second. No matter how often I tried to access the juicy piece pertaining to my abduction, it wouldn't work! With a frustrated huff, I dove into the other articles.

"INTRODUCING PUMPKIN! EVERYTHING YOU NEED TO
KNOW ABOUT THE HEARTY VEGETABLE COMING TO A
NEPTUNIAN MARKET NEAR YOU."

That revealed pumpkin hadn't existed until a week ago. Or at least, none of the public knew it existed. They shared a quote from one of the farmers detailing how the crops required modification to survive the heat and moisture of Gro's climate. Which resulted in a cuttlefishing fest of what other random things I'd potentially be living without. Thankfully, it wasn't much. No one here ate red meat, but it wasn't a deal breaker.

"THANKS TO PRANKSTERS, WEEKNIGHT CURFEW
ENFORCED IN TIGER BEACH!"

This highlighted the non-existent crime across Neptune's three cities. How a few eight-year-olds spray painting a dick in a public restroom sparked public outrage. To the extent that they closed the public beach on weeknights. It was disappointing to learn Neptune had the same workweek as America. There were no afternoon nap breaks like in Europe, either.

Although, who knew if these males would even want me working, I was down to become a trophy wife. Which led to researching women's rights, confirming they were thankfully more equalized than what I was accustomed to. There also wasn't any colorism in the Earthly sense. *Go figure.* Some immortals could have atypical skin shades in prima forma, from greys to transparent for a small percentage of fae. There only seemed to be concern with classism-esque rankings for Classifications on a site called 'Ranked' which seemed to be Reddit equivalent.

Article after article, my eyelids grew heavier and heavier. Realizing it was well past midnight, I abandoned my rainbow scallop.

The slanted roof and skylight gave a picture-perfect view of the stars glistering against the darkness. It was like sleeping in my own cozy Planetarium. Unlike what I was taught in school, Saturn and its rings were neon green while Jupiter matched the apartment. Space felt so much closer here, I could see pink and blue clouds decorating the winking stars, resembling glittery cotton candy.

It was wondrous.

South Carolina might've been where I grew up, but it never felt like home. Especially for the last decade after college. As much as I loathed Isaiah's nickname for me, it was true. I actually *was* a snail stuck in a too small shell. My frequent impromptu vacations weren't enough of a crutch anymore. My future dimmed with each passing month. Honestly each year was more hopeless, I was sitting in total darkness when Aphrodite abducted me.

No more, Nala. You're finally free.

PLANETARY PAIRING PROGRAM HEARTQUARTERS
Hidden Recording Device Transcript
06:32PM

Aphrodite Valtameri: "Hello gents, thank you for coming despite the short notice. We can remain in the lobby; this will be quick. Just in case you missed the details in the meeting invitation, the third and final femme has signed her contract. The six of you are those who shared interest in Nightingale Williams."

Avexeidros Valtameri: "We fucking know! You're thirty minutes late, you don't get to just gloss over that. Not after dragging us here for what could've been an email. Why are there no snacks? And the damn water dispenser is dry. Burt kept us hostage so I couldn't graciously correct those oversights, either. I'm at the end of my patience. Please, get on with it. Which of us meets Na—*her* first?"

Burt Valterson: "You wouldn't have come back if I allowed you to leave for snacks, cuz!"

Aphrodite Valtameri: "Apologies, I had not checked the time. Managing programmatic operations for seven planets has made this mating season more chaotic than the norm."

Timoset Drago: "I thought there were only five participating planets?"

Aphrodite Valtameri: "There *were*. We have two inaugural Programs, although they are not operational yet, they launch within the month. I am sincerely sorry, my prior engagement ran late. I know how valuable your time is. Thank you for your patience. And to get on with it, the femme prefers 'Nala' to Nightingale—"

Yu-Jin Rapax: "Why? 'Nala' wasn't listed in her documentation."

Avexeidros Valtameri: "No one cares about the reasoning behind that boring factoid, pupling. For the love of Karma, share the schedule!"

Aphrodite Valtameri: "Although Nala is admittedly one of the least fearful humans we have discovered, I wanted to begin her dates with the most mild mannered of you—"

Ryloh Cabbage: "Th- That's complete shit."

Avexeidros Valtameri: "Agreed."

Aphrodite Valtameri: "Ryloh, this should not come as any surprise. And you never go first, Avexei. We have been through this. It is your hair—"

Multiple laughs.

Aphrodite Valtameri: "Settle down. Your possessive overreactions to mere photographs of Nala are precisely why Yu-Jin will take the initial courting. I cannot trust your natures to behave given her scent is potent. Yu-Jin has the highest marks in control and—"

Chadwick James: "He's still a suckling—"

Yu-Jin Rapax: "Shut the fuck up before I make you, Chad."

Avexeidros Valtameri: "How mild-mannered of you to say, pupling."

Growl.

Timoset Drago: "Behave. This is about Nala, not your pettiness."

Incoherent grumbling.

Multiple sighs.

Zaire Mensah: "Just share the schedule, please."

Aphrodite Valtameri: "Yu-Jin's date with Nala is tomorrow night. Based on past analyses, we have concluded that one day's break between the first and second date is critical in preventing overwhelm. So, Timoset will meet her on Friday. Ryloh has Saturday. On Sunday we have the Founding Gala, which pushes Chadwick to Monday, Zaire to Tuesday, and Avexei, you are last on Wednesday. This is also based on Earthly astrological compatibility, as reading star charts is one of Nala's hobbies."

Avexeidros Valtameri: "I'm fucking last?! I can't wait an entire week! Mo, switch with me."

Timoset Drago: "Absolutely not."

Ryloh Cabbage: "Don't even look over here. It's bad enough I'm third."

Incoherent grumbling.

Aphrodite Valtameri: "Nala's schedule is set, switching is prohibited. As a reminder, if I learn of any unfavorable behavior, you will find yourself reprimanded by the Queen and immediately stripped from her roster. Understood?"

Zaire Mensah: "Of course."

Aphrodite Valtameri: "Excellent. Before we part, there is one final matter to discuss. Since there have never been this many interested in one participant, we anticipate Nala will have at least two bonded. I understand many of your subspecies grapple with sharing, so this is your final opportunity to recall yourself from her roster."

Multiple growls.

Chadwick James: "I don't know why you fools are bickering, there are two other femmes. Sure, this one is attractive —"

Ryloh Cabbage: "Th- The other two are lacking."

Zaire Mensah: "Really? I found Lakshmi to be quite lovely."

Avexeidros Valtameri: "Good, she's all yours then, Zaire. It's gonna be Mo and I with Nala baby. I'm calling it right now."

Growl.

Avexeidros Valtameri: "Happy to share with you, fae. Which means the rest of you should make other plans. You're more than welcome to attend the mating ceremony, though."

Multiple growls.

Aphrodite Valtameri: "Are there any additional questions pertaining to Nala before Burt lowers the wards?"

Yu-Jin Rapax: "There wasn't anything about her family and friends listed in her summary and —"

Aphrodite Valtameri: "Nala is more reclusive than the other two participants. You have everything we gathered."

Multiple whines.

Timoset Drago: "She has four bullets of interests, that is far too few—"

Aphrodite Valtameri: "It is a positive, I assure you. It implies the femme has nothing to return to. She signed more quickly than any other has. I believe at least two in this room will be mated males within the coming weeks. The Council is pleased—"

Avexeidros Valtameri: "The Council is just thirsty for another dragon to add to their collection."

Aphrodite Valtameri: "Be that as it may, the ultimate decision is Nala's, and only hers. I am trusting you to contain your natures. She is unaware of your truths. You must maintain careful control until she has had the opportunity to adjust to our cultural differences."

Yu-Jin Rapax: "Are you sure? I don't particularly like the idea of hiding anything from her. Not if she's to be mine."

Ryloh Cabbage: "Aren't we allowed to divulge if Nala asks?"

Aphrodite Valtameri: "No sooner than her second week. As many of you seem particularly fond of her for whatever reason, I suggest you keep your lips sealed and true natures contained. I am entrusting you with her safety and emotional well-being, do not disappoint me. Or your Queen."

Zaire Mensah: "Are we free to go now? Apologies, but I'm due back at Sirenuse."

Aphrodite Valtameri: "Yes, I will be in touch. Happy season, gents, best of luck."

END OF TRANSCRIPT

I woke up drenched. A tad feverish, and no, I wasn't sick. Only flustered. My dog-like-panting and boiling cheeks were thanks to *incredibly* vivid dreams. I'd spent my night in an orgy. Which felt real despite starring indistinguishable men I couldn't see or hear. They were no more than ginormous shadows with dark silhouetted fingers, even dicks. *That's what you get for spending all of that time with Homie.*

Shadow droid reminiscent or not, I knew those silhouetted wisps of men—*males*—were from my roster. Wish I could say it was my first wet dream involving one of those headshots, but it wasn't. I couldn't even think of *that* at the moment though.

Despite the erotica I consumed on the daily, majority of my nights were renditions of my near-death experience. Not all, but most. *Except for silvery he—*

No! Can't think of him.

As I attempted to inflate my lungs, leaning upright against the cloud of pillows, the rainbow rays of the sun bounced off every surface in my bedroom. I knew it was the same sun thanks to public school science, but instead of the typical yellow or white glow, there was an entire spectrum of hues reflecting against Thalla's surrounding buildings. Like a disco ball.

"Good morning, Nala. It is 7:00am, Wednesday. The temperature outdoors is anticipated to be an average of thirty-eight degrees Celsius, and sunny skies have been predicted to last through this evening. Would it be helpful to increase the temperature by several degrees before you rise?" Homie's robotic voice carried upstairs, interrupting my bed stretches.

"Yes, please." *Welp, you can't deny it.* I was on Neptune, partaking in an alien mating Program, and a tad obsessed with my tablet friend.

"How was the temperature last night? I lowered it once you went upstairs."

No wonder I'd slept like the dead. "It was perfect. You're the best, Homie."

"I'm glad you think so, Nala."

I took my time breathing it all in, absorbing how much of an improvement this was from my typical routine. After the apartment warmed, I threw back the weighted sheets, racing to the nearest window to witness the blossoming streets below.

Never having lived in a city myself, I'd always visit them to get my fix. Morning walks were a treasured vacation activity. When I could pretend that I was a part of the everyday population, with my little cuppa something in hand. Cairo. Seoul. Mexico City. San Diego. London. Sydney. Marrakech. Rome. Toronto. Istanbul. Those were my top ten favorites I'd traveled to, but *none* compared.

Thalla resembled a fairytale combination of my top cities mashed together. There were several dozen skyscrapers, but otherwise, the buildings were no taller than three or four stories. There was admittedly an ancient European feel from the carvings decorating façades, although it was still an architectural hodgepodge. The only similarity from street to street seemed to be its paint color. Some had thatched roofs, while others were tiled, or tin. Most with flat had a swimming feature in a fun shape; loads of flowers, fruits, and stars. Unlike the boring circles and square pools on Earth. It took me at least five minutes to abandon the window's marvels.

Thankfully, deodorant and other necessities, like a toothbrush and paste, awaited in my rose-gold accented bathroom. After taking care of business, I slapped on some fifty-SPF and grabbed my phone from its charging stand, hurrying downstairs. Despite the eagerness to become acquainted with Thalla, I needed to first peek at the male's outlines in an attempt to discern who'd starred in my slumber. The contract was on the counter, right where Aphrodite left it. That feverish panting resurfaced when I flipped to the page with the six specialty sausages. *Gaaah*. I hadn't exaggerated their hotness.

Mister gorgeous glasses stole the show, winning the gold for sure. However, chiseled cheeks and 'WD,' AKA wet dream, were a tie for silver. Bronze honorable mentions awarded to clover eyed rover and sexier Superman. Both had a bad boy edge that could possibly move them up a spot, we'd have to wait and see. However, brawny beefcake didn't place. He didn't wear sunscreen if the peeling burn painting his cheeks had anything to say. Which led to pondering whether he'd turn leathery despite his immortal-ness. I mean, don't get me wrong, he was still handsome but paled next to the others.

Unfortunately, despite it being my first one-woman orgy dream, I could barely remember anything besides the trifecta's dicks. The lacking correlation only confirmed my theory that it was merely a concoction of my desperate, and smutty mind. *You don't believe in fated nonsense anyway, Nala.*

With creeping somewhat outta my system, I abandoned the loft with a goodbye to Homie. The lobby had walls tiled with undersea scenes from Sirens to Krakens. All in orchid, of course. Although it felt like I was on top of the world from my bedroom, it was only the third level of a Victorian-esque brick row-house. As anticipated my entire street was singularly violet.

I knew the bicycle locked to the railing was mine because my phone vibrated in passing. Also, because it was the same hue as Barney the dinosaur. Instead of wandering and getting lost, I decided to be responsible, and texted Gabriela. She thankfully was down to meet earlier and shared an address. The coffee shop was half-a-mile away.

The Eastern end of Mov Street was an expansive park, at least a block in size, equipped with an Olympic pool slash water park. Hordes of parents watched over their variously shifted tots, while a dozen or so axolotl-headed males ran around its tracked circumference. It was my first shifted, dua forma Dolphino sighting. They really were periwinkle instead of grey, like a Lisa Frank portrayal of a dolphin. And triple the size. I was tempted to get a closer look; however, it was in the opposite direction of coffee.

As I slung a leg over my new wheels, I took note of the temp. It was early morning but felt like a million degrees with 100% humidity. No wonder they stole me from my swamp. With my shell-phone safely tucked in its handlebar holder, I joined the sparse pedalers, delighting in the balmy breeze through my messy bun.

I passed families with backpacks, briefcases, and lunchboxes in tow. There were a variety of sizes, from average to plus, the starkest difference from home was how tall everyone was. Honestly, if not for the animalistic heads, rainbow hair, and wings, I wouldn't have known it was Neptune. Everyone wore modern clothing, with casual shirts and shorts as the majority.

The trees decorating the sidewalks were taller and greener than I was accustomed to. Although palm and palmetto trees were most common, fruit trees were a close second. The swaying trimmed citruses were so ripe and pungent that they perfumed the busy streets. Apple. Grapefruit. Lemon. Lime. Orange. Peach. Pear.

There and then, as I turned the corner from a deep eggplant street, onto an indigo version lined with enormous orange trees, I made a promise to myself. No matter the outcome, I would take full advantage.

The more I marveled at how much I already felt at ease, I became more desperate to stay. There wasn't anything keeping me from doing so, from finally pursuing something. For once. I'd dive in head-first. Even if I never remembered a lick of it and got my awkward self rifted home. No slow burning, I would ash this opportunity down with kerosine.

Picturing each of the six ridiculously handsome males from the contract, my skin literally buzzed. There weren't any names, there weren't any tails, just hot headshots. Yeah, I was nuts and my desperation was showing, but so what?

When I turned down a navy stucco street that reminded me of a German village, I couldn't help but feel like this would be my most memorable vacation yet. Hopefully it would last more than five weeks, but for now it was another temporary escape.

As I sweatily pedaled on and the baby hairs around my face bounced, I couldn't keep the stupidly wide grin off my face.

The streets' paint color lightened as I approached Captain's Café. Before disembarking, Gabriela forced a hug, strangling before I'd stopped pedaling. Nearly sending us both to the cobbles. After untangling and righting my bicycle, I immediately took note of how stunning she was. Her hazelnut hair was in an effortless topknot that put mine to shame, and she was super-duper model tall from the way she had a few inches on me. "So, do you prefer Nightingale, Gale, Nene, *or*…?" Even her voice was enticing, like a husky southern purr.

"None of those. Nala." I extended my palm, momentarily forgetting hugs were exchanged. *She'll learn how socially inept you are soon enough, anyway.*

"I go by Gabs myself, no worries." Instead of shaking, her twiggy arm tugged me through the glass doors and into the line wrapping around the shop. The familiar aroma of beans left me teensy homesick. "I've never heard Nightingale as a first name before, where'd it come from?"

"My parents bestowed the seven of us with the names of birds featured in the Bible. You know, since my siblings and I were their 'flock.' I landed with the most abnormal. Even my brother, Osprey, was luckier. He had Oz, they called me *Gale*." Gabs cringed and I nodded in equivalent repulsion. It was nice, but foreign holding a conversation with someone who understood. Almost a balm to my anxiety. *What a pathetic admission, Nala. When did you even last speak to Isaiah?*

"So how badly are you losing it?" Gabs questioned, interrupting my tabulation.

My reply was a snort.

"That bad, huh?" She pushed.

"I'm still unconvinced this isn't some kind of twisted dream."

Gabs shared an understanding smile as she fidgeted with the strap of her crossbody bag. "Yeah, that doesn't wear off. I still wake most mornings and pinch myself. I'm from Houston, what dump did they drag you out of?"

"At least you're from somewhere. I'm from Bluffton, South Carolina." When I noticed the furrow in her dark brows, I explained. "You've probably heard of Charleston and Savannah?" She nodded. "Bluffton is the sweaty bellybutton of a town between them. It's mostly marsh and the population hadn't grown until COVID. Admittedly, it's better than Sugar Tit. Which is a real place, by the way, I have a cousin who lives there."

"I dunno, Sugary tits sound more appealing than a marsh," she replied. We shared a chuckle as I scanned the menu, deciding on a banana oat flavored coffee and egg sandwich.

"So, you must have a million questions. Hit me already." Gabs demanded with an exaggerated stomp of her foot. And I did have more than a million before, but now, in her presence? I was flustered with where to start.

"There's not much of a difference from back home..." I babbled, aimlessly.

"Not yet, but you'll see. There are differences, not deal breakers, but otherworldly stuff for sure. I found the beaches to be most unsettling in the beginning, there's so many dua forma on display. Once you get used to the inhumanness, you'll find everyone is friendly and helpful. It's way safer too. *Oh!* And there's a lot of polyamory, way more than Earth. But I haven't had a tough time adjusting. After my first week, I was ready to permanently move into my adorable orange place." When she wasn't looking, I grimaced at the thought of *that* obnoxious color strangling me.

"When were you last home?" I changed the subject as the queue moved forward.

"Two months ago, I think. Seong isn't the biggest fan of Houston, so we haven't gone back often, but I have email. My family and friends think we live on a remote island with weak internet access. We told them Seong was an archaeologist, but he's the Queen's hand… No. Don't look so excited. He's more of a bodyguard than advisor. He hates it, but he's stuck." It was unsurprising to hear jobs sucked equally here.

"And what *is* Seong?"

Gabs waggled her brows. "Finally! I was wondering when you'd ask the good stuff." I chuckled. "He's a whale shifter, or Whalen. I've only seen him take that enormous form once, for obvious reasons."

"So, you freed your own Willy?"

She laughed, before explaining, "He's not an orca, Seong's more similar to a blue whale."

"And you're… *Happy*?" I asked, cringing in preparation for her response, because how could the Program be as ideal as it seemed. What was the freaking catch besides kids?

"I'm at my happiest," Gabs replied without skipping a beat. I couldn't find the lie, no matter how thoroughly I scrutinized her friendly smile. The fellow human looked content. We reached the glass case to order before finding an empty two top table in the corner. Once settled, Gabs said, "Seong is leagues above any guy I'd ever met."

"Even better than your daddy?"

"My daddy beat us, so the bar was low. Honestly, all of this has been a dream come true. I wasn't close to my family and worked at the Mac counter at the mall so there wasn't much to abandon. We matched before the end of my second week, it was comfortable from the first hour."

"And now, you live on Neptune forever with Seong?" I'd read Whalen possessed true immortality; they were one of only ten zoatalan subspecies with eternal lives. They were also near indestructible, so it made sense the Queen had one as her personal guard. Gabs nodded, and I probed further, "You don't miss Texas at all? It's been a year that you've lived here now, right?"

"Thirteen months. I do miss my best friend, Cynthia, but we email. It's not like I don't talk to her. Besides, I won't age, and she will. It's better to keep things virtual after the next decade."

The news of sluggish emails wasn't enough of a negative to sour my excitement. "There's no video chat? I saw there's video calling on my shell."

Gabs shook her head. "That only works here, and email is delayed by a few hours because of the galactic separation. You get used to it."

"And you chose Seong out of six males?"

"Nope, I had three, but the other two women in my group had four."

"They both matched?" I questioned.

"Yup, both matched, one tethered to two males. She's already given birth. Three months ago, now, I think." My eyes bugged out from that revelation. "It's a lot, I know. But the population here is low compared to Earth. Seong and I aren't in a rush, but some of the males you'll meet will be gung-ho for babies. Speaking of, not everyone participates willingly, so it's not all rainbows and butterflies. My first scheduled date was a nightmare, his parents forced him, so he barely paid attention. But once I told Aphrodite, she booted him."

"Miss Cupid is trustworthy then?" Gabs smiled and nodded before rising to pick up our noms from the counter. As soon as she was back in earshot, I asked the salient question, the one needling me. "What's the catch, Gabs? There must be one."

She frowned while placing our tray down, opening and closing her mouth a few times before using a careful tone, one she hadn't yet used. It sent my gut through a spin cycle of unease. "Most of the negatives are specific to a male's subspecies. Like as a Whalen, Seong snores heavier than a loud muffler in the middle of the night, which sucks but it's not a deal breaker. I don't want you to get overwhelmed. I can tell you're different, Nala. You don't seem nearly as daunted as others are at this point. The best advice I can give is to be open minded about the males, meet everyone, and then form your own opinions before dwelling on the negatives. That way, you can compare the pros and cons when you have all the information. Don't you agree?"

I narrowed my eyes, because it was an unbelievably fishy response. But impossible to counteract. We were essentially strangers, and she was supposed to be selling me. I eventually tamped down my frustration enough to ask, "So what else do I need to know, Gabs?" I might've changed the subject, but it didn't mean I'd given up. The only negative couldn't be snoring, I wasn't buying it.

"I would avoid the other two women in your grouping if I were you.

Seong thankfully wasn't dating them, but another male in my roster was. One of them, Kirsty, was a real piece of work. She staked out my apartment just to threaten me." *Add another catch, at least this one was loud and clear.*

"Doesn't that go against the rules?" I asked through a mouthful of deliciousness.

"Sugar Honey Iced Tea, I didn't tattle! I wasn't interested in the guy we had in common when she went psycho anyway. Seong and I knew we had something. Truthfully, the rules are difficult to enforce."

"Sugar Honey Iced Tea is 'shit' isn't it? Do you not curse either? I stopped, too." There were two reasons for my avoidance, the first was to keep the peace with my puritanical parents, and the second was the challenge in finding suitable replacements. My life was *that* boring and dull, I was forced to find creative means to entertain myself.

Gabs barked a loud laugh and slapped a hand to the table. "It *is* shit, but I stole it from my mama. I still curse, but the saying stuck. Just like my Texican. You're lucky your accent is barely noticeable. Your accent is all posh and professional."

I attempted to brush off the compliment externally, but internally preened. It took an effort to keep my roots hidden. Gabs must've misread because she added, "Not that I'm saying you're professionally... I wasn't a virgin when I arrived, are you? If that's what– *Oh, God.* I've overstepped. Haven't I?" Before I had a chance to react, she leaned in and lowered her voice. "Seong and I, *you know*–" she said, wiggling her brows, "Before we chose each other."

"Banged?"

Gabs winked. "Can you blame me? We were sure."

"They never found out?" I questioned and she shook her beautiful head, chewing her banana muffin.

"PDA isn't frowned upon. It's legal to bang in the streets here, as long as it's after dark when the kids aren't allowed outside. We couldn't stop ourselves and kinda just went for it."

"*What?*" I whisper-shouted. Gabs shared a smirk before taking another bite. "What's the age of an adult here?"

"Sixteen."

"How? You can't drive in all fifty states at sixteen," I exclaimed.

"I know, it's because immortals are forced to learn self-control at an early age, there's like courses for it and everything."

"That's odd. Did Seong explain why?"

"They're shifters, Nala," Gabs replied. As if it answered everything.

Her circumvention was loud and clear, which was why I shifted gears. "You shouldn't have told me we could hook up because I'm no virgin. I'm a dedicated smut reader and this whole thing is already a buffet of epic proportion. Those headshots of the males were eye candy, especially the one with the glasses." Gabs' eyes widened, and several emotions quickly crossed her pretty face. As I opened my mouth to question it, she beat me to the punch.

"Speaking of six males, remind me to stop at a bookstore once we get to the Xora District. I don't know how much you're into fae, but I just finished this why choose series, it changed my life."

On our walk from the coffee shop, we passed an enormous elaborately decorated stone castle in the middle of a city street. A magenta one. Unnervingly, it matched the Program's lobby perfectly. There were even overgrown bougainvillea vines in a complementary shade circling the towering exterior walls. "That's where Seong works," Gabs explained at my gawking.

"The Queen's castle is Barbie pink?"

She nodded, "It's gorgeous on the outside, but horrid on the inside."

Unlike a fairytale castle, this was far more gothic in architecture. Forebodingly so. There were angry Medusa and Siren carvings sitting atop several of the turrets. I couldn't rip my eyes from the towering spires until they were no longer in view. Which took another few blocks.

The Xora District, otherwise known as Thalla's elite shopping block, put Rodeo Drive to shame. Unlike the remainder of Thalla I'd seen thus far, there were hardly any residential buildings. We passed cutesy storefronts, in various shades of peach, selling anything you could dream of. Since it was late Wednesday morning, the crowds were sparse, making it ideal for people watching. "Gabs, do immortals call themselves *people*?"

She shook her head, explaining, "Beings."

"*Ah*, makes sense I suppose."

"So, what are we shopping for?" Gabs questioned as I eyed a pet store showcasing aquariums with snakes in every shade. *No doggies in the window?*

"Everything. This is what I was abducted in."

"You haven't checked your calendar? The 'Cal' app?" I shook my head and Gabs motioned for my scallop. Her aloof expression became a wicked smirk as she tapped around. In a quick movement, she had her own oversized chrome oyster shell out, sending a message before raising her head.

"What?" I probed.

"Your first date is tonight," she squealed while I panicked. It felt too soon. "So, on top of the basics, we need a dress. A showstopper. I know just the place." She stuffed both of our phones into her crossbody, dragging me towards a store with a flashing 'Prima Formula' sign.

"Do you know *who* my first date is with, Gabs?" I was dying to know but she had my phone, and it wasn't as if I knew which names corresponded to who. However, she kept her lips sealed as we entered the Bloomingdales-esque store. The entire place was iridescent: walls, floors, lights. Somehow, being caught in a rave didn't distract from the tables and racks of clothing. None of which matched the holographic decor.

Gabs promptly found a seven-plus-foot, heavily tattooed salesperson wearing a sleeveless black shirt who could pass as human, except for height. "Hello, my name is Milo and I use they or them pronouns. How can I be of assistance?" They greeted with a wave. It was a comfort to hear pronouns were used, I'd forgotten to cuttlefish LGBTQ+ community specifics from my exhaustion.

"Hi there, Milo. We're both she's. I'm Gabs and this is Nala. She has a first date tonight and owns next to nothing, we're gonna need the works. All hands on deck." As Milo opened their mouth, Gabs interrupted, "Price isn't a concern."

"Are we talking sexy casual or sexy cocktail for the date?" Milo bluntly asked, right down to business. Neptune was growing on me by the minute.

"The male is always in a suit, so you can push the formal boundaries," Gabs replied. She turned to me to whisper, "By the way, no one touches here. No shaking hands, or hugs. That's why I tackled you. I have severe withdrawals."

"Helpful," I replied, preoccupied by the no budget revelation. As Milo motioned for us to follow, I grabbed a stack of tanks seemingly in my size, eyeballing it because the tags only listed materials. Since price wasn't a problem, a first for me, I grabbed a handful of seamless thongs and lacy boy shorts too. However, I was so distracted, I nearly missed a critical detail. "Do you *know* who my first date is with, Gabs?"

She ignored me, again. This time, the squirrelly guide even rushed to walk beside Milo instead. *Unbelievable.* She really was a squirrel, equal parts adorable and shifty. Before I could demand answers, our helper interrupted. "Your skin tone works with most shades. Any color preference?" They'd led us to a changing room with a turquoise curtain wrapping around a raised platform.

Gabs plopped down onto a viewing bench as I weighed Milo's question. Before yesterday, I probably would've replied with lilac, but instead I said, "Whatever you think will look best. I'm not scared to show skin, not in this heat."

When Milo returned with an entourage, each carrying an equally heavy load of feathers and sequins, an uncontrolled squawk left my lips. It was prom shopping all over again, except this time, Mama wasn't gonna ruin my fun with her nonsensical biblical propriety.

As the dresses were hung on a display rack, my eyes caught on three. Each in black, a shade which proper southern Baptist girls weren't supposed to wear unless attending a funeral. Since this date was a possible sayonara to my past life, placing my bets on black felt luckiest. Grabbing the trio, ducking behind the curtain, I didn't waste time stripping.

"What's your astrology, Nala bird?" Gabs questioned.

"Pisces sun and Libra moon."

"No wonder we get along, I'm almost all Aries. Sun, moon, rising, Saturn, and Venus." *Aha.*

"I could've probably guessed. My bestie from childhood, Isaiah, had an Aries sun and moon. What's Seong?"

"Double Scorpio."

I was glad my cringe and mouthed 'yuck' were hidden behind the changing curtain. They weren't the worst pairing, but they certainly weren't the best either.

"Are we playing nice enough for you to share your secrets now?" I tested the waters.

Gabs cackled instead of replying, and I rolled my eyes, pulling the first gown over my knees. It was a mesh, maxi-length with an opaque bra and micro-skirt. Humidity approved and it flaunted my figure. I didn't even leave the curtain: automatically greenlit.

"I'm gonna download the only available Earthly astro app onto your phone. You're lucky, they didn't have it last year when I matched with Seong. I couldn't even look up his chart."

"Why?" I questioned, grabbing the second garment.

"Because the stars' placements aren't the same and Neptunians don't use astrology, it's only recently become popular." *Weird, considering its ancient roots.*

The second dress was incredible, so I pushed back the curtain to show Gabs. She clapped with an overenthusiastic Milo as I spun, modeling how the bedazzled number banded around my boobs, bellybutton, and bum. The built-in bra was corseted so it kept my girls tucked tightly while being just the right length to conceal my stretch marks. Not that I cared to hide. *Screw the haters.*

Gabs started dancing while I chuckled at her antics. "That's the one! That. Is. *It*!"

"I'm gonna need something else to wear outta here, I refuse to put my crappy tee and Crocs back on," I said, earning a chuckle from Milo, who directed two of their minions. "And swimwear too, please!" I called after their receding figures.

Gabs' smile was wider than mine, "You're not gonna last the full five-weeks. No chance. Not with that ass." I snorted as her focus returned to her shell. Trusting my instincts, I didn't try the last dress. I'd just save it for later. Instead, pulling a few more options in various greens and tossing them into the pile. It could be a possible contender for a new favorite color.

When my helpers returned with a variety of crop tops and shorts, I grabbed a set from the stack and left the rest with Gabs. Shortly after, another pair of angels delivered a selection of shoes, from sandals to sneakers. I didn't question how these beings knew my exact size in everything. *Magic, duh.*

By the time we made it to checkout, and Milo was scanning item after item with an incessant *ding* for each, I questioned, "How much do you think this is in dollars?"

"Seong's mom told me it's better to measure gold against nepbloons. A singular US dollar is that insignificant." I cringed in horror as my totals surpassed the two-thousand mark on the fancy register. "Don't worry, Nala. Most of your roster is ancient, they've had thousands of years to collect riches. This is nothing to them. I promise."

"This is giving Pretty Woman without the prostitution," I muttered.

"I thought you looked familiar," my tattooed helper mumbled, but I caught it.

"Pardon?"

Gabs waved her olive arm frantically with an aggressive shake of her head. What was up with this beautiful bitch and her secrets? She then refused to meet my scowl, hiding behind her phone. "You're a freshie then," Milo eventually said. Which did nothing to curb my frustration. They must've noticed and taken pity because they whispered softly, "Beware of the Kraken—"

"Hey," Gabs interrupted, snapping her fingers. "None of that! You'll ruin the experience!"

"The Kraken?" I questioned, pointedly ignoring her with a raised palm to the side of my face, blocking my guide from view. "Why?" When the register crossed the thirty-five-hundred-mark, Milo clocked the 'you owe me for this commission' look I shared.

Thankfully, it worked, and they mouthed, "Chad is bad." Which left me chuckling and nodding. Who would've thought that rule extended to the farthest reaches of space?

"Thank you," I mouthed back, passing my shell to settle the outrageous charges. This haul surpassed my total belongings on Earth.

"Makeup next," Gabs said as she looped an elbow through half my holographic bags. "Then skin care, because I see a zit looming on your chin. My face broke out too. It's because of the shift in the atmosphere, the air is heavier, or some crap like that."

I felt around my face and sure enough, there was a witch's wart brewing. "What a relief! I can't be going on dates looking like a hag. Even if I'm still annoyed with you." I knew she'd ignore the dig, but I wouldn't surrender. No matter how much Gabriela Martinez Rapax dodged, I'd keep throwing balls in her direction.

"The males would still go ape over you, even with a honker. But trust me, skin care on Neptune is something else. I had acne scarring on my cheeks and it disappeared completely in two days. The shop is called Hides and Scales, it's my mecca. Brigitta, the mage owner, will customize a potion for you on the spot. She whips out crystals, a mortar, fresh herbs, and everything."

"Do mages have any fancy features I should prepare myself for?"

Gabs shook her head, "No. They're the most human seeming of immortals. Their ears match ours. The only weird thing is that her hair is neon cyan."

"Naturally?" I questioned, and she nodded.

Gabs grinned at my gaping. "Exactly, it's pretty cool. Just wait until you meet her, she's a gem. Once we're done there, books." Her bottle brown eyes landed on my hands with a distasteful scrunch of her nose as she said, "Then mani pedi… *Ugh*. I wish I could take you to my favorite nail place. They attach scales to lengthen, which is way healthier than gel extensions, but it's Below—"

"You can breathe underwater?" I shouted, and Gabs nodded. "How?"

"It's a long story, but yes. You, on the other hand, can't. So Clawdia's and gels will have to do. There's a cute bistro next door so we can stop there for lunch."

I was tempted to call her out for the deflection. Instead, I settled on, "Thanks for this, Gabs. I'm sure you had better things to do than tote me around all day."

She waved dismissively before linking arms. "The only thing I've been missing is a girlfriend to shoot the Sugar Honey Iced Tea with again. This isn't selfless. You're stuck with me. And I promise everything will be revealed in due time, you just have to trust me for now." My hackles rose as she dragged us down a redder street, Gabs would soon learn I didn't back down.

Or trust, for that matter.

❦ ❦ ❦ ✦

While waiting for lunch, Gabs dug through her crossbody, and in Mary Poppins fashion, piled a trove of items onto the table. Eight lip glosses, or maybe thin perfumes? Potions? A second phone, this one with an orange sand dollar encasing. Four kinds of hand sanitizer, all from Bath and Body Works. An unmarked, full-sized, leather notebook. Several bunches of various dried herbs. Twelve crystals. Two pens. And finally, a Hello Kitty wallet.

Wait, there was more. She shoved the odds and ends back, before waving a tasseled velvet drawstring. "I think it's about that time in our friendship, Nala bird."

Gabs whipped out a worn deck of tarot cards with a wink, shuffling and clacking them against the table. "Have you ever had a reading before?" She questioned, instead of immediately replying, I scanned the packed restaurant in fear of an audience. People or aliens, I assumed both were nosy by nature. Surprisingly, the surrounding bustle didn't pay us any mind though, which wouldn't happen in Bluffton.

"I've had a reading. What kind of deck is that?" I probed.

"Loteria, it's old. I inherited it from my Abuelita. A little worn, but never wrong," she explained. I kept my face nonplus —*by some miracle*—as she whispered something to the deck. "Love or life reading?"

"Both," I said, honestly. Unsure whether tarot was something to believe in. The only glaring certainty was that Gabs and trust were oppositional, like similar magnetic poles, they kept bouncing further and further apart as the day wore on.

She chuckled while doing an accordion-like trick, plucking one card from the top of the stack with her chrome stiletto nails. Two of cups, upright. "Beginning of a partnership," she proclaimed. She flipped the next, also upright. The Lovers.

And squealed like a piglet while I cringed. *Great, just great.*

"Yo, you can't even try to ignore this! The universe has spoken. You're staying. True fucking love!" Gabs did a jig in her seat. I sighed as she made a show of dancing her fingers over the last card. "I bet you this one is the ten of cups: Happily Ever After."

I shook my head, the odds were too slim, one of forty-six cards was near impossibility. But Gabs was grinning maniacally as she flicked the last card across the table, to where it landed in the dead center of my place setting, spinning like a top. She screeched before my noggin counted the number of cups spiraling.

Fuck.

"You cursed!" She accused with a pointer.

"I didn't mean to say it aloud," I croaked. Incapable of ungluing my eyes from the ten of friggin' cups. "Aren't you supposed to read them care-fully, so you know whether or not they've been reversed? This could mean disharmony."

"*Nu-uh*, I checked beforehand."

"Convenient," I muttered, crossing my arms as she clapped. "I don't believe it." My belief altering quota had already been filled. *No vacancy.*

"You don't have to! It's gonna come true," Gabs sing-songed while the waitress delivered our separate plates of zucchini noodles, mine with garlic sauce, hers with tomato. Apparently, mortals had introduced many of our foods since the Program's inception. However, there were plenty of alien options on the menu, like frozen fisheyes served in caviar like tins.

Pushing her hot plate aside, Gabs swiped the ten of cups and started shuffling again. "It doesn't mean there won't be chaos for you to find your lovers. Let's see what calamity awaits you in finding them." Here she was, assuming I was polyamorous… I was. Kinda. *But still.*

Unlike Gabs, I was starving. So, I was chomping away as she *pss, pss, pss*-ed into her deck. From what I already knew of her, there was no way she'd relent, even despite my blatant cringing discomfort.

"Death," Gabs murmured, forebodingly. Although there were no facial reactions shared, my organs clenched. "You're gonna rid yourself of old habits."

Avoiding her eyes, I kept on chewing. "Goddamn," she breathed. Unfortunately, my ears perked. "That hasn't happened to me in a while," she said with a chuckle. And I finally gave in to my curiosity, to find there was a card sitting horizontally beside the vertical death card. The seven of swords. "You'll not only deceive others, but they'll be stabbing you right back. Both upright and reversed."

Internally, the stupid hairs on my body stood on end. Externally, I scoffed.

"Huh," Gabs said, inspecting the final card. "Reversed four of wands: disharmony." She ensured I saw her pitying look before snatching up the deck and tucking it back into its velvet drawstring.

"Fabulous," I clipped. "That wasn't painful at all." And I didn't believe her reading. Not even a little. Nope.

Gabs swerved my incessant questioning *all* freaking day. Unfortunately, I couldn't hold it against her, not after she thoroughly upgraded my life. I know they claim money can't buy happiness, but after experiencing my first ever unlimited splurge, I disagreed. Leaving the shower to find Gabs organized my walk in closet by color was like a shot of joy injected into my veins.

Maybe it was because I'd never possessed similar luxury, but I had to give her some of the credit. Gabs was like a fairy Godmother, and we got on well enough. It was difficult to loathe her. Especially after she spent an hour on my makeup. I'd never looked better. It was an infuriating catch 22. She abandoned me with a pyrite crystal, "for luck," with ten minutes to spare until a bicycle carriage for one would arrive.

Although I was expecting it, I jumped out of my skin at the *trill* of my doorbell. My ticker was tap dancing like I'd never gone on a date before. My legs leaden, and mind muzzy as I trodded downstairs. Everything about this was daunting, and not just the aspects of potentially abandoning Earth, but the idea of actually sharing myself.

This was no Uber.

The tuxedo wearing male had onyx scales that matched the topless bicycle carriage. It was my first up close and personal interaction with a dua forma. The Reptilia male had a karoo lizard head with a thin lime-green forked tongue. "Nightingale Williams?" He questioned with a lengthened hiss on the S. I nodded before taking his offered claw to climb in. It was tough, but I avoided ogling his inhuman parts, even when he wasn't looking. "We aren't going far." He seemed like a decent chap, so I let my defense hackles fall. *Temporarily.*

I'd never feel safe wandering any city, on Earth or Neptune, no matter how it touted its security. It'd been hammered into me from one too many bad experiences. I was sorely missing the kubaton stabbing tool and pepper spray dangling from my keychain back home. We couldn't find similar protective devices in Xora, so I was forced to settle with loosely sewing a steak knife into the zipper of my dress. Gabs teased me endlessly for it, but having protection within reach was my lone protocol. Even if it was slightly scraping the ridges of my spine as we bobbed along the Thallan cobbles. A few scrapes were a worthy exchange for peace of mind.

Mister scales stopped before a deep turquoise glass high-rise two streets from my loft. It was the tallest structure within view, so I'd often surveyed its flat roof and oddly waved glass paned sides. It seemed out of place, too modern beside the surrounding rock faced buildings. "Here we are," the driver announced.

With each passing second, it was increasingly difficult to inflate my lungs, let alone think. Climbing out of the carriage and remaining upright in my five-inch heels was my sole focus. So much so that I accidentally ran right into a wide suited back. One which smelled of the sea, a masculine saltiness with a hint of coconut. My nostrils were inhaling like I was prancing in a flower field when he spun to witness my creepiness.

Chiseled cheeks!

Jin Rapax had perfect bone structure and flawless khaki skin. The pristine midnight suit he wore matched his cropped hair. Strands that looked black in his photo were more indigo as they caught the light. I gulped, finding my mouth dry as he towered, the male had to have been at least seven feet. Thankfully, he was equally as gobsmacked by me. Jin clawed a huge palm through his shiny locks as his eyes undressed me. More than once, his gaze bounced from my face to my sandals. Twice. Thrice. Make it four.

Five freakin' times!

It took the male a few tries to finally rasp, "Nala?" So quietly that the carriage pedaling off was overwhelmed by the sound. I would've been smug if I wasn't equally as stunned by how attractive he was. My fingers crossed as I pleaded, *'please don't let him be rotten inside,'* to the universe.

"Nice to meet you," I mumbled. It was all I could manage. At least I was no longer shaking like a leaf in a storm, had to give myself props for that.

"Fuck," he mouthed, the dark plum of his eyes stripped me down from head to toe, *again.* "You aren't at all what I expected," he breathed, out loud this time. Jin's monolidded gaze was stunning. Those swirling amethyst irises paired with his navy hair made it impossible to deny he was alien.

"Uhm… Thanks, I think?" I muttered back, taking his extended palm. I thought he wanted to shake, but the male's big hand didn't release mine, he clung on. Sparks didn't fly as our fingers interlaced. However, it was the first time anyone's hands completely dwarfed mine. It was nice.

The harmless act left me tremoring, though. Physical touch was something I'd learned to live without, especially in recent years. Outside of sex, which was rare, there wasn't any intimacy in my life. Not like this.

Jin led through a set of heavy glass doors, revealing a modern concrete walled lobby with thirty- to fifty-foot ceilings. There were liquid filled columns with dangling vines trapped within their depths as decoration. Despite my limited plant knowledge, I could identify the greenery as dozens of marbled pothos spiraling down from the high ceilings.

I feigned unawareness as Jin's eyes remained on my ass, but I couldn't keep from smirking. A buzzard receptionist waved an arm and wing from behind an oversized bamboo desk as we passed, but my date didn't spare him a glance. "I hope the arrangement is to your liking, Yu-Jin, sir," the beaked male called. *Yu-Jin's definitely Korean, with that superior bone structure and the monolidded eyes it certainly adds up, but how?*

From what I'd observed thus far, the typical heritage indicators from Earth didn't apply. For example, dark skin didn't gravitate toward dark hair, nor vice versa, it was random. As were facial features, including almond eyes, like Jin's. There was no denying his name's origins, though.

"I'm certain it will be. Thank you, David," Yu-Jin finally seemed to find his voice, which was the smoothest baritone I'd ever heard. Goodness gracious, my ears were singing.

"So formal," I muttered as he pulled me into the elevator, keeping a firm grip on our interlaced hands as he clicked the button for the fifty-fifth floor. Classical hummed through the speakers and we were tugged upward.

"I prefer Jin, by the way," he said with a scratch to the back of his neck.

"Even to sir?" I spouted. It was the first thing that came to mind.

Jin rumbled a laugh as he squeezed our intertwining hands, and my heart skipped a beat. "I'm the Duke of Thalla, so it comes with the territory, unfortunately." My mouth dropped back down to the lobby as we passed the thirtieth floor.

That meant he was the *lone* government representative for the entire city of Thalla, the only higher-ranking official was the Queen. My stun must've been obvious because Jin added, "I won the election after running twice, both times against my father. I'm sorry for making this awkward, Nala. You just..." He licked his plush lips and met my gaze, and I tried to keep from blushing.

The glass cage of the lift dinged our arrival in interruption, revealing sprawling views of the cities and surrounding oceans against a sunset. It was nearly empty, a flat expanse of concrete, except for a gazebo over a table for two in the corner. Unfortunately, the weather was equally sweltering up here, the slight breeze was equivalent to one of those pathetic battery-powered-hand-held-fans. *Useless.*

Jin cleared his throat as he tugged me toward the canopy, mumbling, "As I was saying, I'm sorry. You're far more stunning than the photos and I know it's a horrible excuse, but you're a total knock out, Nala. I wasn't prepared." Taking the seat with the best view of the streets below, I squeaked as the male fell into the closest seat, not leaving an inch between us.

It took me a full minute to recover from his muscular thigh pressing against mine.

"You aren't so bad yourself, Your Grace," I volleyed, and he rolled his plum eyes. "Oh, come on now. You're just as beautiful, if not more so. Although I do appreciate the compliment."

"That's an Earth thing, we don't use those silly titles. And no chance. I already knew I preferred you to the other two, but I mean..." he trailed off, his eyes undressing me again. My grin widened to an obnoxious extent. "I'm doing it again, I'm sorry," he muttered. It was unbelievable. From how insanely fine Jin was to the way the faraway planets reflected onto the endless sprawling waves.

I'd forgotten we were holding hands until he released to point towards five carafes of drinks. "I made sure there were plenty of options, both alcoholic and non alcoholic. What's your preference?" How had I not checked if there were spirits on Neptune? *You were dick-dazzled that's how.* "This is called 'something on a beach' back on Earth, if I remember what my mom called it. Whereas this is more like a blend of whiskey, but we call it a 'zonvon' here. And there's water and —"

"That one, please." I interrupted his flustered mutterings to point to the amber liquid. "So, your mom is human, too?" Now, the Korean name made sense.

"Was. She *was* human and in the Program. She's originally from New Orleans. Also, worked as a waitress before, just like you."

"Small world… Or galaxy I guess," I said, clearing my throat to share thanks. "I can't believe you're the elected official for the largest city on Neptune. It's impressive. And the fact that you beat your dad to win is crazy. Does he resent you?"

Jin frowned as I took a sip, it tasted like a hard caramel and a jalapeño had a baby. The warmth spreading through my limbs took some of the edge off. "Actually, the opposite," he explained, pouring himself the same liquor. "I'm close to my parents. They pretended as if the election wasn't happening during, but my mom still organized the party when I stole his seat."

"Why'd you run against him? You said you ran twice, right?"

"Thalla wasn't anything like it is now. It was unkempt in comparison to most immortal cities because the Queen was dipping into the tax treasury. My father, along with the two past seated Dukes, were too terrified to intervene and do their jobs properly. I've never feared her, so I felt a personal responsibility to run."

"I knew there had to be corruption," I exclaimed, my volume sending him momentarily jolting. "Give me the dirt, the *real* bits about Her Royal Highness, Jin."

"She's excessive in everything. Most was blown on redecorating her palace and throwing lavish parties. She's a nightmare, but all Titans are. I know she loathes what I've accomplished but can't show it. My public support forces her to play nice."

"Titan?" I asked with a frown. Were the ancient Greek ones real?

"Oh, right. Earth has its various theories regarding the Dawn of time. Big Bang? Christianity? Do you believe in either, Nala?" Jin questioned with a blatant cringe. I shook my head, earning a relieved sigh and drooping suited shoulders. The religious fanatics shoved me toward atheism, although I could never admit it to my parents. My mother would undoubtedly host an exorcism to save my soul and invite her entire congregation. If not every Christian within a thirty-mile radius.

"Earth was purposely kept in the dark, it's a result of the sparse immortals there. 13,489 years ago, there were thirty-three Titans responsible for the Dawn of time. Earth's population has been wiped several times, so I know your measured years are much lower. Titans created the planets, and they remain the most powerful beings, their magic is limitless and unmatched. Nowadays, a Galactic Council of thirteen of the originals reigns over the galaxy. Our Queen is the sixteenth Titan, that's why most fear her."

"Are there gods?" I questioned.

"They're children of Titans. Gods tend to be more prestigious than other immortals. However, both are still one of the eight classifications. I assume you know what those are?"

I nodded. "That turns everything I've ever known upside down. So, did you expose the public to the Queen's treachery to win?"

"Not exactly, I campaigned to grant citizens bare necessities. I didn't want Neptunians to merely survive or get by anymore. It wasn't fair. Everyone should thrive, regardless of how they were born. My dad believed providing interfered with natural order, that the less fortunate should be forced to struggle. My stance was unheard of and took years to garner understanding.

"But once the citizens understood what my platform was offering, I won by a landslide. We didn't only revamp Thalla's structures, we ensured every household was outfitted. Ookea and Bahasa were slightly better off, given they were recently constructed, but their dukes replicated my legislation. It's the primary reason Neptune's population finally expanded." Jin spouted off like a pro. His voice even changed; it became deeper, more passionate. He was a poster for political fairness. If I thought the male was hot before, his pot was now bubbling over.

"What's bare necessities to you? Because back home, we don't have anything provided." I considered myself luckier than most, but my parents struggled until their own died and funded their retirement. During childhood, Daddy was an oyster shucker and Mama worked as a maid. My siblings and I regularly plucked apples from the tree in our backyard for school lunches, and we weren't the poorest. Still, I remembered everything we lacked. It left its mark.

Jin smirked. "I know, Mom explained the capitalistic corruption. It's not only healthcare and schooling my legislation covers, but Neptunians are also provided with a monthly stipend. No cost housing. Actually, your apartment's an example of what every immigrant receives upon arrival."

"Wait, wait, wait," I held up my hands as Jin took another sip. "Are you telling me that everyone gets an apartment as ridonkulous as mine?" He nodded his handsome head, but I couldn't believe it. "They move in with everything there? Appliances? Furniture? What about electronics?!" Jin kept nodding as if it was nothing and a noise of disbelief left me.

"Earth is one of the most impoverished and underdeveloped planets, Nala."

"You don't have to tell me, I'm the one who lived there," I hollered.

Jin barked a laugh, and I was crushing hard. When he recollected himself, he said, "I didn't anticipate you being so... funny. What else can I answer?"

From the sudden pressure, I fumbled with, "What's your favorite color?"

"Blue."

"*Hmm.* What kind?"

"Azure. Why do you ask?"

"I'm considering a new favorite after being strangled by the purple in my apartment. Not that I'm not grateful—*I am*! It's just too much of the same. Did you know there's a film stuck to the windows, so natural light is filtered through lavender?" Gabs pointed it out. She also confirmed the rays of the sun were cast as a rainbow by the Queen's design, a fact which now tracked.

"No, that is aggressive," Jin replied. "But it's the trending decor style, especially in Thalla. Transplants prefer it because of the ease in adjusting. It was psychologically proven surrounding yourself in a preferred shade can lead to reduced stress. It took my office over a year to compile the necessary data to prove it." He was so freaking enticing, even while nerding out.

Yu-Jin was the purest soul; I could already tell. Everything the male was thinking was clearly visible on his chiseled face. Unlike dates on Earth, there wasn't any need to evade topics to spare myself– *inequity being a prevalent example.* He seemed to understand. Completely. However, there was still one unknown persistently nagging. I cleared my throat to ask the most important question, my go-to-first date Q. "What's your star sign, Jin?"

"Cancer," he replied with a cheekier grin. As if he knew exactly how star blessed we were. "I'm also only one-year older than you." We were a match made in literal heaven, and it was difficult to contain the squeal clawing up my throat.

I was so stoked by our star alignment that it almost distracted from his age. "You're thirty-three-years old? I thought you were ancient?! Gabs made—"

"*Gabs*? She's your guide?" Jin's plum eyes widened, giving me a better view of their swirling liquified depths as I nodded. "She's my brother's mated."

"What?!" That beautiful squirrely bitch, why didn't she tell me?

"If we're talking about the same Gabs from Houston, she's mated to my half-brother, Seong." Jin waved his hands dismissively, adding, "To answer your question, yes. I'm hardly considered an adult yet, but it doesn't make me any less proficient at my job." A sore spot I immediately took note to poke when more inebriated.

"You have *centuries*, why'd you even sign up for this now?"

"Seong and Gabs actually. I would give up being single to find that. You're as young as I am, so I can ask you the same question," he replied easily.

"I'm not gonna let you off the hook so easily, Jin. How are you certain you're ready to be tied down? The real reason." I held my breath, waiting, a bit scared of what he'd say. As insane as it was, our brief conversation already topped any other first date's.

"Just to be clear, I'm not looking for anyone, Nala," he said, our gaze locking as his brow furrowed. "Gabs is slightly deranged, but she's the right one for my brother." I chortled but he ignored it. "I'm not looking for what they have. Or even what my parents have. None are true partners. I want someone to share everything with. The boring as much as the fun. Someone who isn't scared of challenging me. I've been told I'm intense —"

"I don't find you the least bit intense, Jin." I had to interrupt because I didn't give two clucks what anyone else thought of him. "That's what I want, too. I want someone who attempts to understand without judgment because I'm a weirdo."

"Is that all?" he questioned, glossing over my self-deprecation.

My smile spread. "I'd like to be loved equally. I tend to love too much in relationships. It's never been... I don't think my feelings have been recip-rocated." Then grimaced as the truth left my lips.

"Now that you mention it, I think I've probably experienced the same. Although my family and friends are mostly equated." Jin's frown was deeper than mine, which hardly made sense. "You didn't get along with your parents or siblings?"

"Never. I was seen as problematic for holding any opinions that opposed Christianity with my parents. My siblings were only slightly less unreasonable. It wasn't just about religion, most of my views are unaccept-able. Your platform is a relevant example, they'd side with your parents."

"I don't always get along with mine, but they've been there for me," Jin said.

"And here I was trying to find the holes in your family tree, when they were in your dating history instead," I teased with a smirk, and he barked another rumbly laugh. "So, no immortal exes for me to worry about?" I dared ask.

Jin shook his head, a navy strand fell onto his forehead, and I battled the urge to reach over and brush it back in place. "It was never serious. I always thought I'd participate in this," he tacked on with a genuine grin. His perfect white chompers rendering me swoony.

"Because of your mom?"

"Partially. It's mostly the data, I like to have as many details as I can before making any decisions." That was the third or fourth time he'd used the word like it was the bee's knees.

"Data?"

"The information they gathered about you before you... *Arrived.*"

"You can say abducted, you know," I grumbled. Jin broke mid sip, choking. I patted his back and said, "There couldn't have been many details on me. I barely left my house."

"There wasn't," he confirmed. "You're a surprise."

"*And?*" I drawled. Fishing for a compliment.

"My favorite so far." I was stunned by the ease in which he shared that. "I'm glad you don't have much to go back to if I'm honest," Jin said, shrugging his wide suited shoulders.

"Speaking of the Program, I have to ask since you're more transparent than Gabs," I started. Jin's brows drew together, but I needed to know. "What's the catch?"

"Are you asking about pairing with me specifically, or in general?"

"Both," I replied, crossing my fingers and toes underneath the table.

Jin's eyes got lost in the tie dyed sunset before he finally replied, "My subspecies is Siarc, so you'd only live for five-centuries. There aren't many negatives besides that, I don't have the same urges as others. Were Siarcs included in the Program resources?"

"No, I don't think Homie even mentioned you."

"Probably because I'm rare, our subspecies is only passed through males in my family. I never met my grandpa, he died before I was born, so my dad and I are the lone pair. Mom said the closest relation is a cross of multiple sharks you're accustomed to. Mostly Great White, but larger." *Shark, huh?* I couldn't help but wonder if he shifted like an Animorph or all at once.

Jin continued as I envisioned his mouth widening into rows and rows of sharp teeth. "Most don't know this, but our nature is more intelligent than predatory, one of the many reasons my father and I find politics rewarding. As far as the overall PPP's catch? I think it's the forced children. I've always found that aspect fucked up."

"No kids right away then?" I questioned and he shook his head. "That's a relief, I don't wanna pop one out for a while. It'll probably take a few decades to come around to the idea. I was one of seven kids growing up, there were too many of us, so I never pictured myself as having a family of my own."

"What else do you want for your future, Nala?"

"Besides three males, you mean?" I blurted, and Jin choked. Eventually, laughing it off while I chided myself. "Kidding. Kind of," I muttered, deflecting as my cheeks burned. "I haven't thought about it much. Not in the context of living longer." I decided it was time for a change in subject. "Is Seong your only sibling?"

"No, he's the oldest. My sister, Min, is between us."

"I'm a middle child too, the fourth born. You must be the spoiled brat of the family then," I said.

"I wouldn't say 'spoiled,' per se, but I'm the closest to my mom out of the three of us," he replied offhandedly, as if he could hide his Mama's boy-ness.

"Shocking," I teased.

"So, what do you do for fun? I surf when not working." He promptly U-turned.

"Read. I've probably read for more hours than I've slept," I explained. "Plus, kayaking and yoga. Do you know what those are?" Jin nodded. "Those are probably my favorites. Besides traveling, but that was more to get a break than a hobby."

"Why didn't you leave if you hated it?" Jin asked, unknowingly hitting a nerve. It took a few blinks to gather a proper response. "Unless that's too personal a question," he backtracked.

"It's not. The truth is I tried to leave after graduating college. I spent plenty of time living away but boomeranged to my parents for one reason or another. A lot of it was my refusal to live with roommates. I couldn't do it, not after growing up in an overstuffed house. The other issue was any time I'd save enough it was wasted on travel instead. There wasn't any pressure to move because I paid rent, although below average for the area. My parents lived on the water, so I was spoiled in that sense. It wasn't nice water, marsh front, but there was a dock."

I skipped over how devastating it was to live at home at my age. How our area was cheaper than the national average and I still couldn't get by. How I lost the motivation to change jobs after hundreds of botched inter-views, courtesy of my anxiety riddled ADHD.

"Since the three of us were argument prone, my parents built me an apartment with a separate entrance after my fifth failed attempt to move. We hardly spoke which counteracted the urgency to leave. Also, our town had recently grown with younger transplants. It didn't remove any of the kooks, but it made living there more palatable… Honestly, my hatred just numbed to complacency." I didn't mean to go as far as I had, but Jin wasn't cringing, or disappointed. No, the male was unsettlingly clinging to my every word with a slight curl to his tempting lips.

It gave me the fortitude to voice, "The weeks of 'it'll get better,' became months, then years before I knew it. I'm a severe procrastinator, Jin. An entire depressing decade flew by. That's why immortality excites me, time is something I waste."

"I still can't believe you remained single," he said.

There it was. My opening to share the part that usually sent dates scampering. I downed my drink for courage. "I dated. Never seriously. There was one long-term boyfriend, Andy, who cheated throughout our six years together. We were young, only sixteen, when we first kissed. I didn't know anything but him until my twenties.

"After college, I spent my weekends at home while he partied. Even after we got engaged. I should've been suspicious but wasn't ready to acknowledge reality, not until I was forced to, when he no showed for our wedding. It wasn't as devastating as it should've been. The worst part was the humiliation. I knew calling our relationship toxic put it lightly. Not that I'm entirely blameless, but... I've avoided all serious *-ships* since, even friendships."

This was typically when I'd expect his eyes to narrow in suspicion, because how could anyone get jilted without cause, right? There had to be something horribly wrong *with me*. Never Andy. There had to be some overarching reason he was cheating on me consistently. It was the only reaction I was accustomed to. However, suspicion wasn't reflected in Jin Rapax. He looked pissed... Which was frustrating. "Why are you looking at me like that?"

"I've been cheated on twice; I'd never wish it on anyone. I can't believe the bastard disrespected you for six years. And jilting you with an audience?" He shook his head with a fierce look as my jaw unhinged. "You didn't deserve it and neither did I. In a fucked up sense, I'm grateful because I doubt we'd have met otherwise." Jin's cheek ticked and his eyes darkened, even while fuming he was gorgeous. *How was he betrayed, too?* With that perfectly proportional face? Not to mention his intelligence and kindness. He was the whole package and then some.

"I assume you hold the same no cheating stance as I do?" Jin nodded and my trust in him surpassed every being with a penis I'd ever met. Gabs wasn't exaggerating. That wall I'd erected over the years? It was no more than dust now.

But Jin was laughably out of my league. He was everything good, shiny, and bright. I was nothing more than a dull, sometimes comical, grey area at best. No shark should settle for a snail, which was why I began shooing him away. "Jin, you're way too everything for me. Sexy, smart, successful." I was sweating my makeup off, and probably resembled a drenched poodle. It had little to do with the humidity and everything to do with how he devoured me with his cyclonic gaze.

"Don't, Nala. From what I can tell, you're fucking perfect—"

"No! Not perfect! Anything but!" It was an accidental outburst, but it seemed more acceptable than lunging the sparse distance between our lips. "I appreciate the sentiment, Jin. I do. But I'm lazier than a sloth and a complete mess. A disaster," I said as his nice purply eyes continued searching mine. For what? I didn't know. And it worsened my puddling.

"Can I ask you something?" Jin nodded. "If I'm drenched in these scraps, how are you holding up wearing a suit in this?"

Jin laughed, a rumble which left me clenching my thighs as he tipped his navy head back. How was his laugh this sexual? The better question was how long had it been since I'd been with anyone? Twelve… No, fifteen months. *Woof.*

"Siarcs can adjust their body temperature at will," Jin interrupted my dick-speration as he took my hand in his. "It may not feel like it, but I am at least fifteen degrees cooler."

"I wish I had that. I'm soaked all over." I accidentally let slip, leaving him gulping.

⋙ ⋙ ⋙ 🐟 ⋆ ˚

"So, there's a reason we're dining on this rooftop," Jin said as I chewed on sautéed carrots. We were having a vegetarian stew of sorts, tasty but not something I'd have chosen. Not that I was hungry between my nerves and the heat. "See those Reptilia over there?" He pointed in the direction of an expansive beach where several enormous chameleons with their curved heads gathered.

"On Earth, chameleons are like toy versions of them," I exclaimed, and Jin laughed.

59

"Just wait, this is their practice night."

As I began questioning what kind, at least thirty more rifted in. The purply sun would soon disappear behind the teal waves, it was likely sometime after 8:00pm. A horn blared, sending the lizards into a formation of sorts. The next thing I knew, their skin flashed in unison. Red. Then orange. The colors of the rainbow as they stretched. A routine quickly followed.

"Woah," I breathed as each section rifted in between their shifting friends. There were splits and jazz hands. Several cartwheels. A few flips from the Reptilia on the ends of each row.

"I know you're new to Neptune and our shifted forms, but I thought—"

"You did well, Jin."

"Good. There's a theater they perform at, I'll take you. But the Whalen haven't come through yet, just wait. You'll notice a lot of subspecies gather with their kind." As soon as he said it, I remembered the axolotl headed males running around the track together this morning.

At least a hundred Whalen suddenly appeared, spewing from their blowholes in the water behind the chameleons. They were narwhal-like with enormous sparkly horns. Despite the darkening skies, I could see the sparkle of those spears from our distance. I'd never encountered anything similar. It topped every trip to SeaWorld.

Jin interrupted my stun. "I thought you might be scared or—"

"No way. It's… *Amazing*." Our wide grins matched. The two of us drew in closer, like a pair of magnets, I couldn't resist the pull of duke Jin Rapax. When he interlaced our fingers again, there was a dizzying ambivalence. On the one hand, his touch was already a comfort. Whereas on the other, I was jittering like a bug from anticipation. Or butterflies. The feeling was so foreign, I could hardly breathe, let alone name it.

"You have the prettiest eyes I've ever seen, Nala." That was how he decided to break our stare filled silence?! With another compliment? This male was a dream. Had to be. I pinched my thigh with my freshly manicured nails, but it left behind an ouchie.

"*Nu-uh*, my eyes are boring brown. Nothing special. Not like your grapes, mine are dirt."

"Dirt?" Jin barked a surprised laugh. "It's not about the color, it's your lashes, and the way you use them… Fuck. I sound like a nitwit. I'm so sorry, Nala."

Now I was the one laughing as he struggled and loosened his tie. "And how exactly do I use my eyes, Your Grace?" The way I so visibly affected him was empowering. Addicting.

"I can't seem to string a proper sentence around you—" the Siarc's plush mouth froze as I readjusted the top of my dress. You could say I had him right where I wanted him: booby trapped. When his gaze finally lifted to meet mine, I smirked.

He gulped. "I don't even remember what we were talking about, Nala."

Neither did I.

I was drunk, stuffed, and wishing the moons would slow their roll. Yeah, there were sixteen moons on Neptune, each a different size and patterned crater; some resembled eaten wheels of cheddar, while others were seafoam or mauve.

"Can you explain space travel to me? People on Earth shoot themselves into space all the time and the planets they're photographing look nothing like those," I said, pointing toward Saturn and its neon rings.

"Earth's exosphere leads into a parallel realm with barren planets, many are no more than oversized asteroids," Jin explained, finishing the last of the drinks. We'd drained all five carafes.

"The Titans were responsible for keeping mortals excluded?"

"Yeah, their excuse was protecting your kind. But if you're strong enough, you can rift through their barriers with ease."

"Like Aphrodite," I muttered.

"There's more immortals living on Earth than you'd think, lots of halflings. Especially fae, although they're arguably the most unpredictable. That's why they placed a border around Saturn a few centuries ago."

"Fae are from Saturn?" I questioned and Jin nodded.

"Not all but most. They can only leave Saturn with permission from all three Omni, or rulers. You have to win a year-long tournament, survive being hunted by hundreds to earn yourself the opportunity to petition the Omni, and even then, many aren't allowed passage. Most of the Neptunian fae got here before the barrier. They're considered the wildest and most unpredictable among common immortals."

"Are there any generalities among zoatala?" Jin's opinion seemed more legit than the rankings I glimpsed on Ranker.

"I don't think so. We're pretty varied since subspecies are more specialized. My sister had a worse time with adolescence than I did. Despite our thirteen-year gap, she was still struggling with control when I left for college. It took her till her forties to settle into herself," he explained, shrugging his huge, suited shoulders.

"What's all this 'control' business? Gabs mentioned it, too."

Jin struggled for a beat too long, his plum eyes darting around the darkness. I raised my brows, and he sighed, relenting. "Shifting. We can lose control of ourselves and accidentally shift into dua forma. It's incredibly difficult to break when it happens unintentionally."

"I still wish I could shift. I'm super jealous you're this humongous, scary predator. It must be soothing to swim around and kill things when you're mad."

Jin snorted and shook his head in a 'you're trouble' way.

"I should probably get you home, it's past midnight," he eventually muttered as his smooth thumb circled my wrist. I knew he felt my shiver from the way the corner of his lip tugged. When he caught my frown, he added, "Or not. Whatever you want, Nala. Where do you wish to go? There aren't many options, Wednesdays aren't fun weeknights on Neptune."

"Not if I'm keeping you from beauty sleep, Your Grace. You probably have all sorts of important meetings in the morning." I conceded.

Jin rolled his eyes and tutted. "I'm in no rush to part from you. I thought it would be obvious by now."

As my stomach flipped, I said, "Okay, anywhere but my apartment. I don't have any snacks. It's not fit for hosting the duke of Thalla. Gabs only took me shopping for this." I motioned towards my get up.

"There's a twenty-four-hour market on the corner."

"Jeez, skipping right to the serious stuff, *huh*? Shopping for groceries is relationship territory. Are you sure you're ready to venture there with me,

Jin?" I was mostly joking. I'd never shopped for groceries with a guy before. Andy deemed shopping my responsibility since I didn't have an 'important' or 'real' job like he did. And trips to the Piggly Wiggly for Franzia boxes with my ex-bestie Isaiah and his husband, Bobby Junior, didn't seem to count.

"Almost. There's just one remaining box you haven't checked." Jin replied, seriously. I short circuited, forcing him to help my sputtering ass up. "But I can't allow you to remain snack-less under my watch. Mom taught me better than that."

"What's your mom's name? She sounds amazing." I asked with a smile as his arm swung over my shoulders and tucked me against his suited side.

"Hae."

"Doesn't it mean water in Korean?" I questioned and he nodded with a grin. "That's like the sickliest destined thing ever. Like spook spook fated nonsense."

He laughed before saying, "She's going to love it when I tell her you knew that." Scoring mommy points wasn't a priority but it added to our delightful repartee all the same.

"I spent a month in Seoul last year. Kimchi is probably my favorite condiment."

"Mine too." Jin squeezed my shoulders before leading towards the lift. "I haven't been yet, but I wanna visit at some point. Both of my maternal grandparents were born in Seoul."

"How long did your parents wait to have you?"

"Thirty years after they matched. Seong came first, I think he arrived like a decade in. Min was a few years after him."

"Different dads?" I questioned, remembering he called Seong his half-brother.

Jin nodded before pressing the button for the elevator. "My mom mated with three males... Are you polyamorous as well?"

"Sort of," I replied, and he paused to give me a 'what the —' look, you know the one. "I've never actually been a part of a relationship with more than one person. My sole exposure has been in books that... you could say they sparked my curiosity. Theoretically, I'm open to it. In practice, I'm not so sure. What about you?"

"I think it depends on who my partner is," Jin said easily, unblinking.

"What about me? If I was that who."

"The idea of having *you*?" He gave me a more pointed once over. I was feeling a full bodied tingle in its wake. "I'd be lying if I said it didn't sound ideal to keep you all to myself, Nala."

Damnit. How did we go from fun and flirty to seriously sobering?

It forced me to simmer on whether the Siarc could be it. Jin had already checked my boyfriend boxes. He'd been the one to claim perfection of me, but it was him. Well, *nearly* perfect, the singular negative was his mommy's boy-ness. However, he was better than a regular shmegular suck up, he had plenty of razzle dazzle.

The unchecked box was to confirm that his parts were up to par. *But how couldn't they be?* The dude was enormous, I felt like a petite princess tucked under his heavy corded arm. I wasn't typically a betting gal, but there was a slim chance any of the others even came *close* to sharing our connection. "Jin, I—"

"Don't finish that thought, Nala. We haven't even gotten you snacks yet." He interrupted. My heels clacked against the concrete lobby floors as he said, "My parents made it work. We couldn't have had a better childhood. My siblings are opposed, but I think it depends. It always worked for our parents. I'm sure it wasn't as easy as they made it seem, but." The male shrugged. Little did he know, I'd already made the decision. I didn't care if it meant giving up exploring my sexuality further.

"I dunno if I'd even want to share, Jin. And to be honest, you're—" I stilled when he stopped and tilted his head. The movement sent a few navy strands out of place, and I gave into the craving to brush them back. When his cheek pressed against my palm, we statued like that for a few blinks. "I like you, Jin." I said. *Like a complete and total loser.* The male literally stopped blinking as I cradled his closely shaved cheek.

It took a bit for him to clear his throat and say, "I like you too, Nala." And then we were walking again. Except this time, in a cozy silence as warm and fuzzies spread across my sweaty skin. When we turned the dark and empty street corner, the grocery's neon lights came into view. I nearly sprinted as I felt the air con wafting over. My scallop read thirty-nine degrees Celsius but that was meaningless to my American ass.

"It's ludicrous this heat bothers me so much, I'm from an equally humid place," I mused as we walked through the sliding doors and then immediately lost my train of thought. Instead of those water misting cooled shelves, there was an entire greenhouse in the center of the massive space.

That was just for the fresh goods! Everything else was so neatly organized I went cross eyed. "You're going to have to help me, Jin. This is nothing like home."

"No? Mom never said," he frowned. "What's different?"

"First of all, the produce in our stores is dead or dying. The only freshness is the recent squirts of preservatives keeping it from rotting." The male looked horrified as I barreled on, "Whatever you have that's unhealthy should make me feel right at home snack wise."

Jin cleared his throat before ducking to my ear to whisper, "I don't think we have anything which qualifies."

"No chips? Thinly sliced potatoes that they fry to a crisp until they sometimes chip a tooth?" I asked and he shook his head in equated confusion. "They're also puffs. Or rings?" Nothing. Not even an ounce of recognition on his too perfect face. "*Oh*-kay, any snacks then. Lead the way, Your Grace."

Jin tugged me towards a far corner behind the greenhouse, away from the three workers who snooped by the registers. It was unsettling, but understandable, given the duke of Thalla was in present company.

Once we reached the aisle chocked full of stacks of prepackaged goods, the most familiar item was crispy nori, or seaweed. Everything else was uncharted. I braved half a basket worth before we argued over who would pay. I taught him rock, paper, scissors, and it was a case of beginner's luck when he bested me. I knew one-sixth of my funding came from him, but it was the principle.

As we made our way out and neared the loft, I was spiraling. I didn't want to part with Jin. Neptune was more than I dreamed, and Jin multiplied it. Times a bazillion.

He kept attempting to chit-chat, but my anxiety wouldn't allow me to partake. I couldn't stop questioning whether we'd kiss. And skipping right past that base, and the next, for a home run. Jin had to be phenomenal in bed, the best sampling I'd get a taste of, and I wanted him more than I'd wanted anything. Or anyone.

As the steep hill of Mov Street came into view, I was out of sorts, twisted up, and trembling. When I blurted, "Would you stay if I asked you to?" it resembled a beg.

Jin stilled for an uncomfortably long beat. When I couldn't take another second of the suspense, I ducked from under his arm, attempting to distance myself. Nearly tripping over my sandals in the process.

Of course, Jin caught me before I fell. His adorable gravely laugh was also to be expected. As were his warm smooth hands which fit around my hips like they were made to. What was entirely unexpected though, was how we both lunged at the same time.

Fireworks erupted as his soft lips moved against mine. He was gentler than I expected, seemingly taking his time with each languid swipe of his tongue. Until I bit his lower lip.

Jin groaned and sent me sparking, my nerves were firing off like I was a tween all over again. I clawed into his soft strands as he pulled my body flush to his and picked me several feet off the cobbles. "Fuck, you smell incredible, Nala," he mumbled against my lips.

"Impossible," I panted back. "I'm sweaty." *Way to ruin the moment, champ.*

"That's not sweat dripping down your thighs." Jin replied and I did a stunned double take as a smirk tempted his lips. He placed my feet back on the ground and added, "Siarc, remember? Our sense of smell doesn't function as yours. And speaking of which, if I stay, I don't know whether I can behave."

"Who said I wanted you to?" I teased, dragging the male towards my door before he could argue further. "You know your brother and Gabs didn't play by the rules, right? They hooked up and no one found out."

Several emotions quickly crossed Jin's unblinking face until he found acceptance with a smile. "I didn't know that." I unlocked the door using my shell, relishing the cooler temps chilling my skin, he followed a step behind me. His jacket came off when we reached the landing and he shook out his limbs, clearly having an internal pep talk.

As I unlocked, he interrupted our silence. "I don't expect anything, Nala. I hope you know—"

"Save it." I tossed my phone and snacks on the counter and made my way upstairs, not checking whether he followed. "I really like you and I've never had more fun on a date. After that kiss, I want you. If you want me too, then whatever happens, happens."

"I wish it were so simple, Nala. Unfortunately, it's not. There's a lot you don't understand yet," he said with a sigh as the iron stairs creaked with his heavy footed steps.

"So, explain it to me while I shower. You can park it right there and I'll be able to hear you." I pointed toward the stool beside my bathroom door before grabbing a magenta cami and boy shorts from the closet. "You're also welcome to join me or sit on the counter. I'm not shy." Might as well get the worst out of the way and give him a good look at my dimpled cellulite, uneven boobs, and stretch marks while he could still change his mind. Not that any of those things bothered me, it made me Nala. *However, who knew if guys were petty and unreasonable jerks on Neptune too.*

At least he hadn't questioned my scar… *Yet.*

Jin took the stool, and I shrugged in passing, leaving the door open both physically and metaphorically, hoping he would peek as I stripped. Unfortunately, he kept his head tilted toward the beamed ceiling as I removed what was left of my makeup. He sighed before interrupting our silence, "I don't know where to start. I'm not sure how they explained our compatibility to you. Are you sure you're sober enough for this?"

Crap. So serious. "Yes, aren't you? All Aphrodite said is humans are ideal because the kids only take on the magic of the Neptunian. Which isn't the case if you mix with a femme of your own kind, that the blend can dilute or expedite magic." I hopped into the shower, uncaring how the spray hadn't fully heated yet.

Jin heaved a heavier sigh, near groan, and I began hurrying with the soap. "On a basic level, yes. What they didn't explain is once we have sex, we're bound. Mortals are the lone class to not possess fated mating tethers, or *amoroso* bindings. You're the only classification a bond can be forged with, like a blank page an immortal can claim. Since tethers have been near extinct since the intergalactic war, three-thousand-years ago, there are few negatives. That's how your life is extended, it's an inherited trait from our bonding, your life is tethered to mine in every way. Each coupling has variances, which makes it difficult to know what to expect beyond extended life expectancy. You'll never be able to shift but you'll take on some magical abilities. In polyamorous groupings, everything is shared between all involved."

"Even between the Neptunians?" I managed to ask while processing the rest.

"Yes, everyone shares almost every magical ability between them. My parents can communicate telepathically from my dad, they can breathe underwater without shifting from Min's dad, and they'll live for eternity from Seong's dad, as examples. But there are limits and risks. The primary reason the Program capped the number of mates per bonded was due to an unexpected death. Her body couldn't withstand the magic of four."

Okay… No sex until we were sure. *Roger that.*

As I chewed on how to respond, I felt a line of leg hair I'd missed when shaving earlier. Although I hadn't rinsed out my shampoo yet, I bent over with my razor.

And accidentally slipped with a *bang*.

As I landed on my ass, the razor flew over the shower enclosure, spiraling through the air.

To where it landed in the toilet with an echoing *bloop*.

I was groaning for being such a bruiser when Jin stormed into the bathroom to find me sprawled out like a dying cockroach. You know the pose, when those disturbing critters are trapped on their backs with limbs splayed in every direction. That was me.

"Uhm." I scrambled upright, but the stilled expression on Jin's face was difficult to discern through the shampoo foam stinging my eyes. *Horror? Repulsion? Shock?* Likely all the above which was why I hid in the shower spray, turning my back to him.

When Jin's smooth fingers spun me by the elbow, I gasped, not having heard him open the glass door. "I'm fine, I'm fine," I placated, anticipating him asking. Except he didn't. He just stood there staring at my dripping face with the muscle in his left cheek ticking. "Why are you looking at me like *that*?"

"When Seong told me he knew Gabs was it after their first hour together, I called puffer shit." My eyes saucered as Jin began unbuttoning his shirt. "I'll never admit it to him, but he was right." His plum swirling eyes never left mine once despite my drenched nudity on display.

"What are you doing?" I squeaked.

"Joining you." I gawked, and Jin smirked. "If you want me to, that is. We don't have to bond tonight, but I know I don't need to meet anyone else. I had a horrific date with Dayna. My date with Lakshmi didn't compare to ours either. It's only you, Nala, I'm 100% certain."

"What the —? You can't be serious!" I didn't mean to screech. Or speak *aloud* for that matter, but the sight of his sculpted chest towering over me was like a hit of crack and I lost all sense.

"You're awkward and curse like a cartoon, so what? It's adorable.

You're honest and you speak your mind regardless of how I might feel. You're as funny as you are witty, and I've never met anyone quite like you, Nala." I sputtered as he casually unzipped his pants and let them fall around his ankles. *All aboard the thick thigh train. Choo-choo.* "It seems like our wants are aligned, that you're still figuring yourself out as much as I am. And none of it has to do with how fucking sexy you are. Just say the word and I'll join you."

The desire on Jin's face as his eyes drifted down my naked frame was so tempting it left me in jitters. Coupled with the tremble in the clenched fists at his sides, like there was a battle in restraint, I had to refrain from throwing myself at him. The bulge in his boxers confirmed everything coming out of his mouth, but a tiny part of my brain was firing off warnings. How was he *this* certain?

Wait. Wait a hot minute, aren't you precisely as certain? I already told him I liked him. And dragged him upstairs. Can't forget how I also essentially invited him in here. Jin's smirk didn't falter as I bobbed for apples and attempted to gather myself together. *Gaaah, he's so good looking.*

I was beginning to ache from how badly I needed him, fifteen months of celibacy was torture. However, I somehow dredged up a sliver of restraint and choked out, "But, Jin." Then it took every ounce of my willpower, from all thirty-two years of life, to rip my gaze from his package to meet his eyes. The purple had completely disappeared, giving him a sharper edge. "Obviously, I want you. But I'm damaged and lazy, you shouldn't want anything to do with me. You're a public figure for crying out loud, and I'm just a mess!"

He laughed as he bent over and those boxers fell to the floor, changing my entire worldview. 'Great' took on a whole new meaning and I wasn't talking about sharks. Jin was uncut. From past experience, circumcised guys could go longer, but in this case, it was a relief. The sheer length and width of him was nerve inducing. I had to steady myself against the shower wall as he abruptly climbed in and pressed all his perfection against me.

Jin's nibble to the side of my neck sent my soul from my body. "Will you stop fighting whatever this is between us? Your scent is driving me crazy. I need to touch you. Please." I nodded as one of his hands trailed past my navel. "Just tell me if I need to stop."

"I won't!"

Jin chuckled into my ear as his fingers grazed my clit and I moaned like a banshee. Consequences be damned. Some unreasonable force struck and rendered me desperate. Not just a normal desperation either. *Nope!* It was the kind where your mind becomes mush. Taking that incredible dick for a spin was necessity. Fuck the consequences, I could percolate on those another time. *Or in the next life. Or never. Whatever.*

I spun so my face pressed to his abs, it took an effort to climb high enough to crash my lips to his. When a groan rumbled in his chest as I gripped his velvety thick length, it was game over. I was trembling from head to toe as he palmed my breasts.

"Jin, I need you. *Now.* I don't care how," I panted like a bitch in heat, completely feral.

"Shit," he whispered, swiping a palm down his face. "I want to. Fuck, do I want to. But Nala, do you understand what it would mean? Are you sure? You can't reverse a bonding. There's no divorcing."

It didn't matter, nor could I wait another second.

"Please. Jin, you're more than I've ever wanted. It doesn't bother me if this means I can't be with anyone else, you're worth it." The male's hands were fists at his sides, he tilted his head towards the ceiling for a few deep breaths that sounded like teensy growls. I could see his restraint crumbling, but it hadn't completely fallen yet.

"It's going to be painful this time no matter what, Nala." The 'who cares' ringing through my brain nearly spewed. That little factoid made me crave him more. Why was Jin trying so hard to talk me out of it? It set off my frustration like a smoke alarm needing fresh batteries. I was *done* talking. It was time to smash!

"I want you to fucking wreck me, Jin!"

Finally, he flicked off the water and had me over his shoulder faster than I blinked. When he bent me over the vanity's counter, I started praying. To him. Because Jin was my only religion as he sheathed himself in one thrust that would've hurt far worse if my body hadn't spasmed while it adjusted. I'd never been stretched so intensely, but I didn't care about the damage as he stilled. The overwhelming blend of pleasure and pain wreaked havoc on my vocal cords, and the growl which left him was loud enough to rattle the mirror. It was unexpectedly arousing, leaving my skin peppering as his fingers clawed into my hips.

Then he rutted with such force that I went cross eyed.

Jin was fully in control as my slippery tits slid against the counter and my hands had no hope in finding purchase. I was completely at his mercy. I'd never been submissive, but I loved it. Feeling small. Like he could break me if he wanted to.

When I cracked a lid, he was watching our reflection as he used me. Which was as hot as it sounds. When Jin's growling became a deep groan and he ground my ass into his hips, me and my clit both cried out. That was all it took, I went off like a sparkler on New Years, and came with an unintelligible garble. *Oh my—*

"You feel so fucking amazing, Nala." Jin's whisper was reverent. Each time he slammed into me forced a mewl from my lips. I wasn't sure if we were slippery from sweat or the shower, but the sounds stemming from our slip-n'-slide were sloppy. I couldn't get enough of how rough he was.

Typically, I was a far more active participant and although Jin made it difficult, I managed to clamp down around his girth. Once I'd begun, I couldn't stop from flexing around his length with his every glide. The barbaric roar Jin released as I squeezed as tightly as I could left me chuckling. When he stilled and our gazes locked in the steamed mirror, the wickedness in his dark eyes was more than sinful. It was savage.

"I'm in fucking control here. Not you!" he snarled, and I shuddered as he slammed home with more force.

"More, Jin. Please," I moaned as he gripped my wet hair into his fist and yanked. I melted on his cock as slick ran down my trembling thighs. "Don't stop." Another animalistic sound left him as he picked up the pace and pulled my back flush against his chest.

When a warm hand closed around my neck and he held me up like a doll, my vision darkened, and I climaxed again. Jin didn't slow, he stole the air from my lungs. Sex had never, and I mean ever, been as wholly consuming. It wasn't just mind and body, he had stolen my fucking soul.

"I love how your cunt releases me as you come."

It was the sexiest thing anyone had said to me. A whimper was my reply as he toyed with my clit, and I shook all over. His other fist kept a hold on my throat and tugged so he could whisper in my ear. "So. Fucking. Tight." Jin punctuated each word with a thrust.

"Please!" I didn't know what I was begging for. When he bit my ear hard enough to bleed, it sent a tingle back to my clit. He hadn't relented, not even a little bit.

"I need you to come with me. One more time. I know you can, love," he forced out. His finger was toying with me, but it was difficult to inflate my lungs. Every sensation from the fullness to the euphoria filled dizziness pronounced when he finally pressed with the heel of his palm.

I didn't think it was possible, but we crossed the finish line together with a mirrored rabid noise. Wave after delicious wave, my body shut down instead of slowing. It was like a power outage. And I literally went lights out.

<<*"Someone's going to receive a tersely worded email over the absence of a coffeemaker in this apartment. Mov must be in Glen's district. Should've guessed it was him. That inept fucker."*>

Something was *off* this morning. I'd been lucid for the last hour, and knew I was coming out of a dream, the semi-conscious state of awareness where you'll probably wake at any moment but don't know when. Only none of it was normal, there was just darkness and a strange, distorted echo of Jin's voice. He was chit-chatting about a variety of topics, most of it nonsense.

<<*"I wonder whether Nala will notice I removed the window films. You might've nearly died climbing up there, but she doesn't have to know the specifics."*>

Duke of Thalla, Yu-Jin Rapax. The perfect male Siarc that I couldn't believe existed. The adorable commentary had to be a concoction of my own sick and twisted mind. Which was exactly why I refused to open my eyes. I was concerned I might've imagined our hookup as a fresh means of self-torture.

<<*"Maybe she'll reward me for removing some of the purple. Maybe I'll finally have a taste of her today. Maybe I should wake her with my mouth… Too far again, Jin."*>

Then the pain surfaced. *Sweet baby Kermit.* There was no denying I'd been skewered. It was unnerving. I could typically delight in physical suffering and even sometimes relish the way it challenged me. Not today. Not with the aching pulse stretching from my abdomen to calves sending jolts of agony with each breath.

<< *"Quit thinking with your cock, dumbass. You'll get another dip in that perfect cunt. Stop thinking about how Nala squeezed and fluttered and… Fuck. That's not helping."* >

I cracked an eye, throwing my arms to either side to check if he was nearby. *Maybe that's why you're hearing him?* But the bed was empty. I was also dressed in the pink set without any memory of slipping it on. The confusion was admittedly unsettling, but my pain was worsening by the blink and overwhelming every other concern.

<< *"I'm never going to forget a second of how she felt, though. Fuck. The sex… I would choose Nala again, and again. It doesn't matter that we hardly know each other, it'll make things more interesting. We'll grow together."* >

My dream was continuing to play in my ears. I blinked a few times. No change.

"Good morning, Nala. It is 11:00am, Thursday. The temperature outdoors is currently forty-two degrees Celsius, and cloudy skies have been predicted to last through this evening. Your guest adjusted the temperature this morning, is it comfortable for you?"

<< *"Fucking Homie, I forgot about his morning message. Should've been upstairs."* >

I gathered the resolve to move despite the pain, and shot from bed, to lean over the railing. But couldn't see the male. The pulsing wound between my legs forced me to waddle and whimper each step, resulting in me almost falling down the stairs. Right into Jin's chest. It was clothed, unfortunately. He was in a fresh suit, charcoal instead of the midnight version he wore last night.

<< *"Fuck. Fuck. Fuck. I hope she doesn't hate me."* >

"So last night really happened then."

Here was the thing, Jin's mouth didn't move as mine had, but I totally *heard* him.

"I'm sorry I wasn't there when you woke, I wanted to be," he said. Out loud this time. The distortion of his buttery lilt in my brain was… "How do you feel? How bad is the soreness? Do you need coffee? Tea? Are you hungry, love?"

Oh. My. Jin. I'd actually been hearing *his* thoughts?! It was more than a shock, I was floored. *How did he already care so much?* I nodded as my brain attempted to playback this morning.

"Which one? Use your words, please." Jin was scratching the back of his neck. Nervously.

"Sore and coffee." Then I noticed the mountain of new items on the counter island beside an open laptop, resembling a MacBook without the apple. The towering pile of goods beside it was far more exciting. "What's all that?" Apparently, I could only manage three words at a time in my current state.

"Mostly snacks my mom recommended," Jin admitted as his gaze avoided mine. He then darted behind me and lifted my cami. I was too stunned to move as his warm fingers caressed my spine. "I'm glad your back healed."

It took me a few blinks to ask, "What?"

"You had scrapes down your spine, from that dress I'm guessing." *Why had the steak knife scrapes healed, but not your vag?* Jin cleared his throat and lowered my tank before saying, "I have something to help with the pain, too." He darted over to the pile and made a mess as he searched. The male had never moved quicker, it was like pressing fast forward as he flitted with inhuman speed. It reminded me of watching Shark Week on the Discovery Channel, except he was chasing my well-being instead of prey.

Jin slowed to normal once he found what he was looking for. "Human birth control won't work, but you only need to take this tonic bimonthly." A tiny pink vial was plopped in my outreached palm, and I tossed the cork into the nearby bin. It tasted like cherry flavored medicine, but it was a teeny gulp. What a relief that he was so responsible, I couldn't handle a child yet.

"I'm grateful you thought of everything. Thank you."

"This is for the soreness," he informed, ignoring me before extending a larger vial filled with a black liquid. I tipped back a dropper without a second blink, praying it had an instantaneous effect. Spoiler: it didn't.

"Nala, you're mine now, love. You deserve far more than this. I know we acted hastily last night, but you're my partner for life. Your well-being matters. I'm always going to take care of you. Or at least, I swear to try.

There's no need for gratitude." The sweet sentiment fell flat because Jin's eyes were still darting around the loft.

I'd had enough.

We needed to get over the awkward hump and it seemed I needed to be the one to initiate. I gripped a suited forearm and waited until his plum gaze met mine. "I'm allowed to thank you. No one's ever cared like this for me, Jin. It's odd but nice. An improvement and I'm chuffed, but it's still bizarre. You know I'm one of seven, the only time my parents paid attention was when they had to. My past relationships, even friends, were never as thoughtful as you've been in the last five minutes. It's going to take me a long while to stop thanking you, Yu-Jin Rapax. Get used to it."

His grin was brighter than the multihued rays casting through the film-free windows, and my stomach did a flip. "You aren't the only one who feels odd here, love. Trust me." I huffed before he barreled on, back to business, "This one you have to take daily to mask our scent. It might mute your new abilities, which will lengthen your adjustment period, but we don't have a choice. It's so the other males can't sense our tethering." *Wait, what?*

"Jin, I don't understand." I said, eyeing the soda sized bottle in his palm with trepidation. The liquid was unnervingly bluish white in that one, like chemicals mixed into milk. "You said you wouldn't want to share me. So, don't. I'm delighted to be yours. You are more than enough. We can reach out to let Aphrodite know and—"

"I can't give you any reason to regret me. You should at least meet the other five. It's only your happiness I'm concerned with now." Jin interrupted. I could hardly believe it. I didn't deserve it.

"What if I didn't want to do that to you?" I asked, closing the distance and pressing my cheek to his tie. The male's chest was so comfortable for being so outrageously ripped. And his scent? I hadn't imagined how soothing the salty coconut of him was.

Jin breathed in my hair as his arms circled around my middle. "I was joking when I said I didn't want to share last night. What I should have clarified is my Siarc is too possessive to see you with another. What we have in the bedroom would have to remain between us, we'll have to set boundaries, that's all. If my dad could manage for this long, I can. Besides, you don't even know if it's something you want. What's the harm in finding out? If it's me at the end, then great. If it's not, then we figure it out. I trust you."

I was having a Grinch moment; my heart literally grew three sizes. The other males didn't matter, not even glasses or WD, Jin would be enough. *No regrets.*

"If you insist, fine. I'll meet them even though I don't want to. But do you swear you'll tell me if anything changes? Even if it's for no reason?" I pressed.

"Absolutely."

"Do you hate any of the others? Is there some drama I should be aware of before going in?" I felt him begin shaking his head, but refused to relent, "I'm asking because I value your opinion, Jin." *What's with him and Gabs keeping stuff hidden?*

<<*"I'm not keeping anything from her… At least not anything important."*> My eyes narrowed as his thoughts beat his mouth. "Two are insufferable, but I know you'll see that for yourself. I'm not worried," he voiced.

"That's a lot of faith in someone you've known for a few hours," I muttered.

Jin squeezed me with enough force to suffocate. "And you're one to talk? You said I was your god last night."

Hello humiliation, we meet again.

"I hoped I hadn't said that out loud." Jin's laugh rumbled against my cheek before he disbanded our hug and pushed the milky bottle into my palm. The sip was indeed as gruesome as I anticipated, like a sour Pepto Bismol. After a full-bodied cringe, I asked, "So, are we going to talk about the elephant in the room, or what?"

"I don't know what that is, but sure," he replied with a shrug.

Maybe there aren't elephants on Neptune. "The mind connection now that we've mated. I've been hearing your internal monologue. Granted, I thought I was dreaming through most of it."

"Fuck." Jin frowned. "The suppressant might mute it, but…"

<<*"Shit. Shit. Shit. She's going to panic when she finds out about —"*>

"But *what*, Jin? What else should I expect? Are my fingers wands now? Should I buy gloves? Is that why you stopped touching me? Am I dangerous? I don't have any experience with magic!"

"I'm so sorry. Fuck, if I could go—" He looked near tears, and I couldn't take it.

I silenced him with my hand over the slant of his lips. "No! Absolutely not! I'm the one to blame for this mess. I begged you for it. And if I don't regret it, you don't get to either." A smile spread against my palm, so I lowered it. "Don't be a doofus. Nothing's changed. You're it for me."

Jin was smug as a creepy bug hiding in a rug. "Eloquent as always, love." I smacked him as he chuckled. "For the record, I have no regrets either. I'm here for you, Nala, for the next five centuries, or so." Five. *Centuries.*

"You mentioned coffee?" He nodded before maneuvering around my kitchen and pushing a ton of buttons on a machine that wasn't there last night. "Jin, babe, please tell me you did not run off to buy a spiffy coffee machine this morning."

"Alright, I won't."

<<*"If that fucker, Glen, could do his job properly, I wouldn't have been forced."*>

I withheld a chuckle and picked apart the tower of treats Umma Hae suggested. Thank my lucky tits there were salty rice crisps. It confirmed Jin was the right choice when my stomach rumbled. Although I was crunching away, I felt the second the suppressant kicked in. Jin's thoughts were suddenly muted, and the soreness was no longer stabbing, though I could still feel a lingering discomfort. *No long walks for you today.*

As I gingerly plopped into the stool beside his open laptop, I asked, "Do you need to work? Am I distracting you from running the city, Your Grace?"

"No. I cleared my day." My brows shot to my hairline and Jin shrugged. "I haven't taken a day off yet. They'll manage without me."

"Then what's the suit and laptop for?" I questioned before taking a bite of a crisp.

He shrugged. "The suit is out of habit. The laptop is for… Research, I guess."

"For?" I asked, mid chew.

"You," he tossed over his shoulder.

"*Me*?! Why?" I accidentally spewed some crispies across the counter.

Jin cleaned up, explaining, "Since you're staying now. I thought…" When his sharp cheeks went crimson my belly fluttered. *What did you do to deserve this squishy mama's boy?*

"Spit it out, Jin! Please."

"I don't mean to overstep, and I don't know how you'll feel about it, but I reached out to organizations to explore if they have openings. Charities, local businesses, farms. You don't have to work, not for money. Unless you want to. Not even when we eventually 'pop one out.' It's up to you. I'm not trying to rush you into anything either, just wanted to see if there was something worthy of exploring. Feel free to tell me to fuck off. You can read and practice yoga while I'm at work for all I care, Nala. Whatever you want to fill your time with. As long as you're content."

...

I was experiencing what must've been an aneurysm.

I stumbled for a few beats. Until the sheer thoughtfulness struck my face with a grin. "Well, what are you waiting for? Get over here and show me what you found then." I said, patting the neighboring stool.

Jin and I were trapped in a blissful honeymoon bubble all morning. After finishing lunch, I finally checked my phone for the first time since our date, and there were thirty-two unread texts flashing. To my complete horror. Unlocking with a panic, I soon deflated with an annoyed sigh.

Every single freaking text was from a nosy squirrel.

"I have double digit pings from Gabs. You should know, I'm not a great liar, Jin. We're going to have to tell her and your brother soon," I said as he tossed our food containers down the connecting trash chute.

The sole person I'd been able to fool with my lies was Doctor Vanna, my long-time therapist, which was necessity. After discovering she debriefed our sessions with my parents *without* permission, I was forced to. Not only was what she did illegal, going against doctor patient confidentiality, but *I* was the one paying her bill. I don't know why it took me so long to break things off with her, truthfully. *Because you dragged your traumatized feet with everything back then, Nala.*

"Should we get it over with then?" Jin asked and I spun to find him holding up his *ringing* white scallop. "Video call," he mouthed, and I jumped up from the kitchen stool like my tush was aflame. Suddenly anxious. Meeting the family was a massive deal to him.

"Hey-o Jin-o, what can I do for you little bro?" I snorted as Seong's scratchy voice bounced around the loft. It lessened my nervousness a tad. When I peeked over Jin's shoulder, there was a paler version of him with a squarer face staring back. "Oh, shit," Seong breathed as I gave a little wave and Jin fought with a smirk.

"Nala meet Seong. Seong meet Nala… My bonded."

"Seong! Did Jin… Did he just say what I *think* he said?" I cringed as Gabs' holler crackled through the speaker. "They met last night! I told you! That's what you get for betting against me!" She came on screen with a shove to her male's chest.

"Hey, Gabs. I didn't mean to ignore you." I said in greeting.

"You were clearly preoccupied! *Oh. My. God.*" Her bottle-brown eyes widened.

"Gods," the males corrected in unison. She didn't pay them any attention, bouncing. Then she screeched like at a sporting event, sending Seong into a scowl.

"I'm so stinkin' stoked! We're gonna brunch at least biweekly. Oh, and market mornings! You have to come with Burt and I this week." Then she whooped. "I'm so glad you're staying!"

Seong finally seemed to overcome his stun, asking, "Have you told Mom yet?"

"No, and you have to keep it to yourselves." Jin snapped before I even had a chance to blink. The way his eyes narrowed said he didn't need our telekinesis to know what I was thinking.

"Why?" Seong asked with a frown. Gabs was grinning like the Cheshire cat, as if she knew this would happen. "Aren't you calling Aphrodite to report it?"

We both shook our heads. Jin cleared his throat and saved me from explaining. "Nala's going to explore if she feels a spark with any of the others first."

"You got her a suppressant?" Seong asked and Jin nodded. "Is that what you really want? Our childhood was fine, but are you sure you want to share?"

"I asked him the same thing," I said, meeting Jin's swirling purple gaze. "I am already overjoyed with him but he's insistent I might regret it otherwise."

"If it bothers me at any point, I'll tell you. I swear," Jin said as Gabs chucked. And I believed him. Despite meeting the male last night and hardly knowing much of how our bonding would work, I didn't have a single regret. *How idiotic and wishful of me, right?*

"The animal shelter replied to my inquiry. Apparently, they're available for tours this afternoon if you're interested." Jin interrupted our Holotube break after lunch. He was introducing me to his favorite show, a crime drama that was reminiscent of Law and Order. It was oddly set on Earth instead of Neptune since there wasn't much crime here. However, it was *all* wrong, from the terminology to the mildness of the offenses.

"Yes, I love cats and dogs!"

"I don't know if we have those—"

"What?" I exclaimed, leaping from where I sat across the couch and into Jin's lap from disbelief. How were there no *dogs*?

"We don't have either of whatever those creatures are. 'Dog' is a derogatory term for a Wolven mage, so you shouldn't repeat it. I don't know many Sphinxes so I'm unsure how they feel about being called 'cat.' I would probably refrain from using it as well. We do have tigers, are those the cats you're referring to? Do they keep tigers as pets in America? Isn't that dangerous?" Jin questioned, his eyes wide.

"Only the most deranged people keep tigers. It's illegal in most states because they attack their owners. We don't have the time to get into it. Or how people forcefully domesticated wolves because they were murking too many villages. So, what animals are at the shelter?"

He shrugged, saying, "Besides fish and snakes? Probably raccoons, skunks, and squirrels are the most frequently domesticated. I would assume the majority at the shelter are snakes though. They live the longest."

"That's crazy!" Jin nodded with a frown as if my stunned reaction was out-of-pocket. "Most of those are feral where I'm from. And not many keep snakes because of the rodents or bugs you have to feed them," I explained, and the male mirrored my stun. "What kind of volunteering is it? Are you sure it's something I'm capable of? I do like animals, but I'm not qualified—"

"No qualifications necessary, love. They need volunteers to help keep the place clean and the animals played with. It's ten hours per week, you can manage if it piques your interest. Should we go?" I nodded, then frowned, catching sight of my cropped tank and jean shorts against Jin's suit. One he insisted he was comfortable in.

"I'm going to look like a peasant if I wear this beside you, Your Grace. Maybe I need to change." He rolled his eyes as I hopped up and ran upstairs to my closet. There were an overwhelming number of options, so I closed my eyes and picked the first sundress my fingers landed on. A cotton tank number in a yellow that made my skin glow. My curls were out of sorts after having slept with them unbound and wet, so I did messy space buns and called it. I'd still look underdressed beside him but had a feeling it was something I'd soon get used to.

"Ready," I called, trekking downstairs with phone in hand. "Are we walking?" I'd chosen a pair of sneakers due to the lingering pulsing ache between my legs.

"I know you've been circumventing discussing magic each time I raise it, but have you rifted yet? Do you know what it is?" Jin questioned while staring at his phone. Since he wasn't looking, I took the opportunity to mutely scoff at his magic dig. I wasn't ready to acknowledge further changes quite yet. I was abducted literally two days ago. *So, sue me!*

"Yup, we can rift," I said aloud, taking his outreached khaki palm. Just as it'd been with Aphrodite, I felt nothing but a shift in the air. We were surrounded by the smells and sounds of a pet store: wood chips and fish food paired with a chorus of scratches and squeaks. When my eyes cracked, the first thing I noticed was the stainless steel like surface that covered the walls, floors, and even the doors. A rectangular window behind the desk revealed the neatly organized stacks of aquariums and cages.

"Hello, Yu-Jin sir. It's an honor to meet you. Welcome to our shelter, I'm Penney, the Operations Manager. You must be Nala, nice to meet you too. I'm so grateful you're considering volunteering," a silver haired femme with pale freckled skin waved excitedly. She was insanely beautiful, and her freckles were a neon coral hue, an unnatural one. *Selkie, maybe?*

"Pleasure to meet you, Penney." Jin used a tone that was far too sexy for our surroundings. It would seem I wasn't the only one sweating for him either, Miss was eyeing him far too aggressively.

I strangled Jin's hand as I clipped, "Should we get started?" It was difficult to keep my cool as her gaze undressed *my* male. I'd never been a jealous type. I couldn't grasp where this irrational possessiveness was stemming from, but the urge to punch her in the face was undeniable.

Penney nodded before motioning over her shoulder for us to follow through the swinging double doors. "So, I understand you're from Earth, Nala. Have you spent time around these animals before?" The most common resident were snakes, there were at least a hundred. My last experience petting one was probably in childhood, but they never frightened or repulsed me. The next most common resident seemed to be skunks, there were at least two-dozen. Surprisingly, there were hardly any fish, three in total.

"Transparently, most of these are undomesticated where I'm from, but they don't scare me." I said offhandedly, elbowing Jin and pointing towards a pair of teensy baby skunks cuddled up in a wicker basket. "Look how cute those two are!"

"That's Sugar and Spice. Their parents were thought to have been fixed and the family couldn't keep up with more. Newborns must be fed once an hour. You'd likely feed the pair often. Would you like to hold them?" Penney explained as she made her way over to the plexiglass cube with holes. The exaggerated swinging of her hips left my fists clenching. I worried Jin would be ogling her. However, when my gaze swung back to him, he was zoned out on my cleavage.

When our eyes met, and I smirked, the male gave me a shove towards Penney. "You aren't allowed to hold or touch skunks back home, it's thought to ruin their scent and cause their parents to abandon them," I explained as she placed the pair of strawberry sized critters in my hand. They were so adorable and sleepy. And clones to the black and white striped skunks from back home, too. Which was odd. *Why were the animals duplicative of Earth when immortal dua formas weren't?*

"It's true if you find any in the wild, but we have an overpopulation which led to their domestication. I think you'll do fine, Nala. We mostly need you for feeding and playtime. There will be the occasional aquarium or cage cleaning, but we have staff to handle most of that. Are there any others you wish to hold?" Penney asked as she peered over my shoulder.

When I lifted my gaze to find Jin's grin wider than my own, it gave me the courage to say, "That's okay, I think I'm sold. When can I start?"

Friday morning came and went, I couldn't believe nearly half a week had passed since my abduction. Not to mention, I now had a Siarc for a permanent partner, one I'd already caught scary feelings for. *Two. Days. In.* Although I knew the catch would rear its hideous head soon enough, I wasn't as distraught over it anymore. And it wasn't loud snoring with Jin, he slept like a stone. I was the one disturbing him with my never ending repositioning.

I'd been ceaselessly hunting for clues in our time together but came up empty.

By some miracle, I'd also dodged every conversation regarding the specifics of my new dick magic. It was procrastination at its finest, I was aware the inevitable would come, but couldn't keep from hiding in my shell. Not that I wasn't excited for my new skills too, I just wasn't ready to burst our dreamy honeymoon bubble yet.

It wasn't any surprise my water sign ass cried when Jin left for work this morning. Once I started, it was impossible to stop. Especially when recounting each "love" from his lips. And I don't mean the normal kind of crying, I *wept*.

Every concern I'd been avoiding was squeezed through my eyeballs. I was mourning the loss of my old crummy life, of everyone, and everything I knew. I felt so much better after my weeping show though. I'd made my peace.

Unfortunately, it looked as though I'd suffered an allergic reaction by the time I was finished. Which was great, considering I had a date. One I wasn't too convinced I should be going on. However, I was a people pleaser first, and I wasn't going to let Jin down. So, I sat with cucumbers and ice on my eyes with my favorite dating show in the background. It was called Tentacles for Two, and the contestants were all Krakens. Each time a pair would confirm their match, the host yelled, "Suckered up!" It was quality.

When my doorbell *trilled*, I thought I'd fallen asleep and flew from the couch, but my grape wall clock showed Timos wouldn't arrive for another hour. "Open up, bitch!" Gabs.

When I let her in, she tackled me to the floor with the force of her hug. "Were you crying? What did I walk into? Did Jin fuck up already?"

I raised my hands in surrender before plucking myself off the tiles. "Jin is perfect, too perfect. More than I deserve, but I'm glad I trapped him anyhow. This," I pointed to my runny nose, "is because I got emo after he left and hosted a funeral for my old life. I'm a crier so you can imagine." It was tough to ignore the way my vocal cords sounded like they went through a meat grinder.

"Oh," she mouthed as she abandoned her crossbody on the counter. "I'm here to help, and thank God, because you look awful. No offense."

"Don't lie to me, Gabs. I know you're only here to hear about the mating. But I'm only gonna share if you pinky promise a trade. I'm sure Seong's hung." I held out my shortest digit and she strangled it. With a sigh, I motioned for her to follow upstairs. "Do you know how I should dress for the pier by the way?"

"Who are you meeting again?"

"Timos," I croaked.

"That's the name he gave?" She questioned with a furrowed brow, and I nodded. "*Hmm.* Casual, probably shorts and a crop top. Now spill," she demanded as I grabbed an apple-red top with puffy sleeves and jean shorts.

"I didn't think it was possible to orgasm so often in such an embarrassingly short span. He doesn't even have to last five minutes for me to have five rounds. It's nuts."

"Go, Jin." Gabs mumbled as she picked through my makeup bag on the desk. "I'm so proud of him! Seong claimed he'd resist, but I knew. It's always the innocent ones that cave first."

"Jin is just…" I lost my train of thought. Which was why I asked, "Did you pass out after the first time?"

"Everyone does, I think." Well, that was a relief. "So, there was more than once then? Atta girl!" The second time wasn't nearly as fun as the first. Despite a triple dose of the inky sedative, your girl was waddling. It was more fun during than after.

"Does the feeling of being skewered ever fade or am I gonna be a walking kebab for the next five-centuries?" Gabs howled and I rolled my eyes. *Not helpful.*

"You know it doesn't, I don't even know why you'd ask," she eventually settled long enough to choke out. "I put that black stuff in my coffee every morning, I probably couldn't walk otherwise."

"Fan-flipping-tastic." After changing, I plopped down onto my desk chair.

"I knew you would cave too, you eager beaver. The reason Seong and I took longer is because I had to crack his Scorpio shell."

"And is he soft and gooey on the inside?"

"Not as much as Jin, but enough for me. Speaking of! Sugar Honey Iced Tea, Hae is going to lose it when she hears that her favorite settled down."

I grimaced. "Honestly, I always avoided mommy's boys, but I couldn't resist him. The temptation was like Eve and the apple level. But I clocked it ten-minutes in."

"Whatever you're imagining, double it. Their relationship even freaks Seong and Min out. I can't believe he hasn't told her. You're gonna need at least one more male to make up for how you'll already be sharing half of him with Hae."

Leave it to this Aries to push me over the edge of patience. "You aren't helping, you know."

Gabs shrugged, "Wouldn't you rather know? Hae put me through the ringer, and Seong and I hadn't even bonded yet. I can't imagine how she's gonna react to hearing her precious angel broke the rules *and* didn't ask for approval before mating with you."

I lightly banged my forehead on the desk. My one hard rule was no mama's boys. I frequently dated shorter men, frequently overlooked under-achievers, I even dated my fair share of ex-cons and skirting-the-law types. But *this*, this was exactly why I avoided mama's boys at all costs. *Dun, dun, duuun.*

"I'm exaggerating," Gabs attempted to backtrack, noticing my inner turmoil.

"No, you're not."

The beautiful bitch cackled, "No, I'm really not." It was difficult to believe her after discovering she hid Jin's connection. Maybe the fact our honeymoon bubble hadn't popped was another contributing factor. After our initial awkwardness, Jin and I fit perfectly, like a pair of jeans fresh out of the dryer.

My feelings seemed a lot like real love, true love, the Happily Ever After stuff. Not that I knew for sure. I'd never been in this deep before. Not even with my ex-fiancé, Andy. "Hae and his closeness don't bother me.

Jin is everything. I don't even know why I'm going on this date. We have the best relationship I've seen two people have. Obviously, we're in early days, but—"

"You're going to end up with a harem, Nala. Accept it now." I sputtered as Gabs nodded with hands planted on her hips. How was she so sure when I was anything but? I didn't even know if I'd randomly start weeping again.

"How can you say that so easily? You hardly know me. I've never been able to successfully date one man or woman. There's no chance I can emotionally juggle three plus me." She shrugged, wearing an annoying smirk, which served as a reminder. "Since you did me wrong with Jin, you better reveal which one Timos is."

"Do you remember what you told the bookstore clerk in Xora? Your favorite creature?"

"Dragons, yeah. *Duh.* They're the best." Gabs nodded her head, one too many times, before making a 'there you have it' motion with her lithe arms.

No. Way. She kept nodding while my noggin tripped over itself. "Are you telling me this male is a mother-effin' *dragon*?" The last word was a shriek.

"Timos is ancient, *huge*, and scary. Also *never* smiles. I don't think I've heard him talk. Everyone's terrified of him. Seong told me he's over six or seven thousand years old."

"Which headshot? Tell me. You have to, Gabs. Please!" I was totally fan girling. All my worries about Jin went out the window. He promised me it was fine, so it would be.

Gabs' expression transformed into a devious smirk. "Glasses." I didn't just shout this time, I flew across my bedroom, and started jumping on the bed like a preteen who learned her crush liked her back.

Timos' shell was the dreamiest of the six, from his hazelnut tresses to the bronze of his eyes. I also had a thing for glasses. And sure, it was vain and unhinged to crush over a total stranger, but I was too far gone now.

Butterflies flapping? *Check.*

Mouth drying? *Double check.*

Spazzing out? *Triple check.*

Which was why I skipped outside, propelled from the steps, and flung myself at the huge male in greeting. When colliding with his hard chest, Timos' eyes widened, however, he hugged me back. Albeit, awkwardly. Enormous was an understatement, both in height and width. I'd venture to guess the male had several inches on Jin. And he smelled amazing! Like worn parchment and wood smoke, maybe an antithesis, but it reminded me of reading beside a fire.

When a gigantic, calloused hand pressed against the exposed skin of my back, I realized Timos was *freezing*. I hadn't imagined his chest cooling my cheek through his long-sleeved linen shirt. I didn't react, refusing to worsen the awkwardness I'd already dealt with. Besides, he probably had the same temperature thing as Jin.

Timos' long sleeves were inappropriate for the weather, perhaps that was behind the frigidness, although his shorts and loafers were aligned. He reminded me of a steamy professor. One you'd hope didn't follow the rules about hooking up with his students. *One that would bend you over a desk and—*

Down, girl. You couldn't handle this giant too, get real!

"Sorry for the unexpected physical contact, Timos. You'll soon learn I'm socially inept. Hello, nice to meet you," I greeted.

He pushed up his black spectacles as his face remained expressionless. "Hi, Nala." It was hardly above a whisper sending chills spiraling down my spine. Goodness gracious, he was gorgeous! So much so, I fell into a giddy daze as our eyes locked. Which was when his pupils began to… shift.

The copper of Timos' irises lightened to a liquid gold, which melted into the whites of his eyes. There weren't irises, just a bright canvas behind slitted pupils. Undoubtedly draconic, but beautiful. A few silent blinks passed, until he seemed to collect himself, and gawking transformed into humiliation.

When he sputtered, I deflected on his behalf, "We're walking to the pier?" The male nodded before starting down my street. "I didn't expect these dates to be so similar to Earth."

Nothing. Nada. Zilch. Zip.

After the initial slip, Timos remained silent, I didn't have a clue as to what he was thinking as he towered over the crowd and his spectacled gaze assessed our surroundings. I wasn't the lone ogler, the passersby were stopping and whispering with pointed fingers, it was more aggressive than with Thalla's duke present. Was Timos some kind of celebrity? The passing disgusted reactions were pointing towards… *Dare you say, villain?*

"I chose the pier because I have never been. We shall be on equal footing," Timos finally replied as we reached the park at the end of my street. *No way, he couldn't be the villain.* His calming voice was sound machine adjacent, like ASMR, leaving gooseflesh in its wake.

"You aren't from here then?" I questioned.

"No."

"How long have you lived on Neptune?"

"Over two-thousand years."

"Then how have you never gone to the pier? We're on a teensy island!"

"I rarely venture." That was all Timos gave. Gabs wasn't kidding when she called him quiet, but it wasn't any bother, my mouth ran more than enough for the both of us. I jolted when he eventually tacked on, "You have likely noticed the general public's reactions to my presence."

"What's going on? Are they staring because you're—I don't mean any offense by this, Timos, but you're enormous. Is that why?"

"No. It is because I am a dragon."

"I love that you're a dragon!" I didn't mean to raise my voice, but my enthusiasm hadn't cooled since the squirrel finally shared a juicy acorn. Timos froze, mid-step, as if no one had ever said that to him before. Which was ludicrous.

"You do realize I am the most lethal classification? No element is more powerful than dragon fire," he said with a raised brow. I knew he was attempting to frighten, but it had the opposite effect.

I waved a hand dismissively. "Yeah, yeah. *Sure.* You seem more harmless than a horsefly with your calm demeanor. I never imagined dragons were real, and they've always been my favorite creatures. I mean you can breathe fire *and* fly. *Oh*, and the treasure hoarding! Who *doesn't* like collecting nice things? I honestly can't enjoy a book without at least one dragon." He kept silent for another block, but I couldn't contain my curiosity. "So, what color are your flames?"

Timos halted and canted his gorgeous taupe head, casting me in shadow. "No one has ever asked that." I shrugged in response, and his cheek ticked as his eyes shifted again. "White," he said to my keenness.

"*Woah*. You're gonna have to show me," I squawked, bouncing on my heels.

"It is abnormal to be this riveted, Nala."

"Unsurprising. I'm an abnormal person. I'm not scared of you, though. It's too thrilling to confirm your existence. I'd love to be a dragon myself. I even love the way your eyes shift." I might've broken him with that revelation, since he recoiled with a full-bodied cringe, but didn't regret voicing it.

The aloof mask fell, and devastation crossed as he whispered, "I do not understand why I cannot refrain from shifting in your presence, I apologize if it—"

"No apologizing necessary. Your slitted eyes are as stunning as your prima pair, I dunno if I could pick my favorite, Timos." My skin was itching with the need to know everything about him, and not because of what classification he was, it was the ancient emotionless curtain I itched to peel back most. Having gotten my first taste of how much sexier he was without his tact in place, I needed more. So, I attempted to keep him talking, "Anyway, how common are dragons?"

We crossed a major intersection decorated in various shades of olive with lush maple trees replacing the fruits and palms. It was so similar to London, that if the rows of pillared townhomes were painted white instead of green, it could've passed for a copy. Well, except for the group of varied Phiba and Reptilia heads bicycling past, each sharing trepidation in our direction.

It was more than a little frustrating. How did they not see what I saw? Not even a single being creeped, and he was smokin'. Objectively attractive. Fit, but not in a gross over-muscly way, he was just big. Nicely dressed, too.

"I am the lone dragon on Neptune. My father was the first of our kind and there has never been a high population. I lost count of my nieces, nephews, and their resulting young over the last few millennia. There are likely one hundred of us in total."

"Are you all related?" I asked, and he nodded. "How many siblings do you have?"

"Thirty-three. Thirty of whom are dragons."

"And I thought I had a huge family being one of seven! How'd your mom manage that? Thirty-three kids had to have been chaos." Timos frowned, which was why I tacked on, "I'm so sorry. I don't mean to pry. Or be rude. Or make you uncomfortable. I'm only curious, promise. I never thought I'd meet a dragon, and I find you so..." I blabbed myself into a corner. *Typical.*

"You truly wish to know? It may perturb you." Timos tried with a furrow of his dark brows, and I nodded enthusiastically. "We are born as eggs which are much smaller than typical newborns." *That's a positive for your petunia at least.*

"Do they have to cook in dragon fire before they hatch?" Timos nodded with narrowed slitted eyes as if searching for disgust, or shock, or something.

Naturally, I grinned wider.

We ventured past what seemed like a Bachelorette party wearing paper crowns and sashes, having a grand ole time at an outdoor bar until they caught sight of my date. When they fled, screaming bloody-murder, I honestly didn't know how he could stand it. "The sole reason they're hating is because you're a dragon?"

"The public keeps their distance out of wariness, not that I have given them any cause. It is because I am so rarely seen in this form," Timos explained.

"Everyone acts like this around you everywhere you go, even off Neptune?" I questioned with a grimace. He nodded, sending my gut spiraling. "I *loathe* that."

Timos shrugged his enormous shoulders as if it didn't matter, but it did, which was why I added, "I was considered an oddity back home, my height was atypical. Not that it comes anywhere near how everyone behaves around you, but I was kinda used to it, so I understand. It doesn't make it okay. No one should make you feel uncomfortable because of what you are. You didn't ask to be born a dragon."

"I can hardly believe your lack of fear. Those reactions are what I am accustomed to." He said as he caught me worrying my lower lip. "Since you are stouthearted, what else would you like to know? I find your questioning amusing."

"Do you also wear glasses while in dragon form?" I questioned, and he shook his unruly hazelnut curls out of place. "That's weird. I wonder how."

"Not only have I never considered it, but no one has inquired of that either," Timos replied. "I have worn corrective lenses since youth."

"What about when you eat as a dragon, does it upset your stomach when you shift back into this form?"

"No."

I narrowed my eyes at Timos' uncharacteristically quick reply, but he wasn't meeting them. We turned down a busier street where the buildings grew taller. Our silence was comfortable as we passed a theater with its flashy sign, and I caught him stealing glances when he thought I wasn't looking. It wasn't anything like the devouring stares from Jin, it was far more intense… Serious? Difficult to explain. Like I was a puzzle to him. Did the dragon even have anyone who cared?

"Are you close to your family and friends since you remain a recluse?" I prompted, and Timos shook his head. "And you don't visit home often?"

"No. I remain in contact with my father, we speak frequently. However, I covet the distance from the remainder. As for friends, I have one on Neptune." At least there was one! But who was I to talk? *You had no one and nothing back home.*

"So have you managed to stay single for six thousand years or…?"

"No. Although I have never found a true partner, there were a few centuries with several relationships. It feels as though it were multiple life-times ago now."

"Then why are you in the Program?"

"You." I must have misheard. Timos' voice was hardly a whisper among the surrounding ruckus. My eyes were scrutinous, but his well-proportioned face was unflinching, unblinking.

"Pardon?"

"I have had access to the potential femmes since the Program's inception, I never entertained it until *you*," Timos confirmed.

"You aren't dating the other two participants?" I demanded. He shook his head, and I recoiled in disgust. "*What*?! Why?"

"You are the lone participant I found beautiful. After our sparse conversation, I can confirm your personality is equivalently intriguing. It is your bravery, Nala. Most find me unsettling, especially those unaccustomed to immortality. I believe you are the first to overlook the temperature of my skin."

"I figured you could control it, like Jin."

"No, dragons are cold-blooded."

"All of you is that icy?" I asked, and he nodded. "All of the time?" He nodded again with a slight frown. "Even your tongue?"

It slipped!

Timos eyes slitted, leaving my kitty stirring. From one blink to the next, they shifted back. "Is that a problem?" He inquired, and I shook my head with enough fervor that my neck cracked. There was a vibrator in my freezer in Bluffton so you could say I basically manifested this. *Crap! Mama's gonna have a stroke if she clears your fridge in your absence.*

"I appreciate how you flaunt your every thought on your face, Naliti." He tossed out, interrupting my panic. *Naliti* didn't ring any bells, but I preened, given it had to be endearing. At least, I hoped it was.

"*Pfft*! If that's the case, then what am I thinking right now?"

"That you find me as enticing as I find you," Timos replied. My cheeks boiled as I got lost in his coppery gaze, the way that tiny flecks of copper and bronze made a kaleidoscope. "Even while flustered, you are the most stunning being on Neptune."

His compliment granted me the courage to admit, "I think I'm crushing on you already."

"Good." It wasn't what I expected him to say! I wasn't even sure how to reply. How was Timos this delectable? I was blatantly staring — *again* — so, I diverted to focus on my feet instead of *goo-goo-gah*-ing. My fingers itched to grab him as I kept my gaze on the cobbles, I couldn't help but question whether his curls would be soft. Whether or not the feeling of his chilly skin would quell some of the heat. *How it would feel to have those huge, calloused hands on your —*

Too far! Pivot, pivot! "So, I read this book, and the dragon had two dicks —"

Timos interrupted with a loud rumbly laugh, one which was such a drastic tone from his soft voice that I did a triple-take to confirm it was his. I committed his reaction to memory, even if my ridiculous comment was the cause.

"I apologize if my singular cock will not be enough for you," Timos replied with his first genuine grin. It hung crookedly on his lips from disuse, but it did nothing to detract from his beauty. It felt like I'd won the lottery with that laugh and resulting smile, my organs were doing a cele-bratory jig. I mirrored him after overcoming the shock of the blatant flirting.

"So, what do you do for work?"

"I am Neptune's Protectorate. Additionally, I cohead a division of researchers and scientists focused on scalability. When I first arrived, Thalla was the lone grounded city, besides the twelve below, and it was one-tenth the size. My role began with large scale improvements, such as land usage and zoning, given the limited supply for farming. Now that the population has continued to steadily rise, our work has transitioned towards alleviating more specialized concerns."

"Fascinating." Timos raised his brows as if he doubted me. "I mean it! So, what are you researching now?"

"Since the majority of the population is vegetarian, we are seeking to manipulate the nutritional composition of the most purchased crops."

"Increasing proteins then?" I asked. He nodded with another toothy grin, bringing his slightly sharper pearly fangs into focus, and I gave myself an internal high five. "What are you protecting Neptune from?"

"Malice."

I frowned, poking him in the ribs. "You're gonna have to give me more than that, Timos."

"Chiron's Titan Contessa, Malice, has been at odds with Neptune's Titan Queen since the Dawn. She wishes to thwart the current peace as a continuation of their feud. The same Contessa is to blame for the intergalactic war, she is the reason a Council formed three-thousand years ago. That is eke why there is at least one dragon assigned to each planet, we are the Protectorate, given we are indestructible, and cannot perish."

"There's one of you on Earth?" I questioned and he nodded. "How is that possible without magic there? Wait, what's 'eke'?"

"Apologies, my verbiage is dated. 'Eke' is another term for 'as well' or 'also.' As for my brother, Kronos, and his amoroso, they remain hidden on Earth to my knowledge. Transparently, I do not know much, as I have not spoken with him in millennia. Earth is in far less peril than Neptune."

Huh. I wondered why it wasn't in the news. There wasn't any mention of it being unsafe, not even a hint. "What are you protecting the borders from exactly?"

"Chiron smuggles vampires through our wards. Do you know what those are?"

I nodded, "Blood suckers, right?" I doubted they slept in coffins or had aversions to garlic but made a mental note to question Homie later. Now that they were a real threat. At least Jin sourced me a mini switchblade on a keychain, which was already attached to my phone. Although it'd likely do little against a vamp, it was better than nothing.

"Yes, they are leeches who possess the ability to blend into any society. The last major breach, three months ago, resulted in the loss of sixty-six innocents," he replied.

"That's horrible. How many vampires got in?" I questioned.

"Two."

"That much damage from *two*?!"

Timos' handsome face and shoulders fell as he sighed. "Vampires possess the ability to turn, or splice, other immortals into half vampires. Although two broke through, ten were turned, and in turn, the twelve of them drained the rest."

"*Woof*, that sounds like a nightmare."

The lines of his handsome face deepened as he revealed, "I am to blame. At the time of the attack, I was visiting a planet known as Uru. It was for merely forty-eight hours, so no additional patrols were arranged in my absence. A mistake I will never repeat."

"What were you doing there?"

"Uru is the most advanced planet, and our research frequently requires the use of their resources. We had not experienced any breaches for over a decade prior, so my leave was approved without thought." Devastation cloaked my date, from his tightly clenched fists to the ticking in his cheek. The berth around us grew with every blink, as though the populous could sense his frustration.

"It doesn't seem like you're at fault. You shouldn't be so hard on yourself, Timos. You're just one person... *Er*, male, I mean."

He stilled, as if no one had told him he wasn't responsible, and my corny heart cracked. Timos' voice was softer, more intentional, when he said, "Perhaps not. However, if I were here, none would have perished." The whole knight in dinosaur amour thing he had going was doing it for me. "We have the most border skirmishes of any planet, which is the primary reason it became my assignment. I am the third most prestigious dragon." *There went that stupid triggering word again.*

"Prestigious?"

"No one has mentioned magical prestige?" I shook my head, and he explained. "The more magic an immortal possesses, the more prestige they hold within society. Although Neptune is not nearly as classist as other planets, the one consistency is that dragons are at the 'top of the food chain,' as you humans say."

Jin hinted as much so it wasn't surprising. However, it was shocking hearing Timos' ancient voice spouting a familiar saying. "How did you know that?"

"Avexei has been obsessed with Earth in recent years."

"Your one friend?" I clarified, and he nodded in response at the same time I remembered there was a Avexeidros on my roster. "Is it weird that I'm gonna date your lone companion?"

"Cousin. My uncle is one of Avexei's mother's many bonded. Although there is no blood relation between us, he is more of a brother than any of my true siblings. So no, it is not weird. We have shared plenty in the past."

Innuendo? Or… There went my brain with that 'plenty.' Spiraling down, down, down. I lost her in the gutter. Along with the air in my lungs. It didn't even matter which one of the remaining four Avexei was. "So, you two planned on sharing me?" I wheezed, incapable of plucking that shadowy orgy from my brain.

"That is entirely up to you, Naliti."

This brought up the other bridge we had yet to cross. Which was why I croaked, "And you're fine with sharing me? Even if it's not with your cousin?"

"That depends."

"On what?" I asked.

"Who you desire to bind me to for eternity." *Oh, right, because dragons lived forever.*

"I'm feeling pretty sure about you and Jin."

"Yu-Jin would struggle with you having multiple tethers as a Siarc."

"Jin swore he would be okay with it," I rushed out, unsure if I was trying to convince Timos or myself of that more.

"Yu-Jin is not one of the males who would deter me." Timos stared at the distant sunset as he added, "I have lived for over six thousand turns, you are the first to capture my interest so wholly. Truthfully, who you wish to tether with may not matter."

My heart did more than skip a beat, it somersaulted as his kaleidoscopic eyes shifted the second they caught mine. There were literal sparks crackling in the air between us. How had I truly believed I couldn't form feelings for someone else? I'd always enjoyed polyamorous reads most. In my few relationships it felt as though I had too much love to give to one person. But now I had to noodle on how to explain this to Jin —*No ma'am. Worry about that later!*

Then the pieces fell into place. Ancient. Protectorate. Indestructible. "Timos, are you a god?" He nodded. "What exactly does that entail? Do you have a shtick?"

"What is that?"

"As an example, Aphrodite is the name of an ancient Greek goddess of love back home. So, her shtick is relationships," I explained.

"No. We refer to shticks as domains. Gods are merely the children of Titans. We are more gifted than most, however, only Titans command oppositional domains. As the Queen's daughter, Aphrodite is technically eke a goddess. I am unsurprised to hear she was commonly known, she resided on Earth for several millennia." I made a mental note to question the femme at the first opportunity. How she gained her notoriety had to make an interesting tale.

Thanks to the thickening crowds, I could tell we were nearing the water. When wiggling through a particularly squished section between street vendors and lines of patrons, I noticed a gathering around a podium of sorts beside a small park.

Burnt brunette beefcake!

The male from my roster was center stage, wearing a white t-shirt which gave his sunburn further prominence. *Why does he remind you of a GI Joe action figure? Probably the buzzcut and oversized muscles.* His grating voice crooned into a fancy mic as the spectators gleefully hung onto his every word. "Chadwick," Timos all but growled and I looked up to find him scowling. Which resulted in an instantaneous wide berth around us despite the packed street.

"You know him?" I prompted, earning myself a disgruntled nod. "What's with the audience?"

"He hosts a popular podcast titled, 'Masc Males'," Timos clipped. I didn't contain my full-bodied cringe once noting everyone in audience was indeed male. The title was loud and clear, too. "Exactly. And it is likely far worse than what you are imagining; Chadwick preaches that femmes should only be considered as 'breeders,'" he said with finger quotes. Giving me a conniption.

As we drew closer, we unfortunately caught the dumbasses' attention. *"Look at that!* The dragon's on his date with the human. What do we think? Will he win her affections before I can woo her?" *The sun must've fried his brains too.*

The small mob leered in various states of distaste and on instinct, I gripped Timos' frigid hand in mine. Their resulting booing and shock didn't penetrate. Nothing could as my fingers essentially vibrated against his. Something shifted, but I couldn't put my finger on how, or why.

There was a chill, almost like a block of ice, forming behind the center of my sternum. I didn't know what to make of it, or how to react as it became increasingly difficult to breathe. And I wasn't even looking at the dragon, because if I did, I would've probably melted. No, my eyes were unfocused, there were too many dizzying physical sensations crashing through my consciousness.

"Damn, I thought humans possessed more self-preservation. Look at her! How are you so unafraid of the dragon, Nightingale Williams? Don't you possess any sense?" Chad's pesky voice crackled through my stun. I caught him smirking as his followers rallied. He was as demented as the worst Earthly Podcasters.

Suddenly, the jeers became squeaks. They were scampering. I could feel the furious shift in the air as a bleached cloud of smoke billowed from Timos' lips paired with a menacingly low growl. He didn't scare me. If anything, his threats got me revved up. Honestly, I was equally infuriated by this podc-asshole. "From where I'm standing, you're the only terror here, bad Chad," I volleyed. *Kinda lame, but effective.*

The male's nostrils flared as he fumed. Krakens were arguably some of the most disturbing immortals, the possums of Neptune. *Suckered arms? They were no dragon wings, that's for sure.*

"Wow. Nightingale must be damaged. How else—"

A deafening *roar* sliced through the atmosphere, silencing Chad, the speakers, the spectators. Everything. The last of the lingering jeerers scattered as Timos erupted. "Say whatever you wish of me, Kraken, but you will never speak ill of Nala again. *Do you understand me?*" Then the screaming resumed as the pearly smoke spread, creating a thick cloud cover over the surrounding city block.

Timos was godly, alright. His slitted eyes were aglow as more smoke left his pouty lips. As I struggled to keep from lunging at him, the mic went staticky. My attention flicked to Chad nodding with his eyes downcast. *Tail between his legs!* Even his idiotic followers had abandoned him. *Bad burnt Chad's a real bigot alright.* I couldn't contain my cackle of glee.

Spinning towards my date, I found him thrilled. "Told you, dragon," I said, daring to inch closer as the icy sensation in my chest worsened. "I'm never gonna be terrified of you. If anything, that was the hottest threat anyone's ever made on my behalf."

Timos' grin spread, but he hesitated. It's not as though you don't know how he feels, so what's holding him back? I had no such qualms.

Nor could I withhold my urge to get my hands on him for another second. I lunged, gripping his stubbled cheeks before my fingers finally tangled in those unruly curls. *Softer than expected.*

Our lips locked and I moaned from the balm of his frigidness against the humidity.

When our lips first met it was like an earthquake. Timos groaned when I tugged his hair. His minty tongue left every bit of me tingling. He wasn't gentle, he was rougher than rough. Demanding as his icy tongue pushed past my lips. I knew his eyes would be slitted without needing to peek.

Timos kissed me as though the world was ending. The dance between our tongues sent chills through every inch of my being. I wrapped my legs to cling and claw onto him because I couldn't get enough.

It didn't matter that we were in the middle of the street, once I felt the freezing hardness pressing against me through his shorts, I whimpered into his mouth. I was gonna die trying to take that joystick for a spin but didn't care! Nothing mattered but this gorgeous dragon.

When he withdrew, an embarrassing squeak of disappointment escaped, and that was when those fangs pierced my lower lip. Oh, my sugary effin tits, I felt that bite in every nerve ending, every muscle, everywhere. I was trembling all over as our foreheads met. "Naliti, you are so—"

"If you don't shut up and kiss me again, I'm gonna pitch a fit!"

It took us probably another ten minutes to untangle, but we eventually made it to the expansive pier. It was disturbingly similar to Los Angeles, a near replica of Santa Monica's. From the raised wooden planks to the brightly lit Ferris wheel, and hordes of unhinged children running amuck. It was larger with far more attractions, along with a dock below, but they were similar.

"Aren't we going over there?" I pointed towards the carnival-esque park, and Timos shook his head. Instead, he tugged me down wooden steps off the side by our interlocked hands. The inexplicable sensation behind my sternum hadn't settled, but I was attempting to ignore it. And failing. It did at least keep the surrounding heat at bay, I wasn't drenched for once.

"We are scheduled for a tour. The docks are below." Timos turned to add in his low voice, "We could explore the pier when we return if you would like to."

"A tour?"

He nodded. "Of the undersea cities."

"*Really?*" I shrieked like an owl. "Are we going by submarine?"

"I do not know what that is."

Why would they have submarines, you dolt? "Can dragons breathe underwater?" I asked instead.

"I am personally able because I command water. However, it is rare among dragons, I was one of three to inherit the ability from our mother." Timos stepped onto the floating dock and caught my frown as he aided in my footing. "Do not fret. The tour is bubbled, you shall be able to breathe normally, eke our clothing shall remain dry for the duration."

There was one boat docked, a double decker resembling a ferry, and it was packed like a can of sardines. "So, this curved bow is meant to get us under those waves? Seems impossible."

"A shifted Whalen shall fasten the hull to its back with a harness."

"*Huh*," I mused as we climbed the gangplank. Timos pulled a black conch phone from his shorts and swiped it past a hologram scanner, unlocking the turnstile to climb aboard. The entire crowd went still at the sight of him. I fumed. *What's up with the dragon persecution?!*

Did they blame Timos for those deaths? The thought knotted my stomach. It didn't seem like he deserved it, he only left for another work trip for crying out loud. Ignoring the rudeness, I asked, "Should we go to the top floor? Where do you think will have the best view?"

"Whatever you wish," Timos replied. When we passed a pair of femmes who literally spat in disgust, I shared the most scathing expression possible. If looks could kill, the scowl I gave would've incinerated them *twice*. Timos caught the way my hackles rose and pulled me under a heavy arm before leading towards the stairs. "As I have said, they do not bother me, Naliti. Do not fret for me, please."

"It bothers *me*! If they're gonna be rude, I'm gonna be *rude-r*," I huffed as we found a pair of empty seats on the upper starboard. "And here, I thought Neptune was this idyllic utopia, but nope! Y'all have just as many bigots!"

"Y'all?"

"Sorry, my hick comes to the surface when I'm feeling spicy. I try to keep it hidden."

"No more unnecessarily apologizing," Timos whispered into my ear with his icy breath. My every nerve in body popped like kernels in a microwave. Coupled with the chill behind my sternum, I was struggling. Big time.

"I can't help it," I breathed in little more than a whisper, rubbing my free hand across my chest. *What's happening to you?* I'd never encountered a similar sensation, not even when the suppressant waned around Jin. I could physically sense Timos beside me through it. His calm.

"Could I inquire something of you?" Timos questioned, interrupting my internalizing, and I nodded. Now creeping heavily on his tantalizing lips. "How are you so comfortable in my presence? You did not hesitate to kiss me." I couldn't contain my chuckle, then grin.

"What you mean to ask is why I'm so forward when we barely know each other?"

"I suppose." He said with a perplexed furrow.

"It's because of how I feel around you. You help quiet my insanity. I can't explain it, Timos, but I feel it here," I gestured to the center of my chest. "You're not only handsome, but you're also caring and interesting. And lonely, I know what that's like more than most. Which is why seeing these disgruntled reactions sent your way grinds my gears. Even if you were the one blamed for those sixty-six deaths. You don't deserve any of this leering."

"I was not blamed. The public does not know because the Queen refused to share the deaths with the press. Only I carry that burden."

"What? How?" I exclaimed.

"She used her gifts and position to conceal the truth."

As I chewed on that, the cresting of an enormous humpback-like whale beside the pier sent the boat into a frenzy. "Welcome to the Reef Rider Tour! Thank you for joining us this Friday, we have quite the schedule, as we plan on taking you to all twelve Reefs! Before we dive in, there are two safety precautions to be aware of! Although you may roam the vessel freely, if any of your appendages extend beyond the railings, you will no longer be protected! So, no pointing overboard! Claws and paws to yourselves, ladies, theys, and gents! Please settle in, our Whalen, Kristoph, will keel in ten seconds!"

When that huge ass whale made us bounce ten feet in the air, I *screeched*. Timos had me secured underneath his weighted arm, but it wasn't any comfort. It felt as though we were nothing but a speck of glitter. I'd been too daunted to research what beasts called Neptune's seas home, so who knew what lurked below. "Nala, I would not risk your safety. You must know that."

There was a loud *click* before a groaning of iron that distracted my reply. Before I could blink, we were descending. *Rapidly.*

The sudden shift from the humidity to coolness was a shock to my system. Kristoph's distant maw remained downturned as he took us deeper and deeper. The sun's rainbow rays were lost within moments, encasing us in a terrifying gloom. There wasn't any wetness, but I could hardly keep up with the warring sensations between my chest and the ride. It felt like a rollercoaster more than a boat, given we were flying at the speed of a big drop.

"Are you alright?" Timos asked softly, and I managed a nod with my eyes clamped shut. From the velocity in which our Whalen friend tugged, I worried my ears would pop, or worse, my eyeballs. *It's possible, people's eyes can plop out from abrupt changes in atmospheric pressure.*

It took an entire collection of breathwork to settle me. Timos was frowning when I finally cracked to discover all was fine and dandy. We hadn't reached the first city yet, but I could see the distant spatter of lights. There was a clear sphere around the boat and whale, one I could see bubbles drifting around. Its tangible magical shield, or ward, was unnerving to witness. Especially because my life relied on it.

It was a good thing I grew up on boats, because several around us fled from their seats with seasickness. *Bless their hearts ... Not.*

It was karmic retribution for their hating on my date.

"Our first stop is Pike Reef! Established in the year 10001, the Reef was named for its most common inhabitant, the pike fish! This city below has a population of 2,300,000 and as we near, you will notice that they have chosen to replicate the Thallan pier that sits directly above its depths," the speaker boomed. I caught sight of the Ferris wheel illuminating the center of the buildings made of grains of *sand*! Freaking sandcastles. It looked like a fairytale, so much so, I had to pinch myself to make sure it was real.

"*Woah,*" I breathed, getting a bird's eye view of the streets below our Whalen. There were not only plenty of immortals walking around on the grassy seafloor, but millions of fish swimming between. There were cafes. Shops. Even a hospital, it had the same cross symbol and everything. It reminded me of a hyper-realistic Pixar movie with our bubble acting as the 3-D goggle's lenses.

"I believe they brought in a mage to spell the sand to keep its shape"

Timos explained, and I nodded wordlessly, too caught up in the unbeliev-ableness. We were coasting above the tallest buildings, but it was still incredible. "Are you alright, Naliti?"

"More than alright," I breathed. "Timos, thank you so much for plan-ning this. It's amazing! I don't even know where to look. I didn't think I'd get to see these cities!" When I caught the huge grin Timos wore, I got sucked right in, he was the eye of the hurricane. I had to fight the urge to close the distance as his tempting icy lips were inches away.

"You are so beautiful, Naliti," Timos said in little more than a whisper. My cheeks boiled as he brushed a coiled strand behind my ear with a chilly finger. "It is difficult to avert my eyes from you." The closeness of his chilly breath was sending my heart thrashing against my ribs while that frigid sensation in the center of my chest worsened.

"Same," I rasped.

The speaker broke our staring contest to announce the next stop, and we were once again surrounded by darkness. Since we'd crossed second base, I nestled closer into Timos' side tucked underneath his heavy arm. When he took my other free hand in his, so we were essentially pretzel-ed together, I knew he was mine. No insecurity, no questioning, none of that. "You said I'm not like anyone else, but it's truer about you, Timos."

"My lone stipulation prior to bonding, is that you meet with the other males. Chadwick is irrelevant, but the others may not be."

"You're *that* sure about me already?" My lips twitched, tempted into spreading to an obnoxious extent.

"I am. Do you not feel the same?" He asked. I nodded as our stupidly wide grins matched. Between Timos' slitted sunny eyes and the abandon-ment of his inscrutable mask, he'd managed to brighten the gloomy depths of the ocean.

"Okay, I'll meet with the others. It's not going to change how I feel about you though… Or how I feel about Jin." Instead of the cringe or grimace I anticipated by raising Yu-Jin, Timos only nodded. Still wearing that smile. I couldn't seem to erase mine either.

⋘ ⋘ ⋙ ◖ ⋆ ˚

The other Reefs were completely unlike the first, both in structures and the populations of fish. Angler Reef's fish bone buildings were hardly visible and resembled ancient ruins. The sole illumination stemmed from the creepy fish's dangling appendages resembling curved book lights. The scary guys and their huge gaping jaws with rows and rows of pointy teeth were giving haunted…

Porgy Reef was an entire city of interconnected glass domes. The weirdest part was seeing the unbelievably lengthy tubes sucking air from the surface for its residents' survival. Their population was the most intermixed and the closest to Bahasa's shores. Apparently, there were plenty who couldn't breathe underwater and commuted in oversized hamster-ball-looking bubbles. When I told Timos how people killed themselves trying to cliff dive in similar inflatables, he laughed so hard he snorted…

Tarpon Reef was a near replica of Thalla, at least, from what we could see from our distance. The rainbow pattern of the streets and architectural mashup reminded me of the view from my bedroom window. That is if you removed the kelp, sponge, and seaweed decorating the façades…

Dory Reef was a bust as I didn't see a single dory fish. All their buildings were also sandy, which felt unoriginal after our initial stop. Although they did have the most bioluminescent creatures lighting their streets…

Slippery Dick Reef had the best name but was disappointing because it lacked any structures. The immortals lived under the seafloor. Admittedly, it was a gorgeous reef, reminiscent of the Great Barrier in Australia. But normal…

Timos laughed at my reactions to Wobbegong and Lumpsucker because I couldn't believe my ears. So much so, it distracted from paying attention to those two as I got sucked into the dragon instead…

Once we arrived in Jelly Reef, I jumped from my seat, and Timos wrangled me back from the railing. Every single illumination was a jelly-fish. The humongous, oversized jellies were assigned to act as streetlamps, while I could see their smaller relatives peeking through the windows of the passing skyscrapers. It was undoubtedly the brightest city…

Our three-hour ride on Kristoph *flew* by. The flirty conversation with Timos was as entertaining as the sights. By the time the speakers buzzed to announce our final stop, my cheeks were sore. "We saved the best for last, my friends! Welcome to Bristle Reef! Founded in 12334, it is the *only* city below that possesses spelled oxygenation! That is why it has the highest population, with a whopping 5,200,001! This is your sole opportunity to explore for yourselves! Please do not venture too far. We will reconvene in thirty-minutes!"

The Whalen slowed in front of an empty parking lot-like stretch of dark sandy ocean floor and the gangplank extended. Given the reactions around Timos, I forced him to wait last to disembark. The male kept insisting he didn't care but I did. I couldn't be liable for punching someone in the face on his behalf.

As my platform sneakers hit the glistering navy sand and reacquainted with solid ground, I could hardly believe the packed street sprawling before us. It was exactly as I imagined Atlantis might look. The most surreal part was how I couldn't tell much of a difference once we abandoned the boat's spelled bubble. I could feel the pressure of the water on my body, could feel its frigidness against my exposed skin, but remained totally dry. The only applicable comparison was like wearing a waterbed.

The majority of the buildings had pointed conical roofs which gave Bristle Reef a witchy feel. Especially with the lacking illumination, the streetlamps' flickering cerulean flames did little to expose the winding passageways. There were as many fish as there were beings walking or swimming up and down the shell lined sidewalks. I could hardly function as I took it in.

The tourist trap shop and its attached restrooms seemed to be owned by the boating company, as it had teensy replicas of our boat with Whalen attached. There were the typical knick-knacks and trinkets. Magnets. Tees. Hats. There was even a holiday section with ornaments. "Timos, do you celebrate Christmas on Neptune?"

"No. Those are for celebrating Yuletide, many hang them from their windowsills from November to January."

"Are there gifts exchanged?" I questioned with a frown. A bit disappointed there wouldn't be a Neptunian equivalent to the holidays since I finally had a reason to celebrate.

"Gifts are typically only given during anniversaries."

"*Huh*," I mumbled as he pulled me through the towering aisles of junk.

Then the cutest drinking glasses caught my eye, and I jumped out of my skin. "Timos! *Look* at *these*!" I picked one up to get a better look. They were so unique you could only hope to find them on Etsy. Each had a normal stem in a different color, like any wineglass, but an oversized shell replaced the cylinder. All with a different shell, from conch to oyster.

When Timos began picking out a set, I raised a brow. The dragon shrugged and dropped, "I am purchasing these for you."

"You don't have to do that! You already helped fund my entire life here. Besides, I'll never forget this date. I don't need any reminders. It's ingrained forever, trust me."

He ignored me, asking instead, "Is there anything else that has caught your eye?" I shook my head. "What about one of the magnets?" he pressed, pointing toward the miniatures of the boat and Whalen. The ones I'd been eyeing since their background images were spelled to switch from Reef to Reef every few seconds.

"Fine, but only because you insisted."

"I could never refuse you, Naliti." I believed him even without peeking at his expression. Once I had though? I was done for.

"What does that mean, Timos? Naliti?" I finally mustered the resolve to question, meeting his bronze kaleidoscopic gaze.

"Fearless little Nala," he replied as his cheeks dusted with embarrassment. An unbidden squeal escaped me. No one had ever bestowed a cuter nickname. It was such a simple thing, but that didn't make it any less significant. The dragon and his genuine shy grin as I lost my noodles compounded my emotional chaos.

This whole tour, his thoughtfulness, and his *laugh*? Good grief, his laugh! Timos was under my skin, and he'd burrowed deep. Sometimes I loved being a softie Pisces, but not tonight, not around this attentive male. The one who had been starved for any positive consideration or TLC for thousands and thousands of years.

We grabbed shrimp-po-boy sandwiches before returning to Kristoph. I was relieved to learn that despite his work, Timos wasn't vegetarian, unlike Jin and Gabs. I finished the sandwich in seconds and thankfully he hadn't judged, not even when I licked my fingers like a heathen. It was another reason added to my 'keeping him' list.

Yeah, I was tallying and keeping mental lists. I knew not to compare Timos to Jin but couldn't help it. It wasn't that I was looking for a winner, my obsession with duke Yu-Jin Rapax was clear, it was solely in attempt to understand the abrupt shift in stance. How I could feel so certain about

Timos in such a short span. In all honesty, I didn't feel nearly as certain about the Siarc at this point in our date, our tethering resulted from my deadly case of dick-speration.

Thankfully, Timos allowed me to indulge in my internalizations as the Whalen tugged us back to land. The silence was comfortable, the sole reason I remained unsettled was because of the chill in my chest. The ice cube behind my sternum hadn't melted and it was perplexing as to which organs were responsible.

"Can I ask you something?" Timos questioned as we reached Thalla's now, darkened and near empty streets. I nodded. "How did you obtain such a noticeable scar? You could have it removed if you so desired."

My stomach's plummet stole the air from my lungs. Not even Jin had questioned the mark yet. Most of the time, I avoided thinking about the six-inch-long slash that encouraged my singledom. Since it was on the back of my calf, I hardly noticed unless looking for it. Yes, it was tempting to have it lasered, as it drew attention over the years, but I wanted to remember what resulted from not trusting my instincts. Timos must've noticed my discomfort because he opened his mouth to backtrack, but I silenced him with a shake of my head.

"I'll tell you, but you have to promise not to judge." I was gathering my strength as he nodded with a deep-set frown on his gorgeous face. "You probably remember the one long-term relationship I mentioned?"

Timos grunted as his eyes lightened, then slitted. "The abomination with the 'hick' name who cheated, yes." I chortled as he regurgitated my terminology in his ancient lilt. It calmed my nerves a tad.

"Him, yeah. After Andy deserted me in front of every person we knew at our wedding, I tried sending everyone away. They fought with me about it at first, my parents along with friends, but I just wanted to be alone. We'd already paid to rent the oceanfront venue through the night, and I couldn't go home because I was living with him. But they were freaked because I wasn't reacting.

"That was the worst part, Timos, the humiliation he dealt so publicly. Andy had a million opportunities to cancel the whole charade. I wouldn't have been surprised; we weren't happy. But it wasn't him who made me cry that night, it was my ex best friend, Isaiah, revealing he knew Andy cheated the entire span of our six-year relationship—" Timos interrupted with a teensy growl and an accompanying puff of smoke.

Despite the traumatic topic, my lips were tempted to stretch into a smile. "Don't worry, we haven't been friends for several years, it was a betrayal which led to our eventual collapse. Isaiah and his husband were pissed I wasn't crying. Or like, suicidal, or something, I dunno. His exact verbiage was, 'Andy abandoned you because you're an emotional train-wreck, Gale.' Obviously, I didn't take that very well.

"Once I shed those tears, thanks to Isaiah, they all left. When I was finally alone, I had an entire bar to myself, and got hammered. We paid for a fireworks show towards the end of the night, so I dragged my drunk ass out to the sand to watch. We have these inflatables back home, called pool floats, which are essentially the size of a blanket. I used one to keep my dress from being ruined by the sand. But I passed out at some point.

"The tide rose, dragging the inflatable and me into the ocean's depths. I thought I was dreaming at first, that the waves were nothing more than a realistic nightmare. Until a hook accidentally caught my leg. I'd drifted out to where the fishermen anchored, and they hadn't noticed me. Not until I began screaming when said hook ripped through my calf and popped my pool float. I almost drowned by the time they toted me to the hospital for thirty stitches."

"You could have died," Timos breathed with his draconic eyes wide. I shrugged off the shivers that mentioning the trauma always dealt. Unfortunately, he noticed and scowled. "Why that reaction, Naliti?"

"I still have nightmares. Or I used to before arriving on Neptune. My therapist insisted Andy's loss is what caused them, but they were only about what happened after the abandonment, of when I was out in the water. Bleeding. Choking. Drowning. They're always more horrifying than the reality of the memory. Don't tell Jin this, but sometimes I used to wake up screaming from picturing sharks ripping me apart."

"Why did you keep the scar if it pains you?" Timos asked with another puff.

"As a reminder. I left it there because I didn't listen to my instincts. I didn't put myself first and I let fear win." A chuckle left my lips, and the male observed as if I'd lost it. "It's funny. I stuck around because I cared about Andy's feelings more than mine. I didn't think he'd accept a breakup without—"

"*Accept?*" Timos question was near snarl. *Oh, snap.* I hadn't meant to mention that.

"Ah, yup." I started shifting nervously from sneaker-to-sneaker because this was typically the part of the story I left out. I'd never spoken it aloud to anyone other than Doctor Vanna, my untrustworthy therapist. And I brought it up with her *only once* because her reaction was so condemnatory that I lost the courage to repeat it. Not even Isaiah learned the truth. I buried it deep. It was probably time to dig it up, though. Timos felt safe. He hadn't balked at any of my quirks. But even so, voicing it was daunting.

The dragon patiently waited as I gathered courage. I'm sure I looked like a lunatic as I kept opening and closing my mouth while nothing came out. No matter how many attempts.

It took him pulling me under the comfort of his cool heavy arm to eventually coax the dreaded words. "My relationship with Andy was physically abusive—"

Timos interrupted with a growl. One that was so loud that the sparse beings in the street ran in the opposite direction hootin' and hollerin'. "Does this cretin still live?" I nodded as another rumble shook Timos' enormous chest and a larger billow of smoke escaped his lips. I didn't deserve this reaction which was why I kept spewing.

"It only happened when Andy was drunk. I'm not making excuses for him. I don't remember him raising a fist until we left college. We used to black out a lot from drinking back then, so I can't say for sure, though. He'd randomly bash my ribs when he'd come home from the bar to find me asleep. My therapist claimed that might've been why I had such vivid nightmares, because I'd been awoken to beatings so often…"

I wasn't finished, but lost my train of thought, catching sight of several moons surrounded by pink clouds. I was swept into the memories. Of how Doc had judged the ever-loving crap outta me, of how I lied and swore that it happened once. But every single fight resulted in rough sex with Andy. I was beyond damaged. He pavloved me into getting off on pain before pleasure. I'd still not recovered nearly a decade later.

There was so much self-loathing for enjoying the abuse that I could drown in its depths. For sticking around out of a sick and twisted need for more. I knew my desires could've been sated in a safer environment with the right partner, but I was too chicken to even vocalize it. Dark romance novels were beginning to sway me in moving in the right direction, but… I knew Andy's beatings should've been associated negatively. He *was* trying to harm me after all.

Instead, they fed my perverse desires.

It's why I never attempted to date. It's also the reason why I reveled in Jin getting rough. The fact that he checked a secret fantasy box without having to voice it probably was why I was so obsessed. The resulting wounds were far worse nowadays. I could go an entire waitressing shift on my feet and not need Tylenol after going to blows with Andy Shmandy. Whereas now, I'd not be able to stand from the ache without triple the inky sedative.

It was unsettling I had my sights already set on this even more enormous male, my who-ha was doomed. I peeked and caught an internal struggle blanketing Timos, it looked a lot like sympathy painted in his grimace though. *Yuck*.

I gripped his stubbled chin and forced his gaze down to mine. "Don't you dare pity me. I fought him back each and every time. Andy's bruises were usually worse than mine in the morning. I never back down from a fight, I can be vicious. There's something seriously sick and wrong with me for feeling satisfaction in mentioning that. I know. But I'm a fighter, always have been, I enjoyed it sometimes. And because I struck him back, I'm at fault too—"

"It is pride I feel for you, not pity," Timos interjected, his voice with a bit more dragon gravel. I didn't know what I expected, but it wasn't that. "You cannot blame yourself for the actions of others. Your resilience is admirable. It is difficult to hear the details of your past because it is not the same defiant and self-aware femme who stands before me. You have grown, do not be ashamed of the kindling you once were. Nor should you be ashamed of how your flames rise now. I covet your fire, Naliti."

That...

That was the sweetest thing anyone's ever *said to me* or *about me*.

I burst into tears.

Timos scooped me off the ground and held me tight as I sobbed into his frigid chest. I couldn't find an ounce of embarrassment. "I wasn't supposed to weep all over you," I eventually cried into his linen shirt.

"At least you did not apologize unnecessarily." I gasped and stilled in my teary tracks. *How?*

How did he know how to abruptly stop my weep show? Barking a raspy laugh, I wiped away the tear tracks. "I'm grateful you're the first I've shared that with, Timos. Thank you." In response, he gripped my wrist and pressed a peck to my palm. I short-circuited from the feeling of his chilly soft lips. When he pressed my same hand to his chest, the whisper of the chill disappeared immediately. Timos' sternum was boiling.

We both gawked for a few seconds. Then it hit me, like a mallet over the head.

I tugged his icy hand from my wrist and pressed it against the ice cube in the center of my chest. The inexplicable *thing* that'd been nagging me.

Once his enormous hand decorated my sternum, Timos' mouth popped open. There was a buzzing under my skin, but I was too worked up to discern the source. The lone sensation I could confirm was the way his body mimicked whatever mine was doing. "What is it?" I rasped as his eyes flicked between our hand-to-chest placements.

"Truthfully, I do not know." Timos' slitted eyes searched mine. "My nature has oddities not even my father completely understands." The corners of his lips tugged downward as he withdrew his hand. All night this male had been objectified, but the only time he reacted in self-loathing was in regard to me.

"I don't care what it is. Nothing's gonna scare me away from you. Get it through your thick skull."

The gorgeous smirk across Timos' face instigated a hunger that left my entire lower half clenching. The male placed me back onto the sidewalk gingerly and immediately loathed the distance. I bit my lower lip to quell my craving, but it was no use. The menthol tingles in my chest were spreading to my limbs.

We started walking again, hand in hand, and when I knew we were one street away, I was experiencing a full body zizz in anticipation of taking his icy lips for another spin. "Nala, I must thank you for tonight. I do not think I have ever laughed as freely. You reminded me how enjoy-able new experiences—"

"Timos! You're making me emotional again, that's not allowed to happen before a kiss! I don't wanna sniffle all over you!"

"No?" He smirked as I shook my head. "What is allowed then, beauti-ful?" He leaned down within reach. So, I went for it and grabbed those

ridiculous cool stubbled cheeks of his. I hadn't imagined a lick of how good
he tasted.

And it seemed the snail caught herself a dragon, too.

When I unlocked my front door, discovering a shirtless Jin eating cereal on my sofa, I didn't know how to behave. Besides placing the paper bag with my new trinkets gently on the ground, of course. *What's the protocol for how to act after having a mind-blowing date with someone else?* I didn't know!

Figuring I would've at least had an hour to myself, I hadn't prepared for this conversation so soon. I hadn't even spent a second pondering the best approach to spare Jin's feelings. So, when he neared, I burst into tears. *A-freaking-gain.*

"Nala? Are you alright, love?" He asked, pulling me into his toasty arms. "What's wrong? I'm sorry if I surprised you by being here, Gabs gave me the codes to get in." That only encouraged my sob fest, the male was worthy of far more than this.

"Welcome home, Nala. I attempted to prevent the duke from remaining and surprising you," Homie tacked on, clearly annoyed. "However, the male was insistent."

Jin frowned as he asked, "Would you like for me to leave?"

"NO!" Crap, I didn't mean to holler. Get it together, Nala. "I'm sorry! Sorry! So sorry!" Timos would be so disappointed by your unnecessary apologizing.

The thought sent me for another loop. I backed out of Jin's arms and sprinted up the stairs. Mature of me, I know, but I just needed a minute. *Alright, maybe five minutes.* How was I supposed to spill the beans without hurting Jin? Would cuttles have a clue? *Damnit, you left your stupid phone downstairs.*

"Nala!" I knew he was trailing from the way his giant feet shook the entire second story. "Please, tell me what's wrong." Out of desperation, I did what anyone in my position would do... And locked myself in the bathroom.

"Nala, did the dragon harm you?" Jin demanded.

"No, Timos would never!"

"Please, talk to me."

I felt horrible, but still called back, "I can't yet!"

"Should I leave?" Jin's voice cracked and shattered my resolve along with it. I opened the mauve door to find devastation painted across his handsome face. Which only tightened the noose of guilt strangling my gut.

"No... I needed a minute to—It's... I'm sorry, I don't deserve you, Jin."

He sighed and ran a hand through his inky strands which made his ridiculous abs flex. "I thought we were past this, love. You're stuck with me until I kick the bucket."

"Nope," I shook my head with a sniffle as his swirling eyes met mine. *"Forever."*

"Siarcs don't live forever," he replied as I flung myself at his warm chest and squeezed.

"That's true, but dragons do."

Jin pinched my chin and forced my eyes to his. He opened his mouth to speak a few times before finally managing to rasp, "You're already certain about Timoset?"

"Timo-*set, huh*? Even his legal name is ancient sounding."

"Nala."

"I'm sure about him... Not as sure as I am about you. Well, actually. Obviously, nothing happened—That's not true either. We kissed. But that was it. Twice—"

Jin interrupted me with his lips. It was a claiming. A rougher one than usual. His hands fisted in the hair at the nape of my neck with enough force to hurt as our tongues thrashed. He tasted like oat milk and frosted flakes and home.

Jin withdrew a few inches and groaned. "I knew I would have to share you."

"I'm so sorry," I replied with a sniffle.

"You didn't do anything wrong, love. I told you to explore when you offered not to." He planted a sweet kiss on my forehead as he released my hair. "The dragon isn't problematic. If anything, I'm relieved. Timoset will protect you more than I ever could. Besides, living forever is a plus. Mom will be thrilled."

"We ran into Chad the rotten egg. I definitely don't like him." Jin barked a gravelly laugh, and I immediately felt a million times better. "Is he one of the two you dislike? Timos hates him too."

"I'm surprised you cracked the dragon so quickly, knowing how anti-social he is," Jin replied with a smirk, totally avoiding my question. "Can we go back downstairs now?"

"I'll meet you there, I need to change first." I hopped to my closet and dropped my jean shorts to trade them for a cotton pair. As I made my way to where Jin was snacking on the couch, I said, "You're going to have to tell me, you know."

Jin groaned but it was more of a gargle because his mouth was full of cereal. Once he swallowed, he grumbled, "Yes, I despise Chadwick. The second is Ryloh, and I'd venture to guess Timoset agrees. There. Happy?" I flicked his cute nose before getting up to turn on the Holotube. "Love, what are you doing? Your phone's right there. You could also ask Homie to turn it on."

"Yes, I would be happy to help you, Nala," the droid's voice carried.

I spun with my mouth agape. "Is that why there's no remote?" Jin burst into laughter and my cheeks boiled. "Okay, bully shark. I don't remember asking you to move in!" His face fell and I instantly regretted my sass. "Sorry, didn't mean it."

"You're all twisted up."

"I know," I exclaimed, falling onto the couch, and using my hands to hide. "I'm a complete mess, I don't know how to act in a healthy relation-ship. I warned you!"

"Would you rather talk through it or eat?"

"Are there new goodies?" I questioned, lifting my head.

"Brought over a surprise for you actually." He jumped over the back of the couch in a move I could never manage. I'm not ashamed to admit I ogled his perfect butt as he fetched the gift from the fridge. "My mom's kimchi."

"You didn't!" My weep volcano nearly erupted again. "Did you tell Umma Hae?!"

Jin's plum eyes narrowed. "Why are you constantly asking me that? No. I didn't, wasn't even tempted to. You know I want you to be there."

"Gabs got to me, I'm sorry." He huffed when I snatched the container and fork as I mouthed another apology. And then proceeded to think of Timos' disappointment.

I told Jin.

It was time. He deserved to know more than Timos. However, unlike the dragon who interrupted then swallowed his rage to listen, Jin sort of short-circuited. He just gawped.

I dunno how much time passed, but it was a miserable amount. My left knee hadn't stopped bouncing like a po-go stick as I awaited any reaction. Perhaps it was my fault, I randomly spouted the entire story as the male chewed on kimchi. Was he even blinking? Breathing?

<<*"Fucking Earth. No wonder she bound to you so quickly. What a clusterfuck that must've been. And she didn't even flinch once. Nala's been through so much. I wish I could tell her I love her. Nope. Can't. Way too soon, psycho. Not the best moment for it either."*>

I didn't know how his thoughts broke through the suppressant, but it was a relief. Jin made sure I felt his love through action, but hearing the distorted voice of his brain's confirmation was chicken soup for my soul. Maybe the magic stuff wouldn't be so bad. Just as my lips pursed to raise the topic I'd been avoiding; the male beat me to it.

"I despise every bit of what you shared with me, Nala, I can't deny that. I'm glad you're okay. Proud that you didn't shed a single tear."

"Stop! Now you're gonna make me cry again!"

The Siarc chuckled as he pulled me into his warm chest. "You told Timoset?" I nodded. "He didn't burst into flames?"

"He growled a titchy and there was some smoke, but no." I shrugged.

"I'm surprised he didn't burn down the block. Share your trauma with him in Ookea or Bahasa next time, please."

I pulled back with a scowl, "Don't you dare talk about him like everyone else does, Jin. He's calmer than you are! Dragons aren't mindless monsters." Instead of the apology I expected him to return, he gifted me with a scratch to the back of the neck. The uncomfortable one. "Spit it out, Jin!" It wasn't just the male pestering me; the inexplicable creepy freezing returned to my sternum at the mention of Timos. He was still somewhere close by, too. I could *feel* him. Like a string attached between our chests, the closer he was, the less taut the pull became.

I was failing to ignore or rationalize any of it.

"You're right that he's calm, it's because he's ancient. However, once you're mated to a dragon, you're more than just theirs. A dragon's greatest treasure is its tether. He's going to be obsessive. With you, with your safety, even past harm will craze him. Anyone who betrays you in the future is signing their death warrant. It's his nature. Dragons have no subspecies for a reason, they share the same aggressive nature."

"Don't you dare try to distract me with fun facts." I stabbed Jin's chest with my nail. "Timos is harmless!"

"To you? Absolutely. To me? *Probably*. Timoset is a trustworthy male, I'm not claiming otherwise. He's quiet, sure, but we've always gotten along. Although I won't lie, I found him terrifying as a kid." When Jin caught my furrowed brows he explained, "Timoset worked closely with my dad, too. He's always been Protectorate, since the first hundred who lived on land."

"Well, I don't think he's done anything to deserve the hate. Regardless of what his nature entails, he's a saint as far as I'm concerned."

Jin snorted.

We woke that Saturday morning to Gabs' thundering with an equally booming Australian voice in tow, Homie emitted an alarm. Which caused Jin to lunge out of bed and over the balcony of my second floor, to landing on my couch with the grace of a cat.

"Chill, Jin and Homie! It's me," Gabs announced with a cackle that echoed off every inch of my loft. Thankfully, my shadow friend recognized her voice and abruptly stopped. "It's market morning, we're here to take

Nala! You remember Burt." It took Jin a few moments to lower his haunches with a grumble.

"G'day, Yu-Jin and Gale snail! I see you're rule breaking already, not even a week in, *gewd* for *yew*," the Aussie teased with a smirk as I made my way downstairs. "I won't dobber, don't worry," he winked, tucking his hands into the pockets of his shorts.

Jin was scratching the back of his neck with discomfort while Gabs and I hugged. "Hello again, Burt. Gabs, you bitch, you could've called before giving Jin a stroke. What time is it?" I asked with a yawn as I plopped onto a stool. "Babe, can you please work your coffee magic? I would but I have no idea how to work that thing. Too many buttons."

"It is 10:00am," Homie responded. "I can also make your coffee, Nala." Jin scowled at the interjection, and I swallowed my chuckle. He and Homie had beef as of late.

"Dang that *is* a fancy machine," Gabs said as she peered over Jin's shoulder. "Seong forces me to use a coffee press, it's the worst!"

"How was last night?" Burt questioned, leaning his elbows against the counter-island.

Before I could answer, Jin announced, "Nala chose her second."

"No shit?!"

"Dragon dick!"

Burt and Gabs yelled in unison, and I cowered under my elbows.

"I can't believe it! He's such a reclusive enigma, that Drago. Aph's been thirsting for him to participate for*ever*, but he refused until we sniffed you out," Burt said.

"Who do you think the last one's gonna be?" Gabs asked Jin, as if I weren't present, earning an eye roll from me. "My bet's on Ryloh! He's the most enticing one left." I groaned.

"I think it's gonna be Zaire," Burt volleyed. "Gale's been collecting the rare ones, and turnu are less common than dragons."

"What's a turnu, again? I forgot."

"They can take any shape they desire. There's only five in existence."

"With that logic, I still win. Ryloh is the *only* fae to possess the ability to shift." Gabs said, poking her tongue out.

"Jin and Timos both hate him, so you might wanna rethink that," I shared with the class.

Gabs waved me off, "Trust me, I'm never wrong. My tía inducted me as a bruja when I was six because of my accuracy."

"Well, you're meeting Cabbage tonight," Burt said. "Ryloh already withdrew his interest in the other two. I heard through the grapevine that he refused to speak to either. He only involved himself for you this season." My ears perked at that.

"Cabbage? That's his last name?"

Gabs pointed her hip to say, "Don't judge a book by its cover! Fae have weird surnames."

Just as I prepared to ask what Ryloh's subspecies was, Jin distracted me with a kiss to the forehead, passing around mugs before taking a neighboring stool. "I'm surprised neither of you said Avexei because of his closeness with Timoset." Burt and Gabs exchanged a loaded glance before hiding behind their coffees.

"What was that look for? Sharing is caring."

"My cousin is damaged, I doubt he'll be the one," Burt stated matter-of-factly. *How many of them were cousins? Good grief, you need Homie to build you a family tree.* "He also withdrew from the other two already. Not to mention, that bugger's thrown his hat in every round since the Program's inception, and never matched with anyone."

"How many rounds is that?"

"Sixteen hundred, at least —"

"Avexei and Nala will hit it off, don't fucking tarnish her opinion," Jin interrupted with a scowl. He really was the squishiest little boy scout, and I adored him for it.

"Also rare," Gabs exclaimed with an excited little clap. "The first male Siren crossbreed. *Ooh!* I might change my bet..." She scrutinized me for a few blinks before shaking her head and taking another sip. I have no idea what she saw, but she eventually said, "No, no, never mind. I'll keep Ryloh." *Which one's sexy Avexei, though? Or Ryloh, for that matter.*

"This is bizarre," I repeated for the hundredth time as Burt and Gabs led me through the market. It was an oversized, incredibly modern, glassed arboretum spanning half-a-mile in the middle of Bahasa. Thankfully, it was air conditioned, although not to my preferred ice out. There weren't any vendors or booths, you just roamed freely, and picked items as your phone automatically kept track to charge you upon leaving the greenhouse.

"How did you two become friends?" I questioned as the pair wandered a few steps ahead to exchange whisperings. *Again*. It was the fourth instance thus far, and I was about ready to jet.

"Gabriela was the first participant in the twenty-years I've worked for the PPP to hold me hostage upon waking. I typically ensure I'm on the phone, or pretend to be, when I see one of you stirring. But this loon attacked and tackled me to the floor before I had the chance. We became fast friends after. I mean, I knew she would stay on Neptune. Aph calls puffer shite, but I knew she would pick Seong. He's quite the character as well, wait until you meet him, Gale snail."

Gabs rolled her eyes. "You left out how you laughed in my face and pinned me to the floor until Aphrodite returned from lunch like an hour later. And technically, we didn't have a friendly conversation until *after* my mating ceremony."

"When we discovered we were both artists," Burt added.

"I watercolor and he sculpts," Gabs explained. "Nothing serious, but we host artsy days together. Lots of drinking and ripping into each other's work."

"I'm not the least bit surprised," I said, reaching on my tippy toes to pluck a cucumber from its vine, placing the oversized veggie into my new netted shoulder bag. A much-needed gift from Gabs. Observing the chunkiest tomatoes I'd ever seen, I mused, "I wonder which of these vegetables Timos has packed with more proteins." The duo exchanged perplexed looks. "What? That's what he does, he said that he leads a team of researchers."

"*He does*? I thought he was just a scaly police force," Gabs replied.

Burt chuckled. "Planetary Protectorate not police. Whenever I go to the beach, I always see his bronzed bum bobbing about on patrol."

"In dua forma? Fully shifted?" I questioned with wide eyes, and they nodded. "Does he look like the dragons from Game of Thrones? Even though those are technically Wyverns since their arms are wings. Or is he —"

"Nerd alert!" The force of the Australian's bellow shook the surrounding glass.

"Kinda, he's way shinier though," Gabs said as she leaned over to pluck a few eggplants. "And speaking of the dragon, now that Jin's no longer chaperoning, I need dick deets."

"No dick deets. At least not yet, and who knows if I'll even survive to share the tale," I grumbled. Gabs giggled as Burt shook his head in disgust. "It was an incredible date. The best one I'll ever have. I dunno that I even need another, two kids are already too many to be totally honest." They both laughed in my face, and I frowned.

"You're going to get three, Nala! I'm never wrong!"

Burt was on his knees pulling carrots as he proclaimed, "Yes, you're going to end up with a third, Gale, and the babes that come with that. You're the first to have six interested males in roster, it's impossible to not end up with a trio. You heard Jin, he knew it too. However, since we've learned things with Drago aren't official, I may alter my bet. *Hmm.*"

"No, Timos is for keeps. He's the opposite of Jin. It's a perfect balance. And we had a run in with bad Kraken Chad, who's out."

"I wouldn't agree," Gabs said over her shoulder. "The two you've chosen are both chill and composed. Predictable. Which is fine, but a total snoozefest. That's why I think Ryloh." I couldn't handle the anticipation for another second and whipped out my phone.

"Gabs, you genius," Burt exclaimed, "I'm copying your bet! Don't tell Seong I switched."

"Can either of you tell me why I can't find any photos of this male when I cuttlefish him?" I questioned over the screen of my scallop.

"You're obviously blocked on purpose! Here, allow me the honors. Burt, please record her reaction so we can replay it for Seong." He did as told.

"There's clover eyed rover, rainbow himbo, and sexier Superman," I muttered, mostly to myself as I counted on my fingers to be sure. They heard and completely lost it. Gabs was howling as she passed the search results of a steamy male. "No, no, not *him*," I breathed, stealing her phone and scrolling through more. *Your other two loathe this one, his sausage is not for sale!*

"Yeah." Gabs said with an 'I told you so' look that left a sting, "Seong is so jealous of my crush that he gets all snarly. I've never had a chance to interact which means you gotta take one for the team here, Gale snail. You know how I feel about fae!"

"Not you too, I left my snail trail behind! I'm named after a bird for crying out loud," I thundered as they cackled. "And I *can't* even consider liking Ryloh, Jin and Timos both despise him. I can't have dueling baby daddies for all eternity." Also, how were there so many paparazzi images of him? *What else are you blocked from see—*

"You can do anything but sex," Gabs interrupted with a waggle of her brows before snatching her chrome oyster shell back. "Sorry, Burt, I know you find my cock-talk insufferable. That was my last bit, I swear."

"I'm giving you a free pass because of the freshie, but it will expire with Gale's mating ceremony." Burt said, "Besides, I've only seen the other side of the Program which is duller."

"How did you get your accent then?"

"My mummy! I'm Program spawn, proof in the pudding. I also pop to Earth often. It refreshes my lingo and traveling is a real treat. I love the clubs in Ibiza and Mykonos, the ones here are complete and utter trash."

"He's a Siren and forty-six years old," Gabs said as I opened my mouth. "I know that's what you were gonna ask. *See*, besties already? For the resties too, now that you snagged Drago." She linked our arms and skipped, forcing me to follow along begrudgingly. Although I admittedly was warming to her, the taunting and whispering reached new heights.

When my phone vibrated, I jumped from my skin. Gabs managed to claw the scallop out of my tote bag before I had the chance. Her dark brows got lost in her bun as she showed Burt. They held an entire conversation in silence before I snapped, lunging for my shell.

… Welp.

As I typed out a reply, the duo sprang over to rest their chins on my shoulders. Gabs was the devil on my left, while Burt was the angel on my right.

Ryloh Cabbage
4332 Seahorse Dr, Bahasa
Expecting you at 7:00pm sharp

Nala Williams
Hiya! Nice to meet you too, Lolly

I'll cancel if you call me that

Your loss not mine, Lolly dolly!

You'll be paying for that later

"You know what? No. Nope! He doesn't get any flirting. I'm only going because Jin and Timos are forcing me. Lolly's a douche canoe, I'm gonna sink in less than an hour."

"Shite! That address is *his*," Burt hollered, rendering me deaf.

Gabs bit her lip, "I love a rule breaker. Seong's so lucky that one wasn't in my roster."

"Oh, sod off! We all know you're a sap when it comes to the nutty Whalen."

"What do I even wear? And don't even think about it, Gabs!" I accused with a pointer, "I'm not gonna ask him." She chuckled as we ventured deeper, probably imagining his response, just as I was. It would be something far too flirty, like 'nothing.'

We were *so* not going there. I decided I hated Lo-Lo, Lolly, Ryloh. There. *Done.*

"He initially refused the other two," Burt dropped like a missile, right onto my resolve. "Aph forced him to meet them."

"Great," I mumbled. "Then I'm going as a nun. Where can I find a habit?"

Gabs burst into laughter and heaved, "Sexy! Nun!"

"Truthfully, the fae can incinerate anything you wear. It made the papers when he did it to another in public —"

"What else have I been blocked from seeing in *the papers*?" I interrupted, and they both stilled. "Give me your phone again, you sneaky squirrel," I demanded. No wonder I couldn't view the article regarding my abduction.

Burt cleared his throat after exchanging a grimace with his partner in crime. "It's better if you don't look yet —"

"No! Fork over the phone! Now!" It was immature, but my foot stomped from my annoyance. There'd been too many secrets.

Eventually, Gabs relented. "You don't have to worry; they legally have to blur your photos out." That wasn't any comfort. As soon as I had her shell, the first place cuttlefished was *The Salt*. And lo and behold, Timos' handsome smile graced the headlining article with his arm draped over my pixelated shoulders. However, the title instantly soured my stomach.

"NEPTUNE'S LONE DRAGON PUBLICLY SPOTTED FOR THE FIRST TIME IN CENTURIES GRINDING AGAINST GUTSY HUMAN PRIOR TO CURFEW."

"I shouldn't have looked," I relented with a sigh, scanning the horrid article. *The Daily Mail* didn't have jack on *The Salt*. Our entire date had been staked out. There were even quotes from the Bachelorette party who screamed bloody murder. *Ugh.* "I hate the way everyone talks about him. Timos is literally the kindest person I've ever met." My sternum iced as I raised my head to find the duo sharing *another* secret.

"Nala, hon, I love you. But Timos isn't a person. He's a dragon," Gabs replied.

"They don't even have subs, Gale snail. Even turnu have subspecies!"

I scowled, demanding, "What does that even mean?"

"You can't!" Gabs hollered, but the Australian nodded. *Thank almighty Gandalf.*

"Fuck the rules, Gabs. She's already mated," he said before turning back to me with an apologetic look. "Dragons strike fear because they're *too* powerful. They're the lone classification that cannot be killed, every other has at least one weakness. Plus, there are rarely differing species born from dragons. There have only been three exceptions, Timos' sisters. That's it. Three, Gale snail, no other classification holds such genetic dominance. It's seen as unnatural."

"I'm still not getting it! Dragons are the only reason everyone's protected!"

Gabs interrupted Burt. "That's what I argued, too. But Timos' entire family is apparently equally as huge as he is, which also skeeves the public. Seong thinks our giant myths stemmed from the dragons assigned to Earth." I wasn't biting on her distraction attempt. Although it *was* an enticing factoid.

"The older an immortal family's roots, the less critical they are of dragons. My family regularly hosts the male for dinner and ignores the hubbub," Burt explained. "As for the general population however, faith is spreading in prevalence." Gabs and I groaned. I thought I'd finally rid myself of widespread religions. "It's Karma. The Creator." *Why did that sound familiar?*

"There's no proof she's real," Gabs exclaimed.

Burt nodded, "I didn't say *I* believed, little loon. There's debate over whether she's the true Creator, but 50% of immortals believe. They preach that half of each Titan is blessed with what they call Karma's 'chaos magic.'"

"What does that have to do with hating dragons?"

Burt replied, "Followers insist Karma demands balance in all things. Because dragons are atypically blessed with power, they're also seen as cursed. The unluckiest of immortals."

"Nonsense! And *everyone* hates Timos, not just half," I couldn't withhold my shout of disdain, earning us a few disgruntled glances.

"That's because the half who don't believe in Karma, believe in self-control above all else. Dragons are notoriously poor with restraint. Timoset's dad tore an entire planet apart with his bare prima hands when the Stars captured his amoroso. It's a tale as old as time."

"Why does everyone keep talking about stars like they're people?"

"Because they were. Until Timos' dad slaughtered them into literal extinction. That's the ending of the story Burt just referenced," Gabs informed, and I barked an unbidden laugh.

"If anything, that's insanely romantic," I said as they stared me down. "Timos doesn't have that issue. He won't lose it for me. I know he won't."

Burt clicked his tongue as Gabs frowned. "I mean no offense by this, but he has the same nature as his father. He's better than most dragons at hiding it, I admit. But—"

"Fucking nonsense! I'd bet my life on his control, damnit," I lost it. Between the public's reaction, Jin's reaction, theirs, *plus* that cursed article; the leash on my frustration snapped.

The glass panes shook as my chest froze into a block of ice. The pair were more stunned by the outburst than the passing strangers. It took Gabs a second before she elbowed Burt with enough force to leave him grunting.

"*See,* you broke her, Burt. She doesn't curse, I told you it was too soon!"

Biking through Bahasa's modernized streets towards Ryloh's apartment, I wasn't nervous. I'd dealt with my fair share of douches back home and could keep my wits. I would pull a 'hi,' and 'bye,' and flee. Gabs and Burt were about to lose their bet.

Although the buildings were as tightly packed as Thalla's, Bahasa possessed more minimal glass structures and skyscrapers. And no rainbow paint, everything was white, black, or grey metal. Sometimes façades were all windows and reflective, others just concrete. The palms and fruit trees painted a starker contrast against the gloomy palette.

I wasn't personally loving the vibe, but it was still beautiful in its own way.

It was no surprise Ryloh lived in the building with the least character yet, a monstrosity of windows towering over a black sand beach. Not that I knew where any of the others lived, it was just my hateful mood.

When I pressed the button for the duke of Bahasa's penthouse and the door buzzed wordlessly, I rolled my eyes. With each stomp on the white marble floors, I cursed him alphabetically. *Ass. Asshat. Asshole. Bastard. Brat. Bum.* It continued in the elevator, and by the time the 30th floor *dinged*, I was on wildebeest.

With my resolve set in stone, I took a final deep inhale as the chrome doors slid open. To reveal the interior of a bright apartment, one which its owner was already scrutinizing me from. Ryloh was perched on a white lounger facing the lift, sexier Superman all suited up, and staring me down like a total creep. His lair was immaculately clean, decorated solely in creams and whites.

How long has he been parked there? You were forty-five minutes late on purpose!

Lolly reminded me of a king atop his throne, there was just the right amount of superiority reflected on his sculpted face. No pleasantries were exchanged as I sauntered over. The male didn't blink once, it didn't even seem like he was breathing; the lone indication he was alive was the tick in his cheek.

When noticing he had one white pupil in his flashy silver eyes, I gasped. The unique pupil was also shaped like a star. It was far more distinct than those with heterochromia, his mismatched eyes were a beacon, and I couldn't look away.

However, my awe was short-lived when he finally opened his mouth. *"That's* what you decided to wear? Y- You do realize this is a d- d—" His jaw clenched audibly as his expression morphed into fury. "date?" *Is he really that mad about an outfit?*

Oh, Hell no, clearly a psycho. How dare he insult this strapless white romper? It was weather appropriate, and my wedge sandals fancied it up just fine.

I closed the distance to leer over him, stabbing his shirt with my pointer. "Wrong! *Rude* and wrong, you're the one who seems to be confused here. House calls do not make for first dates, you insufferable dickwad!" He seemed to be pleased with my outburst.

I was seething as Ryloh's lips formed a terrifying smirk, clamping my eyes tight when his chrome headlights started distracting me. The next thing I knew, our lips were locked. He *kissed* me.

I know. I couldn't believe it either!

Nor could I believe that his lips shocked with static. *Hello, divine intervention!* That's when I came to. Using his chest to spring myself backwards, I landed on my ass with a *thump.* It would likely bruise, dousing my rage in gasoline. "How dare you?!"

Ryloh laughed in response. Wickedly. Right in my face. *Par for the course with this one.* Even his lips tasted of sin, like an evil temptation simmering underneath his handsome shell. *He's the villain!*

I groaned with frustration, picking myself off his pristine floors. Then the pointy-eared maniac stood to sneer down his straight nose. Ryloh possessed a disdain that only middle school bullies could dole. So, in equated maturity, I reveled in the fact he wasn't super tall, definitely the shortest male in my roster thus far. Admittedly, it wasn't saying much as he was probably close to seven feet. But still, it was something.

"My home, my rules. You agreed to play as soon as your feet left the lift." He licked his pink lips and leaned in, sending my pulse into spasms when he added, "Careful. Don't give me further cause to reprimand you."

Those words in *his* deep voice? In *his* accent? It was slightly Irish, and ten thousand percent delicious. *Fu —*

Wait, no. Not gonna work! There were no safe words here, this was not the daddy to try on as a Dom. *He's sick and twisted and...* As I stood, my resolve had solidified once more.

I would never.

Nope.

And then we were kissing again. Those foul fingers gripped my jaw with enough force to bruise which was why I clawed my nails into his scalp. Unfortunately, he liked that.

So did I.

Ryloh tasted like pop rocks. That static shock earlier? Yeah, it was *him.* He was literally electric, or some ish, and each swipe of his sparkler tongue lit me up all over.

He. Was. Smoldering.

I was little more than putty in his rough hands. This was just my luck, the only one I couldn't withdraw from was the same I could *not* keep. It took me longer than I'll admit to rip away with a weak, "No."

"That's not what your pulse says, Nala spice." The sick fucker was enjoying this if his clownish grin had anything to say.

"You aren't allowed to give me flirty nicknames, you're too demented and vile!" I backed away in a feeble attempt to regain sanity, but he wasn't having it. When I dashed for the lift, he caught me around the waist, and slung me over his shoulder like I weighed no more than a napkin. "Put me down, Ryloh, I said *no.* No means no!"

He did. Dropping my ass unceremoniously onto the floor. It would leave a bruise if the first tumble didn't. Then he spun to tower over me and snarled, "You're *mine*. I- I locked the lift, there's nowhere to run."

I did not experience a normal person's reaction to that. Thankfully, I had to focus on remaining upright instead of my suicidal lady parts. Because that's what this male was. Poison, and subsequently, death. "I'm not yours!"

"Y- You are my soulmate, Nala. *Mine*," Ryloh said in the most ferocious tone. So… Most fae smut was 100% accurate, but nowhere near as sexy. More feral. More immature. More like a nightmare.

Okay… So, I lied. The fae was blazing hot. When he ran a pale hand through his messy chin-length dark locks with a scowl, my thighs clenched. *The traitors!*

A whiff of him reminded me of a summer storm back home. Which wouldn't do. *You can't be comforted by this creature!* Which was why I started breathing through my mouth in avoidance.

When Ryloh gripped my curls to lift me off the floor, spinning me, so my back was against his chest, a moan left my lips. I didn't mean to, but it slipped. His sardonic chuckle in reply intensified my regret. "If you behave, I'll allow you to select your punishment, spice."

"You're going to give me a stroke," I hollered.

"My static can restart your human heart."

"This is *not* how a date should go," I tried again.

"Y- Your sh- shitty attire is to b- blame for th- that." His jaw clacked shut in my ear, as if he was angrier than I was, which hardly made sense.

"The audacity of you. Nope. Let me go! I don't like you—I want out!" Ryloh released me and I stomped back towards the lift with my middle finger over my shoulder. Except when I tapped the button, it wouldn't light up. "Let me leave, I'm not staying here!"

Next thing I knew, my hair stood on end, like when you touch one of those zappy balls at a science museum. Even the air in his sprawling apartment grew thick despite the blasting air con. I turned slowly; a bit scared of what I'd find.

My trepidation was warranted. The fae was terrifying. Ryloh was pitching an electric fit. His eye with the starry pupil went blank as tiny lightning bolts danced all over him. He was gonna murder me. *Fry you up like a chicken drumstick!* Manson bells were ringing in my ears.

"Take y- your punishment and I will release you," Ryloh snarled, becoming scarier by the second.

When my heart stilled and the room swallowed me whole, he tacked on, "Can't y- y- y- y- you..." Despite his rampaging, he coughed, then cleared his throat. "Take the punishment for that mouth of y- yours?" *Take*?! His comment sliced through my petrified stun and pissed me right off.

"Oh, I can *take* it," I seethed. This sociopath wasn't gonna relent and I wasn't in the mood to be deep fried. Raising my arms in exasperation, I stomped to where he lounged on a white sofa. "For the record, I'm not going to enjoy it, and I'm—" Once I was close enough, his lips crashed into mine as his fingers dug into my hips, and I yelled into his mouth. "*Nu-uh*! Hurry up with whatever you have planned, you psycho."

"Fine." When he withdrew, planting his elbows on his knees, I was cringing in preparation for the insanity that would surely come from his tempting lips. "Palm or ropes?"

My mouth went Sahara dry so all I could manage was a breathed, "What?"

Ryloh was grinning now. "Would you rather I spank you with my palm or would you rather I tie and suspend you from the ceiling with my static?" My face fell into my hands, it was the lone place to hide as I unpacked that. It felt as though I was trapped in a haunted house, except the scaries weren't the fun kind, the saw still had its chain on.

From what I'd read about shibari, or Japanese rope play, it was far too intimate. There needed to be boundaries and trust. However, the idea of being spanked made my skin crawl in a bad way. There were no spankings from Andy, only punches. However, my parents had broken plenty of wooden spoons on my misbehaving butt over the years. I was the black sheep after all, but this was... *Okay, actually. Ding, ∂ing, ∂ing, we have a winner!*

Reliving the childhood trauma had to douse my lust, right? That was exactly what I needed, to hate Ryloh, to loathe him, to never wish to see his mismatched eyes and flawless porcelain skin —*Focus, Nala!*

"Palm," I said shakily, with my ears tucked between my knees. Before I had a chance to blink, the male's warm hands spread me across his dark suited thighs. As my head dangled, I questioned how his floors remained so clean. There wasn't even a speck of dust. *He must be scrubbing them with a toothbrush, just like Nana used to.*

"By my count, you're at eight offenses," the murderer said, and I harrumphed. "This is going to hurt, spice." That was the exact moment I *knew* I'd made a grave mistake.

But it was already too late.

Slap!

Oof. Ryloh spanked me right over the shorts of my romper. That wasn't what bothered me though. *Oh-ho-ho-no-no!* It was the electric zing to my clit his palm left behind as a little parting gift. He'd managed to arouse me so much that I couldn't even inflate my lungs. By the fourth slap I was mewling over his knees and clenching my thighs.

I was past enjoying it.

When my legs began twitching, Ryloh stilled, and a rumble shook his chest. "Nala spice." *No. No. No. Anything but that!* I could handle anything but that cute nickname coupled with my preferred name. My trembling ratcheted up to a full body shake as he leaned down to whisper in my ear. "I knew you needed this as badly as I did."

"No!"

He laughed. "I can scent your lust. You can't keep secrets. You're *mine.*"

"Not. Yours." I panted unconvincingly. Then shrieked when a warm finger swiped against my soaked panties. I attempted to flee, but he kept me pinned. Far too easily.

"Let me taste you," he demanded with another snarl. *Gaaah,* I wanted him to.

I mustered a sliver of resolve and garbled, "No."

Ryloh spanked me again, except this time, he added triple the electrocution and I came with a silent scream. My vision darkened while my body flooded with bliss. *You're completely and totally damaged.* Might've also been dying as I was flying far too high, and gonna get burned alive... *That orgasm wasn't the best you've ever had, don't even think it!*

"Please. Grant. M- Me. Permission. Nala." Ryloh panted in that maddening accent.

It took a while to recover, but I eventually mumbled, "I can't. I hate you. I don't want you." It was far too breathy to be believable.

The bastard released a throaty laugh and spanked me again, with a bigger jolt this time. One that left aftershocks in its wake. I wish I didn't revel in it, but of course I did. "Wh- Why can't you? And if you attempt to lie, I'll know… D- Do not test me."

"It's against the rules—"

He interrupted with a *tsk* and spanked harder, leaving a searing heat behind on my asscheek, one I knew would leave a burn. Third degree, at least! *Why did you like it so much? He straight-up branded you. You're the psycho here, not him!*

A mark I'd also have to explain to Jin. *Oh, no. No. No.* Yu-Jin Rapax. My actual perfect match. The one who held my heart. Who *hated* this male! So, I tried again, "I hate you."

"I ordered you not to lie to me. Th- The truth. *Now.*"

When he zapped the ever-loving crap outta me, to the point my teeth clacked, I was the one who growled. "Jin and Timos despise you!"

Ryloh repositioned with a speed that gave me a mouthful of my hair when I straddled his trousers. It was difficult to ignore his stiff erection, but I feigned unawareness. He clawed my shoulders with trembling palms as his mismatched blinkers flashed. "Wh- Why do their opinions matter, Nala?" As my gaze wandered around the singularly—*maniacally so*—white apartment, he grumbled, "D- Do *not* attempt to lie to me again."

That was the moment when my common sense decided to join the party. *Late's always better than never.* Call me all the names you want, but I was always carrying. For this lovely meeting in a complete stranger's apartment? I had my teensy switchblade tucked into my romper pocket.

I waited until Ryloh thought he had the upper hand, until the most vicious smirk I'd ever witnessed crossed his pretty face, one that said he could whittle my resolve down to smithereens. I mirrored it. Then whipped the pocketknife out and pressed it against his pale throat until I saw a red droplet painting its tiny, but sharp, blade.

Initially, Ryloh was struck with shock. His peepers widened, giving me a perfect picture of his metallic irises. In under a blink, his stun was gone, stealing the smug look from my face along with it.

The killer wore a maniacal smile when he zapped me near blackout. When he forced a bolt of literal lightning to steal the knife, along with the shell-phone, from my grip and fling to across the room with a loud *crack*. I orgasmed right after, when he sent another firework right for my clit. This time, with a twitching fit against his suited and delicious scented chest.

The worst part? I *loved* every second. A heck of a lot. At some point the pain had intensified my pleasure. Our entire altercation had flipped me upside down and shaken my brain out of place. When I raised my head to meet his gaze, Ryloh growled, "T- Tell me why the Siarc's opinion matters, Nala."

After spitting out some of my errant curls, I scowled. "It's none of your business, is it? I took your punishment so let me leave. *Please.*"

We exchanged three blinks. I couldn't read a single emotion that crossed his face as his plush lips twitched. "As you wish," Ryloh relented with a sigh, giving me whiplash. He helped me stand like a gentleman while I gawked at his outwardly nervous face. *Doctor Jekyll and Mister Hyde didn't have jack on tall, dark haired, and electric chair fae.* "I- I... d- d- did prepare d- dinner, but it seems y- you have made y- y- your d- decision. If my lacking self-control is to blame for th- that, I- I apologize."

"*What?*" I thundered. "*Apologize? Are you serious?*"

He nodded and steam must've shot from my ears from outrage. *How. What. When. Where. No. Absolutely not.*

I punched him. Right in his stupidly carved stubbled chin. With a proper fist and all. I wasn't sure which one of us was more stunned as I shook out my aching hand.

I also wasn't sure who lunged first. The other kisses were nothing like this. They were a warmup to this violence. Teeth. Tongues. I didn't know why we were dueling with our mouths, but we were. When I bit his lip to the point that we both tasted metal, he slammed me against a wall and took a bite out of my neck. So blitzed I didn't even care about the bruising. Every bit of euphoria from Ryloh came with the sweet agony I'd been craving. "Give me permission, Nala. P- Please."

He seemed equally affected, panting as the silver of his irises disappeared. His neediness shattered the last of my resolve. "No bonding," I breathed.

"I can't promise you that, spice. N- Not with how aroused you are, Nala. *Please.*" His begging sent a shot of adrenaline straight to my heart, but I couldn't give in completely. So, I tried shoving his chest. And failed. Again, and again. Granted, I wasn't trying too hard.

Eventually it worked and he relented with an eye roll and nodded. "Fine! No bonding. *Yet.*" When he fell to his knees and stripped me naked in the same movement, my eyes fell out of my head. I didn't have any time to detail the scene for my memoirs before he was on me. Running his tongue up the slick on my inner thighs.

Jeeezus!

"He isn't real."

"I didn't mean to say—*Ah, ah! Ryloh!*" I'd had plenty of tongues and toys on my privates, but never one that accomplished the feeling of both. The electricity. It was like a vibrator on crack. The fae didn't give me the chance to breathe, every second was a shift in sensation, each more overwhelming than the last. Ryloh wasn't eating me out, he was feasting. And when he added fingers to the mix and zapped my g-spot I came once. Twice. Thrice.

My vision blanked as I came a fourth time with a scream that shook my eardrums loose.

"I can't wait to feel this perfect cunt around me, Nala spice."

"Shh," I whispered as he rose and got back in my face with a lick of his lips, like the heathen he was. *You seriously just allowed that to happen.* "I'm gonna need a minute."

"Mine," Ryloh taunted with a nibble to the pulsing hickey on my neck, smiling against my neck. Not even giving me a second as he grinned from ear-to-pointy-ear when met with my shock. "Mine to breed. Mine to cherish. And most importantly, mine to punish." *Oh, the mistakes you have made.* Ryloh won the regret tournament.

I wanted to loathe him as much as I loathed myself. Spoiler: I didn't. Which sent the flames of my self-loathing rising higher. "Knock it off! You can't claim someone without ever sharing a single conversation. You know nothing about me, Lolly. Well, except for how I taste. And apparently how much I enjoy being spanked. What a dreadfully enlightening discovery that was!" Then I hysterically giggled realizing I was naked, then pulled the romper up from my ankles.

When Ryloh opened his mouth to say something that would've turned my wrath up another notch, I silenced him with, "At least feed me before I have to pedal home and fester in my regret." He made a noise like one would call their dog or giddy up their horse, and then *snapped* over his shoulder for me to follow. I didn't know if he was this horrendous or if it was a twisted sense of humor. Either way, I hated him. Hated myself. I especially hated the uninterrupted view of the ocean from the dining room. All I felt was hatred when Ryloh pulled out my chair and kissed the top of my head. *He really just did that. Just like Jin, the love of your life, since you forgot him! Again.*

My nerves were shot.

When the clock on the mantle shared I'd been here for only twenty minutes it shattered what little sanity I had left. Ryloh found me scowling when he blessed the table with an All-You-Can-Eat buffet of seafood. Crab. Lobster. Oyster. Scallops. All my favorites and everything I'd been hankering for. My little pescatarian heart did a trick for him. The shrimp-po-boy sandwich from last night didn't sate my fix. But *this*, this *master-piece*? Kimchi might've been my favored condiment, but shellfish was my most treasured meal.

It had to have been one huge joke that *he* was behind it.

Ryloh leaned against the table and waited for my reaction. "Nala spice." The gentleness in his pleasing accent made it worse. "W- Would you rather eat in the bath?"

He couldn't have offered that. So, I ignored it all. Him. The clock's mocking face. My emotional chaos. And slurped down a vinegary oyster instead.

"L- L- Let m- me."

I couldn't ignore his offer to feed me though. Not when his pale hands perfectly cracked the crab leg I'd been eyeing. "P- Please, N- N- Na- Nala. It's the least I can do after my beast got the best of m- m- me." He even plunked it in a perfect amount of butter before presenting it to my lips. His eyes were darting around the dining room as he grumbled, "Th- That wasn't the first impression I wished to m- make. I'm sorry. It won't happen again."

Slowly opening my mouth with narrowed eyes, I scowled. After I chewed and swallowed while he watched with his *too* alluring, yet angsty, and grumpy, and sexy —*stop it, Nala.*

"What are you promising not to do again, Ryloh? That you'll never degrade my clothing? Or trap me with threats to fry me? Or punish me? Or bite me? Or spank me? Or burn me? Or eat me out until my eyes go black? Or claim that I'm yours? Or skirt your way around the repeated refusals of all the above? Please, do tell."

To his credit, the male did look mighty guilty, and possibly mortified, but now that I'd started spittin', I was *fuming*. That teensy cut and the punch weren't nearly satisfying enough! Neither left a mark on his stupid flawless skin.

"You managed that in twenty mother effin *minutes*! I don't know why I'm sitting here and letting you feed me crab legs, but I'd rather not find out. All signs point to crazy town."

"N- N- Na- Nala—"

"*No.* Don't use that name, you aren't allowed to tarnish it for me too!"

Ryloh's face crumpled and I felt a twinge of guilt, not enough to take any of it back though. He was grown, if he was gonna dole it out, he was gonna have to take it, too. I kept my glare firm as his Adam's apple bobbed. Even when he tried and failed to speak a few times.

"It- It's a terrible excuse, but I l- l- lost control. Y- Your tempting scent and the way you stormed in, I…" he exhaled and averted his eyes towards the ocean. "I- I… I f- felt fifteen again. Y- Y- You brought m- m- my beast forth an- and I couldn't control m- myself. I am s- sorry."

This domineering daddy did not just stutter like that!

It reminded me of my brother, Hawk, who also suffered from a stammer. How he explained the worst part was knowing what you needed to say but feeling too scared to try. Ryloh, the big bad duke of Bahasa, was hiding one. Likely fighting it all day, every day. And… The shield I'd erected toward him cracked.

I placed my palm on his suited elbow and squeezed.

The sheer devastation in Ryloh's shiny gaze as it swung back to mine, stole the air from my lungs. It was clear that the male never lost control. Not like this. He was equal parts frustrated and vulnerable. It was more than just me seeing him for who he was though; loath as I was to admit, I felt *for* him.

"I- I know I- I've ruined this, Nala. I- I… I'm very good at ruining th- things, especially relationships. Th- That is why m- most find me i- in- intolerable." I opened my mouth and motioned for another bite, causing him to scramble. It was all too…

I was making *him* flustered? The way he clenched his jaw didn't match his gaze, his eyes were near black with desire, scalding against my rapidly warming cheeks. *How in the world did you make the monster so nervous after that?*

The better question is why you're ten thousand times more attracted to him now that you know he's as imperfect as you?

Ignoring my internal monologue, I said, "I will give you a chance,

Ryloh. One. Tonight. If you're willing to get to know each other, and *only* that."

"D- Done." He paired with a nod before passing me a tasty scallop dipped in a yum sauce.

"This is my favorite meal, holy moly! So good!"

"M- M- Mine too. No one eats meat here, it's ridiculous. I was forced to catch these myself."

I gawked. "You *did*?! How? Do you have a boat? Wait, no. What *are* you, I mean? Besides fae." He grimaced and I frowned. "I'm sorry I didn't mean to make you uncomfortable." Now I was unnecessarily apologizing again? *Ugh, Timos would be disappointed.*

Ryloh shook his head, brows drawn. He coughed. Then shook again. And I now knew why.

"It's okay, Ryloh. You've seen every bit of me, it's only fair I get to see you too. Take your time. I'm not going anywhere."

"Th- Th- The af- aff- affliction crops up most when I'm n- n- nervous. Around y- y- y- you especially."

"I like it… It's cute. Real. No one's perfect. There's no need to be nervous around me."

He growled, but instead of cowering, I smirked. "N- Not cute," he ground out and my smile leveled up to a grin. "It's weak," he eventually rasped. "I hate it."

I shook my head. "Don't. It's not a weakness, Ry. It's a strength. You've overcome it. I didn't even notice it before."

"It- It's because y- y- you're m- my soulmate," he said, now fully raging. As I opened my mouth to argue, Ryloh stuffed a juicy piece of lobster in my trap. "P- Please listen to me, N- Na- Nala. I have to get this out." He closed his eyes and gave me a better view of his sickeningly long dark lashes fluttering against his pearly cheeks.

Ryloh fell to his knees, with his head landing in my lap, and I might've gasped. "I- I've n- n- never known what I am." He sighed, as my fingers tangled in his hair, seemingly quelling. Don't ask me why I went for it, but I did. "I was abandoned in an orphanage in Moonscape as an infant. Fae children are born with their gifts, and mine *always* drew attention. I'm the lone member of my classification to possess the ability to shift, so I became a spectacle. Some claimed I was zoatala who could take the form of an electric eel, despite solely shifting my lower half. While others swore, I was unsanctioned Titan kin. Hundreds of genetics tests never revealed me to be anything more than fae. As powerful as a Titan, although I share no direct genetics, which has always painted a target on my back with the Galactic Council.

"M- Most of their testing was torture, especially two-centuries ago. That is how this speech i- im- impediment surfaced. From the age of three or four years when my only interactions were with scientists poking and prodding. It worsened when the testing shifted toward caging me with rabid creatures. I struggled to communicate properly until I forced myself to relearn and practice in adulthood."

I nearly bit my own tongue off attempting to withhold a reaction. "I'm sure you don't want my pity, but I despise that, Ryloh." He nodded in my lap as I tangled my fingers in his luscious hair. Ignoring the way his tresses sent heat zipping from my fingertips to trickle down my spine. "How did you escape?"

"Th- There's no escaping, if you're powerful, you're subject to testing. Yu-Jin and Timoset experienced the same. I survived and continue to. Many covet my prestige as it is rare among fae, but I can tell you it isn't worth the nature destiny paired with it. The reason I'm sharing is because my beast consumed m- me and prevented you from leaving, I wasn't in control. There is another consciousness in every immortal.

"When I say there's a monster inside of me, it's unfortunately not metaphorical. He and I coexisted for most of my life amicably before you. Y- Y- You were the cause of my first slip since childhood, spice. No one has ever spoken to me as you, none have ever managed to drive my nature to the surface, it's because you're mine. Even if we never accept our tethering, the bond will remain. Your heart will always beat to the same tune as mine. We are indisputably fated. You are my amoroso."

I choked on crab, eventually rasping, "Humans can't have one!"

"Th- The truth is I'm technically unclassified despite my ears. Who's to say my tethers function as others?" I couldn't even begin to unpack the validity of that. Or the seriousness in his gaze.

The sudden humanization of this male already had my emotions spinning like a top. However, it wasn't just Ryloh weighing me down, it was how his revelation clicked the last piece of the immortality puzzle into place. I hadn't considered these males to be all that different from humans, foolish as it was.

I hadn't questioned why Jin was uncharacteristically rough when we were intimate. How Timos' eyes shifted uncontrollably yesterday and the why behind his resulting embarrassment. It was a bit too late for panic as well, so I did what I did best, and shoved the mounting concerns aside. "Cabbage is the last name they give to orphans on Saturn?" I questioned to deflect.

"C- Cabbage is the most popular crop on Saturn. I- I- I'm uncertain as to how it became the surname they granted to orphans. Although it wasn't initially meant to be derogatory, it became so over time. By my birth, the name was no better than 'garbage.'" I blanched.

"What about Ryloh?" He shrugged his suited shoulders. "You truly don't know?"

"N- No, and it isn't common," he murmured.

"Burt and Gabs made you seem like a man-whore—"

A rumbly laugh cut me off. "Appearances, spice. I have not touched another since my arrival on Neptune. Static may have been used in a sexual sense a time or two, but it was always for another purpose, never to sate myself." Not that I cared about the stammering, it truly was endearing, but I noticed it cropped up less when the male was smiling. As though his lighter spirits helped ease his suffering.

"Why?" I had to know. Ryloh didn't seem to be lying, he'd earnestly held my gaze since my initial question.

"You," he replied, and my brows furrowed. "A Seer prophesied my soulmate's existence. I knew our meeting was on the horizon. You have consumed my thoughts since," he said with a softened smirk.

My heart pinched over that. However, I ignored it, asking instead, "And you're how old?"

"Two-hundred-thirty-three," his maddening accent replied.

I chewed my lip, knowing I was running out of deflections. "Why do you call me 'spice?'"

He raised from my lap to meet my gaze, asking, "D- Do you dislike it?"

I wanted to say yes, for a host of reasons, but the truth was, "No. I'm just curious."

"Because I'd like to eat you, Nala spice," his grin spread, "again."

"You can't just say stuff like that," I exclaimed, feigning offense. In reality, my pussy wept.

Ryloh's eyes flashed as he chuckled. "I'm behaving," he purred.

"Barely!"

"I think I'm growing on you," he said. There was no ignoring the way my heart danced around in agreement with that. Until he asked, "How would you feel about a collar?"

Snorting, I drawled, "On you? *Absolutely*. For me? Not so much."

"Intriguing. Would you desire a leash for me as well?" His eyes flashed as I bit my lip and nodded. "What else?"

"The rope stuff you brought up, but later. Once I feel like I can trust you to not fry me."

"Fair enough."

"Your stutter is gone again, I dunno whether I'm proud or if I miss it," I deflected—*again*.

Ryloh's eyes flickered with lightning as they searched mine. There was something about him, outside of the obvious attraction, that drew me in. *Maybe it's the whole forbidden fruit thing. And you also struck him twice within minutes of meeting him.* An eternity of me drowning in his silvery gaze passed before he asked, "D- Do you believe our fated bond, Nala?"

"Let's say I, theoretically, do." I voiced shakily. "Could you see yourself playing house with Jin and Timos? I don't wanna have kids in a broken home, where their dads can't get along, I won't do it. Not for all eternity. No way." Ryloh scowled, then scoffed, crossing his arms as he formulated a reply. It wasn't his stutter this time, he was weighing his words carefully if that raised brow had anything to say.

"Y- Your concerns are unfounded. I- I'll save the details of why I relocated to Neptune for another time, but I was nominated as duke after serving the Queen for thirteen months. I'm controlling and get shit done when others cannot. I have a professional persona to uphold."

I sighed, crossing my fingers before muttering, "Don't tell me you're a Capricorn."

"Virgo." Ryloh bragged, as if it weren't *minutely* better. "And as I was attempting to explain, my work façade is all they have witnessed of me. Not that you have seen much better, but I will make amends. For you? I'd happily play house with whomever, Nala spice."

"You're *serious*?!"

"Why are you so concerned with those two? They are the only males you have met. Yu-Jin does not share a fated bond. You will never feel the same for him, and you have yet to explore if you share tethers with the others. Y- You must."

I bit my inner cheek before the truth escaped, mumbling instead, "How can you tell when I'm lying?"

"Th- There is a string between our two hearts, when yours speeds it pulls mine along with it. Also, your pulse flutters when you lie."

I gaped for a few seconds before the vehement denial kicked in. *Magic? Believable. Mating Bonds? Sure. But this lie detecting?* "You can't be serious!"

He smiled and nodded. "You likely could not feel the distinction from your arousal, but I noticed it the first second our eyes met. Should I demonstrate?" I nodded as he rose from the floor to take the seat next to mine with a wide grin. "If it becomes too uncomfortable, tell me to stop." He closed his eyes. And Ryloh demonstrated.

I could *feel* it when my heart suddenly sprinted. Could feel him. Sense his emotions.

Yup. Yup. Yup.

This was real. It wasn't just an attraction. We were physically connected. Our hearts were actually, I-shit-you-not, *tethered*. And well...

I fainted.

<<"*Where is she?! Please, no bonding. No bonding. No bonding. Did that barnacle harm her?! No, you'd feel it. This is exactly why you should've been selfish when you still had the chance. Keep your cool. You can do this. Breathe. She must be fine. Nala's just sleeping, you idiot.*">

I woke with a front row seat to Jin's panic attack. Which meant… I jolted out of the plush bed that smelled of a storm, yelping when I found Ryloh there. Perched in another throne, staring from across the bed, one which I apparently slept —*In your birthday suit*?

The shirtless fae rose *slowly,* his grumpy scowl accentuated with static. Which left my heart whizzing unnaturally. Although, granted, I couldn't tell if it was potentially coming from his end with our heart thing. "N- N- Naughty, n- naughty, N- Nala spice, you." He growled, shook out his limbs. *"Lied. To. Me."* He punctuated each word with a bolt of static bouncing like a yo-yo from his downward facing palm.

The suppressant was outta my system and he knew. I shook my head and backed a step, landing my burned ass onto the mattress with a wince. "Y- You did. By omission," he snarled.

"Are you gonna tattle?" I squeaked as he loomed over me. Tattooed in all the best places with a random collection of lines, some curled, others

146

straight and sharp. A painting I had to forcefully pry my eyes from. How had he hidden that under a suit? And was everyone carved like a statue here, or what? *Get it together Gale, now is not the time to ogle the fae who's gonna ruin Jin's day!*

Ryloh shook his head with disgust as his upper lip curled back. "Wh- Why would I? It would ensure the pupling keeps you to himself. It's bad enough he had his turn before I could. You're mine, he should be grateful I'm willing to share."

"I can explain," I rushed out, but Ryloh shook his handsome head.

"N- No need. It's already crystal. I underestimated Yu-Jin Rapax, I had him pegged for a rule follower to a fault, but no matter. He has no part in us. We're going to bond right now, Nala spice. I'm not waiting another second." That was the moment when my traitorous eyes noticed the prominent tenting of his tight black boxers. "If the shark already staked his claim, there's no reason I can't."

"I love him! I don't know what I feel about you," I screeched.

Ryloh laughed as I tried to flee. Multiple attempts failed. He dragged me to the edge of the bed by the ankle. "You might believe that now, but *no one* and *nothing* exceeds an amoroso bond. I own the other half of your soul. You were *made* for *me!*"

Ryloh caged me with his larger body in the most compromising position, I was at his mercy as he used his outrageous abs and boner to pin my hips down to the mattress. *Gaaah*, did he smell amazing. Just like a hurricane back home, which was fitting, considering he was equally destructive. Once I had nowhere to run, he met my gaze and growled, "You are the only gift fate has ever granted and I *refuse* to let go."

"No." It was all I could think to say to the too-cute sentiment.

"N- No?" His thick brows hid behind his perfectly imperfect messy hair as he lowered onto his elbows, putting us nose-to-nose. "I can scent your lust. You can't hide from your soulmate." I'd hoped ignoring my kitty would keep her tamed, but clearly not. *That traitorous bitch!* We already had ourselves overstuffed with shark and dragon sausages. *Mayday! Mayday!*

"No bonding until you prove you can play nicely with others!" *Don't make promises you can't keep, you slug.*

Then the fae was on me. When our lips locked it was nothing like last night. Ryloh was sweet and gushy. Even the strokes of his tongue were languid and soft. I was melting as he moaned into my mouth. Which wouldn't do. Not like this, I was too naked. And I'd already proven I can't be trusted with him. "Ryloh, please. We can't." I breathed as he rested his forehead against mine. "Not yet." *Dagnabbit*. I didn't mean to voice *that*.

"D- Do you swear it?" I sputtered as he tugged my heart into another gallop. "D- D- Do you swear to accept me if I can play nice with your male?" Not the worsening stammer. Paired with his too-perfect face? I was doomed. The hope in his pretty chrome eyes blasted the last of my defenses.

"*Males*. Plural."

Lightning sparked in Ryloh's starry pupil. "Th- The dragon is m- more agreeable, I assure you."

"I dunno, Ryloh. Jin said Timos probably despises you, too." I regretted it as soon as it left my lips. Especially when his face crumpled. *Oh, bologna*. From the little he shared; I knew he didn't enjoy being the bad guy. Even if he couldn't help it. Send me to the looney bin, but I couldn't allow Ryloh to feel less than.

Was he unhinged? Completely. Was he theoretically dangling me over the edge of a cliff with every moment spent together? Absolutely. Was he gonna go full beast on me again? Probably. However, I knew what it felt like to lose control and couldn't hold it against him.

I'd also never had anyone *zippity zap* me until I orgasmed before and was unashamed to admit that I more than liked it. Along with his stunning headlights for eyes. And the scent of him. And his—"Ryloh, I swear. If you prove that you can play nice, then I'll be yours too... *Oh*! And no more abusing our attraction. You can't keep using it to take advantage of me."

"Done." He hopped up and brought me with him, plopping a kiss to my forehead before pushing a pile into my arms. Of clothes which weren't mine.

"Are these yours?" I questioned.

"No. I sent my assistant out while you slept."

"Where's my romper?"

"In the trash where it belongs," he said offhandedly.

Asshat! I harrumphed, pulling on the stretchy black skort. He was lucky it reminded me of a set I was missing. Once I had the matching cropped tank on, he inspected from head to toe with a look of smug approval. And I battled the urge to clock him. "Where's my phone? I've been hearing Jin's panic. I need to call before he loses the plot."

"Your minds melded telepathically?" Ryloh questioned with a scratch to his stubbled chin and I nodded. "Interesting. The shark is not a complete dud then, that will be incredibly useful for us to share."

A hornet's nest could've hidden in my gaping maw.

"H- Here, it's been vibrating incessantly all morning." Ryloh stomped over to where my phone was on his charger before tossing me the rainbow with its dangly broken switchblade. At least the screen hadn't cracked.

Spawn of Satan! A grand total of one hundred thirty-four texts and fifty-six missed calls. I ran a shaky hand through my hair, and the motion caused the bruise on my neck to pulse angrily. I had to take a breath to quell my arousal from pressing it. When I dove towards the mirror above his dresser and found the noticeable hickeyed bite, I whimpered. "Jin's going to completely snap when he sees this."

Ryloh barked a laugh. "I can heal it, come here."

"Thank you. Please. Fix me." His warm calloused palm spread a silver light over my skin. "Will you fix my ass from where you burned me?" I bent over and his huge dick twitched in my peripheral. *Goodness gracious, you gotta get outta here and as far away from him as possible.*

"I would rather not heal that."

"Ryloh! Please! It hurts!" I feigned frustration and he sighed, as if he flipping knew.

"F- Fine," he eventually relented.

After his warm palm caressed my freshly healed bum, I flew from the bedroom, and sprinted for the elevator. When I was smashing the button like it was a high stakes game of Hungry Hippos, Ryloh rifted over to whisper, "I'll be delivering a dress for tonight, I suggest you behave and wear it. That is unless you'd prefer another reprimanding."

No goodbyes. No processing. Nope. I couldn't even form words while staring at my phone screen with dread. Then stumbled into the lift, pressing for the lobby with equal fervor. It wasn't until I reached the ground floor that I realized I'd abandoned my wedges. There was no turning back now. *Sayonara, shoes.*

Once out of Ryloh's building, my bare feet led towards the black sandy beach stretching behind it. The grains between my toes were a comfort. It still had to have been around dawn since the sun's rays were a peachy pink collection cresting over the obsidian waters. The humidity and setting, although drastically alien, still felt homey.

When I forced my trembling hands to video call Jin, and noticed my reflection on screen, I knew he would notice my feasted-on disposition. However, it was too late to course correct, the male answered the first *ring*.

"Nala, where are you? Are you alright? Do you need me to come get you? What are you wearing? You weren't wearing black when you left!" I opened my mouth, but no words left my lips. "Did that barnacle do something to you?! I'm going to *kill* him!"

"He didn't," I shouted.

Jin's plum eyes narrowed in well-earned frustration. "Where did you spend last night?" I was going to *kill* Gabs for granting him an all access pass to my place.

"Nothing happened! I fainted. That's why you haven't heard from me. I'm on a beach in Bahasa, I just need a few hours to decompress, then I'll bike home. I promise."

"Nala—"

"I'm fine, I promise! I need to lay on the beach for a bit. It's nice here."

"Nala, love—"

"Please. I need this, okay? I didn't bond with Ryloh. I'm unharmed."

"Why did you faint?" He pressed. I hiccuped instead of a proper response and Jin's nice eyes narrowed in further suspicion. "Nala, what did that fucking barnacle do to you?"

"Nothing!" The guilt from my lie stung, but I would fix it later. Selfish of me, I know. However, I needed a second to process the last however many hours since I rang that callbox. Then remembered the one thing I needed to share. "He knows we're bonded though. The suppressant is outta my system, I'm so sorry. I didn't mean for him to find out."

He growled. "Fuck!"

"Ryloh won't tattle," I rushed out.

"Of course he fucking won't."

My brows furrowed. "Then why are you worried?"

"Did you forget your reaction to our telepathic connection? What are you going to do when more abilities surface? You've avoided every conversation about it!"

Oh, right. That. Meh. Jin looked ready to rip me in half as I shrugged. "I'll be fine! I mean it. I'll call you if anything happens. I swear, Jin."

"I don't like this." He was clawing his navy hair out and I felt something awful, but I needed time apart to process. I'd propelled past my social interaction limit since arriving.

"Please, Jin."

"Fine. Be careful, alright? I'll see you when you get back."

I gaped at the screen after he hung up on me. That was not a boy scout reaction.

<<*"How in the fuck am I supposed to care for her when she can't even hold a conversation?!"*>>

It was the longest I'd gone without taking the suppressant, which also meant I couldn't escape the mind-meld. I never thought in a million years I'd be missing that bleachy stuff, but every few minutes, like clockwork, Jin's unsettled thoughts projected and sent me spiraling further. Our honeymoon bubble? It'd popped. *And would likely deflate before lunchtime.*

My aimless stroll around Bahasa's beaches did nothing to ease, despite their otherworldly beauty. The further I trekked, the more remote the black sandy beaches grew. Despite Bahasa seeming as tightly packed as Thalla, my barefoot hike proved otherwise. There was a generous span of dense jungle a stone's throw away from the bustle, one I'd ventured into.

I decided braving the bugs would be worth enveloping myself in the peace of the greenery. Luck must've been on my side, because I hadn't been bitten yet. Despite the dark sand underneath my feet, I was surrounded by neons. Overgrown ferns and monstera plants overwhelmed the bases of the knobby tree trunks. I was forced to hop over a handful of vipers slithering past, but it was otherwise delightful.

<<*"This is exactly why Nala remained single, Jin."*>> *I couldn't deny he was right.*

In any other situation, the serene and picturesque setting would've been more than enough to quell my internal storming. However, that was before I fell in love. Before my entire life changed. The easily distracted, listless version of me was long gone, her too-small shell obliterated. Strange as it was to admit, given it'd been less than a week since my abduction, the old Gale the snail was no more than a distant memory.

That was what irked me, the fact I hardly knew this brand spanking new me. It shouldn't have been a priority. It should've been guilt I felt about the situation with Ryloh. It should've been remorse for sharing my love of Jin with someone else first. It should've been panic over how I was going to break the amo-whatever news. But instead? I only felt out of sorts, like my skin no longer stretched over my bones properly.

<< *"You're going to have to tell her, Jin. Programmatic rules or not."*>

The most terrifying part wasn't even the magic conversation anymore, it was questioning how to embrace who I'd evolved into. For the first time in my life, I felt kindred to my namesake and wanted to fly. But I didn't know how to spread my wings properly yet.

<< *"If Ryloh did something to harm her, I'm going to swallow him whole. No question. That barnacle is deader than dead. I'll be stomping on his fucking grave too..."*>

I'd been dodging my buzzing phone and attempting to ignore Jin's musings. However, the beautiful squirrel, Gabs, hadn't taken the hint, and refused—*go figure*—to relent. When my scallop vibrated with her thousandth video call, I answered with a raging, "What is it?" The pest was smiling like a maniac. My glower sprouted and grew.

"Are you in Gro? Why are you in the jungle?" No greeting. No explanation for her aggressive stalker-like tendencies. *Just more prying, of course.*

"Why are you blowing me up, Gabs? Is there an emergency?" I clipped.

Her chocolate eyes widened as she finally caught onto my moodiness. "I was curious to hear how things went with—" *Knew it!*

"Listen, Gabs—"

"I can see you're off-kilter. Are you okay? Where are you, Nala? Do you need help?" I sighed as Gabs switched gears and her sepia face lined with concern. However, I wasn't about to apologize unnecessarily. She'd rung in triple digit territory. *Unacceptable behavior.*

"I'm fine. I've been exploring Bahasa's beaches. I started in Bone Beach, I dunno where I am now, but it doesn't matter. Nothing of note happened with Ryloh—" She interrupted with a cross between a laugh and a scream.

"Yeah, right! Like I believe *that.* Jin's been avoiding me and Seong. I know something happened. You're wandering around fuming—"

I hung up and tucked my shell into my tank's built-in-bra. One thing was for certain, this new version of Nala was done with Gabs. *That nosy, fu—*

When I was suddenly cast in darkness, my gaze lifted to find an enormous real life dragon soaring overhead. *No. Way.* It only took one flash of his scales to identify who it was, I'd recognize that coppery shade anywhere. My jaw unhinged as a singular flap of Timos' wings mimicked a landing helicopter, the male was flying at least a mile above the tree line, but my hair tangled as if there were just a dozen feet between us. That's how humongous he was.

<<"Should you call her again? No. Don't be an idiot. Your incessant calling is why she didn't come home in the first place. You're being way too intense."> *That thought left a mark I felt from our reaching distance.*

But I now had a distraction.

The sun's prismed reflection against Timos' scales made his enormous dua forma glitter. He was the best dragon I'd ever seen, with his spike lined spine and matching wings. It was difficult to discern his size from our distance, but his thorny diamond-shaped head seemed comparable to an SUV. A large one, think Escalade or Yukon, not a crossover. Possibly a school bus.

"You should not be roaming, Naliti." Timos' voice was unrecognizable, deeper and scarier, as he circled above the palms. "I caught a vampire nearby, it is unsafe." In the next blink, the male stood before me in prima forma, wearing a black long t-shirt and matching shorts. He'd kept the wings though, which caused a squeal to escape my lips. They were fitted to his current size and unlike a bat's, their skin was smooth and shiny like a snake's scales.

"How do you have clothes? Is it magic?" I demanded, lunging for a hug. The second his long-sleeved arms circled my waist, the freaky chill returned to my sternum. However, he didn't respond, just growled against my cheek. "*What*? What's—"

Timos interrupted by flinging me into his arms and *flying* towards the beach. "There's another one, Timoset!" A deep rumble carried through the jungle. Once we left the shade of the fronds, through my dancing curls I caught sight of clover eyed rover standing in the onyx sand. He said, "Hello, Nightingale Nala Williams." The dragon gingerly placed me down beside the water's edge, before lunging into the sky within the span of a second. I couldn't avert my gaze as the soccer-field-sized reptile soared away. Then dove, clawing a distant speck before black sludge splattered onto his scales.

<<"Where in the fuck could she be for so long?!">

"It was another vampire," the Black handsome stranger explained. His voice was *really* deep, like an old obnoxious engine. Stealing my attention from the dragon's carnage, I whipped my head around to get a better look. The male was far too *fine*. His skin? Flaw-less. His long locs were pulled back and showing off the sharp cut to his chin. He was staring into the ocean with his palm cupped over his eyes, dressed in an olive button up and khaki swim trunks. What was up with Neptune, seriously? Movie stars didn't have jack on these aliens.

"Which one are you?" I didn't mean to sound like a doofus, but it'd been a day.

"Zaire Mensah," he extended an umber palm without looking over, which I shook. "Nice to meet you."

"You too," I said, turning back towards the water to find the dragon now MIA.

<<*"Fuck this shit! You have to find an outlet! She's not coming back anytime soon."*>

"Why has your scent blended with Ji-Ji's?" Zaire questioned, with a perplexed look. I caught sight of his nose ring and got momentarily distracted.

Unfortunately, Timos rifted over and definitely heard. Both males swarmed me, leaning in. I frowned at their matching exaggerated sniffing. *Do you smell?* I checked under my arms and found pear scented deodorant still intact.

"Pardon?" Also, who in the fork was *Ji-Ji*?

A puff of smoke left Timos' lips. "Your scent, Naliti. Have you bound yourself to Yu-Jin?"

Shit.

Timos' eyes shifted into bright draconic slits, the rage lining his face palpable as he loomed over me on the beach. Zaire, now terrified, distanced himself by backing a few steps behind the dragon. I gulped. *Maybe you should've taken the warnings seriously.*

"Don't attempt to lie, Nightingale Nala Williams. Please. Not to the dragon," Zaire begged. He raised his umber arms in placation when the growler spun towards him. "Allow her to explain first, Timoset."

When Timos circled his anger back to me, where it belonged, I might've cringed. Instead of intelligently thinking my wording through, I blurted, "Jin and I bonded."

"When?" Timos demanded, crossing his burly arms while his bronze scaly wings shook. "Your scent was not intertwined prior, and you were scheduled with Ryloh last night." Then something widened the dragon's gaze before his disapproval worsened. I knew, no mind reading required, he'd caught a whiff of my zappy buffet.

"Explain," Zaire urged from his growing distance down the beach.

"So, *uhm…*"

"Tell the truth." Timos demanded, I sputtered.

"Tell him! Tell him Ji-Ji did not force you!" *Oh. That's* why Timos was growly?

Hiding behind my hands, I forced the humiliation out. "We bonded the first night. It was completely my fault, he attempted to stop it. I was on a suppressant when we met because Jin insisted I stick with the Program." Instead of the explosion I was cowering in anticipation for, nothing happened. Eventually, I lowered my hands and cracked an eye to find Timos no longer glowering. Perhaps he was a bit peeved, but his eyes were a prima pair of pennies.

"I *knew* I could trust you, dragon," I exclaimed, throwing myself at him for a hug. "I knew they were all talking out of their asses!"

"I would *never* harm you, Naliti," Timos confirmed, returning my squeezing. The sensation in my chest enjoyed it far too much, leaving my skin prickling.

"You have nothing to say in response to my tethering to Jin?" I pressed as I withdrew from the dragon's peppery scent, and both males shook their heads. Zaire, now less spooked, crept a few cautionary steps closer. "How?"

"Although it was not entirely honest, you shared your intent with Yu-Jin," Timos said with a shrug of his spiky wings.

"He's one of my closest friends, we were born within a month of each other. What do I care if you're mated to him? I know Ji-Ji would share." Zaire explained as he neared. From our closeness, I noticed male's green eyes were also in motion.

Like my *Ji-Ji*'s. *Gaaah*, he was never going to hear the end of that nickname. "I'm not going to rat," he said.

Timos heaved a sigh. "I am disappointed you withheld it from me."

"I know, Timos. I shouldn't have. I'm so sorry—" I was interrupted by Zaire closing the last few steps and lifting a strand of my curls to sniff. Aggressively, with huffs and all. The turnu's handsome face was screwed in confusion as his nostrils flared.

"Why do I also scent you on her, Timoset?"

What's with all the scenting?

<<"*Scenting? Nala, where are you?!*"> *That answered whether or not our mind connection worked both ways.* <"*Of course, it works both ways! If you hadn't been avoiding the conversation, I would've told you as much.*">

- — *"Touché, Jin. I promise we can finally discuss the specifics of dick magic later. I'm still in Bahasa. Timos and Zaire are here. I'm safe. Back soon, bye."*-

"I thought I imagined it. You are certain?" Timos questioned Zaire, who nodded stiffly. "Shit," the dragon said with a pinch to his brow as his wings trembled, in what I assumed was agitation. "It must have resulted from my beast's obsession with her. Not even my father understands the intricacies of dragon curses, I may have marked her unintentionally." Another beastly mention. *Fantastic.* Which reminded me of-

"Ryloh, too." Zaire added, with a grimace this time. *Great, another Lolly hater.*

<<*"The list of those who despise Ryloh is endless, love."*>

"I can explain," I interjected, ignoring Jin's commentary. Timos released a puff of white smoke, while Zaire backed a sudden terrified step. "Ryloh says we're fated. Amo-something? I didn't believe him at first, but I felt the heart thing. It was kinda hard to deny after... What?" I asked as they held an entire conversation through their eyebrows towering over my squinting head. *Sunglasses would've been nice, but you don't even have shoes, Nala.*

"Ryloh believes he's your amoroso?" Zaire regurgitated each word slowly, and I nodded. He chuckled and shook his head before murmuring, "Ji-Ji is going to off himself." Timos grunted in affirmation, ping-ponging my attention back to him.

"You're joking, right?"

"How are *you* going to deal with this, Timoset? I don't envy you. No offense, Nightingale Nala Williams." Zaire said with the most condescending smirk, *ever*. "Your fated family is pure chaos. Dragon, Siarc, and a freakish faerie, you will never know peace again."

"It is not as if Nala chose him. Yu-Jin and I must both accept it," Timos replied with a deeper furrow. "Amoroso tethers are irrefutable." *Wait a hot minute.*

"It didn't feel *that* serious," I interjected, "Besides, if Ryloh can't play nice with the both of you, I'll refuse to bond with him. Simple as pie." Zaire barked a laugh while Timos' frown worsened. "Why's he laughing while you're devastated?"

"Because you have no idea how wrong you are," Zaire choked out before the dragon could explain. The turnu was a nuisance, a pot stirrer to the max, reminiscent of my three brothers. No matter how fine his shell was, I wasn't interested. Which was a relief for more than a handful of reasons, the primary being I'd claimed three apparently.

My eyes pleaded with Timos, who relented with a sigh. "Ryloh holds the other half of your soul, Naliti. If you do not accept your tethering, you shall never feel true happiness. No immortal willingly refuses their bonded, it is untenable."

"What?" I hollered. Zaire chortled as my knees buckled. Timos prevented me from face planting into the black sand, sharing an uneasy smile as he kept me propped up by the shoulders "But you're not stuck with me, Timos. Even if Lolly and Ji-Ji are—"

"Untrue," Zaire interrupted. "Timoset's scent is smothering yours, just as much as the other two. Amoroso or dragon curse, difficult to say, but it is clear. Whether you fucked them or not, you have three bonded, Nightingale Nala Williams. There's no denying it."

"Aren't you just a peach?" I muttered with an eye roll.

"Does peach have a duplicative meaning on Earth?" Zaire probed.

Instead of answering that, there was a far more pressing concern. "Timos babe, are you sure you're alright? You look queasy." The dragon shook his curls out of place as he attempted a smile. And failed. Quickly, I might add, which tugged my own lips downward.

"My stress is not because of you, Naliti. It is because I am concerned *for* you. It is your fifth day, you hardly understand the intricacies of immortal culture, yet you are now caged for all eternity with males you hardly know."

I threw myself at Timos' frigid chest and squeezed him tight, sighing as I was enveloped in his delicious scent. When his arms and wings wrapped around me, I couldn't withhold my hum of content.

"She's unnervingly brave for a mortal. I've never witnessed similar," Zaire murmured but I couldn't give him any of my attention as I stroked a hand down Timos' smooth frigid scales.

"I'm glad to be stuck with you, Timoset Drago. Don't worry, I'm fine. I probably would've chosen the three of you anyhow." He scoffed as his cold palms circled my waist. "I swear. Ryloh told me about immortal beastliness, I understand there's stuff the PPP hid. Jin's already in my noggin, I know there's more to the dick magic, and—" Zaire snorted in interruption. I forwarded a scathing look before finishing my thought. "I know Ryloh can be an asshat, but I *do* like him.

Plus, he swore he'd make things right for everyone involved. He seemed genuine."

"I will hold him to that," Timos proclaimed, entirely too seriously. "Ryloh must prove himself worthy of you first. Then he must rebuild trust with Yu-Jin and I, second. It will take time, and it is not your responsibility to make amends on his behalf. I am truthfully disappointed you did not meet with the other males prior to tethering. However, I am not disappointed in you. I will manage."

I heaved a deep sigh and pinched my brow, withdrawing from the dragon's cool embrace. "I hope you know that 'manage' is literal, Timos. It's gonna be messy. How in the Hell am I supposed to break this news to Jin? He hates Ryloh, too." I rubbed away the dark spots in my eyes.

Zaire abruptly stopped howling to say, "I'd like to be there." I reopened my peepers and raised a brow towards Timos who shrugged. "I can walk you home. Timoset should fly another lap around the island," Zaire tacked on. *Vampires, right.* I'd forgotten about that fiasco.

<<*"Vampires?! What the fuck, Nala?"*>

"I will see you tonight anyhow, Naliti." Timos said. Without waiting for my reply, he planted a kiss on my forehead, and lunged towards the sky. It was insane how quickly the guy could grow a hundred times over.

"He took that horribly," Zaire said as soon as Timos was out of earshot, earning himself an aggravated groan. "I'm curious to compare the dragon's reaction to Ji-Ji's."

"You're not helping, you know," I clipped as the handsome male smirked. Condescendingly again, obviously.

"You live in Thalla, correct?" He questioned, completely ignoring my sass.

"Mov Street, yeah."

"You're really gonna come inside?" I tossed over my shoulder, swiping to unlock the door of my building. The air conditioning was such a delight that I couldn't withhold from dancing as my feet were met with the cool granite tiles. The walk resulted in forty minutes of hot asphalt burning my soles while tugging my bicycle along. Although they did heal as I lifted each foot, a neat trick thanks to the lacking suppressant.

"I wasn't joking when I said Ji-Ji would off himself," Zaire said with a chuckle as he rearranged his loc bun. It'd been an enlightening conversation. I'd discovered the male was the duke of Ookea, which seemed secondary to his entrepreneurial pursuits. A Leo, avid traveler, and music obsessed. Also, since he was turnu, he shared his favorite shifts. Most of which were lower halved because he was just that into himself. Granted, he was finer than fine, so the ego wasn't entirely misplaced. "It's best you have backup for this conversation, Nightingale Nala Williams."

"I don't know if he's even still here," I said, waving my scallop over the doorknob. "He could've-... *Oh*. Hey, Jin. Sorry I was gone for so long." I said with a wince as he rose from the couch, suited arms crossing.

"Welcome home, Nala," Homie said from where they were charging on the fridge.

"Ji-Ji," Zaire greeted with pearly whites on display. "You could've told me about the feisty human you chained yourself to." I rolled my eyes as they did some kind of bro handshake. Jin had mentioned his closeness to another duke from childhood, but I hadn't pieced it until witnessing the similarly sized males together. They were besties despite Jin's unflinching fury, he held onto his scowl through their entire chest-bump-filled routine.

"Why the fuck were there vampires in Bahasa?" Jin's first question. The second followed less than a full breath later, as his furrowed navy brows spun towards me. "You swear that barnacle didn't harm you, Nala?" He stormed over to where I'd stilled by the entry. Zaire's grin clownishly spreading behind him. He performed a full-body inspection as I struggled to recall the script I'd prepared after tuning out Zaire's ramblings of how Neptune sucked compared to Venus.

"Nala, love, why do you look as though you might be sick? What happened?" When I couldn't seem to muster a response, Jin spun towards Zaire who burst into a giggle fit. "One of you better share!"

"*Ryloh's my amoroso,*" I blurted. It was from the pressure. I shouldn't have shouted, but it just sort of happened.

Jin froze in place with fists clenching at his sides. Every possible emotion crossed his chiseled face as I chewed on my lower lip. "No fucking way," Jin finally boomed. Thankfully, that finally shut Zaire up. "Is it true? You scented him on her?" He asked his bestie, who nodded. He then started pacing, or more accurately, *stomping* from one side of my loft to the other.

The air whooshed from my lungs when the doorbell suddenly *trilled*.

Homie's screen became a video feed of the entrance to my building. I was silently praying that Jin wouldn't catch sight of Ryloh Cabbage standing there with a zippered dress bag in hand, but I had no such luck. Zaire cackled, fully erupting. Which caused Jin to see, then stomp past, and out the door. I followed with Zaire on my heels. Who I elbowed, for good measure. He pushed me back. We already were acting like siblings as we fought our way down to the lobby.

"What the fuck are you doing here?" Jin thundered. His feet made the building quake as they slapped against the landing. Zaire and I shoved each other, scrambling down the steps to catch sight of Ryloh smiling maniacally from the other side of my glassed entrance. I shook my head in a feeble attempt to warn the fae to behave himself. But who was I kidding? My muscles were taut in preparation, bedlam was in the air.

"I bring a g- gift," Ryloh said, that psychotic gleam sparking in his headlights, "For *my* amoroso." He was also in another suit, just like Jin, which only rattled my lusty brain. It wasn't the time, but my lady parts weren't listening as I observed the pair.

It took him a second, but Jin roared, throwing open the door to tackle an incredibly smug Ryloh. Zaire held me back when I tried to follow, explaining, "It's best you allow them to get this out of the way." Despite Jin's clear advantage in height, the fae held his own. I sputtered in horror, failing to muster a reply as I watched Jin get zapped down with a spider web of lightning bolts.

The suited male was flopping like a fish over the side of the iron railing while Ryloh picked at his nails, bored. "Cabbage will win this round. Ji-Ji's advantages are in dua forma," Zaire whispered seriously in explanation, as if he was announcing at a golf tournament.

"Behave, Ryloh, you promised!" I finally found my voice to defend my poor Siarc.

He rolled his chrome eyes and said, "He started it." Then extending a wary hand towards where Jin was crumpled. Who ignored him and rose with further hatred flooding his expression. "You see, spice. It's the pupling who struggles to behave. Which makes sense, he is the most immature in current company." *Oh, no.*

Jin fell for the taunting and lunged for Ryloh's neck with a growl. However, the fae only barked a laugh. I soon realized it was because his skin zapped Jin's palms. He withdrew the steaming fleshy appendages with a roared, "You're such a fucking freak-show!"

"We share a soulmate, so what does that make you?" Ryloh volleyed. Thankfully, Jin's hands healed. I gasped as a khaki palm slapped the fae with a *crack*. Zaire and I exchanged a wide-eyed glance. But unfortunately, Jin wasn't done, he snarled, then Ryloh shot another zap with a sigh before crossing his arms.

"Have you settled? Will you allow me to present Nala with her gift?"

"You aren't good enough for her! No matter how you attempt to win her over, I know what you are," Jin erupted once more. At least he kept his hands to himself, but his chest was still rising and falling rapidly as he glowered in Ryloh's orbit.

"Why do they hate each other so much?" I whispered to Zaire. Unfortunately, the duo heard and stormed over to yell their own explanations. *Good grief!*

Stomping back up the stairs, I plugged my ears. There was no need to check if they followed, I felt the ground tremoring. It was too reminiscent of my violent zoo of a childhood, and I was ready to punch the trio in their stupidly hot faces.

"Enough," I yelled in intervention, slamming my door for emphasis. The terror triplets froze in various positions around my living room. Zaire even stopped his bum mid-air above the lounger. "You two are going to calmly explain why you despise each other. Jin, I'm sorry you found out this way. I am. However, I didn't ask for any of this either. Can you please sit down for me?" I pleaded as he continued with his enraged pacing.

"She only l- l- loves you... *For n- now,*" Ryloh conceded with a scowl as he crossed his arms. I was dumbfounded. Might've even blacked out from anger momentarily.

"He didn't know that yet," I seethed as Jin grimaced. There was a singular means to solve this. "Get out, Zaire, leave. *Now!* You too, Ry. Thank you for the dress, but you gotta go," I shooed them with waving arms when neither immediately heeded.

The turnu booked it upon receiving my lasered glower. But Ryloh — *obviously* — had to plant a sloppy peck to my cheek before slowly sauntering towards the exit. There was a wildfire-esque flash of static, and he was gone.

Finally, alone at last.

I swallowed a grimace and put on my big girl pants to face the heat. "Jin, I don't know where to start—" The second I turned, my lips were pressed to the coziest warm pair I knew. It wasn't a part of the plan, but I wouldn't refuse the deflection. When we rifted into my bathroom, I pulled back to ask, "Are you alright, Jin?"

"Fuck no," he replied without skipping a beat. The male then ripped through my black set with his hands before tearing through his suit and tugging me into the shower. "I have to remove his foul fucking scent before we attempt to discuss this," he clipped.

I bit my lip as Jin carefully soaped me up from head to toe. In raging silence. The fervor in which he clenched his jaw made a creaking noise, but his hands were gentle. There wasn't anything I could say or do to improve our circumstances. At least, I couldn't think of-... *Actually, there was a potential solution.*

There wasn't any need to fall to my knees, I just slightly bent at the waist and found myself face-to-cock. As Jin opened his mouth, I mirrored the action as our eyes met, and extended my tongue to lick the head of his partial boner. He groaned, and I took it as acceptance in my olive branch of a blow job.

Jin's plum eyes rolled back into his head as I wrapped my lips around his length and swallowed the best I could. Granted, there was a lot of him that wouldn't fit, even choking. But I did my best as his fingers tangled in my hair under the pouring faucet.

"Fuck that feels amazing, Nala," he breathed as his navy head tilted towards the ceiling. A sexy little shudder wracked his body as he hardened between my lips. When I forced him past my gag reflex, the male groaned.

I whimpered as his fingers tugged on my hardening nipples. It only egged us both on. I was dripping as his thick thighs shook under my fingertips. "Your lure, love," Jin breathed. I didn't know what he meant as he pulled me upright from underneath the shoulders.

"But you didn't even come yet," I pouted. Instead of responding, he flipped off the water, and yanked me out of the glass stall over his shoulder.

"I can't while you're luring me," he said. We were both drenched, but I couldn't care less as he tossed me down onto the freshly laundered sheets. When the male fell to his knees on the rug, I did a double take.

"Why are you kneeling?" I sputtered as Jin bowed his head and I got to ogle his perfectly carved dripping frame. And that glorious dick twitching against his ripped abdomen.

"You're luring me into submission," he croaked. I didn't know what to make of that. My brain was no more than mush as I licked my lips. We exchanged a heavily lidded and lusty blink.

"What?"

Before he could respond, I heard my scallop vibrating on the counter downstairs. Homie announced, "Ryloh Cabbage is calling. Would you like to answer, Nala?"

"No," I shouted.

When I met Jin's stare he explained, "You lured him. What the fuck?"

"I've done no such thing! Explain," I demanded, sliding to the floor, so we were face-to-face. Jin's pupils had overtaken the typical plum swirls of his eyes. "What's a lure for immortals?" I asked as I brushed an errant soaked lock from his forehead.

"Immortals cast lures when they require their soulmates. It's part of the magic conversation you've avoided—" he stilled when I gripped his throbbing length. Then he shook his head, quickly forcing out, "Anger, anguish, and arousal. Anytime you feel one of those three emotions, you apparently force us into fulfilling your wishes."

"But I haven't done anything?"

"You have," he rasped as I gave his shaft a languid twist.

The loud vibration started up again. "It is Timoset Drago calling, would you like for me to share you are busy, Nala?" Homie questioned and I couldn't muster a response from my stun. Instead, I decided to finish what I'd started in the first place.

Jin moaned as I bent to lick a trail from his balls to his tip.

"Fuck, you can't do that right now," he breathed. "Your lure is too strong, Nala. I can't orgasm until you—"

"We'll see about that," I replied, accepting the challenge with a chuckle. When I climbed and slid down his dick in the same moment, Jin's whole body shivered underneath me. I clung onto his muscled shoulders and bounced. Unlike every other occasion, the male remained still and let me do my thing. His fists were clenched beside his feet as he watched me, still kneeling. It was what I needed, I loved being in control of each and every delicious stretch. "God, you feel unbelievable without the suppressant," I moaned, and he whimpered.

"What is it, Jin?" I stilled after grounding my clit against his public bone and his chest stilled. "Are you alright?" The male's eyes were clamped shut.

"You," he whispered before taking a deep inhale through his mouth. When I rose, then fell down his length while clamping around him, Jin's groan was sinful. "I can feel everything you're feeling, I don't know how, love. But it's so intense, I can hardl—FUCK." He ran a palm down his face and slapped his cheek.

Despite his out-of-pocket reaction, I was having a grand ole time, so much so that I didn't want to come. But it was tough.

"I'm close," I said with a shiver of my own. I didn't even need friction or movement; every sensation was intensified without the suppressant. Bliss didn't even begin to cover it. Especially with how solid Jin was kneeling underneath me.

"I fucking know," he replied in a single breath, through clenched teeth.

Homie's robotic lilt carried, "Ryloh Cabbage and Timos Drago are downstairs—"

"Don't you dare let them in," I hollered.

"Understood."

"You need to come, Nala. Let go, please," Jin begged as he pinched his brow. The male still hadn't touched me once since I started riding him. I hated it. Which was the reason I gripped his palms and placed one on a boob before grinding against him. "Fuck, Nala. How are you this powerful?" He groaned.

It only took a few more thrusts to cross the finish-line and drag the male along with me. It was so overwhelming that we crumpled onto the floor together, with my body strewn across his. It was a complete KO. I could barely take in a breath and Jin's eyes remained clamped tight.

When I finally mustered the energy to crack a lid, with my cheek against the rug, I *wanted* to bask in our afterglow. Instead, my peripheral caught suspicious shadows casting through the skylight above our heads. *You were definitely feeling their nearness then.*

Unlike with Jin, I could distinctively feel Timos in my chest... And Ryloh.

Turning onto my back, I mouthed, "I'm going to murder you two," toward the creeps peering back. One guilty, the other grinning as he shared lewd gestures. I was in no state to process their boundary crossing. *Congratulations, Nala, you played yourself.*

Knowing Jin would lose his noodles if he noticed, I cautiously but aggressively, motioned for them to get outta dodge. Ryloh didn't want to go, scowling and pouting. But Timos, thankfully, rifted them seconds later. *Phew, close call.*

"I hate the suppressant," I panted, noticing right away that there wasn't a residual ache this go around. However, Jin seemed dead. Not even his chest was moving. "Jin," I said before shaking him by his huge shoulders. He cracked a plum swirling eye but only shook his head once. "Are you okay? Is it me? Am I still messing with you somehow?"

"I don't know how I survived that," he rasped.

It took him a few moments to come back to me wearing a smirk.

When I felt the fresh boner under my stomach, I knew why. Jin didn't waste a breath, he picked me up and tossed me on the bed. I didn't have a chance to blink as he threw my legs over each shoulder and slammed into me. "Christ, Jin," I gargled as his fingers dug into my ass.

"You're fucking *mine*, Nala," he all but yelled as my body attempted to adjust. Whatever spell he was under was long gone, as was his normal voice. He was speaking in a choral combination of tones.

Jin didn't waste a second as he leaned over me and bit my lip until it bled. Then the male gripped each side of my waist and slammed into me. A *roar* echoed through my loft as he thrust with enough force my eyes darkened around the edges. Each of his breaths were a growl as his eyes widened. They were too large for his face as he snarled, "Not theirs, *mine*. I don't care that you lured them, this pussy is fucking mine. All mine. Say it, Nala!"

"Yours," I wheezed.

The sensations were too much to care about his shifting, I lost myself. All my muscles went taut, I was so close as he demanded, "They've never felt you melting on their cocks, have they?" When I moaned in reply, Jin stilled, and moved a hand to decorate my neck and squeezed.

I could only muster a twitchy shake of my head before he pounded that humongous dick into me again. I saw stars, likely from the lack of oxygen as he hadn't eased his grip. It felt as though I was flying. *At least you'd die happily.*

"No dying," Jin commanded, in that same weird multi-tonal voice, with a sneer before releasing my neck. I felt him thicken as he increased his pace. Then, I orgasmed again, unexpectedly. Which sent him over the finish line with a slew of curses. We were both a panting mess as he rifted us back to where we'd started.

"So that's luring, *huh*?" I questioned with a breathy chuckle, and he nodded.

Since my legs were too shaky to stand on, he leaned me against him as he rinsed us off with the detachable shower-head. "I'm sorry if I was too rough, love. I lost control after how intense your lure was," Jin mumbled as embarrassment darkened his chiseled cheeks.

"Don't be, you weren't. If anything, this is my fault," I relented with a heavy sigh. "I should've come back. You didn't deserve my avoidance. I was being unreasonable—"

"Neither of you explained the vamps," Jin interrupted with an accusatory snarl, one with a hint of more voices. I raised my palms in placation.

"I barely glimpsed one of the two who breached. Timos clawed it up in the faraway waves. I dunno why Zaire was with him, but," I shrugged, "then there was a sniffing fest and Zaire walked me home while Timos went on further patrol." Jin grunted as he flicked off the spout and helped me out. He then assisted in toweling me dry before taking care of himself.

The domesticity left my heart skipping and I couldn't keep the sentiment to myself any longer. I didn't care whether he'd ever make up with Ryloh. The beastly stuff that had just gone down didn't matter, either. I loved Jin, every flaw, every alien bit.

"I love you, Yu-Jin Rapax. Real, real love. True love. You're the first I've felt this crazy about. You've changed my entire perspective on relationships, you've even helped me learn to love myself, Jin. I love you more than I've ever loved. And I'm so sorry I told your nemesis before you, it was an accidental slip. I didn't mean to—"

"I know, Nala," he interjected as his plum eyes met mine with his first toothy grin of the day. I swooned, and my heart was so thrilled it made my eyes blur. "I've heard your thoughts when the suppressant wanes, I know how you feel. I love you too. Equated, remember?" I nodded before flinging my arms around his warm neck and clinging on. "You're still the one. I've not questioned that, love."

I withdrew with a smirk. "Not even this morning? When I chickened out?" He shook his head and I chanted, *Li-ar. Li-ar. Pants on fire.* Before admitting, "I heard your frustration, Jin. Will you explain why you hate Ryloh so much?"

"He's abusive," he replied, all contentment replaced with fury. "You remember how I told you I'd been cheated on?" I nodded. "Both instances happened to involve Ryloh." I gasped, palming my mouth in horror as Jin rifted us into the closet. "He claims he didn't know I was dating the femmes. But that's beside the point. None of my hatred has to do with the cheating, it's the burns he left behind." I threw on a t-shirt and some boy shorts as the male took one of his four suits. He'd been slowly moving in, I didn't know why he was doing it one item at a time, but it was a discussion for later.

"He used his static on them unwillingly?" I questioned, hoping Jin didn't notice the tension in my shoulders. He wasn't going to like where this conversation would go.

"No, it was supposedly consensual. Although both admitted to regretting their consent later," Jin surprised me by answering. Then his brows fell as he asked, "How do you know the male calls his gift, 'static,' Nala? He's the only being to possess static under his command." I blanched. *That didn't take long.*

"Jin, you should probably be seated for this," I started, before tugging his shirtless self towards the edge of my soaked bed. "How much of it do you think you can handle without your beastie raging?"

He threw his head into his palms, and I fell to the carpeted floor at his feet, so our gazes could be parallel. "Ryloh revealed our natures?"

"He kinda had to. I got a glimpse of Timos', too." Jin groaned through his palms. "It's okay, it doesn't change how I feel. It makes sense, it doesn't bother me, I literally don't care."

Jin raised his head to shout, "You should care." When I shrugged, he added, "If I'd been able to fucking keep it together, we could've avoided this!"

"What?"

"It's my fault you're tethered to Ryloh," Jin roared before jumping to his feet. When I began shaking my head in denial, he shouted, "I fucking am, Nala. I'm the only reason you're no longer human! How else did you think you were able to sense your bond?"

"Oh." Hadn't thought of that.

Jin nodded with a grimace, which felt like a sucker punch to my stomach. "Fate chose you for *him*. Not me, Nala. Amoroso bonds are the only ones that matter! Even if you never accept him and complete the tethering, you'll still feel a pull to him whenever Ryloh is near, your souls are essentially magnetized by destiny." I stood and wrapped my arms around his middle, but it did nothing to quell him.

"It might've been Timos," I conceded, hoping it could help.

Jin gripped my shoulders and shook as he demanded, "Explain. Right. Now."

"That's why they were sniffing me. Timos said something about unintentionally dragon cursing me into being his or something."

"You've got to be fucking kidding me!"

"You're the only one I'm in love with, Jin," I said with a smile. He heaved a sigh, which was an improvement, so I carried on. "If you asked me to never bond with them, I wouldn't. Seriously. You're my priority. I don't care about the spooky soul stuff. Ryloh promised he'd play nice, but if he doesn't, then I'll never speak to him again. I swear—"

"I do love you. So much so that I can't be the reason you reject your amoroso and live your life with a piece of your soul missing." Jin interrupted, his warm corded arms circling me in return. "I swear to you, Nala, I'll try. I despise him, I hate him more than anyone. But that is nothing compared to the love I have for you already. I'm sorry I've reacted so poorly, it's not what you deserve. I'll behave around the barnacle."

"I love you too, Jin. There's no rush. We can let you simmer with it for a bit. We'll keep our distance for a few days—"

"No. I don't have a choice but to accept this now. We're seeing Ryloh and Timoset again in less than two hours for the Founding Gala. Why did you think he brought a dress?"

Fan-flipping-tastic.

<<*"You don't have to tell me, love."*>

The Founding Gala was hosted in the littoral caverns of Thalla's Quartz Beach. Once the lone housing on Neptune, the extensive sea cave system was repurposed to serve as their largest event venue. It was another initiative of Jin's, he explained how they converted the inner-city's more walkable venues into apartments in exchange for the caves. It was the only topic that brought his smile out to play as we dressed.

The theme of the Gala was "No Shoes, No Rules," and the hick in me couldn't wait.

We rifted in at 8:00pm to find the flushed sunset reflecting like a window-catcher onto the towering caves jutting from the sand. At first, it seemed reminiscent of any pebbled beach, until realizing the stones were smooth quartz crystals between my toes. *That's why it's named Quartz Beach, you dingbat.* The patterns in the towering walls were further confirmation, there were flecks and streaks within their depths. It was idyllic, otherworldly. And a complete struggle to focus my gaze on any singular thing.

The décor was elegant, mostly in gold to complement the beach's natural beauty. Until we went into the caverns, which were an explosion of color. Initially, I thought the bouncing lights were strung on string, but after closer inspection they were whizzing robotic orbs. Each with their own assigned hue to cast in a specific direction, painting our faces in a full-spectrum as we moved through the expansive caves.

Most of the party was circling among the gathered standing cliques, there were a handful of those groupings bobbing along the shallow glittering waves with their fins and tails out. While tables and loungers were tucked into the naturally formed cave corners. Hundreds in attendance was an understatement.

It felt like thousands of eyes were following where I dangled from Jin's arm. The crowd orbited as though my date was the sun. His duke mask was super glued onto his chiseled face, and he knew the names of who approached, wished belated birthdays, asked after family members, etc. Honestly, Yu-Jin Rapax was a total pro at crowd pleasing. Barack and Michelle Obama-at-a-gay-wedding level cherished.

When anyone commented on our abnormal closeness for my first week, which happened often, the duke of Thalla chuckled politely. Jin was hiding it well, but I could feel the triggering effects, how his grip on me kept tightening. It was an easy price to pay after our afternoon chaos.

Jin refused to let me wander and as much as I feigned exasperation, I was grateful he took care of everything. The best part was I only had to smile and nod. Which gifted the opportunity to snoop, there was oddly no music playing, making an ideal setting for it. Actually, now that I thought of it, I hadn't heard any tunes on Neptune yet. Which was nearly as weird as the outfits.

The theme resulted in a random fashion collection, each immortal wearing a different decade from the next. Togas and robes were more common than suits. It seemed more college rager than Gala despite the iridescent drink glasses. There was a plethora of shirtless and topless, others totally nude, while many also resembled Disney princesses. *I'm looking at you, copy-cat Jasmine.* She had a headband, teal genie pants, and everything but the tiger.

However, the strangest part wasn't the outfits or the lack of music, it was the smells. I didn't know if the dick magic burst through my suppressant or if I'd just ignored how everyone had such an easily accessible scent prior, but it was perplexing. I could pick apart minute notes, whether someone was drinking or not. If they'd had sex recently. If they drank coffee or tea this morning. It was so bizarre that I could hardly focus on anything else once noticing.

By the time Gabs found us, I was three-whiskey-tipsy, meaning the 'you little shit' look she bestowed slipped right over my skin, like a spill on a plastic covered sofa. "How have the honeymooners been since last night?" She poked.

"I haven't met Seong yet," I said, holding out a palm as Gabs' left eye twitched. If we were in a cartoon, steam would've shot from her ears. "Hello, finally, Seong Rapax."

Seong, the Whalen, was less like Jin in person. His face was squarer, hair longer, and his height a bit shorter. He was wearing a black t-shirt, matching his eyes and straight locks, beside his dolled-up Houston honey in her silver dress. The male was still handsome, but as was the entire alien population. "Nala, sweetie, we've met," Seong drawled.

Definitely a double Scorpio.

"Nope, video chat doesn't count! C'mon, you can't leave me hanging," I pressed when he refused to shake my waving palm. Eventually, Gabs elbowed him into it. "Aren't you just a pesky sand gnat?" I added once he withdrew like I'd stung him.

There was something *off* about their conjoined scent. It wasn't the typical sexed out smell I'd been picking up from other couples, there was an undertone I couldn't quite decipher. Which was infuriating since I hadn't struggled with anyone else's. *Earthy, maybe? Gabs does tote handfuls of dried shrubbery around.*

"Aren't you a little too drunk?" Seong volleyed, and I poked out my tongue.

"Trust me, this is nothing," Jin muttered into his glass, and I raised both brows. "What? I've seen you in action, love. You nearly drank me under the table and still balanced in those insane heels." I couldn't believe he remembered. Or that he winked before turning towards his brother to say, "Nala's not drunk until her every line is a rhyme."

"You two are all good and gooey then?" Gabs pressed with a pout, and I narrowed my eyes at her too obvious antics. Thankfully, despite being edgy, Jin didn't pick up on it.

"Gooey? Does that have a duplicative meaning on Earth?" Zaire questioned, joining our gathering beside the appetizers. There wasn't anything tasty if you were wondering, just carrots and celery without any accompanying dips. *Highly offensive.*

"Hello, nice to see you. Looking lovely." Zaire's locs were pulled back to show off his suit. After an umber palm gave a wave to us gals, the guys went full bro, sharing fist bumps and chest thumps. Gabs mirrored my cringe.

When the squirrel realized she'd found her opening, she clawed her chrome nails into my shoulder, dragging me a few steps from the males. "Spill, you bitch. Right now!"

Honestly, I didn't want to. She didn't deserve to know how Jin hadn't stopped losing it since Ryloh and Zaire left, or the way his voice kept accidentally shifting mid-sentence. She only saw us thriving because of my being glued to him all night.

I suddenly felt weird.

There was something to say about fate, because it chose that exact moment for Ryloh Cabbage to appear through the parting crowd. When his headlights found me, and he rifted to the empty space behind us, I thought Gabs might keel over. "Sugar Honey Iced Tea! You scared the crap outta me!"

"Gabriela, always a delight," Ryloh monotoned as his eyes never left mine. Instead of greeting me though, he forced a head-to-toe inspection. He even made a motion with his pointer for me to spin. *The audacity!* Naturally, I chomped down onto his extended finger. Ryloh chuckled before zapping me off, with enough force to rattle my teeth.

Gabs sputtered until she breathed, "Did I just imagine you biting him? I didn't imagine that, right?" I shrugged as the fae smirked and slithered an arm around my waist. The sleeves of his black button-up were rolled to the elbow and those delicious tattoos of his were on display.

"You're a vision, Nala spice," he purred before leaning in to murmur, "Did y- you miss me? I haven't stopped thinking about y- you for a second." I momentarily stopped breathing from the pull of his nearness. It was unnatural.

Then my heart suddenly galloped into hummingbird overdrive, and I wasn't sure if it was from him, but I managed to get it together enough to whisper, "That depends on whether your assistant picked this dress out."

"No, I did. I'd n- never permit another to style you. You should know that," Ryloh chided, anger peaking. *Crispy Kit-Kats!* Destiny really was a tricky little treater.

"But we bought that dress together on your first day?" Gabs screamed and we both recoiled. It was true, Ryloh bought me the same mesh number

I initially tried at Prima Formula. Jin pitched an actual fit when showing him the duplicate.

"We did, yes. Electric fae here bought me a backup." Then I stood on my tippy toes to make sure Ryloh saw my lips draw out, "It's unfortunately more fated fuckery." I couldn't help it, taunting him felt like cliff diving. I was addicted to the thrill, although I was well aware the cords could snap, and result in my demise.

Ryloh grinned from ear-to-pointy-ear. It was a wicked thing as his chrome eyes flashed with teensy sparks. Then he bit my neck in the same exact area he'd healed this morning. It took a beat, or two, or ten, for my soul to return from space.

Mother-flipping-fae-floundering-

Cameras flashed. Gasps rang through the crowd. Everything slowed to an ESPN replay as Ryloh's nose trailed up the side of my neck. Instead of butterflies, lightning struck all my organs at once. "I'm disappointed you wouldn't allow Timoset and I to join you earlier." My vision went blank as I heard the grin in his voice.

He just said that, yeah?

Two words: shadow orgy. The addition of this holy trinity's faces to my prior dream unplugged my brain. I knew it was incredibly unlikely, given Jin's possessiveness, but you couldn't stop this Pisces from daydreaming. It was a doozy, too.

When a *roar* sounded, I came to my senses. Spinning in Ryloh's arms to discover Timos grimacing in a well-fitted black suit. If my noggin was unplugged before, it was now tossed in the trash at the sight of the gorgeous goggles all spiffed up.

However, it didn't seem as though the approaching dragon was the source of the disturbance, only the freezing in my chest. My eyes searched until Gabs pointed to where Seong and Zaire were holding a raging Jin back. Ryloh noticed the same moment I did, barking a laugh. Which, unfortunately, compounded the Siarc's anger.

"He fucking bit Nala! Let me go!"

This was far too public for the duke of Thalla to lose his noodles. I attempted to free myself from Ryloh, but he kept me in place with ease. When a frigid palm circled my upper arm and I tilted to find Timos, the male was more than unsettled. Then came the screaming from the crowd. As I readied to ask what the heck was happening, I caught sight of Jin's mouth shifting wide and sharp. I was dumb-founded as Ryloh commanded, "You g- grab him, Timoset. I'll take her."

"Third Quarter," Timos confirmed with a nod before storming over to the others. *Whatever that means.* Zaire, Timos, and Seong scrambled to capture Jin as he began rifting around the caves. Like a very messed up version of chase where he terrified bystanders. The crowd went completely ape, I'd never seen equivalent calamity.

I gawped as Jin's oversized smirking maw suddenly appeared behind a white-winged male, who immediately shifted into dua forma from sheer terror. His oversized white goose body and accompanying *honking*, sent the spectators into further hysteria as Jin let a multi-tonal laugh rip.

Ryloh and I couldn't contain our giggles as the male goose circled, flapping above our heads, and—*literally*—began flinging his shit around the cave. Except this was no normal bird poo, it was the size of a great Dane's as it *splat* on innocent heads. When Seong appeared nearby to catch Jin, he took off again. I was gasping for air when my unhinged Siarc appeared in front of Ryloh. And bitch-slapped him before disappearing. Sending me into further howls.

Lolly didn't find it nearly as hilarious, though.

Another loud *crash* sent the throng wild before we disappeared. I'm not gonna lie, I was peeved to abandon the entertainment. Ryloh teleported us into an open-mouthed and empty cavern. It was still made of variously colored quartz, but I could no longer hear a hint of the bedlam, so we must've gone far.

Vast, unending, teal waves lapped along shards of jutting crystals through the lone opening. It was just wide enough to showcase the neat row of rising moons tucked between blue and purple clouds. Unlike the Gala, these caves were claustrophobic, with low-hanging stalactites. *Poor Timos is gonna be hunching in here.*

Ryloh shoved me behind him as the pair rifted into the waves, with a half shifted and snapping Jin. He momentarily stilled the second my gaping face reflected in his oversized eyes. Timos had somehow changed into the same casual apparel from earlier, with wings intact, and his hands as coppered scaly paws.

The Siarc's head was a shark's that fit his humanoid still suited body. I couldn't look away or move as he chomped and growled, attempting to get past the aggravated dragon to where we watched from fifty feet. Ryloh was chuckling with a rotating ball of static in an upturned palm.

Majority of the movement was Jin, flapping around in the water, it wasn't really a struggle. When one of the Siarc's teeth *cracked* on Timos' claw and started gushing red, I understood why the public feared dragons. *Ouchie.*

Timos wasn't just my professor, he could also double as our rodeo handler apparently.

"Nala unfortunately belongs to Ryloh as well, Yu-Jin." Timos used his typical lilt, but his eyes were glowing like a pair of suns.

When Jin's roar caused an array of quartz icicles to rattle, and subsequently fall, Ryloh took us to my loft before we could hear a resulting crash. "Welcome home, Nala," Homie echoed from the fridge, inciting more of my frustration.

"Take us back, Ryloh."

He shook his handsome pale face in refusal. "I will not risk y- you, Nala. The Siarc is 'in frenzy.' It's best you allow —"

"*Frenzy?*" I interrupted, scrunching my nose in confusion.

"Think of it as untethered fury that knows no bounds or l- logic. In frenzy is a more aggressively feral state than what you witnessed of my beast. Jin is dangerous at the moment. He will not settle in your presence. Even with your suppressant intact, I can scent both Timos and myself on you. I'm not sure how it's possible. It shouldn't be —"

"Jin will calm for me!" He shook his head with more fervor, so I raised my voice. "Take us back, Ryloh! *Now.*" Thankfully, the fae relented once I screeched.

Within the next blink, we were back in those caves. The chill in my chest stole my breath away as I watched the pair struggle. I don't know what I expected to find upon our return, but it wasn't an enormous fully shifted great *navy* shark mid-argument in the waves with a half shifted Timos, who'd grown several sizes.

Jin's dua form was thrilling to witness. The patterns on his skin matched his hair. He was also far more regal than any real-life sharks I'd seen, flawless and unmarred. Huge, possibly comparable to Timos in his dragon form. While Jin's eyes were no longer monolidded, they were as round as they'd been when we were intimate, their purple swirling irises the same familiar pair.

I knew the second I'd captured his attention because Ryloh dove head-first into the waves and sprouted a flipping *tail*. I barely had a chance to inspect his dark holographic scales before an enormous shark opened his maw and white light filled the cavern, effectively blinding me.

"*NO*," Timos' reptilian rumble echoed before a loud *pop* sounded. The resulting dragon's shout was guttural, like a huge boulder falling off a cliff and cracking into millions of pieces upon impact. The pebbles under my bare feet trembled. I didn't know what else to do, throwing my arms over my head and ducking for cover.

"It's alright, spice," Ryloh's alien lilt echoed off the surrounding caves. "Timoset contained Yu-Jin." I cracked an eye to find my Siarc had been trapped in an enormous bubble floating in a distant corner of the cavern. Timos was cleaning his glasses with humanly taupe hands while Ryloh shifted back into his formal attire on the shore. Jin was repeatedly slamming his pointy face against the clear sphere. Probably in an attempt to reach me. Each bang against the barrier resulted in a *bloop* that was far too hilarious for our predicament.

"Can he breathe in there?" I questioned and the pair nodded. "I'm fine, Jin. I swear. You can stop banging around," I called. Earning myself a set of mirrored scowls and shaking heads as they approached. "What? My Ji-Ji's still in there."

"You see, she would never fear me!" The Siarc beastie's voice had so many different tones echoing at once that I did a double take to ensure it came from his sharp toothed maw. It was far more evident than it had been earlier, he sounded like a superdome full of trapped spirits.

"Do not encourage him, Naliti," Timos chided, "his beast is currently untethered. It is straining to keep him contained."

"Is this frenzy what everyone's scared of you doing, Timos?" I asked.

The dragon turned a glare in Ryloh's direction, but the fae only shrugged, uncaring. The chrome in his eyes sparkled more brightly than the surrounding crystals and I had to remind myself it wasn't the time for ogling. Especially when I turned back and got lost in Timos' gorgeous copper gaze.

"N- Nala deserves to know, Timoset. There's no question as to whether she's *ours*."

"Yeah, no more secrets," I tacked on, crossing my arms as the males held a silent argument. "What's the goal here? How do we get Jin back?" They shared an uncomfortable glance before both avoided my gaze. "Tell me, I can handle it!"

Timos shook his head as Ryloh nodded, and I groaned. "Listen, Nala spice," Ryloh started while the dragon continued vehemently flinging his curls in disapproval, "Yu-Jin is technically i- in there, but *not* at th- the same time."

"What does that even mean?"

"You cannot trust him in this state," Timos ground out.

"I'll always trust Jin, beastie or not," I said, earning myself another *bloop*. At least he made a handsome predator. It made me less weary of the fact he could very much swallow me whole.

"I could've told you Nala wouldn't be fearful, Timoset. She hardly reacted when my own beast accidentally surfaced." It was possibly the worst thing Ryloh could've revealed to our current audience. And he did it while flaunting—*you guessed it*—an evil smirk. The Siarc went into a thrashing fit, while we landed in the smoking section, I had to fan the bleached fumes to spare my eyes.

The dragon lifted an accusatory pointer towards Ryloh who held onto his taunting. "Then you also understand how dangerous and entirely misplaced Naliti's lacking caution is. You should care more for her welfare. How am I to trust you?"

"You're lucky I'm willing to share in the first place," Ryloh snapped back with a sneer. I didn't know why he was so ballsy against the male the *entire* galactic populous feared, but he took a menacing step towards Timos without hesitation.

"Nala carries my scent as well, you dimwit!" My dragon bent down to growl in the fae's unflinching face. Ryloh, surprisingly, didn't even blink.

"The femme is mine, and mine, alone," the spirit-box rattled in the background.

"If anything, she's yours the *least*, pupling," Ryloh yelled. I went to whack him in the shoulder, hard enough to hurt. Except, instead of landing the blow where intended, he turned the last second, and I accidentally Hulk-smashed his stubbled chin. A *crack* sounded as his eyes sparked with surprise. *How did you even manage that?*

We were both equally perplexed, exchanging frowns, before staring at my hand. I rotated it, but nothing seemed awry. I'd never known I had it in me. I might've broken his jaw. "I'm sorry, Lolly. Are you alright?" He nodded wordlessly as he felt around with a wince, so I knew I got him good.

<<*"Let me out, you fucking shitty piece of —"*> *Aha! Dick magic was the source.*

"*Jin,*" I thundered, sprinting towards the shore. Unfortunately, Timos caught me around the waist and held me back with a stern expression.

<<*"Shit. Your suppressant is gone, love. And I didn't think this night could get any worse. I'm so fucking sorry."*>

"Jin, don't apologize, you doofus! Can I help you regain control?" I probably didn't need to shout but did anyhow. "Timos, you gotta let me go. I can help him!"

"Th- Their minds melded," Ryloh explained to the perplexed dragon once his mouth healed. "Her suppressant waned; can't you scent it?"

"Fuck," Timos replied. "That will infuriate his beast further."

"Look, I'm not scared. You can float Jin over here and I'll pet him, just to prove it. He won't harm me. I know he won't. He loves me." Both males shouted equivalent concern, then disdain. When a deafening sound interrupted their hollering, reminiscent of a crash of piano-keys, I spun towards the water to find it was the Siarc's unbidden laughter.

<<*"That's a horrible idea, love. I'd rather you didn't, my beast is psychotic."*> *So, they weren't the same consciousness? Unsettling.*

<<*"Exactly. We're very much separate."*>

"The femme is fucking mine! Allow her touch!" *Welp, that tracked.*

"N- Not until you shift back. I refuse to risk Nala. She hasn't tethered to the dragon yet, she's far too breakable," Ryloh snarled as he pulled me from Timos, shoving me behind him once more. I flicked one of his flappy ears in annoyance before side-stepping and returning to the edge of the lapping waves.

"Jin, how do I get you back?"

<<*"You might have to leave until my beast gives up, love."*>

-—*"I'm the reason your beastie's going berserk?"*-

<<*"Unfortunately, yes. Your scent without the suppressant has melded with both of theirs. Although I'm fine sharing you, my nature is not."*>

"You weren't fine about my bonds with Ryloh and Timos either, Jin." I accidentally voiced aloud. Sighing when I realized I was being cornered by the other two, now further disgruntled.

"He doesn't wish for you to accept our b- bonds?" Ryloh raged, and Timos released a puff of smoke in equated anger.

"That's not what I said," I exclaimed in exasperation. "Jin swore he would attempt to get over his loathing for you. And he's always liked you, Timos. He just wasn't stoked," I lowered my voice, "because you have the destined droll and he doesn't." Ryloh snorted while Timos shook his head with a teensy curl to his lips. It was such an improvement that my own grin spread, and I nearly forgot our circumstances. Not quite. Not with the incessant *bloop, bloop, bloop* echoing.

<<*"It is unfair that they share those bonds with you when I don't, love."*>

-—*"It's not. It doesn't change a lick of what I feel for you, Jin."*-

Fighting a pout, I said, "The four of us have to figure this out. I know it's going to take some effort. Especially between you three, but Zaire was right earlier, you are it for me. I love you, Jin, but you're gonna have to get over it. You're the whole reason I even met this pair in the first place."

<<*"You had to attend each of the first week's dates to not get sent back to Earth. It was spelled by the Queen, there are no loopholes."*>

"Is *that* the reason you told me to?! Are you telling me you didn't actually support me being with anyone else, Yu-Jin Rapax?"

"Now wasn't the time to tell her," Ryloh mumbled, but I caught it, and narrowed my eyes. "D- Don't look at me like that, spice. I'm certain I've revealed more to you than they have."

He was probably right, so I turned my fury towards the other secret hoarder. "Is that why you insisted I go on the dates, Timoset?!" The dragon shook his head one too many times under the pressure of my glower. "The truth, *now*!"

"Perhaps it was a minuscule part of it," he relented with a sigh as his copper eyes pleaded innocence. "Not all of it though, Naliti. I swear. It was primarily because I desired you to meet Avexei before tethering." *Womp. Womp. Too late for that.*

<<"I knew you would have more than me, love. I'm just trying to be okay with it."

>

Jin had proven himself worthy of my implicit trust. However, I'd still had enough with the endless secrets. "What else are you hiding?!"

"I don't kn- know whether it's the right time for revelations, Nala spice. However," Ryloh cleared his throat, and his cheek ticked a few times before he added, "It is time for something else." He took a deep breath with his eyes clamped before turning towards Timos to say, "I apologize for how cruel I was under her Majesty's orders. I should've refused th- the wench. I'm sorry. Nala deserves more than a peaceful nest from us." Ryloh extended a pale hand. "I swear to improve your opinion of m- me."

Timos accepted the truce. "Nala's happiness matters above all else. You have my forgiveness for as long as you do right by her. However, you should apologize to Avexei."

"Done." Ryloh spun to face the bubble with my shark to shout, "I apologize to you as well, Yu-Jin. Although the past no longer m- matters, given we both have spice, n- now."

I hopped into Ryloh's arms, relishing his summer storm scent, and whispered, "I'm so grateful, Ryloh." When I went to give him a kiss on the cheek, he moved and caught my lips instead. I gasped when cold hands ripped me from Ryloh's mouth and wrapped me into their own.

Jin's beastie did *not* like seeing Ryloh kissing me. "She is not yours! *Mine!*" The accompanying roar that left the Siarc, caused Timos' copper spiked wings to spring from his suited shoulders. I raised a brow, and he shrugged as his fingers became long russet claws around my middle. That was the moment I looked down and noticed the mesh of my dress was decimated. *Fate strikes again.*

"You should take her home to change, then return to the Gala, Timoset. One of us should resurface after the mayhem. I will remain until Yu-Jin overcomes," Ryloh offered. The fae shrugged when met with my surprise. "Allow m- me to be useful. I owe it to Timoset after how easily he granted his forgiveness. Besides, Yu-Jin and I should have a conversation before we return to y- you."

Timos teleported us to the front door of my building before I could thank Lolly for his service. With a sigh, I pulled my shell from where it was in my bra, and unlocked the lobby door, motioning for him to follow. "You don't seem surprised by Ryloh offering to handle the situation," I mumbled.

"He must prove his commitment, but it is encouraging," Timos replied as I unlocked.

"Welcome home, Nala," Homie said as I trudged upstairs to change into my duplicative outfit. The dragon followed and stood uncomfortably in a corner, fidgeting. "You can sit down, you know, Timos." He shook his head, and I noticed his eyes were slitted as I skipped into the closet. "Why not?"

"I can scent the activity," he said in little more than a whisper. *Whoopsie.*

"I'm sorry, I didn't mean to make you uncomfortable. I also didn't mean to ignore you and Ryloh after luring you earlier. I didn't know I was doing it." Hearing a soft groan, I hurried with flinging off my ruined dress. "Are you okay?" I questioned, leaving the closet in a bra and panties to find him pacing from one side of my bedroom to the other.

"These are difficult circumstances for me. More so than anticipated." I rushed over and did the only thing I could think to do, which was pet the spine of his wings. Timos' draconic eyes widened in surprise as a purr-like rumble shook his chest.

Fighting off my grin was difficult. Anytime we touched, the sensation grew. There was no more questioning it, I welcomed the piece of him that made a home inside my chest. "Can you walk me through what's troubling you, Timos?" I asked with another stroke down his cool scales. "Maybe I can help. I'm the cause of this catastrophe."

"It is not catastrophic, it is just—" he paused when he met my questioning gaze, "I did not anticipate sharing my partner, no other dragons do. Not that I was opposed. I just do not know how to properly support you. Ryloh and Jin have acted rashly—"

"They haven't. I'm fine. I swear."

"It is not in regard to your welfare that they have acted rashly, it is..." He sighed and pinched his brow, turning his russet wings towards me to stare at the lofted high ceilings.

"What?"

"I feel more than I have ever felt, Naliti. For anyone. For anything. My beast is more than merely scratching at the surface for you. I fear what I am capable of—" I interrupted him with a gentle smack to the chest.

When he lowered his chin to meet my gaze, I said, "No, Timoset Drago. You would never hurt me, nor would you ever lose control. I probably shouldn't say this, but I knew Jin would lose it. You missed the pandemonium when Ryloh was here earlier. I knew that Dumb and Dumber would struggle. But you?" I shook my head, "Never you, Timos."

"But I potentially marked you," he replied with a frown. I shrugged, uncaring as my chest iced over. I moved my hand from his wings to where I could feel his heart burning for mine. "I may have marked you when we initially embraced. Your feelings may be a result—"

"Nope, none of that," I chided with a scowl. My chest chilled further. "I signed the contract because of you. I don't give a shit as to whether you marked me. As far as I'm concerned, Lolly's the one who took me by surprise. I *chose* you and Jin. And I would do it again, even despite the Siarc beastie losing his cool."

The male was dumbfounded.

"It's 100% true," I pressed, anticipating his denial or argument, but instead, Timos frigid hands gripped each of my cheeks. He kissed me with enough force to bruise. I didn't care, I clawed his shoulders and climbed him, kissing him back harder. I might've only been in love with Jin, but my feelings for Timos were rapidly encroaching.

If you're honest with yourself, babe, they probably already caught up.

When he withdrew with a toothy grin, my smile was immovable. "Do you feel better now?" I pressed and he nodded as his wings disappeared.

"You seem to know how to ease me, Naliti."

"Duh," I said with a nibble to my lower lip from nerves. There was a need to be patient with Timos, I knew that, but restraining myself was difficult. I wanted more than he'd been giving. It wasn't the same dicksperation I felt with Jin. There was a craving to treasure this precious dragon who already meant so much to me.

"Timos, when was the last time you..."

"What?" He pressed, his copper eyes searching mine behind his lenses.

"When was the last time," I palmed his stiff length through his suit trousers and he released an unbidden moan, "you were intimate with someone?"

"I truthfully do not know," he panted as my fingers drifted towards his zipper. It was the answer I expected, but still didn't appreciate hearing it.

"Do you trust me?" I met his hooded gaze. "I know we're bound by some external force, but do you feel safe with me, Timos? Because I don't think I have ever felt as safe around anyone else."

There was a mask of perplexity on his gorgeous face, but he nodded. My hands shook with anticipation as I slowly tugged his zipper, then unbuttoned, sliding his boxers down so he sprung forth. Nothing could've prepared me for how perfect his dick was though. Huge in a terrifying way, but temptingly so for me. I waited until his gaze met mine before taking his velvety hardness in my fist. Twisting slightly. He shuddered and I couldn't tell if it was good or bad. "Is this alright?"

"More," he demanded, sending an icy thrill barreling down my spine.

"How much more?" I taunted. Then suddenly, I was on my back, bouncing against the couch downstairs as cool hands gripped my knees and pushed them apart. "Timos...?" I didn't know what I meant to ask as he loomed over me. His upper half was still suited, and it was nearly as distracting as his dick. He raised a dark brow, and I forced out, "Are we gonna bond right now?" My voice was breathless. His response was pushing aside my thong as an icy finger leisurely slid into me. A whimper escaped as he curled into my g-spot.

"That is your decision, not mine." His grin was boyish as his pupils blew wide. The ice cube in my chest was all but vibrating from our closeness.

"I want to touch you too. Sit," I ordered.

"It is of far more importance that you—" I silenced him with a pump to his length. When I leaned over to lick the tip, he groaned loudly enough to rattle the windowpanes. My smugness was immovable.

"Timos, lay flat on your back." He didn't argue. Not even when I climbed on top of him, in a semi-sixty-nine, but our difference in size made it impossible. Taking his dripping crown into my mouth, the moan that left his lips was one of the biggest turn-ons of my entire existence. Then another frigid finger pressed into me as I attempted to prevent myself from choking.

There was suddenly a foreign sensation, but I couldn't look, nor did I care to. However, it *felt* like a tongue. An icy one flicking against my clit. When his fingers were replaced, confirming it was an oversized tongue dipping into me, my entire body shook against his. And the frigid bumpy muscle kept snaking deeper and deeper, enough that I cried out. *Wooah, there.*

I was a drooling mess as his hardness twitched at the back of my throat.

Is his tongue forked? The Cha-Cha Slide Timos was doing on its way in couldn't have been possible otherwise. There were two legs to that tongue! I could hardly breathe, let alone pay attention to how he was throbbing in my mouth.

That frigid tongue swished against my cervix in such a way…

Oh, my, fucking-

I came. Nearly dying as my gag reflex bobbed on Timos' hardness.

It took me a second to recover, but I dove into action. A needy garble left him as I quickened my pace, using a fist to twist around the length I couldn't possibly ever hope to swallow.

The sensation of his tongue languidly withdrawing before circling my clit nearly sent me over the edge again. Which just wouldn't do. Out of desperation for him to finish, I tugged on his balls. Timos' resulting groan as he released into the back of my throat probably sent the entire street into a tizzy. He tasted, *surprisingly*, like his scent. Which led me to wondering if the same would be true of the others. *Only one way to find out.*

After withdrawing, I hopped to the kitchen to clean us both up. "It's kinda creepy getting feisty with Homie as an unwilling bystander. Feels wrong," I muttered, passing them on the fridge.

"My warding shut him off," Timos replied.

"What do you mean?" I questioned, tapping the tablet. Sure enough, Homie was dead on their charger. Grabbing the kitchen towel from the sink, I dampened it.

Spinning, I caught Timos explaining, "My wards ensure our privacy both physically and electronically." He lowered his voice to no-more than a whisper to add, "There are surveillance concerns in Thalla. I can never be too careful when it concerns you, Naliti."

"*Huh,*" I mused, wiping his stubbled chin, "another reason to get out of this place." Then straightened his glasses although I didn't want to, they were adorably askew. The male was grinning from ear-to-ear as he tucked himself back into his trousers, and I couldn't help but match.

"You do not like this apartment either?" he prompted.

I chuckled. "Initially, I found it massive. But with you sitting here it feels like a toy house. It's not gonna work for much longer, is it? Which sucks, because I'm obsessed with Thalla, it's my favorite. Though, to be fair, I haven't seen Ookea. Thalla is just so pretty. I adore how old the architecture is here. The colors of the streets, the winding alleyways, it's packed with character."

Timos' brow furrowed as he said, "It is quite modern actually."

"Is this when you tell me you live in a cave? Dragon thing, right?" He nodded sheepishly. I snickered before asking, "Is it bigger than here?"

"Not enough to fit all of us. Although truthfully, Naliti, nothing will ever feel large enough."

Nodding, I said, "We're gonna need lots of space. The other two can be annoying."

A fresh grin split the dragon's face as he said shyly, "I am not though."

My heart might've skipped a beat as I said, "No, you're not. I don't think I could ever get my fill of you either." Every silence with Timos was comfortable and this was no different. I didn't know how he-*hold up. Have you already forgotten?*

He just mega forking tongued you!

Kinda difficult to, considering my insides were tingly with a lingering chill. I didn't get a good enough look of his dragon form to notice his tongue, but it *had* to have been forked. I mean, the more my noggin attempted to replay, the more wound up I became.

There were alarm bells dinging in my brain that I needed to be gentle in broaching the topic. However, I was itching to know every single detail of what he just did. And *how*. I couldn't help myself from breaking our quiet with, "Was it a half tongue shift?" like a total doofus.

Instantaneously wiping Timos' joy. There was a deep-set frown, then his cheeks darkened three shades, before the dragon sputtered, "Did you not—"

I silenced him with a kiss, before pulling apart to explain, "Timoset, stop. Of course I did. That was amazing. I didn't mean to ruin our afterglow. I was just curious, but you don't have to answer." He still looked like a kicked puppy, which pushed me into admitting, "I want you to do it again."

Timos gaped for a second. Just one, before rifting me to the kitchen counter by the wrist. My thong which was already in trashing territory was incinerated with icy bleached flames. Then my bra. *Dragon fire!*

And it didn't burn! Just glittered around my body with a chilly caress as bleached ashes fell to the floor. The echo of my delighted peal in finally seeing his flames was likely heard for miles.

The dragon laughed as he forced me back onto the kitchen island. "Timos, I want you undressed too," I said breathily.

He stilled, face falling, chest deflating.

Oh, no.

Timos' cool palms slipped from my knees. *What did you do to break him?!*

"What is it?" I croaked, stomach cycling with worry.

All I received in return was a pained shake of his head. Which threw salt over the flames of my desire. Something was horribly, horribly wrong. "Timos?" I questioned, palming his cheek as his copper eyes darted around the loft.

"You do not wish to see, trust me," he rasped.

"Nonsense," I murmured, tilting his gorgeous face to meet mine. "Talk to me, Timos." The way his eyes blurred with tears cracked my heart. "You aren't disappointing me. You don't have to do anything, okay?" I assured, slithering my arms around his chest and legs around his middle. We embraced like his life depended on it.

We stayed like that, with us both clinging on like a pair of tightly wound clamps.

Whatever caused this reaction told me everything I needed to know. Memories of our scar conversation ping-ponged around my skull. Timoset Drago healed me then, his words closed the wound I allowed to fester. I craved to do the same for him.

This gentle dragon was mine and I didn't care what was wrong, whether he was disfigured or disabled or whatever, it didn't matter. I wanted to be everything for him. He deserved more than everything after all these years alone... *Fuck. You're in love with him. Like lovey dove love.*

Inside. Outside. Timoset Drago was a dream. This was the exact kind of person I always imagined myself with, someone who could counteract all of my crazy.

Squeezing him tight, I whispered, "You're going to have to let me in, Timos. Maybe not today. Maybe not tomorrow. But please, let me in. Nothing's gonna scare me away, I swear."

"Only because I marked you," he mumbled into my hair, heaving a sigh.

That's it.

"No, you can't keep bringing that nonsense up." I didn't mean to take such a snarky tone, but this wasn't gonna fly. We'd already covered the dragon cursing and I thought we'd moved past it. Gripping his chin, I forced Timos' bright eyes to meet mine, they were still glassy and a bit red, which only solidified my resolve further. "You're mine. It's not fate, it's not the weird thing in our chests, it's *us*. You and me." The voice that left my lips was so ferocious I surprised myself.

Timos' eyes narrowed. Does he not believe you?

Is it the right time to tell him? I didn't know.

However, the words hadn't stopped circling my thoughts since the realization solidified.

"Why is your heart racing, Naliti?" he murmured.

Now or never, Nala.

Fuck. I was nervous. Far more nervous than I was with Jin.

"I love you," I blurted, tears and words fleeing in one swoop. My heart managed to speed further. It was on the highest setting as he placed a taupe hand against my sternum. "Please don't push me away I don't think I can handle it," I mumbled before the weeps dragged me under at the sight of his shy smile.

"Truly?" Timos questioned with so much hope that my sobs worsened as I nodded like a bobble head and pressed my hand to where his chest was burning for me.

He seemed too stunned to function for several seconds.

Then we were kissing. This one was nothing like the last several. Timos was being so tender that my tears worsened in severity. *You love him, you really, really love him.*

"I worry I will disgust you," Timos admitted breathlessly when we pulled apart. "I do not wish to keep things from you, Naliti. You must understand. I loathe refusing you."

"I know," I said softly, brushing an errant curl from his forehead. "There's no rush in you showing me. I'm here. I'm always gonna be. I swear." My weep show abruptly stopped when Timos removed his suit jacket, draping it over a stool. I gripped his chilly fingers as he started on his shirt buttons, stilling him. "You don't have to."

"I do," he replied, going back to unbuttoning. It only took him four or five before I saw the first mark on his broad chest in my peripheral. I waited, holding my breath. It was impossible to fight back the fury I felt in witnessing each additional scar as he went. I wanted to demand, *'who did this to you?!'* But instead, remained silent and still, holding his gaze as he finally undid the last button and tossed his white shirt to the floor.

"Can I touch you?" I whispered, near sobs all over again.

"Please," Timos said. The insecurity in his eyes crushed me.

"You're just as gorgeous as I knew you would be," I said, my fingertips tracing the lines of his shoulders. The black scars were jagged, about three inches in width and at least a foot in length as they crisscrossed over his otherwise flawless chest. His arms had the worst of it, they almost looked like tattoos. Slashes. *Was it a monster or another immortal?* My gut sank with the realization that *this* was behind the long sleeves. Worse yet, how he would be objectified further if he didn't hide. And I hated it. Hated everything about how difficult the world had been on him.

He was perfect. If Jin had sixty abs, Timos had over a hundred. *Now is not the time to be turned on, Nala!* My fingers continued tracing the planes of his chest as his heart thundered. I didn't touch a single mark. Not yet. There was too much trepidation in his gaze.

"Why did you worry? You know how I feel about scars. Yours only add to your appeal." He only scoffed in reply. "Do they hurt?" It was on the tip of my tongue to ask how it happened, but I kept myself in check.

"Not with you touching me, Naliti"

That's your cue.

When I traced the first mark, one of the smaller ones across this abdomen, he shivered. I waited for him to swat me away. A beat passed where he didn't stop my path, so I traced every scar. Memorizing them. Memorizing him. It didn't matter that he hadn't returned my sentiment.

I loved him enough for the both of us.

When I pressed the first kiss to the scar on his forearm, Timos' entire body trembled underneath me. The overwhelming emotions wrapped around my throat like a fist. I couldn't muster another word, but I could show him, continuing from each and every uneven line. The visceral reactions from him were as healing as they were upsetting.

By the time I'd finished, we were both quietly sobbing.

"I have never shown another," Timos whispered, "and I am glad for it now. It was always meant to be you." I met his tear-filled gaze as his palms cupped my cheeks, thumbs brushing away my own waterworks. "You are my strength as much as you are my weakness."

Gripping his arms, I promised with a sniffle, "You don't have to be anything around me. I love you as you are, Timoset Drago. Every single flaw."

"It is more than love I feel for you. No one has ever cared for me as you do," Timos choked out weeping, and my eyes flooded like a fire-hydrant. "I swear to be deserving, Naliti. I swear it to you, here and now."

The teary kiss we shared was my favorite yet. This was where we were both meant to be. I knew it with absolute certainty. The thing in both our chests was singing as our tongues explored. My hands roamed all over him, invoking groans as I went.

I knew it wasn't the right time to reveal how this happened to him. However, that didn't mean I wasn't raging inside. Mostly in anger *for* him. The rest was for revenge. Because if whoever did this was still alive, they wouldn't be for much longer. The fighter in me was thirsting for bloodied retribution. I didn't care if that made me a monster.

"Are you alright?" Timos interrupted our kiss. I hadn't realized I'd stilled from my murderous thoughts. I nodded back with a smile, attempting to hide the storm brewing within. "Thank you. I feel whole with you," he said, and my stomach did a flip.

"Me too," I replied with a watery smile, wiping his cheeks. "I'm obsessed with you. Scarred skin, scales, it doesn't matter." Tapping his chest, I said, "This enormous heart of yours is why I can't get enough of you, Timoset Drago. I'm honored to be yours."

"And the others?" he questioned weakly. "It is not that I do not wish to share you, Naliti, you deserve as many loves as you desire. I do not know how to—"

"I don't know how to either. None of us do," I interrupted. "But what I feel for you is entirely separate from what I feel for them. My love for Jin doesn't feel the same as my love for you. We're going to figure this out together. There's no pressure. What you did earlier was perfect, just talk to me, okay? Open communication is the only path forward."

Timos nodded before enveloping me in his chilly embrace.

"Ryloh was right, we should head back to the Gala," he said in his normal voice with a sigh.

"Alright," I conceded, knowing I'd already blown through all of his limits. "I'm proud of you," I whispered as he helped me off the counter. It was difficult fighting back the weeps after they'd started. "I know this isn't easy, Timos. Loving me. Sharing me. Sharing yourself. And I'm proud of you. I'm proud of myself too, I never thought I could ever get to this place."

Our grins matched as he grabbed his shirt and started buttoning. I didn't expect to trust these two enough to share that I loved them, but here I was. *Who cares? Shame on you, listening to societal norms from a society you aren't even a part of anymore. Pah!*

I wouldn't change a thing anyway.

WEEK TWO

We were holding court with Gabs and Burt, hiding in a cave corner to keep our distance from the Gala's relentless paparazzi.

I'd lost count of my drinks and was drunk as a skunk. Seong and Zaire were there, mostly chit-chatting among themselves. While Timos, Gabs, and I were thoroughly entertained with Burt's play-by-play of the unfolding drama between three fae.

Pixies. Except they weren't teensy Tinkerbells, they were still taller than Gabs, with insect-reminiscent wings sprouting from their shoulder blades. A dark-haired femme with moth wings was attempting to smother a redheaded butterfly with the surrounding pebbled sand. However, it didn't stop the butterfly from responding with whooshes of air, sending the moth into a Marilyn Monroe, revealing embarrassing granny-panties. The enby they'd been fighting over, another Pixie with bumble-bee wings, was caught in the middle attempting to de-escalate.

At least Jin's disruption wasn't the lone maelstrom. Besides the fae, there were kinky public displays gathering miniature crowds in every direction.

Suddenly, Gabs interrupted with a screeched, *"Minny!"* Flicking my attention towards Seong who embraced a lavender haired femme with matching monolidded eyes. Her silky dress put all of our outfits to shame. She had silvery freckles that made the swirl of her light eyes glow brightly against her matching straight tresses.

When she and Gabs exchanged a hug, my guide was bouncing on her heels. "This is Nala, Jin's... *Uhm.*" I shrugged, also iffy over how to explain. 'Sister-in-mate' was at the tip of my tongue, but I swallowed it down and shared a forced smile instead.

"Nala is Jin's mate," Seong revealed with a maniacal grin. Timos and I both scowled, but his lips only spread wider. "What? Everyone here knows. Minny isn't going to tattle. Grow up."

"Jin isn't here. You can't just drop his secrets like they're hot," I snarked. Burt and Gabs both proceeded to drop it low, to Timos' perplexity.

"Ji-Ji broke the rules?" Min asked, hugging Zaire next. He spun her as if she were also his little sister, but then grabbed her bum. With both fists. I gawked, eyes darting, but no one else noticed. "You're definitely no longer human with that scent," Min added.

"Nala just refreshed her suppressant. How have you circumvented it?" Timos questioned as he pushed up his glasses. I'd *quintupled* the dose before we left.

"Because I'm Leviathan," Min replied, "charms don't work on me."

"What does a Leviathan look like?"

"She's similar to Ursula, but with scales, and far more terrifying," Gabs explained.

"I don't understand your reference, Gabriela, but Min is rarer than I am. There are only two Leviathans, just her and her father," Zaire said. "Even rarer than Ji-Ji since they have been the only pair to ever exist in their line. There were dozens of Siarcs prior to the intergalactic war."

"I'm not done discussing Jin," Min snapped her squared french-mani-cure. "So, Nala, you do realize his best friend is our mom, right?"

"Don't be cruel. Yu-Jin's the best! I'm madly in love with him!" They went mute from stun, and I nearly smacked my forehead. *Not the time to share feelings with the class.*

"No shit." Burt breathed as Timos painted a forced smile. *More of a grimace.* I gripped his frigid fingers to include him in the sentiment.

"You love Timoset as well, don't you?" Min guessed with a warm smile and a pointed glance at our hands. Feeling my cheeks boil, I bobbed my head. Gabs gasped, knocking Seong's glass out of his hand.

Zaire said, "*Woah*, feisty human. You work fast! Has it even been a week?"

I rolled my eyes. It might've seemed quick to them, sure, but I'd spent the last three decades with my nose tucked in a book. On escape mode. Idle. Hardly coherent. The only time I lived was on vacation. The rest was a blur.

"Do you love her in return?" Seong demanded.

"Don't ask him that," I snapped. "It wasn't an invitation for you to snoop." *What in the Flubber?* Gabs didn't come to my defense either, smirking over the rim of her glass. Spiking my annoyance.

"Of course I am in love with Nala," Timos said, his free arm snaking around my middle, tugging me against his chest. It was difficult to contain my squeal as my heart sprinted, but I managed. "Distant family we may now be, Seong, but you best watch your fucking tongue. If you upset Nala, you shall have me to contend with." I couldn't help but smirk as the clique gawked. Timos didn't raise his voice and there wasn't a puff of smoke in sight. He was himself, fully in control. And he loved me!

Obviously, I knew, but it was extra special hearing it with an audience. My skin peppered as I leaned against him, finding a grin peering down at me. I'm not going to lie, when he leaned in and kissed me, I was more shocked than the rest. When we made out in the street there weren't friends watching. There was a loud throat clearing before things progressed. *Definitely Seong.*

We disbanded, and I whispered, "Thank you for being my back up." So the others couldn't pry, hoping they'd given up on creeping by now.

"Always."

That's it, you gotta take him back to yours. Like now.

Timos' eyes shifted as if he could sense the direction of my thoughts. "Do you wanna go?" I pressed, internally crossing fingers and toes that he would.

"The others are still in the caverns, are you certain you wish to return without them?" Timos' eyes returned to coppery normalcy. It *was* a valid question. Unfortunately.

Everything changed tonight.

I didn't blame him, but Jin could've harmed me irreparably. As much as he loathed our situation, he needed the others as much as I did. He couldn't come first anymore. Timos and Ryloh were meant to be with us. Ryloh's offer to remain behind also solidified my opinion of the fae. Despite the calamity, the pieces had landed where they needed to fall. We were a team now.

A fearsome foursome. Blergh, no. Yuck.

With a sigh, I relented, "I think the two of us have unfinished business after earlier, but if you wanna play fair then maybe we shouldn't. I still don't know what I'm doing, Timos."

"They should be aware of our intentions prior," he murmured in reply. "However, I cannot refuse you." My stomach wound tight like a coil with the promise laced in his words.

However, we couldn't. Reality whacked me in the head in interruption. I gave a queasy smile, because we'd forgotten the hiccup. "We can't until I'm off the suppressant. I will literally die. I'm not saying it's a bad way to go, but you'll hurt me if we don't wait." He grimaced, and with a defeated grumble, I spun back to the party. Expecting our 'friends' to have moved onto their own conversations, merriment, etc. *But no.*

Most were ogling. Burt and Min were the only pair who'd carried on, chit-chatting among themselves. Timos narrowed his gaze until theirs scattered. Gabs and Seong exchanged a suspicious glance. I was fed up with their antics.

"I'm happy for you," Burt said with a squeeze to my elbow. "I saw how dull your life was before, Gale snail, you deserve this. And you too, Timoset, you've waited long enough." I gave his warm arm a pat back, the Aussie had landed himself into friendlier territory.

"Alright. I've had it with the silence," Zaire interrupted. "Any takers for the after party?"

"Only if we go to Sirenuse, the other DJ's are complete shite on Sundays," Burt replied, earning himself a high five from Zaire. He was flaunting his tanned abs in a partially shifted form, with citrine scaled micro shorts over his privates, the rest of him bare. Apparently, Sirens were known to roam in the nude after the childfree curfew.

"Zaire owns Sirenuse," Timos explained. "Do you wish to join them?"

"Yes! I haven't heard any music yet," I said with a clap. Burt grimaced and mouthed, "It's awful." Likely to not offend Zaire, but he did reset expectations.

"Gabs and I have plans first thing in the morning," Seong interjected. When his mate opened her mouth, readied to argue, he clipped, "You know you can't handle the ice plunge while hungover and your back's been cracking too loud for you to skip."

I barked a laugh, hollering, "Goodnight, Granny!" She glowered before her hubs rifted them.

There was something fishy between Min and Zaire. Burt knew it, Timos knew it, the only ones who didn't seem to acknowledge it were the pair themselves. Each time they'd tumble into a flirty repartee, they'd completely forget about the rest of us, then awkwardly resurface mid topic. The further we ventured, the more I questioned why the turnu was a part of the Program, because they… Well, I wasn't sure *what* they were. The ass grabbing coupled with their aggressive flirtation wasn't confirmation. Not yet, anyway.

We had a lengthy walk. Ookea was on the opposite end of the island from Quartz Beach, but they insisted the Sunday funday streets were worth experiencing. There were food vendors scattered underneath the fairy light decorated lamp posts. Cafes and restaurants had moved their tables into the sidewalks for patrons to enjoy smoking devices resembling hookahs.

Thankfully, no shirt Burt didn't subscribe to the widespread bigotry when it came to dragons, so there wasn't any need to play referee when something captured my attention. Namely, food. Since the Gala's snacks were severely lacking, I was currently on my fourth crispy thing on a stick dipped in delicious.

Majority of the adults seemed to be out and about while they basked under the sixteen moons' glow. It was far more relaxed than the Friday crowding. Probably due to the absence of munchkins. It was hours past curfew and children weren't allowed out again until morning.

Loads stopped Min, most fan girling, and begging for selfies. Almost all thanking her profusely, and strangely calling her 'Doctor.' By the tenth occurrence, I gave into my overwhelming curiosity to ask, "How are you so well-known, Min?"

"I host a podcast," she said with a nonchalant shrug. Zaire *clucked* his tongue until she sighed and added, "It's the most listened to podcast in our galaxy."

"What?!"

"And it's only available on three of the thirteen planets, that's how successful she is," Zaire supplicated with a grin, puffing out his chest in pride. *Far too much for a friend.* "She has her doctorate in psychotherapy, it's a dating show."

"For the queers and femmes," Burt tacked on. "You should tune in, Gale snail. She does a live Q&A for Neptune, Hell, and Venus at once, it's quite the crossover."

"Should I assume it's to counteract Masc Males?"

Min nodded, disgust crinkling her nose. "Absolutely. That heathen and the misinformation he's spouting is why I began hosting."

"I thought rights were more equalized on Neptune?"

"It's bad for us, too. Not as bad as Earth, but still. The queers and femmes band together because of the inequalities and dangers associated with dating the unhinged. I can't complain too much as it keeps my bills paid," Min replied.

Timos explained, "Several Titans are to blame for the widespread toxic masculinity. Unfortunately, femmes on some planets are treated as no more than wombs. Chadwick's followers subscribe to the belief femmes hold less prestige than males. As you can imagine, they respect the LGBTQ+ community even less due to their 'unnatural' means of procreation." My entire body cringed as I recoiled in disgust.

"I thought I'd left all of that nonsense behind!"

"Trust me, I'm trans," Burt revealed with a scowl. "I transitioned almost twenty years ago. It's just as fucking miserable here as it is on Earth for us, Nala bird." My heart sank and I couldn't help but skip over to give the Siren a hug he returned. He murmured a thank you into my hair before we disbanded.

It sucked to hear. Neptune *seemed* more equated from how most chose to actively offer pronouns, but I was clearly looking through rose-colored glasses. Just because it was better than where I came from didn't make it acceptable.

Hello, Aphrodite sexually harassed you!

Min tacked on, "Neptune still has a long way to go, despite 35% of the population being queer, which is why I reside on Venus." My eyes flicked to Zaire. This was sounding mighty familiar. "Venuvians are more accepting. Plus, there's nicer beaches, and the cities are livelier." Interestingly, Burt rolled his eyes and shook his blonde head, as though he didn't agree.

"Zaire told me the same," I said with narrowed gaze. Unfortunately, no one caught onto my innuendo. And my statement threw Romeo and Juliet into another flirtatious bout when they thought none of us were looking. But I was.

"Don't you hate being a celebrity, Min?" I probed, and she shook her head, which caused a lavender strand to fall from behind her ear. One which Zaire tucked back into place with an umber hand that cupped her jaw with a swoon. *They're definitely together.*

"She's a Leo," Burt said in explanation. Which only further confirmed their thing. *Star blessed.*

⋘ ⋘ ⋙ ✦ ⋆ °

I knew the first instant we'd stepped into Ookea. While Thalla's buildings were an architectural mashed up rainbow, it was anything but. All the façades were in a red brick. No matter how tall, there were no variances in the architecture, only the window shapes and sizes.

When a blaring horn sounded, I accidentally tossed my half eaten yum stick in terror. Unfortunate, as it was the tastiest one. *RIP carrot curried crunch.* I frowned as I picked it up to toss it into a nearby bin. A trashcan hidden underneath a fern. I'd never get accustomed to how Jin's legislation beautified every inch of this place, including the garbage.

It was official: there weren't unkempt parts of these three cities. Which I didn't know what to make of. Mostly, it just felt unfair.

Timos grimaced, saying, "It is the wards. I must investigate but will return shortly. Please do not leave Nala unattended." With that, my gorgeous gent with glasses disappeared.

"So Timoset really is the po-po around here, *huh*?" I asked, and Burt guffawed but the love birds didn't catch my joke. "Planetary Protectorate, it still works!"

"Po-po," Zaire repeated. "Your Earthly dialect becomes stranger by the minute."

Min elbowed him in my stead. "Rude, Z. I can't wait to go to Earth, I haven't been yet, but our moms are always going on about it. Even after all this time."

"I can't wait to meet Umma Hae now that I've tried her mashisoyo kimchi."

"You speak Korean?"

"Just a teensy bit," I said with a pinch of my fingers. "I spent a month in Seoul and loved it. I can't wait to visit with Jin, actually."

"I'm inviting myself on that trip," Min insisted. "I've never been either."

Burt nodded, saying, "Me too. I'm coming."

"Ditto," from Zaire.

The conversation left me missing Jin so much I texted to let him know the additions to our travels. Not that I expected him to reply, he was probably still trapped in the cave with Ryloh. Which was why I also texted our intended location. While I typed out a third message to explain how Timos rifted off, Burt dragged me down a thumping stairwell.

There was something unsettlingly fecking familiar about these caverns. They were reminiscent of my past. Most compact spaces were. The tang of blood filled my nostrils as memories swarmed. My first slaughter played in technicolor against my eyelids, it was always the death I never wished to deal, the Chupacabra who sacrificed himself so I could flee.

This imagery would likely terrorize most. Not me. No, the haunting beckoned me forward, extending a hand from the pit of darkness. A temptation to continue what I begun. Because I became worse than a nightmare after that Chupacabra's demise.

Why be haunted when you could become the source of fear instead?

It became a mantra.

However, the tantalizing whispers of my past made containing urges more difficult.

Urges were all I once was. Riding one dark high to the next. I became a machine. Year after aimless year of sameness, lacking despite the plethora of bodies, monies, and opportunities. Life became a game I grew bored of winning.

That was in the later years though, the earlier were abysmal.

Most would claim Ryloh Cabbage was incapable of feeling. Perhaps I once was. Truthfully, though, my stutter caused their speculation. Plus, there was never cause to appear as more than an enigma. Until her manifestation thirty-two years ago.

One fated night, I met Nala in a dream. Then she appeared in the next. And the one after.

Although I didn't know when, or how she might appear. Not initially, those details came later. However, the mere idea of her was enough to uproot who I'd been, alter the soil, and start anew. My current state was nothing like the past version.

Thanks to paying closer notice and emulating 'normal' beings. I begrudgingly learned emotional cues. Empathy to an extent. Appropriate conversation topics, etc. Even made a friend. It took decades, but it had to be done.

However, *none* of that prepared me for babysitting an emotionally inept pupling.

This wasn't how tonight was meant to unfurl. I *thought* I would've been spinning Nala around the Gala. Hearing her sexy giggle echo off the crystalized caverns. Perhaps find a dark secluded corner to see if I could surface one of her fecking madness inducing lures.

Not only had *none* of that transpired, but the exact opposite. Leaving me twitchy. Twitchy wasn't great. *You cannot kill Yu-Jin Rapax, don't even tempt yourself with imagining it.*

The night had spoiled.

What was I thinking volunteering myself for this? Of all things! And for this loaf of overgrown muscle. *You were thinking your soulmate would reward you handsomely, that's what.*

Except, I couldn't keep my shit together around Nala spice last night. I failed. After my slip, this frenzy duty was of significance. A test of will. For her.

I hated myself for the stuttering far more than the beast escaping. Silly at my age, but the truth. I'd grown accustomed to my speech pitfalls, trained to overcome through ceaseless practice. I rarely stumbled to the point of no longer finishing a sentence; so, when the inevitable slip occurred in recent years, I hardly noticed...

Until her. Every pause made me feel like an idiot. Like that helpless child. Damn, how I loathed myself for it. There was at least a century of not pausing or masking —*or quite frankly, caring*— and the second she came into view it all went out the window.

Because Nala was perfect and I was lacking.

"You shouldn't have released me, fae," Yu-Jin's beast roared as Timoset's warding disbanded. He immediately began thrashing. Sending waves in all directions. "Bow to my superiority!"

Superiority? I doubted the pupling was fulfilling Nala's most simplistic needs.

Yu-Jin was a nuisance. He probably wasn't aware her favored 'book boyfriend' had a frenum ladder. He likely wasn't aware of how she preferred drinking her coffee iced due to her self-proclaimed 'belly sensitivity.' And he, *definitely,* wasn't aware of how she came four times on my tongue in less than three minutes.

Sure, perhaps I was more sensitive to Yu-Jin's grating than the norm. Primarily because of aforementioned piercings. I obtained six.

Six metal rods through my fecking shaft just this afternoon.

The mere memory resurfaced the freshly inflicted trauma, leaving me wincing.

Following the lure letdown, I required an outlet. It was a moment of weakness, I admit. Timoset, oddly, insisted on accompanying me to the nearest piercer. The rest was history. Thankfully, due to my quicker healing, my cock didn't fester or ooze for long, but it was tender still.

As was I emotionally.

It was back breaking withstanding the urge to check my feeds immediately after Nala and Timoset left, nearly as galling as remaining behind. But if I gave in, this unhinged twat could glimpse how I'd been *lightly* stalking her and worsen his immature fit. It wasn't worth the risk. I already held the bottom tier ranking in the harem.

You love being the scoundrel, though. It was true. I *lived* for the fire flashing in Nala's endless eyes as she held that puny blade to my neck. Her defiance was my favorite drug. It was already our game, this push and pull. She loved how rakish I could be. I was questioning up-ranking. There was little chance the others could compete after—

"You should fear me in this form. Submit to me," Yu-Jin attempted, and I rolled my eyes. Of course, the Siarc could easily swallow me whole. It would be foolish to willingly place myself within reach. However, fae love to scuffle, myself more than most. He understood this, he knew the prestige rankings. How my skin decorated in thousands of deals and duels won.

I was forced to battle an overwhelming craving to cook him and take a bite. *His meat's likely rancid, though.* Since my baser impulses were clawing, I gave into pettiness and taunted, just a tad. "The only being I'll ever kneel for is *my* Nala spice."

"She is not yours!"

"She is," I replied, already regretting the interaction.

"Not!"

See? Jejune and anything but entertaining. "Listen, pupling, you need to get y- yourself under control. I understand you're still scoring poorly on the m- maturity spectrum, but," I shrugged. He didn't appreciate my blatancy if his growl had anything to say, so I adjusted tact. "Y- You're disappointing our soulmate, Yu-Jin. Nala deserves more." It was a gross understatement, but I knew I'd hit my intended mark. *Time for the final nail in the coffin on your corniness, Ryloh.*

"Sh- She loves you," I spat, disgusted with the statement and myself equally. And for the *second* cursed time on this *wretched* day, my throat burned like I'd swallowed a vat of acid. It was illogical, I knew Nala would soon —*very, very soon*—love me *loads* more than him. Undoubtedly.

And yet... I nearly hurled my guts. It was excruciating to voice.

Yu-Jin stilled, scrutinizing my visceral reaction. "You love her," the Siarc rumbled, his echoing platitudes rattling the stalactites. *Congratulations, captain obvious, you're useless.* "How are you in love with her already? You hardly know her!"

I couldn't have schemed a more opportune opening. There was no preventing the curl to my lips as his distasteful shark face scowled. With a smirk, I revealed my most treasured secret. "I dreamt of Nala. Of us. Before she arrived. For the last thirty-two years, Y- Yu-Jin." He nearly drowned as he digested that factoid. It was delightful.

Also, quite freeing to voice the secret aloud to another. It had been ages.

Each slumber was as much of a boon as it was an anathema. I quickly deduced we would meet on Neptune, through this uncouth Program. I also learned of the others. Sharing wasn't any issue, group bedroom activities were far superior, anyone who claimed otherwise was a lying sod.

Sometimes the visions repeated themselves, other instances not. It wasn't in any discernible sequence, and I never dreamt of our first meeting.

That's where this overflowing patience I currently leveraged stemmed from.

"You have the Sight?"

"No," I shook my head, "the dreams came after I perished in testing. It was 7:03pm on February 19th, 13457." Her birth date and time, down to the minute.

The Siarc's purple eyes widened in shock, and I shrugged. It wasn't *that* uncommon. Many resurrected attested to experiencing destined dreams afterward. "Athanatos and Olorun reanimated me," I explained, "They claimed my demise was n- not yet due." *Now he can share with Avexei and Timoset, one task off your to-do list. Bravo.*

There was quite a bit I glossed over. However, the Titan Seer's predictions hadn't exactly come to pass. That unsettled me most, he was never wrong. Perhaps Nala altered things, I wasn't quite sure *what* changed, but there would be consequences for someone. Just not me, because she was, very much, still mine.

"You knew about Timoset?" Yu-Jin pressed, and I nodded. The dragon was almost always present in the premonitions, he hardly ever left her side.

"Did you know of *me*?" He demanded with a growl, and I shook my head. *And therein lies our problem.* Our harmonic union, the future we'd been waiting on for thirty-two years, wasn't our current reality… *Or, at least, not yet.*

"Who then?" Yu-Jin pressed in his multi-tonal echo.

My gaze narrowed since I hadn't revealed the existence of a third. The Siarc possessed a more intelligent beast than anticipated. Concealing the truth was futile though. *The chaos doesn't involve you.* However, my stomach didn't get the memo, taking a plunge as I voiced the glitch, "Th- The Uktena."

Yu-Jin sucked in a harsh breath. "Did you dream of *that snake* with *her*?" He sneered in those scratchy vocals, taking what he likely thought was a menacing buck in my direction.

It wasn't.

I sighed, pinching the bridge of my nose. "Does it m- matter?" We were straying from the unresolved situation at hand. And I'd hardly gotten the chance to absorb how resplendent Nala was in the dress *I* rightfully *chose*. "You must shift back. I wish to return to Nala. Don't you?"

"Obviously!" I nearly clapped but refrained when the male's prima lilt *finally* returned. "You didn't answer my question, Ryloh! Have you dreamt of her with that stupid god instead?"

"I swear to answer honestly if y- you shift back."

Thankfully, that did the trick. Yu-Jin and his destroyed suit swam to shore wearing a scowl. "She was meant for him?" he demanded, and I rolled my eyes.

"Clearly n- not, Yu-Jin," I didn't have to feign my agitation, it was incredibly real. "Destiny changes. You know this, it's not fixed... Which is exactly why we must make amends. I apologize for our past. Nala doesn't deserve our petty dueling. What do you require for reconciliation?"

The male grumbled incoherently, like the petulant child he was, and I couldn't help but *tsk*. It would've been preferable to have *any* other in our arrangement—*well, not Chadwick*. But who was I to question Nala? This harem was hers. Besides, *his* heart wasn't beating in sync with ours, so I could feign amends in the meantime.

"You didn't see me with her at all? Not once in thirty years?" He looked so devastated that something pity-adjacent gripped my black heart. I was—*shockingly*—tempted to lie. *Oh, so* very tempted because it would not just appease the Siarc, but also stir the pot. Something I typically delighted in doing to this stunted male. But eventually shook my head. It was Nala. The reformation she'd sparked apparently didn't require her proximity.

The male cursed and stomped for several minutes as I fought the urge to lower to his level. My beast was raging to eliminate our zoatala problem. It would only take one zap to his heart, and he would no longer be a bother. *The clock's ticking, he'll be indestructible once she porks Drago.* "It's so fucking unfair!"

"It isn't. You don't see m- me falling into frenzy," I sneered.

"You've had thirty-two years of seeing her with other males to get used to it!"

An unpreventable grin danced across my lips. I sassed, "I still would never act as you have, Yu-Jin. It's time to move past this resentment. Nala wishes for us to play nicely." *For now.*

"I'm only going to forgive you if you swear to not harm her." The male crossed his arms with another scowl, and I laughed. Loudly.

Lowering my shield, I stepped into his personal orbit, forcing my static to escape and cover my form. In threat. "If you knew her, you would know Nala *craves* pain. What she and I do is none of your concern. I will make no such promise to you." A growl from my beast escaped. When Yu-Jin's teeth began shifting in size, I sent a bolt towards his heart, and he stilled. *Good, he can be taught.* "Listen, Yu-Jin. Whatever issue you have with me is upsetting Nala. If you can't seem to overcome it—"

"I'm going to fucking overcome it," he shouted back, lowering to scowl in my face. This sheltered brat could never understand how perfectly imperfect Nala truly was. How her broken and jagged edge matched mine. And the other pair's. The four of us were highly flawed individuals.

Yu-Jin had experienced sparse hardships, laughable blips. I'd done my research on him six years ago. He'd *never* been faced with strife. Never even had to work or try, he was *that* lucky in the lottery of life. Also, the male was overtly popular and well-liked. Infuriatingly, so.

"Forgive me then," I clipped. It was difficult to comprehend how this overgrown toddler wooed my soulmate enough to alter the path of destiny, though. "You're only delaying the inevitable. Nala will soon put y- you in y- your place."

"What you're insinuating is impossible for an ex-human!"

"Deny it all you like, pupling. It doesn't make it any less true." I mutely threatened him with another raise of a staticky finger, and the male heeded.

He relented with a step back, and shouted, "Fine, I forgive you." Then he grumbled as he whipped out his phone. "But I swear to fucking—" the male paused as his eyes darted across his scallop's screen. "The dragon abandoned her with my sister at Sirenuse, we've gotta go!" *Interesting, never expected Drago to leave her side.* However, if Min Rapax was nearby, Nala would be protected. Nothing got past a Levithan's sixth sense, she was nearly as defensible.

"I- I- I'll follow in a few. I have a call to m- make. You should probably change anywho," I said. He glanced down at his ripped suit and groaned before disappearing.

Once certain of Yu-Jin's absence, I dialed Avexeidros Valtameri. My… *Well,* he was my one friend. The close tie nearly no other in this galaxy knew of. The Titan Seer was aware, given he introduced us, but *no one* else. Not even Timoset.

The male had attached himself like a symbiote and we'd been inseparable since.

Vex never judged my past. Likely because his was just as riddled with indiscretions. He was the first and only male I'd lowered my guard around. *And you have plenty in common: Nala spice, non-existent parents, Nala spice,*

He also suffered from the dreams. It took us all of ten minutes to discover Olorun, his and Timoset's uncle and the aforementioned Seer, planned our meet-cute. That was thirty years ago. So, yes, he was likely the closest I'd ever come to having a permanent fixture.

As expected, Vex answered on the first ring. "Aren't you at the Gala? What's up?"

"You would know if you attended for yourself," I taunted.

He sighed. "Just tell me why you're calling during Nala time."

"Th- The Siarc fell into frenzy —"

"Of course, that immature piece of —"

"M- My point is," I raised my voice and he quieted, "I revealed the dreams —"

"Yours or mine?"

"C- Clearly mine, Vex! Yu-Jin isn't aware she lured you," I said in exasperation. "And he took the dream revelation swimmingly, as you can imagine. I admitted how you were consistently there, and he wasn't." A delighted laugh sounded on the other end and my own devilish grin spread. "Timoset also now believes I'm mending our relationship. We no longer have to lie around him, at least."

"Listen, I honestly don't give a fuck about any of that. How's Nala? The pupling didn't harm her, did he? What was she wearing tonight?"

"You aren't on her roof?" I questioned, moving the male to speaker so I could witness the reality for myself. There he was, the little red Avexeidros dot, right atop Nala's skylight in the center of my phone's screen.

He seemed to realize his conundrum, sharing a resigned sigh and a snipped, "Obviously. I can't bring myself to leave. Not unless I'm forced to for patrol shifts."

"So, you've seen what she was wearing then…" Pinching my nostrils, I withheld my giggle while he groaned.

"She made-out with Mo for like *twenty* fucking minutes before they went downstairs. He locked me out with a ward. Probably assuming I was up here snooping after earlier, the fucker," he replied. *Timoset's near the precipice as well then.*

Clearing my throat, I resurfaced the cause for my call. "We didn't remain at the Gala for long thanks to Yu-Jin. Nala's fine, wasn't fearful, not even of the Siarc's snapping dua f- forma —"

"Where's she now?" Vex's voice oozed jealousy. Which admittedly tempted my wiles.

"Th- There's another reason I called…" He grumbled for a bit, forcing me to wait until he settled. "Malice is after her. I saw it a few n- nights ago, and hoped it was a fluke, but then it cropped up again with Nala lying beside me and—"

"*Fuck.* You laid beside her *all night*?"

It was like speaking to a tadpole. "Avexeidros, did you not hear?"

"*Duh*, Malice is after Nala! She despises you, me, and Mo more than any other males in the fucking galaxy. I'm sure there's a vamp Seer trapped on Chiron with her. Why would I be surprised by that?" he asked with a sigh. "Which is why there's no point in discussing it."

Now or never, rip the bandage off.

"There's m- m- more," I cleared my throat, praying the stammer would remain hidden. With a deep breath, I said, "Af- After Timoset and I left Nala's earlier, we sort of went to a piercer. I kn- kn- know you and I agreed to go but…" *Feck.* I fecking hated my swollen cursed tongue.

The silence on the other end was telling.

Vex hardly withheld reactions, unlike Timoset and most gods. Whereas their Titan sires were split between two categories: little more than walking corpses, or emotionally untethered. There were sparse exceptions.

"Are you fucking kidding me, Cabbage?! You went with *Mo*? Did he get one, too?"

A smile teased my lips. "No, he's an oversized wuss. The way he strangled my hand as he watched was as painful than the piercings themselves." *Perhaps an exaggeration.* It was worse than being stabbed.

A frustrated hiss rattled my hearing. "I can't believe you've *already* broken a soulmate mandate. We wrote them two decades ago," he heaved another sigh.

There was a terse beat of silence.

Then Vex asked, "So. How bad was it?"

"Far worse than you're imagining. It healed hours ago but it's still tender… Don't even get me started on how strange my first erection felt."

"At the Gala?" Vex questioned earnestly. If there was an opportunity to speak of Nala the male would steal it and sprint, like the idiotic sport humans watched with the misshapen ball. I grunted in reply. "You're so fucking lucky to have met her already. I could slaughter Phro-Phro for making me go last. I'm dying. I dunno how I'm gonna act on Wednesday. It's worrisome because of the pupling, Jin's gonna—"

I tuned him out, knowing he needed to vent. Heaving a sigh over our mess. Chaos.

A fated frenzy, that's what this fecking is.

THIRTY MINUTES EARLIER

Sirenuse was a madhouse.

The sprawling club was packed with dancing bodies. Thousands of changing neon strip lights lined the walls, giving the space a dizzying, almost drug inducing, effect. The waitstaff consisted of miniature waiter robots floating around, their mirrored shells reflecting the casting hues.

A humongous aquarium filled with various species of dancing gilled femmes, theys, and males domed around the dance floor. There were four bars, two shallow swimming pools, and far, far too many for Sunday night. I checked my scallop to find it was 1:00am, technically Monday early morning.

At first, the music was merely a blaring drumbeat, but as we squeezed through the crowd, I picked up on the slight undercurrent of a band similar to Empire of the Sun. It was okay, not horrific by any means. Zaire was pulled aside by a bald ginormous male with a headset and Sirenuse t-shirt. The turnu demanded we use his tab before disappearing behind a 'Staff Only' marked door.

We laughed as Burt was dragged into the aquarium. When catching sight of his green and yellow mer-trident-tail, I squealed. Burt's scale pattern reminded me of our childhood brindle pit-bull's pixelated stripes, a blended canvas of intertwined greens and yellows.

Min insisted she order at the bar, returning to the table I snagged with two fizzing highball glasses. After clinking in cheers, I nearly yelled at the explosion of flavors in my mouth from the initial sip. The liquid was a peachy shade but tasted like a pink starburst mixed with banana, and I couldn't get enough. While I guzzled half the drink, Min dropped, "Give me your phone. You're going to need my number with all these males of yours, Nala."

"We can keep in contact despite you living on Venus?" I eyed her tiny heart-shaped flip phone bracelet; it made a stark contrast to my glittery oversized scallop.

Min nodded. "Most planets can, regardless of the differences in our devices. Since we're family now, I feel responsible for easing your adjustment. It's gonna be *rough*."

"You really think it'll be that horrible?" I questioned shakily.

Min barked a laugh, before quickly schooling her features. It was alarming to say the least. She placed a milky hand atop where mine was fidgeting on the table. "You're bonded to two of the most powerful males, not just on Neptune, but in the damned galaxy. Once their gifts surface, it's not just your body that adjusts. Your emotional state will regress. Unlike most immortals, I can relate. My transformation took far longer than most."

"Don't say my period will get worse or something, Doc," I grumbled.

"Yep, it does. That's the least of your worries."

Since Min seemed to be the first to speak freely in my presence, so I decided to ask, "What else?" She grimaced, handing back my scallop.

"They won't always get along with how dominant their natures are. Even in the best circumstances there will be tiffs. You're going to have to force them to submit. It's not pretty, Nala. My mom went through insanity with my dads."

"What?! Jin made it seem like your childhood was rainbows and butterflies!"

"That's because he's the youngest. He barely saw half of what Seong, and I had. They were more in control by the time Ji-Ji came around. The best advice I can give you is to wait on the babies, give it six or seven decades."

"Okay," I breathed. "How do I force them to submit?"

"Everyone's different. You're going to have to figure it out... And quick. They're unhinging. Timoset is frazzled already. He's carrying loads of tension."

I recoiled like she'd slapped me. "It's been days!"

"That doesn't matter with immortal males. Especially not with gods. They've lived for too long. Time is meaningless."

It still felt as though I forced his hand, whether he marked me or not. "I hate that. Timos has enough on his plate without me piling on. If I hadn't convinced Jin to bond, I have to wonder if things would've gone differently." My internal musing accidentally slipped. Which was why I quickly forced out, "I don't regret it." Now terrified Min would judge.

"No, you were meant for my brother, too. I'm not surprised he caved, to be honest. He's always been too careful. Ji-Ji was bound to crack and surrender to something. I'm glad it was for you, for love. I can see why they're drawn to you, if anything, they're lucky to have found a mortal who isn't daunted."

Min was right. In more ways than one. The gratitude for her understanding gripped my heart, I heaved a sigh as my shoulders fell. "I'm the lucky one. I don't even care about Jin's slip. He'll figure it out."

"I can tell," she said with a twinkle in her lilac eyes. "You seem to understand more than any other humans I've met." As the femme downed her drink and rose to get us another round, a wave of relief washed over me. It wasn't the alcohol. It was the fact I finally made a *real* friend. One who didn't judge or keep secrets. The feeling was almost foreign, one I hadn't felt since Isaiah owned up to his deceit ages, and ages ago.

You actually have grown. I would've never trusted a stranger with my business in the past. My sharing with Min had little to do with our familial ties, and more with how unflinchingly transparent she was. *Maybe you just needed honesty to feel safe.*

When she returned with fresh drinks, I blurted, "I have to thank you, Min. No one else has been as forthcoming." There were a few tipsy tears threatening to fall so I averted my gaze.

"I don't know why," she grumbled with an aggravated sigh. "You should be aware." I bobbed my head in agreement. *You're gonna have to demand the triplets share their secrets.*

"Can I ask you what the worst part will be?"

"There's more than just one complicated facet, Nala." I motioned for her to continue, and she frowned. "Testing is traumatic. The Council is going to keep a close watch because no other human has ever snagged males as powerful as yours."

"What else?" I questioned. At least Ryloh had prepared me for the science stuff. Albeit I didn't know I would be forced to participate, but it kinda made sense.

"Your moods. Actually, your entire emotional state will be in upheaval. It may be painful to witness your own actions. Like you're trapped in a cage watching yourself sometimes. Especially during periods and—"

"I think I already suffer from that," I interrupted. We shared a laugh, and I had a strong desire to get to know her more. "Did you learn all of this during your doctorate?"

She painted a sad smile. "Mostly patients actually."

"You've never been serious with anyone?"

Min avoided my eyes as she replied in a resigned tone, "I'm in the Program, but I doubt I'll ever find a human. No offense, but men are terrible, lacking in comparison to immortals. I can overlook the difference in height, but not their entitlement."

"I'm well aware," I replied with a grimace. "Why are you wasting your time in the PPP then?"

"It keeps the Council off my back," she mumbled, continuing to avoid eye contact.

As I went to question why that was, Jin suddenly manifested in a fresh suit. He lunged for me first, wrapping me in his salty masculine scent before Min ripped him away.

"Where were you?" she demanded, squeezing her brother.

"I was in a state, then Ryloh and I had a conversation," he explained, then spun towards me. "Timoset shouldn't have left you, Nala. You should've called." I nearly spit out my drink at his deep set scowl.

"Burt, Min, and Zaire were with me, it was more than fine. Calm down."

"No," Jin replied, taking the stool between us. "It's not fine. You still carry our scent despite the fucking suppressant. You aren't safe anymore."

Min poked him in the shoulder to ask, "Who's her third? I can't tell."

"Ryloh."

"Cabbage?" she shouted, leaving me cringing. Jin nodded with a furrowed brow.

Unlike Jin, I felt Ryloh before seeing him. My heart did a happy flutter with his nearness as he pressed a chaste kiss to my cheek before plopping into a stool. I readied to prod about their conversation, but Min interrupted. "Damn. I can easily scent you on her too, Cabbage. How did you manage to mark her already? You should be ashamed of yourselves," she scolded with a pointer.

Jin raised a brow in my direction, and I made a slicing motion across my neck, hoping the meaning was universal.

"Timoset and I haven't y- yet accepted. There's something abnormal with our tethering. Nala l- lured us this afternoon," Ryloh said with a furrowed brow and Min gasped. She looked towards Jin who gave a pained nod. *Here they go with this nonsense again.*

"You *lured* them?" She shrieked, and I shrugged. "Nala, that shouldn't be possible. Most immortals can't *ever* lure their amoroso... I've never heard of a dominant nature attaching to a former human, but it doesn't make it impossible, I suppose."

"Timoset came to th- the same conclusion," Ryloh said as Jin started groaning. "That's why Yu-Jin went into frenzy, Nala's our *kontrolü*." *Controlling the loo?*

I muttered, "I didn't do anything."

"You did, you lured me from clear across the island while already preoccupied with Jin," Ryloh confirmed with a proud smirk. Min nearly fell out of her chair. Jin shook his navy hair out of place as he gawked. Again, I hadn't *done* anything though.

"That's crazy," Min screamed. "Nala, you're going to need to text or call me after you bond to the other two. You might need to be restrained during the transformation. I had to be." *What the —* I searched my males faces to uncover serious concern and was too flabbergasted to reply. Downing my drink.

"You've left her in the dark?" Min hollered.

The chill's return to my sternum distracted me from the conversation. I knew Timos was back. Somehow could sense the male standing behind me. *Jin would lose it if he knew you couldn't feel him the same way.* My stomach plummeted in guilt although I had zero control over any of it.

"We were not yet certain," Timos said, and I spun to find him scratching his neck, uncomfortably. *Just like—* I turned and found the other two mimicking the motion. It was far too adorable for our circumstances. Being around the three of them in less stressful circumstances was messing with my equilibrium, my brain was floaty.

The three were so outrageously handsome that I could barely suck down a full breath. So very different, too. From Timos' warm features to Jin's blue hues.

Despite Ry's height, he was a wide shouldered short king. And honestly, not even that vertically challenged given he had half-a-foot on me, but I would tease him if he were ever mean enough. I never knew what to expect from Ryloh's organized chaos, it was probably why I was so drawn to him.

Gabs was right. Again. Unfortunately.

"If Nala is indeed our kontrolü, then we shall have more than Malice's breaches to contend with. It was a Wraith, by the way," Timos tacked on, and everyone at the table lost their minds and began shouting. Zaire chose that moment to return, mirroring my confusion.

As the turnu dragged stools over for him and Timos, I explained, "It was a Wraith."

"That's concerning and incredibly problematic. I certainly don't envy your role, Timoset. She's gotten through the fresh wards," Zaire replied with a shake of his head.

"*Who?*" I questioned.

"Malice," they responded in unison, which only left me in further confusion. Obviously, this was a malicious attack, I got that... *Hold on.* "Are Wraiths floating ghosts?"

Timos leaned in to explain in his soothing volume, "Wraiths are vampires. Specifically, Revenants who have been reanimated to become more blood thirsty. Although they are not quite as lethal, they are their second most dangerous subspecies. They can shift from solidity to porosity, enabling them to pass through structures with ease. There are few means to decimate a Wraith, one of which being dragon fire."

"Holy bologna! And one got in?!"

"I caught it over the Varvaros Sea," Timos raised his voice to share with the others. "It is concerning she only sent one. However, I alerted the Council nonetheless."

Zaire was tapping away on his oyster-phone with a frown when Ryloh said, "It was likely a trial, knowing her."

"Fuck," Jin thundered as the others nodded grimly in agreement. They were sobering my buzz. As was the music, which shifted to Alvin from the Chipmunks belting over Avicii. "We're going to have to reach out to the press. What if one slips through the wards undetected next time?" *There he is!* Mister Mayor Jin, always thinking of everyone else, the squishiest Siarc. I had to restrain from leaning over to pinch his chiseled cheeks.

"Th- There's nothing they could do to combat a Wraith," Ryloh replied. "If they see it, they're as good as dead. Giving the press ammunition to spark widespread panic will make it seem as though we can't protect the public."

Timos gave a stern nod. "The Council said the same, we must keep it quiet. Only the Skerry can learn the truth."

"What's that?"

"The Queen's Court sessions are referred to as Skerry meetings. She just sent an invite for Code Aqua, which only includes Timoset, us dukes, and her hand, Seong," Zaire explained as he stared at his gold oyster shell.

"Code Cobalt includes the twelve Reef's dukes along with Timoset's father," Ryloh tacked on. "Code I- In- Indigo is the most severe, as it also requires a judiciary representative from the Galactic Council."

"Typically, my mother," Timos explained, before turning towards Ryloh and Jin to ask, "Which of you will remain with Nala during?" Then he used a taupe finger to adjust his glasses. I honestly loved watching him do that, it was the simplest of actions, but it made his enormous size feel smaller. Cozier. I would live on the bridge atop his nose if it was possible...

Maybe you're a tad past tipsy.

"There's no point in sleeping, the meeting is in three hours," Jin said over the rim of his white scallop. "Are you tired, love? You have your first shift in the morning." *Oh, right.* I'd forgotten about my new gig.

"No, if y'all are staying, so am I. And who cares? I'm going to be rinsing out cages and playing with critters, I've managed worse hungover."

"What's th- this, Nala spice? You found her a *job*, Yu-Jin?" Ryloh's headlights flashed.

"She's volunteering at the animal shelter, so what? It's only two mornings per week."

"I think it's time we abandon the foursome," Min said to Zaire. And with that, those two took off with a wave. However, not before I caught their hands interlacing and the resulting grins before they vanished into the ruckus. It was the moment I decided I'd be using my date with Zaire to discuss my new sister.

Ryloh and Jin were having a glare off when my attention returned to the table. "Y'all are gonna have to explain this control-oo-loo nonsense."

"You're as powerful as we are. Perhaps m- m- more so, spice," Ryloh explained with a furrowed brow.

"No way," I said with a snort. "He's a dragon! There's no way I'm as strong as him. Timos can eat me in one swallow. Actually, so could Jin." Except, instead of the smiles I anticipated, my Musketeers were grimacing. "What am I missing here?"

"I'm not sure how, but your scent confirms it," Jin added with a frown. "You luring him from across the island is past abnormal. The probability of that has to be in the negative."

"Ryloh and I have both felt and sensed Nala's emotions on multiple occasions, Yu-Jin. You must accept what she is," Timos dropped, like a literal bomb. Jin gasped loudly. Ryloh hadn't seemed to agree with sharing that, his starry eye twitched.

"Polyamorous amoroso tethers have only been recorded among Titans!" My eyes were ping-ponging and attempting to follow, but it was a lot. I didn't know whether to laugh or cry about being as much of a freak here as I was back home.

"We have more pressing concerns than the specifics of our tethering considering the breaches are worsening in severity. Did you settle your differences?" Timos demanded more than questioned. He was going full professor on the pair. It was hotter than Hell in that spiffy suit.

"Yu-Jin accepted my apology," Ryloh supplied as Jin grimaced with his arms crossing. "I will remain with Nala during the Skerry. The Siarc's strengths aren't on land, if a Wraith takes her by surprise, I'd rather test my static than risk her completely. Timoset is the most critical attendee, otherwise I'd in- insist he should remain with her at all times."

"At all times?" I screeched. "Timos is too important!" Plus, I refused to give up the trickle of freedom I possessed. When I looked for support, they were shaking their heads though.

"You're not even going to give me a say?"

"If you truly believe we are willing to risk your life so you can pedal around without a chaperone, Nala spice, y- y- you're not as intelligent as I thought," Ryloh growled.

"Hey! No calling Nala an idiot! Or your spice, for that matter, you barnacle!" Ji-Ji and Lolly were dueling again. Literal sparks were flying. *Surprise, surprise.*

"Naliti, you will be free of us during your dates and if you desire privacy in your apartment. However, I do not think it wise to venture without my nearness," Timos said into my ear. I ignored how my traitorous skin peppered. Along with the pulsing block in my chest.

"You're clipping my wings then, Timos. All of you are caging me," I volleyed, and he frowned in consideration. "It's not fair!"

The other two heard and stilled their scuffling. A trifecta of disappointment reflected back.

Timos eventually said, "We must, Nala. As much as I loathe it. Your well-being is my priority. Malice is a considerable threat."

"Shit," I said, face and shoulders falling in resignation. Cursing couldn't be helped these days, it was necessary. Nothing else could perfectly encompass what this felt like.

The catch, it would seem, had finally reared its ugly head. I landed myself a danger ranger dragon, a control freak of a fae, and an emotionally untethered shark.

This is what you get for thinking with your clit.

Solitude was an addictive self-infliction. Truthfully, other's contributions to conversation were lacking, rarely warranting my attentions. In my six-thousand-sixteen years of life there has been a lone absolute: the vast majority of beings were drawn toward processing in extremes. Good versus evil, me versus them, right versus wrong, etc. The classification or planet has not mattered, that binary logic remained glaringly true, and it typically resulted in overreaction. The widespread lack of emotional restraint I observed in most was untenable. Emotions were a puzzle in which the pieces never quite fit properly.

Or they had. For an age. *Before, however, now?* I wrung understanding from both fists.

Since Naliti's arrival, I had become one with the masses. Except my lone extreme was that *she* came *first.* My beautiful former human with the widest grins and raucous laughs.

She loves you, Timoset. No other had ever shared the sentiment. Never.

Having Naliti at my side became necessity. I was completely out of my element, not having clung to hope for something as fickle as love. There were only meaningless trysts in my past, mostly with those who treated me

222

as a spectacle. Oftentimes unpleasant, if not outright traumatic. Over time, I eventually curbed my urges alone.

Until a fearless, defenseless, human flung herself into my arms. The instant Naliti's jasmine scent reached my nostrils, I knew. It only took one blink and the unassuming prey had captured the predator. How could I not be captivated by the first being to not balk in fear of me?

Her addictive essence still lingered on my tongue, leaving me on the precipice of rabidity. It was dangerous for a dragon to delay a claiming. But once she was marked and mine, my possessiveness would peak. Significantly worsen. There were tasks to cross off prior to succumbing.

Father would be —*unfortunately*—thrilled. Delighted, even. Although he would be forced to find a replacement for my role as Protectorate, and quickly. I doubted it would detract. He had been lying in wait for this moment…

Just as Malice apparently had been. There were personal vendettas between the vampiric Titan and our family spanning millennia. Malice's amoroso happened to be one of my brothers. Dmitrios spliced himself for her and became a monstrosity. The timing of the breaches was not coincidental. *There must be traitors among us.* Ryloh and I discussed as much after his traumatic stabbing incident. The piercing session. *Fuck.*

I shuddered from the mere memory.

Hopefully Naliti shall not request the same from you…

That is the fucking least of your worries, Timoset.

"Indeed, you should not be thinking with your cock at present, dragon."

Damned ghost. The abutting and prying spirits were atypically restless. It had been centuries since they last paid any mind. They began whispering once the attacks grew in fervor. Like a plague, the phantoms were following, pestering, crowding from every direction with their iridescent forms and dated apparel.

Supposedly, this was a gift, my capacity to converse with souls. Inherited from my father and complicated further by the demonic genealogy of my mother. Neptune's specter population was, thankfully, lacking. Especially in comparison to Nirvana. Nonetheless, it was irksome.

"We cannot abandon you until the bonding has been enacted. Balance must be restored."

Gibberish.

"Once you bind yourself to your femme we shall relent."

An unfounded promise from an untrustworthy intruder.

Regarding any other topic, I would ignore their hushed mutterings. Now I could not, not when they mentioned her. Majority of the comments were nonsensical. *However, not all.* Instigating further fretting. As if I did not have enough.

Naliti's pout circled once again, as it had been. I could not escape her discontent, a stabbing reminder of how I managed to deeply dissatisfy her. Clip her wings. Steal her agency. Refuse her. *You are failing Nala, Timoset.*

"*You are not failing your femme because of what you lack. It is because you have not bound.*

Instead of improving my standing with Naliti, I was here. Feigning to care for the safety of the remainder of this hexed island. A minute without her was overwhelming. I had now gone without her for... Checking my phone, I cursed aloud. *Seven damned minutes.* It felt far longer.

I was damned with the knowledge of every possible danger, every pitfall in our protection. Trapped within the confines of my own panicked worry. Irrational as it was, given Ryloh would be a worthy opponent against *nearly* any...

"*The abnormal one keeps her safe.*"

"*For now.*"

The spirited ramblings were as comforting as a blanket made of sharpened spikes.

Quell yourself, Timoset. Do not tempt your beast into frenzy.

"*Your femme is amoroso bound. That is why you are teetering into frenzy.*"

Their claims were impossible. Nala was divinely bound to another. The tethers were near mythical since the war...

You owe Aphrodite your gratitude for discovering her.

The Program's pageantry was perverse, so I refused earlier association or involvement, despite the Council's pleading. It was not until five turns ago that the PPP lifted the ban on participants returning to Earth after tethering. They had allowed families to believe the worst became of them prior. It was barbaric to say the least.

However, Aphrodite, ever the brown noser, begun sending me the programmatic emails of candidates without my consent. They were filtered to spam. *All but one.*

One lone message made it past, the one which held Naliti's candidacy photos. I cannot explain what possessed me to open it. There wasn't anything particularly outstanding about the loose-fitting smock Nala wore. Her wild hair piled atop her head while she stopped metallic vehicles so that a family of ducklings could cross a road to safety. Of course, she was strikingly beautiful, but it was not what caused my heart to stir.

The means in which her curls bounced with her every step entranced me. How her dress caught the light and accentuated the curve of her hips. Every bit of Nala was alive and clamoring. However, her melted chocolate eyes were miserable, there was an incredibly forced and pained curl to her lips.

That feigned happiness sunk its claws in.

I dreamt and fretted over her disgruntlement for the following three days and nights. Until caving and texting Aphrodite my interest. Then anxiety and panic ensued. I was shit with social interactions. Femmes. Males. Did not matter. I had never felt at ease with others. Perhaps Avexei, but we had been inseparable since my parents assumed custody when we were hatchlings, so he hardly counted. The male was one of the sparse few who never balked at our classification.

Naliti had questioned if I wished her with Avexei, but we drifted a decade or so ago. In public settings, my cousin often acted as my shield, he possessed enough charm for the both of us. We complemented the other's strengths. However, Jin would likely fill the gap. He was not nearly as carefree and effortless, but hardly any were.

Perhaps I initially coveted the inclusion of another in our mating circle equivalently adept at protecting Nala in my absence. *Temporarily, until Cabbage came along.* I once loathed the pompous fae, but unexpectedly, Ryloh wasn't nearly as problematic as the one seated at my opposite fuming.

The tension in Yu-Jin had not waned. I could not ascertain whether the male struggled due to his frenzy, or if it was in result of his discussion with Ryloh. The cause was irrelevant though, we required peace before enacting our bonding.

"What ails you, Yu-Jin?" I kept my expression flat as we awaited the remaining attendees in the Palace's Command Centre. As per usual, they were late. "I thought you came to a resolution." The male groaned in response, his discontented rumble echoing through the cavernous and grotesque room.

"This is why it is so critical for you to tether to your femme. The others only cause discord."

I averted my gaze toward the windows in a feeble attempt to detract from my frustration. If it were not for the impressive views of Thalla, this castle had no redemptive aspects. The long magenta table for fifty with Siren trident-tails carved into its legs was hideous. As was the matching chandelier comprised of scales. Unfortunately, the entire grounds was this garish. If the opportunity arose, I would gladly burn the heinous monstrosity to the ground.

When Avexei appeared, wearing his typical grin, I released a minuscule sigh in relief. Yu-Jin, however, experienced the opposite. It was difficult to decipher why the Siarc's shoulders inched upward as his cheek ticked. "Why were you not at the Gala?" I asked of my cousin.

"Why would I go when Mother didn't?" Avexei fell into the seat beside Yu-Jin. "What's your problem, pupling?" he raised a brow.

When Yu-Jin remained silent, I replied, "Ryloh, I believe."

"No, the Siarc's murderous desires are directed toward the Uktena."

Avexei's grin spread with an, *"Ah."*

"When's your date with Nala?" Yu-Jin demanded more than questioned.

"Wednesday," Avexei responded. "Why?" My breath caught as I awaited the Siarc's reply, hoping Ryloh kept his lips sealed. By the concern reflected back in Avexei, I knew he mirrored the sentiment. It was not as if we were proactively deceiving Yu-Jin, only temporarily omitting information. The *pupling*, as they rightfully coined him, required further marination.

"The Siarc will never settle."

Apparently, I held more hope than the ghosts.

"Apologies for my lateness," Her Majesty interrupted, storming in with her typical, inappropriate, silk robe loosely tied. I averted my eyes from repulsion. A glimpse of her dark hair was enough of a warning to proceed with caution. Yu-Jin crossed his arms and ignored his brother's greeting as Seong and the Queen scurried toward the head of the table. "Where are the others? Should I send a reminder?"

"Zaire's phone shows he's still at Sirenuse and Ryloh isn't coming," Yu-Jin explained on a sigh, glaring at his screen. "He sent me in his stead."

"Unacceptable," she shouted, storming back out to the hall. Likely to ring the fae. Seong raised his brows at his fuming brother, who shook his head.

"What's up with you, Jin?" Seong persisted. "So, you had your first frenzy, who cares? Everyone has one eventually. At least yours was for good reason, I wouldn't want to share my mate with Cabbage either. You can still get out of it. I can ask Imera to release you from the tether—"

"Don't you fucking dare," Yu-Jin roared, standing and flinging his chair against the wall, where it splintered. Avexei and I exchanged a concerned glance. "I'm already Nala's spare," the Siarc's multi-tonal voice proclaimed. *Fuck.*

I kept my expression nonplus. Avexei on the other hand, grinned. Foolishly. When Yu-Jin caught sight of the clown, his jaw began expanding. "Ryloh fucking told you, didn't he?"

"I don't know what you're referring to," Avexei held fast.

My fists clenched as my beast demanded I force their resolution on Naliti's behalf.

Zaire rifted in, completely disheveled, his t-shirt backwards, locs askew. "Sorry, didn't realize the time," he mumbled, taking the seat beside where Yu-Jin's chair previously resided. "Ji-Ji, are you having another fit?" Seong chuckled and shook his head in answer to Zaire as his brother paced. His maw shifted between Siarc and his own with every slap of his foot against the tiles.

I cleared my throat, hoping my earnest expression would settle him, but it was no use. "What is it you believe Ryloh shared with us?"

"That he saw the three of you with Nala in his reanimation dreams! Not me!"

"It makes fucking sense, given she lured me too," Avexei hissed.

I gawked momentarily, then scowled. Ryloh should not have mentioned our secret. Avexei should not have taunted Yu-Jin either. I could not decipher which was more deserving of my wrath. The Command Centre quickly filled with flurries as I attempted to diffuse myself.
"You are the lone sensible male present."

"*What?*" Yu-Jin demanded of Avexei. Thankfully, my cousin had the smarts to ward his voice so that Seong and Zaire were not privy to our worsening situation. However, they were far too curious for my liking. Especially Seong.

"We should not discuss this here," I interjected with a growl before they could respond. There were hidden recording devices in every cranny. Many which could supersede wards. They were well aware.

Fortunately, they heeded my warning as the Queen returned. Yu-Jin stormed to the furthest seat from Avexei, throwing himself down in a huff before continuing to growl on every exhalation. My cousin shrugged when met with my glower.

"So, that cunt sent a Wraith through the wards?" The tyrant questioned.

"Charming as always, Mother dearest," Avexei clipped.

I heaved a sigh.

"Tell my Lolly that his flimsy excuse won't work twice." Yu-Jin nodded towards the Queen's command as she took her leave. Although his mood had settled, I knew we would experience another implosion before morning's end. The revelation of Ryloh's dreams haunted me for the duration of the Skerry, I could only imagine how much worse it was for Yu-Jin.

I anticipated Avexei-related complications, due to the luring, he felt her from the furthest distance. However, it should have remained unmentioned. Nala's strength was unheard of. The majority of immortal femmes merely possessed the ability to lure their nearest mate, for Nala to have lured all four of us…

It was deeply, deeply disconcerting.

"You're coming back with me," Yu-Jin angrily whispered as he gripped Avexei's elbow. The pair rifted and I shook my head with a snarl as Seong and Zaire opened their mouths.

Landing on Naliti's doorstep, I was reunited with their raging. The pair were in a standoff, both evidently struggling to contain their natures. "Fetch Ryloh he should be here for this too," Avexei ordered. I grunted in acknowledgement, sending the text. "Jin, stop freaking out. Your beast is showing, dude. Get it together."

"I'm not fucking 'freaking out,' alright? I'm pissed. Rightfully so."

"Nala loves you," I conceded, although I loathed doing so. My dragon was not pleased by our mate loving another prior. Despite her love for me. The sensation behind my sternum was boiling furiously.

"Why are you so insecure if she loves you already, pupling? It's not adding up."

"Because he's a toddler," Ryloh said with a scowl as he appeared to join our huddle. "I- I... I didn't tell the pupling shit. Yu-Jin can't handle it. Not yet."

"You told him something about a reanimation though, *why?*" Avexei pressed, the curl in his lips faltering. "You didn't mention that to me —*us*, Cabbage."

"Yu-Jin had to be the one to explain. I took a blood-oath to keep my trap shut around the pair of you, godlings," Ryloh relented with a sigh. Avexei mirrored my perplexity as we both turned our attention towards the scowling Siarc.

"Athanatos and Olorun reanimated him. It was on Nala's birthday, he's been dreaming about her, and the four of you bonded, since," he revealed, pulling at his hair in frustration. "I'm never in the dreams. Not in thirty fucking years." When my questioning gaze met Ryloh's, he nodded with a frown.

...

My composure faltered as I digested the severity. Of my father *and* uncle's intervention. They *rarely* involved themselves in personal matters.
"They intervened on your behalf."

"That is why you must tether to your femme."

"This is a clusterfuck," Avexei murmured, his gaze fixed on Naliti's window. "They won't allow Nala to keep four mates. Especially not us four. Our spawn could likely usurp the Council." I grimaced as Yu-Jin cursed and began shifting, again. "I haven't even met Nala. We could hate each other. Fate can change," Avexei said, and I had to refrain from exposing the scoff clawing up my throat. He was lying through his fucking teeth.

But why?
"The Uktena spins webs of falsehoods."

"Th- This is up to Nala spice. I don't like that we're keeping it from her. Can I wake her?" Ryloh pressed and we shook our heads. "Why? She deserves to know. She could meet Avexei now and settle this mess."

"I agree it is Nala's decision. One which has already been made." I said, turning towards Avexei. "You should attend your courting with friendship, and only that, as your intent. It is unfair to her otherwise." Futile as my efforts were, I had to attempt to dissuade further calamity.
"The only solution to avoiding chaos is your binding."

"Don't look so smug, Yu-Jin. If Avexei also shares an amoroso bond, you're out, pupling," Ryloh sneered with a smirk. Earning himself a growl from the Siarc. I stepped between the pair and gave the fae a pleading look. One which he immediately relented to with a frown filled nod. "It's true though, we might as well put it out there. Why pretend otherwise?"

"I wouldn't take her from you, Jin," Avexei… *lied.*

Ryloh and I exchanged an unconvinced glance. Yu-Jin seemed placated. *The nitwit.* "You wouldn't?" Yu-Jin questioned, hope lacing his innocent tone.

My stomach plummeted as Avexei shook his head. The male could likely fool anyone, except myself. *And Ryloh, apparently.*

"You two should head upstairs," I interjected, checking the time to deflect my perturbance. Although it was likely obvious, given the fumes seeping from my pores. "I must discuss the adjusted patrol schedule with Avexei prior to accompanying Nala to the shelter."

Ryloh conveyed further apology in his gaze, so I clapped a palm to his shoulder before he followed behind Yu-Jin. My opinion of the fae was swelling.

Once the hatchlings were out of earshot I hissed, "Why did you fucking lie?"

Avexei shrugged with one of his maniacal smirks. "If she's not mine, it won't matter."

"It will. You do not know her as I do. Naliti is stubborn."

"*Naliti, huh,*" Avexei jibed. "I didn't realize you were in this deep already." I withheld a growl. However, my beast shifted our sight. Avexei's eyes widened as he witnessed how fleeting my careful discipline had become. "Why do you care if I deceive the pupling? Mo, this is me. Us. If I have a bond with her, you know he eventually won't matter."

"Nala *loves* him," I snapped, incapable of withholding it. The male shrugged, forcing my resolve to shatter further. "You *cannot* pursue her."

"It's not as though you can stop me, Mo. I don't know why you'd even try to. The two of us are already family, it would make her adjustment easier."

"That is not enough," I ground out. "She made her decision."

"After hearing about Ryloh's reanimation, I'm even more convinced I have a shot." The revelations coupled with my neglected sleep left my beast raging. Although I contained the urge to bash Avexei's teeth in, my wings sprouted.

My cousin frowned. "Why's this bothering you so much? You're loyal to me, not them. This is how it's supposed to go, especially if Uncle Atha and Olo interfered."

Avexei was and always would be my closest companion.

He may have been the last to draw a laugh from my lips, but it was centuries prior to her arrival. With Naliti, I was more than merely accepted and cared for, I felt alive. Nothing compared to her touch. Her laugh. Her fire. All past relationships paled in comparison.

"Avexei," I said, "now that I have found her, I have changed. Even my opinions of the pair upstairs have already shifted. It is just as it was when you met Julianna."

The male shook his head, tension drawing his brows together while his hair darkened with distaste. "Nothing changed between us with Jules. It's not the same. I can't believe you're talking like this. Kontrolü or not, there's always been the two of us, I thought there always would be —"

"You will always be my brother. However," I heaved a sigh as my beast urged me forward, "Naliti is more." As Avexei frowned, I voiced what unsettled me most. "She *chose* them, if you attempt to sabotage that, it will not end well for you." My dragon escaped towards the end of my sentence, growling in threat.

I had never, not once, sent a threat in Avexei's direction.

We exchanged a wordless blink.

"I've been dreaming of her too," Avexei blurted. Then flung his palms over his mouth, as if further secrets might flee.

What. The. Fuck?!

My wings flexed in equated agitation and disbelief. "And you kept this to yourself?!"

"Can you blame me? I don't know what to fucking do here, Mo. My reanimation dreams didn't start immediately after the war, they waited until she was born, thirty-two years ago. It's why I was so insistent about meeting Nala first. Why did you think I went feral during the PPP sessions?"

I shrugged a lone wing, incapable of mustering another response.

"At first, I thought it was impossible since the version of Nala in my dreams was immortal," he said with a cringe. *Shit.*

"Because Yu-Jin turned her," I rasped. This spurred an entirely different set of concerns.

"Immortal or not, your femme remains in danger until you accept your tether."

Avexei nodded with a pained frown, "I knew her preference was Nala not Nightingale. It was torture keeping it to myself since her photo appeared in the Program potentials. You don't know the extent of how close I am to her in slumber, Mo. What I feel for her is... *Overwhelming.*"

The unshed tears glazing his dark eyes clenched my heart. I could not imagine experiencing the same. I was past enraptured with Naliti. Ryloh and Avexei had spent entire days with her, time which may or may not ever come to pass, it would drive me beyond madness.

"You are already mad for refusing your femme, Timoset Drago."

"It's fucked up," Avexei said.

"You saw Ryloh and I with you and Nala?" The confirmation was necessary.

"I didn't see Jin either. Not once... It makes sense Lo-Lo—"

My brows furrowed in confusion. Avexei paused, before correcting, "*Ryloh* also dreamt of her. He seemed resistant to the typical abuse my mother demands of her Hand. He was never as bad to me as he could've been. Seong's far worse."

As much of a relief as it was to hear the fae was not the villain I once assumed him to be, there was one unavoidable facet. Avexei's mother, The Queen, was the Titaness of bonds. Her domains granted her free reign over contracts and divorce, any bindings untouched by destiny's divine hand were at her discretion. "The tyrant will cut Nala's tether with Yu-Jin if it remains untouched by fate. Nala will never forgive you; I have witnessed her love for the Siarc."

"I know. She has to meet me, and I don't know how I'm gonna behave on Wednesday. I'm not gonna be chill. Not even a little bit. She's all that fills my brain, I can barely stand here without losing my ever-loving mind," he wheezed.

As if this were not complicated enough, I now had to worry for Nala's safety in Avexei's presence. "Ryloh's beast surfaced when they first met," I revealed, terror lacing my tone.

"The murdering abnormal one is unworthy of your femme. As is the Uktena."

I could not muster an inkling of disagreement with that particular spirit.

"You know mine are worse than his," Avexei replied, his shoulders falling. "And that's the least of my worries. We have a lot of fucking enemies. Too many. She's a target without me, but *with* me?" He threw his hands over his head, while I attempted to withhold a shift as my temples pulsed and claws extended.

There was a solution. "I refuse to leave her side," I announced, more beast than male.

"That's unsustainable and you know it," Avexei chided, flicking my forehead as though we were still hatchlings. "There's at least three breaches per day. I can't keep filling in for you on patrol so you can play bodyguard. The second you leave her side Malice will have an advantage. You should've already bound yourself."

"You can drop everything, and you will. If what you have shared is true, then the moment I am inevitably forced to leave her side, you are the lone male capable of protecting her properly. I will request a replacement from Father, so we no longer have to patrol."

"You cannot trust the Prince."

This was exactly why I could not heed the ghostly commentary. Avexei was the only male I had *ever* trusted. The lone being to have rescued me from every brink. Ryloh was not quite trustworthy, and Yu-Jin was continuing to teeter. Avexei, though, I could rely on implicitly.

Or so you thought.

"I hate it when you're right," he replied with a smile. I wished I could mirror the sentiment. That I could cease my incessant panic. Unfortunately, it was not within my nature. "But you still need to accept your tether to her, Mo. So does Lo-Lo."

Grunting in reply, I began questioning why Avexei was referring to the fae so casually.

How close are those two?
"Far closer than he has let on."

I scrutinized the male I knew better than myself. The Council would undoubtedly force the unimaginable if the five of us tethered. Which was why I said, "Go. I must call my father, then Olo. You are six minutes late for your shift." The male shared a lewd gesture before rifting. Abandoning me in agony.

"You will never know tranquility if you lose her from inaction."

It took twenty minutes to coax my dragon into quelling before prima fingers replaced my claws to dial the Supreme. The galactic off planet fizzle I had become accustomed to preceded the initial *ring*. It was mid-afternoon on Nirvana so I knew he would answer. "Mo-Mo, are you following up regarding the Wraith?"

"No," I grunted, struggling to keep myself from slipping. The spiraling I felt from Avexei's revelation left my vision darkened around the edges. "I may have found my amoroso or dragon cursed her. However, I believe you already knew that. I also learned of Ryloh's reanimation. But did you know she would be ex-mortal?"

There was a lengthier pause than usual, sending my frayed nerves twisting further.

"I knew." Then Athanatos Drago sighed, the force rattling my hyper-sensitive hearing, another terrible sign. "Olo has known since your birth, Timoset. It took fate some time to reveal Nala was formerly mortal. However, you know how I feel on the subject of Olo and his musings." Father, having been twin to the Titan of Sight, loathed referring to destiny as anything other than randomness. "I owed Olo a favor and he leveraged it for Ryloh's reanimation. In typical Olorun fashion, he revealed his reasons to us afterward. Your life was at risk," he explained.

"You know that meddling has fucking consequences," I growled. Then recoiled. Not because of my emotional slip. *Fuck no*. I was past unraveled. It was the recognition in how I could no longer wish for my own demise. It was rare, a dragon's death, but possible.

It was not widespread knowledge, but there was one means to slaughter a dragon. It was not a curse. Nor a physical weakness. My sister, Etania, was the first and last of us to ever perish. It was the death of her unbound mate which brought forth her own demise.

"If your femme perishes as will you, Timoset Drago."

Father leveraged a placating tone, "I did not wish to risk Nala nor you, Mo-Mo. Your mother is unaware, and it should remain as such. I do not recommend a mating ceremony or press announcement of any kind. You must keep her hidden until she can withstand the scientific torture."

I harrumphed incredulously. "How do you plan on accomplishing that?"

"Aphrodite. I outrank her flimsy mother. She would never refuse a personal request. It will buy you at least a month. Nala deserves the oppor-tunity to adjust without the hubbub. I refuse to risk either of you unnecessarily." It was not only true, but I knew that my father was Aphrodite's preferred parent. Like Avexei, she was raised under our roof, he forcibly assumed custody in both instances. Imera was a tyrant in all things, but especially parenting.

"Thank you," I replied, finally reinflating my lungs.

He chuckled. "You are welcome, my son. Osri and Persis have agreed to co-assume your position as Protectorate. Imera requested they remained in the Palace for their initial slumber but will require permanent lodgings tonight. You and Vex must both train them, and quickly. I know how difficult the mating urges are. The pair thankfully understand the influx in breaches but lack your warding capabilities."

"Vampires are breaking through regardless," I replied. "The sacrificial breaches only the beginning, you should consider raising it to the others. Osri and Persis' lacking warding capabilities will not matter. Majority of my role has been elimination."

"Why are you so certain of Malice's personal interference?" There was a slight growl that always came when the original vampire's voice fled his lips. They forced her name upon her, the other Titans, most claiming she earned it. Malice loathed it; one of the plethora of inane reasons this petty feuding continued.

"She would never send one Wraith if she intended on wreaking havoc. It was a trial as to whether or not undetected entry was accessible. She will send more, clearly her goal is undetected entry. We both know Chiroptera populations were decimated, why would she willingly sacrifice three per day unless actively splicing? When was the last the Council sent scouts to Chiron? I would bet she has visibly expanded housing. She may already possess an army."

The only means for vampirism to spread was splicing other immortals, none were born. Malice's desolate planet, Chiron, became a prison for her and her closest following their surrender in the war. There were several thousand permanently confined. *Or had been.*

I thought it obvious, but for good measure, supplicated, "It is not an overreaction nor your personal hatred. She has been lying in wait for three-thousand turns. I would not be surprised if Dmitrios was involved. War is on the horizon, has Uncle Olo truly made no mention?"

"Your mother and I can attempt to convince several more to assist your siblings on Neptune, however until Malice breaks intergalactic law, we are incapable of interference. Wraiths are not Revenants. Even if we sent a scout and witnessed an entire military camp, there is no more than a slap on her wrist for such a violation. Loath as I am to admit we conceded that."

"Alright," I replied, "we shall train the others. I appreciate you readying replacements this quickly." My phone beeped with a coinciding call. After hurriedly exchanging pleasantries with Father, I answered his twin. "Uncle Olo. You have much to explain for."

A laugh was my greeting.

Running on a few hours of sleep after heavily drinking wasn't anything new. But for whatever reason, it felt less miserable. However, despite the abnormal pep in my step, I was sour.

The trifecta were suspicious this morning. They collectively decided to refuse my questions. When I cracked Ryloh and he started to answer, the other two threw him in a warding bubble. Then, without skipping a beat, Timos rifted us to the animal shelter. I didn't even have the chance to pull my t-shirt dress over my ass before he grabbed.

Naturally, I spent my entire shift in a state of aggravation. At least it was mindless and soothing work. Just as waitressing used to, it served as a temporary fix to my annoyance, like slapping duct tape over a leaky hole. By the time lunch came around the only thing I could focus on was this dreaded afternoon date.

Biking through Ookea under the sun's rainbow rays solidified Thalla's superiority, the brick and uniform buildings were boring. And Tiger Beach was the first to resemble an Earthly equivalent; it wasn't anything special, from the soft ivory sand to the teal-blue waters. Well, everything but the glittery dragon flying overhead and dozens of tails poking through the waves.

Oh, and can't forget the tigers. Jin explained how the beach was named after a pair that someone accidentally rifted here centuries ago. Since then, the terrifying predators had made the Ookean jungle their home. So, when I noticed the encroaching rainforest on the Western side, it wasn't any surprise. However, actually witnessing tigers swimming in the shallows, like pigs in the Bahamas, was something else entirely. *Nothing* could've prepared me. Dragon shifters didn't scare, but those feral big cats did.

I was twenty minutes early for my date with the sucker named Chad. It didn't take long to find him. The familiar oversized, and shirtless, beefcake was doing lunges beside a makeshift gym on the sand. *If he intends for you to partake in physical activities, he's in for a rude awakening.*

"Chadwick," I greeted, nearing the shirtless jock with the too-ripped bod. You know the sort, roided, and far too veiny as a result. Or worse, there were no steroids here, and the male was just that obsessed with working out. I felt a whole lotta ick without starting on his misogynistic beliefs, the podcast, horrid followers, etc.

"You can't join me in a bikini, Nightingale," he groused petulantly.

"I don't plan on it. You said beach date and I dressed appropriately."

He grumbled near incoherently, but I caught something along the lines of, "You humans are all the same."

"Cool?" I volleyed. Hoping my glower flayed his peeling cheeks further.

"It seems you are slow as well. It is currently fifty-two degrees Celsius, not at all cool. I thought you might be more intelligent than the other two, given you enticed the poindexter dragon." The Kraken continued, but I stopped listening.

There was no point in chatting with this insulting orc. Not to be mistaken for the sometimes-tantalizing kind. No, he was the equivalent of a grubby and muddy-mouthed Lord of the Rings orc.

"It seems you are nothing more than your womb though," Chad finished off with an eye roll.

I scoffed. "This date is over."

Spinning on my heel while kicking sand in his direction, I put as much distance between us as possible. The dragon seemed to be enjoying himself, swimming in the faraway waves, and despite our beef, I couldn't demand we head home yet. He dropped everything to babysit, so I could entertain myself until he wanted to leave.

"Nala! Over here!"

Who? It definitely wasn't the orc I'd abandoned to his weighted jump-ing-jacks, not with that British accent or feminine lilt. I spun in a full circle before finding a gorgeous gal waving.

She was a few paces over, and I plopped down beside the pleasantly plus bikini wearing stranger. She must've had Indic lineage from her glowing chestnut skin and midnight wavy hair. "What's up? Do I know you somehow?"

"Lakshmi," the beauty extended her hand.

She didn't seem immortal, which was why I asked, "You're a Brit? I thought the Program only abducted from sweltering climates."

She grinned. "No, I'm from Chennai. My accent is from work."

"Sorry my stupid American assumption-ism is showing! I meant no offense," I quickly forced out.

Lakshmi smiled. "None taken."

"So, you're in the Program, too?"

"Yep, it's just the pair of us left. Dayna was sent home last night."

Interesting. Especially since Jin said his date with her was horrible. "What'd she do?"

Lakshmi chuckled. "You didn't see?" I shook my head. "She got drunk and threw herself at every male at the Gala. She shagged a random bloke in public."

"No way," I shouted, and Lakshmi fell into a giggle fit. Once we settled, I probed, "How are you liking things so far? Do you have any serious contenders?"

"I'm at the end of my first week. I went through the same bit with that bastard just this morning, he was my final initial introduction. The two males I have left are promising, though."

"You're telling me that bad Chad's been here all day? With the weights and everything?"

She nodded with a grimace I matched. *Despicable.*

"Who are your others? I wonder if I know them."

Lakshmi shared a dazzling smile. "Zaire the Atlanti duke and Vepar the demon duke."

Cringing at Z's mention, I focused on the other, "A demon, *huh*?"

"I was initially opposed for obvious reasons. However, Aphrodite insisted we were the most compatible of my options, so I relented. Our first date was over video chat and he won me over. Zaire isn't as attentive. I've spent far more time with Vepar." *Unsurprising.* I'd venture to guess he was busy on Venus with Miss Min.

"Do Vepar's eyes glow like laser beams?"

"They're dark, more burgundy than red. Actually, we took a selfie at the Gala," she murmured, digging through her netted bag. She passed along a twin shell-phone to mine, with a photo of her grinning beside a handsome ginger with deep skin. His demonic tells were indistinguishable.

"Y'all are cute," I said with a grin she mirrored. "So, he lives here?"

"For half the year, the other half he resides in Hell. It's apparently just another planet with its own cities and such," she explained, conveniently holding up a pamphlet on the subject. The cover was of a Halloween-themed city. There were jack-o-lantern carriages, black gothic buildings, eerily barren trees, and everything.

"Sounds perfect, then."

"Anything is preferable to returning home and likely being forced into marriage with someone I didn't choose for myself," she muttered with a frown. "Vepar insists there's a means to shift his appearance, so they'll believe I've been wed to their standards."

Lakshmi's unfocused dreamy stare into the waves was more for the demon than it was for me. It was comforting witnessing that I wasn't the only one falling for aliens. "I love how he's already thinking proactively, it's sweet. I haven't even thought of our return to Earth, it's gonna be real weird…" I couldn't help but question which of my three would meet my psychotic family.

There wasn't a chance that I could bring them all. Jin's blue hair and purple eyes would send my mom into hysterics. Ryloh's shoulder-length hair and tattoos would spark World War III. Timos could work, but how would we explain his size? *Retired athlete? Hmm…*

"I saw you from afar and I'm not going to lie, I was shocked you could stand to be near Ryloh. Yu-Jin I understand, and *somewhat* regarding the dragon, but the frightening fae?" Lakshmi's pleasant voice crashed through my musings.

"Ryloh's mine. He's a menace but he's *my* menace. It is what it is," I replied with a shrug.

Lakshmi shared a flabbergasted look. "You aren't frightened by him?"

"You're the one dating a demon," I accused, and she barked a laugh.

"Vepar is pudding compared to Ryloh! He's got those psychotic peepers!"

"I call them headlights since one is out, and I love them. Ry's just misunderstood."

Lakshmi didn't seem to believe me, changing the subject, "Are you staying in Ookea, too?"

"No, I'm in Thalla. What'd you tell Aphrodite your favorite color was?"

"Silver," she replied. Damn, her apartment probably dunks on yours. "What about you?"

"Purple."

Our repartee was interrupted by a dragon's shadow blocking the sun. Timos manifested in the sand wearing a dark long-sleeve t-shirt and shorts with his arms crossed, like a genie without the bottle. "Hello, I am Timo-set," he said in greeting toward Lakshmi who waved and exchanged her name. She wasn't terrified or ogling him too much, thankfully.

"Why are you not over there with Chadwick?" he questioned.

"Because he sucks," I said, eliciting a laugh from Lakshmi. "I talked to him, isn't that enough?"

"I suppose." Timos replied, typing a message. "Yu-Jin is better versed in programmatic specifics."

Lakshmi shared a perplexed look, so I explained, "You've gotta meet all the males on your roster to not get sent back to Earth." Before she could reply, the Thallan duke rifted in and sent us both into momentary shock. *"Gaaah* Jin, you can't keep appearing like that!"

"Hello again, Lakshmi," he said. Then I was in his warm arms, being yanked from the sand. "How many sentences did you exchange with the Kraken?" I shrugged and Jin pinched his brow, saying, "Guess."

"Probably like three or four sentences."

"Then yeah, it's enough," Jin said as he patted the sand from my shorts. "I'm done for the day I can walk you back." Our group peered back at the orc to find that his tentacled arms were stretching from his back. Now incorporated into the workout, each lifting a weight, and I had to withhold my urge to gag.

Lakshmi hopped to her feet. "I should get going too. Nice meeting you, good luck."

"Same to you with Vepar and Hell," I replied.

Jin and Timos whispered the entire walk while I cycled a few paces ahead. They refused to share. Not even when I probed. Consistently.

Each block needled me. Poking until I was past the point of return. I couldn't keep from stomping upon arrival, flinging my bike aside before rushing upstairs. My blood was thrumming furiously as they quickened to keep up.

"Welcome home, Nala," Homie greeted as I swung the door open.

"Nala, love, I have to meet my parents for dinner tonight and—"

"Whatever," I interrupted Jin with a dismissive flick of my wrist.

Timos approached, bronze gaze tracking me with caution. *Intelligent of him.* He extended upturned taupe palms, as if in surrender, saying, "Naliti, you must attempt to understand—"

"No, actually. I refuse just like you two are," I said wryly. "You want to repudiate the advice of his sister, who's a mental health professional? *Fine.* You want to keep things although I've shared my trust issues? *Fine.* You want to ignore my questions? *Fine.*" I stomped up the spiraled stairs, tossing over my shoulder, "I'm no longer partaking in this sham of a relationship. Congratulations, you've earned yourselves my silence. Don't come pleading unless you're ready to spill every fucking secret."

When Jin started chasing after me, I spun, glowering. <<*"Please don't shut me out, Nala. I love you."*> He was cringing, big shoulders by his chin.

"Do you really think you're acting like a partner who *loves* me right now?" I seethed. Jin recoiled. "If you loved me as much as you claim, you wouldn't constantly be hiding shit! I'm done with the whisperings. Seriously. You might as well leave. Both of you."

"Please," Timos tried, but when faced with my daggered gaze, he grimaced. So, I continued upstairs, slamming my bathroom door, and locking them out.

My skin was reddened and waterlogged after two extended baths. All of it for naught because it didn't calm me. Jin's unsettled thoughts barreling into my brain caused the fury to reproduce en-masse, like imaginary rabbits. My seething was thumping around every corner of my skull. The pair were *still* attempting to come up with excuses.

For the first time since my abduction, I was filled with regret. Regret for tethering myself so quickly. Regret for refusing Jin's initial offers to discuss the dick magic. Regret for voicing my love. Regret for deciding to stay. Essentially, my rage was boundless.

So, when someone had the audacity to knock on the bathroom door, I shrieked loudly enough to wreak havoc on my vocal cords. It didn't quell an ounce of my frustration, but it felt good. There was *pss-pss-pss*-ing on the other end, though.

More fucking whispers? They've asked for it, Nala. Unleash.

I left the tub without toweling off. Unlocking, and swinging the door open with a *bang* which sent the males jolting back a step. Revealing Ryloh joined at some point, so I deigned explain, "Unless you're planning on spilling your plethora of secrets, I'm not talking to you either. I don't know why the Tweedle-Dee- and Tweedle-Dumb-asses are still here!"

Unfortunately, my nudity distracted them. They were gawking like they'd never seen a woman's body before, despite all having seen mine. Which only compounded my irritation. I stomped my foot with a growl. Three sheepish expressions met my now —*nuclear*—fury. "Aren't the lies twisting you up?!"

"I have not lied. I'll tell you anything you wish to kn- know, Na- Nala spice. You've seen proof of that," Ryloh replied, crossing his suited arms. He did have a point, which was why I narrowed my eyes in the others' direction.

The gorgeous dragon opened his mouth a few times, but nothing came out. I raised a pointer and stabbed his broad chest. "I'll revoke your access to my apartment. Don't. Fucking. Test. Me." The male had never looked more distraught. It wasn't any relief though.

"Don't," Jin fell to his knees at my feet and gripped a slippery hand. "Nala, please. We can feel your frustration. You need to remain calm—"

I shrieked from anger —*again*—except this time, the other two males fell to their knees. It would've been distracting if I wasn't ready to curb stomp them. "Explain or get out!"

"Yu-Jin told us you were refusing to discuss the specifics of your inherited—"

"*Wrong*, try again!"

"You're going to have your first heat soon," Jin rasped.

He gulped audibly when I demanded, *"Heat?"* Internally praying to the universe that it wasn't what I thought.

"Heat, as in your nature calls to ours to instigate procreation. Once you accept their bonds, it's likely to surface. It'll be extremely uncomfortable. That's why you noticed my anxiousness each time I raised the discussion, and subsequently, why the topic wasn't pushed further," Jin explained in a rush. I was shaking my head in horrified denial when Ryloh and Timos both nodded.

My world suddenly came crashing down. Not this. *Anything but this!*

"It can last up to n- nine days at a time," Ryloh cursed my reality further.

"What am I supposed to do horned up for nine days straight?!"

"It's difficult to predict how often you might experience it from my nature because my mom had multiple mates," Jin piled on.

"What do you mean 'from your nature?'" I questioned woodenly. "Isn't heat just a biological cycle, like my period? It'll show up when I'm most fertile, right?" When they shook their heads, my gut plunged into a black hole. "How then?" My voice was little more than a rasp.

This was the worst catch imaginable.

Timos cleared his throat, stealing my attention from Jin's sorrowful plum gaze. "Heats are unpredictable. Unlike the mammals you are familiar with, immortal heats are not tied to a menstruation cycle. It stems from your nature and your body's reaction to ours." I didn't like the sound of that. *Not one bit.*

"Hold on. I just want to make sure I'm understanding this correctly. Is heat as mindless and all-consuming as I think it is? That my skin will itch unless one of you is rutting me? Literally, for hours on end? *Oh, gaaah.* For *DAYS* on end?" I found three heads bobbing and screeched, "What the fuck are you three gonna do during? Take the whole week off work?"

"It will be uncomfortable for everyone," Timos mumbled as he readjusted his lenses.

"Gabs didn't explain to you why she doesn't work full-time?" Jin questioned and I shook my head in horror. We were too busy discussing stupid Earth stuff. *That squirrel!* The Musketeers exchanged another 'uh-oh' glance and I knew this was going to get a whole lot worse.

"They grow in discomfort," Timos said, keeping his slitted gaze on the rug.

"Y- Your heats will worsen the longer we go without babies, spice," Ryloh expanded, sending me toppling to the rug beside them. "Y- Your first shouldn't be too intense. However, your transformation has already been atypical. It is difficult to know h- how to prepare you properly."

My eyes narrowed. The word was giving me a drunk-addled déja-vù, but I couldn't place it. "What transformation? The dick magic surfacing?"

"It's the process of you stepping into your power. Since you were human before, it'll happen when your body accepts our shared magic, which could take anywhere from days to a week after the suppressants left your system and you've bound yourself to them. You'll—*uhm*—," Jin's eyes darted as he cleared his throat suspiciously, "lose yourself for a bit. It's sometimes a coma-like state, other times… Not." I made a derisive noise they ignored.

"Sometimes it lasts a few hours, sometimes a week. Many describe transforming as feeling trapped without your senses intact, others say it's like a drug induced trip. You might also experience your first heat during. It varies by class, love. I assumed you were zoatala because we tethered first, but with how you've been frequently overwhelming the suppressant and luring us, we aren't sure," Jin explained.

"Ideally, since we're the destined pair, y- you're fae. I've heard it's only the ears that're a pain." Ryloh leaned over to tuck an errant curl behind my ear. "However, there's no proof *I'm* fae instead of my own unnamed species. From what we know, no dragon has ever passed their nature to th- their bonded, *but* you're also the first former human mate. Plus—"

"Do not," Timos snapped. Our eyes swiveled to where he rose, then began pacing as he fidgeted. "Do *not* overwhelm her. We shall answer your questions, Naliti. However, I do not agree with voicing conjecture and hypotheses when you could tip into heat *or* transformation from the mildest stressor. There are far too many unanswered questions, now is not the time for theorization."

I frowned. "How are we supposed to get to the bottom of it?"

"Olorun," Ryloh and Timos replied in sync.

"My Titan uncle instructed us to call him when yours begins. He possesses the resources to ensure you are comfortable during. We may be forced to travel, but it depends on several factors. Your final date

Wednesday night will likely…" Timos scratched the back of his neck, exchanging a suspicious blink with Ryloh. "Wednesday shall determine how we proceed." He was secret hoarding. *A-fuckin-gain!*

Painting the most disapproving look I could muster, Jin mumbled incoherently and started rising to his feet. "On that note, I've gotta go. You know how to reach me," he said on a heavy sigh.

"You won't be missed," Ryloh whispered, stealing my scowl for himself.

"Be *nice* to Jin," I roared, incapable of mustering a modicum of calm. "You promised, Ryloh. You fucking *promised*." Timos flicked one of his pointy ears, and the fae winced.

"Good luck," Jin announced, sharing an uneasy glance before rifting.

There was no containing my growl as I crossed my arms. "You two are going to tell me everything. Right. Goddamn. Now."

Surprisingly, Timoset was the first to give in with a curt nod. Ryloh said, "Why don't you call Gabriela to hear her experience with heats first? I swear to share whatever y- you wish afterward." *Ugh.* I knew he was right. Scurrying downstairs, I grabbed my phone, and heard their whisperings halfway back up. They jumped like a pair of guilty pogo-sticks when I *clanged* on the last step.

"Once I hang up with her, you're both telling me everything. Are we clear?" I said over my scallop with the first ring. Phone call because of my nudity.

"Mercury's in retrograde, gimme the bad," Gabs greeted.

The males' faces crumpled as I hollered, "HEATS, GABS. THAT'S WHAT'S BAD."

"I'm so fucking sorry, it's the Program! My tongue is spelled, we can only discuss things you already know," she cried.

I flung myself onto the mattress in frustration, struggling to find a position that didn't piss me off further. I settled on crossing one of my ankles over the opposite knee, laying horizontally. Now comfortable, I demanded, "How bad?"

"Worse than you think," Gabs conceded. "It's why I ice plunge, Seong discovered it can delay them. He can't leave when I'm in one though, not even for work. Hae typically delivers our food during. He's been tying me to the bed lately because I become so… It's chaotic as fuck."

"It's unbelievable none of you told me. Not even a peep," I replied. Lifting my narrowed gaze to find the duo staring at… *Welp, that's what you*

246

get for being on display. I muted the call to raise my brows with a clipped, "Can you act like you've seen my pussy before, please?"

Ryloh barked a laugh as Timos sputtered. I rolled my eyes, unmuting the call as Gabs said, "You have to ask me questions for me to explain."

"How long does it last on average for you?" I questioned before muted her once their eyes flew right back to my privates, like suicidal flies after the lamp already zapped them. "What's with you two? Do I need to get dressed?"

"I'd rather you didn't," Ryloh purred, falling to the mattress with a smirk. I felt him inching closer but became distracted.

Because Gabs replied: "Two weeks."

Rendering me useless.

The air in my bedroom grew thick as I attempted to compute that. Timoset, typically aloof, looked terrified. Eventually, I unmuted to shout, "FOURTEEN ENTIRE DAYS?" Then a whimper escaped. Ryloh's warm tongue plunged into me without any preamble as static shocked my clit.

Whatever Gabs was saying was no longer heard.

Timos groaned as Ryloh went to town. "Knock it off," I tried breathily. Ryloh didn't heed, adding more zaps to the mix as my lower half clamped around his tongue.

"Anyway, it won't be that bad once you birth your first according to Hae," Gabs said.

Her voice was a mood-killer, I began flinging my legs in a feeble escape attempt.

"Are you saying I don't have your permission to worship you in apology?" the fae taunted. Like lightning, his inky hair disappeared between my legs before hearing my response. I went cross-eyed as he swiped at my clit roughly.

"Naliti said no," Timos growled. Ryloh ignored him. As I went to protest, a zippy climax from his talented fingers joining in the ministrations distracted me. My mind went fuzzy as the adrenaline liquefied my brain. He was lucky I wasn't nearly as furious with him as the others.

I only caught the tail end of their argument, when Timos said, "We cannot accept our bonds. Not until Yu-Jin is aware, he will frenzy again."

"H- He doesn't need a calendar invite," Ryloh scoffed. There was some stomping as my eyes remained clamped. "Remember how I mentioned tying you up, spice?" I nodded as he chuckled. It was a low rumble, a wicked sound that left my skin peppering.

There was a snarl as my limbs were suddenly pulled taut. I cracked a lid to find my wrists bound in static above my head as Ryloh and Timos looked on with enough heat in their gaze to strike a match. When my legs were spread with several bolts, and Timos' eyes shifted, I knew there was likely no turning back.

"See?" Ryloh elbowed Timos who hadn't averted his eyes from me, not even to blink.

"Nala! Are you there?" Gabs interrupted. *Whoopsie.*

Ryloh snatched my discarded phone and unmuted with, "Nala's busy at the moment, Gabriela. She'll ring later." There was a squawk before the line went dead. I couldn't begin to react to that as the burn around my wrists and ankles worsened. Delightfully so.

My tormenter swiped a finger up the slick dripping down my inner thigh, holding out the glistening proof. "You see, Timoset. Nala loves this shit."

"Ryloh, you cannot—" Timos started.

"Tell me you can't sense her desperation," he ground out. "Tell me you can't sense how the loaf isn't satisfying *our* mate's needs!" Timos' eyes were glued to where I was dangling.

"You've seen that isn't true, you peeping Tom! Can you please stop dissing Jin? I mean it!"

"No," Ryloh replied with a shrug as he loosened his tie and tossed it aside. "I cannot because he's not enough for you, Nala spice. It is fact. And I swore to never lie to y- you."

I tossed my head to ignore the sexy slow way he was unbuttoning his shirt. Once the tattoos came into view I'd be a goner. "You promised to play nice," I scolded, attempting to keep my voice steady. And grossly failing.

"I do play nice in his presence," Ryloh said, trailing a pale finger down the center of my chest. The male was cut like a sculpture and had hundreds of lines swirling and snaking over every muscle. Many of the lines sharp and jagged, like him.

Before I could protest, his discarded shirt was stuffed into my mouth. My eyes bugged as Timos stormed over and shoved Ryloh aside, ripping the gag from my mouth.

"Do you desire *this* or answers, Naliti?" It was a valid question. A zinger. *What does Nala actually want?* I didn't know, not anymore. The bitterness coupled with my recent climax left me boneless. I found myself swallowing thickly, and Ryloh hummed.

He sent a zap towards my clit, and there was no withholding my moan. Ryloh raised a dark brow in Timos' direction, in clear conveyance of 'told you so.' The dragon shook his chestnut curls out of place before plopping onto the edge of the bed. "If she grants permission, then I shall relent."

"Wh- What do you want? Tell us." My attention went back to Ryloh, who now was naked and grinning as he fisted himself. When I caught sight of his six piercings laddering his dick, I might've whimpered. Ry was big, but big in human-terms, like a European cucumber versus an American one. He would probably still do damage, but not enough to…

No, he's growing under your fucking gaze.

Plus, those bells and whistles would definitely leave an imprint.

"Could you please quit gawking at his cock, Naliti?" Timos whined.

Ryloh cackled in glee. "I told you she would prefer my dick to yours!"

They exchanged several magic tricks while I was too gobsmacked to muster a response. The dragon seemed to have control over all the elements, as each bolt of static diffused differently.

"Please do not force me to do the same," Timos begged, and I burst out laughing.

"It wasn't that bad. You are such a wuss!" Ryloh chided, his taunting smile spreading.

"You *shouted* through each stabbing and strangled the life from my palm," Timos volleyed.

All but slapping me in the face with the revelation that he was there. With Ryloh. At his cucumber adorning appointment. "*Woah*, wait," I interrupted, causing them to spin back towards me. "Timos, you went with Ryloh to get his dick piercings? *When?*" It left me in a squeal.

"Yesterday," they replied in unison, and I squealed louder. Then took another look at the goods. Ryloh did have a pretty one. And my favorite book boyfriend also had these same piercings in the exact same ladder placement. *What're the odds?*

"N- Nala," Ryloh groused, "you never gave permission." He clenched his jaw before whispering, "B- Behave."

"Can you let me go free, then? Maybe we should get dressed," I said, earning a sigh in relief from Timos. But I wasn't letting either of them off so easily. "I want the answers you offered since it's not sexy time." *Yet.*

Ryloh's would be my first and final pierced member and I couldn't wait to take it for a spin. I took another gander at the goods before he tucked them out of sight.

The fae winked his starry pupil before his static disbanded, and I plopped into his outstretched arms. Since the suppressant had waned, the red marks around my wrists and ankles healed near instantaneously.

Skipping to the closet, I threw on the first satin midi-slip within reach and trotted back out to find Ryloh fully clothed. "So," I started, unsure of what to ask first. My eyes swung towards the last of the sun backlighting the purple skies. Along with... *A shadow?*

Yup. That's a humongous being up there.

"Did you just see that?" I questioned with a pointer. "Is there someone on my roof?" Ryloh and Timos exchanged a glance before each took a hold of an elbow and rifted us downstairs. The fae whipped out his phone while Timos filled the room with smoke.

"I- I'm checking the feeds now," Ryloh muttered.

"Pardon?" Has he been stalking you?

"Your entire block is under surveillance, Nala. We weren't exaggerating last night. We refuse to risk you," Ryloh replied nonchalantly. He continued tapping away before saying, "F- False alarm." There was a silent conversation shared with Timos who seemed to slightly quell.

"False alarm? As in it wasn't a vampire? Just a random creep in my skylight?!"

They nodded, which didn't count as a response. I wrapped my arms around my middle, feeling incredibly unsettled. "What about the Wraiths? Is it even safe in here?"

"Y- Yes, you have multiple wards. This apartment is likely the most guarded place on Neptune. Now that Timoset no longer has to protect the island—"

"What?"

"It is true, Naliti. My father sent two of my siblings to replace me, Osri and Persis have already begun taking patrol shifts."

Two more dragons to ogle! I couldn't help but ask, "What colors are they?"

"Blue."

"We're getting off topic," Ryloh interjected, "we must chat through the unfairness and answer your questions."

My mouth went dry. "Unfairness?" I choked.

"We understand you love Yu-Jin because you've spent the most time with him, Nala, but it truthfully makes me a bit uncomfortable. For more reasons than one," Ryloh explained.

Timos surprised me by nodding. "I feel the same, Naliti. Despite the equated feelings we share, I had not realized the male was residing here with you."

"Equated f- feelings?" Ryloh's face fell, and my heart slowed.

Meeting his mismatched gaze, I gripped his hand to cushion the blow. "I love Timoset, too. I'm sorry if it upsets you. It wasn't my intent to hurt or leave you out, Ry."

"C- Call me that instead of Lolly and you're forgiven," he grunted. "The Queen calls me L- Lolly." The clear discomfort on his face worsened the blow.

Oh, no, no, no. Every new story I heard of her was worse than the last. The guilt buried me deeper than eight-feet. "I'm so sorry, Ryloh Cabbage. I'll never do it again. I swear."

He nodded. "I still wish for Yu-Jin to move out."

"Because?" This was my first-go at building a polycule, I didn't know what I was doing. And most of the rules I'd read put emphasis on having open communication. But I was nervous… *And a scaredy cat.*

"We deserve just as much of you." Ryloh lowered his voice to mutter, "If y- you deem he stays, I'm moving in too."

I rolled my eyes, but it was to keep from crying while my heart pinched. You're wanted badly enough for the OCD Virgo to live in a sardine tin with his nemesis.

"Agreed," Timos said. "I understand your disdain for my constant protection, but I can no longer fathom not having you near, Naliti."

"I didn't ask Jin to move in, it just happened, but —"

"We do not wish to upset you, please do not cry," Timos begged, rushing forward to pull me into his chilly embrace. He stroked my hair, murmuring, "You demanded our honesty."

He's right, you dingbat. Get it together! I wiped my tears and schooled my face after a deep breath. "Okay, you two can move in. What else is bothering you?"

"We need a plan to quell Yu-Jin, obviously."

Once upon a time, I looked forward to these weekly dinners in Bahasa. Seeing my parents placated some of my anxiousness. I never delved too deeply into the why, but the forced nostalgia helped. That was no longer the case, though. I couldn't be more unsettled as Hae Soo-Ah Kim Rapax glared at me over the rim of her glass. As if Nala's raging wasn't enough, I now had hers to contend with.

Mom always forced the hostess to seat us at a too-large table so my parents could be side-by-side, as a united front. Tonight was no different. Since retiring, the quadrant were becoming more and more alike. Even in appearance. My dads had grown their hair to the shoulder length of Mom's. It was extremely unsettling. I could barely tell my sire, Appa, from Min's dad with their dark hair. The lone outlier was Seong's father, who only stood out because of his dark grey skin and silver highlights.

I've kept my mouth too occupied to participate through each course, avoiding the inevitable PPP inquisition, nodding while chewing throughout my dads' chit-chat. But unfortunately, my luck ran out. I'd licked my plate clean, and our robo-waiter hadn't returned to refill my drink. I'd even chewed the ice cubes.

Cheap and inefficient fucking bots. This is exactly why your legislation refused to allow these abominations into Thalla.

"Hey, hey," a male voice interrupted. I lifted my gaze to find Seong approaching. *Thank fuck.* My savior. I quickly rose for a hug, taking the distance from Mom as a karmic blessing. Even if he pissed me the fuck off earlier.

"I didn't know you were coming," I grumbled. There was something unsettling about his scent… Couldn't quite place it, though.

"Neither did I," he said, hugging Dad next. "I never know when the wench is gonna dismiss me for the day." It was a wonder he'd held onto this job for this long, the Queen was the worst. *Not that Seong's much better.*

"Language," Appa warned, but my older brother only rolled his eyes as he took a seat beside me, facing our parental unit.

"He got his lip from you," Father accused, and our dads quickly fell into their typical blame-game banter.

"So, what'd I miss?" Seong asked Mom. The fucker looking me dead in the eye as he did. That malicious curl to his upper lip telling me everything I needed to know. He wasn't my savior tonight. No, he was my damnation.

"Nothing. Jin's been radio silent," Mom clipped.

Seong's grin sliced through his face. If it got any wider, he'd shift. "Why would that be, Ji-Ji?"

I attempted to remain calm. Counting to one thousand. Ensuring my nostrils didn't spread across my face. *You aren't eight and useless anymore, Jin, you could take the shithead.*

"I know he had his final courting last week," Mom started. When her narrowed eyes found mine in preparation to deflect, she added, "Before you deny it, Yu-Jin Kim Rapax, Aphrodite confirmed as much no more than an hour before we left." A groan crept up my throat, but I swallowed it down and waved towards a robo-waiter whizzing past.

"He *is* acting suspicious; I'll give you that." Appa chortled, before angling toward Seong. "Why don't you tell us. You clearly seem to know something."

My glare held the force of a thousand winds. It would've made any other male balk. Not Seong, though. When he clapped my shoulder with his overheated palm, I mouthed, "I'm going to murder you." And the pest giggled.

I had to say *something* to Mom. I knew that, but… *What if you lose Nala?*

The topic demanded my attention. It was no longer avoidable.

Ever since Ryloh mentioned those fucking dreams, I haven't been able to shake the persistent, agonizing fear that my time with Nala might be temporary. We shouldn't have tethered before she finished her first week. It was completely irrational to believe she was *my* ideal match.

Destiny intended her for *three* others, all fucking godly in prestige. *How're you supposed to compare?* And none of that had anything to do with how queasy I was when faced with the idea of sharing her. Every facet of my circumstances was humiliatingly hopeless.

So, then, why don't you regret a minute spent with Nala?

- —*"Because we're in love and great together, you doofus. I'm sorry I was so angry before you left. Are you okay? I can feel how stressed you are, babe. You can tell your parents without me there. I don't care."*- *Just the sound of her husky lilt was a balm to my anxiety. However, feeling her concern? Her care for me? From across the island? It was the kick in the ass I needed.*

Nala was mine. Fate, Avexei, and who —*or whatever else*— attempted to come between us, could fuck right off. <<*"I'm okay, love. I'll be back soon."*>

"Listen, I *do* have news," I interrupted, rendering the table silent.

"What's going on, Yu-Jin?" Mom questioned, accusation shifting to concern as the others cringed in preparation. Except for Seong, who clung onto his taunting expression.

Ignoring them, I continued, "I *have* met someone —"

"It's a little bit more than that, don't you think?" the useless hunk of blubber interrupted with a *clink* of his glass against mine. "If anything, we should be celebrating." Our parents seemed to hold their collective breath, their gazes swinging between us like a pendulum.

"Out of respect for Nala, I'm not going to say any more than that. Neither should you, Seong. You four deserve the chance to meet her without preconceived —"

"Are you telling us you've mated, and *I* did *not* meet her prior?" Mom slammed her fork down with a *clank*. Seong nodded with a howl. I fought back a grimace when faced with Hae's fury. Her wrath was nearly as upsetting as Nala's. *Not quite though. Don't you dare balk!*

"Yu-Jin wouldn't do that," Dad said with a chuckle, roping the rest of them into sharing a laugh at my expense. *Typical.* It was always them against us in a sense. My parents squabbled, of course, but it never lasted long. They were a clique of their own. Min repeatedly advised to not take their jibes seriously but was tougher than forgiving myself.

"You're right, he's far too neurotic," Mom said, sending my stomach churning from the whiplash.

Neurotic.

That fucking word always unlocked a barrage of memories. A chorus of the three worst statements repeated to me for as long as I could remember.

You're neurotic.

You're so intense.

You try too hard.

Again, and again. Like an endless carousel ride I couldn't get off. It wasn't just family and friends who used them. Citizens. Colleagues. Classmates. Girlfriends. Mentors. The Press. Teachers. You fucking name it, they've repeated at least one.

- —*"You aren't any of those things, babe. They just didn't understand you."*-

<<*"You're the first to not share that sentiment."*>

- —*"That's why you love me. Well, and my ass."*-

<<*"Every inch of you, love."*>

- —*"I'm blushing, Your Grace."*-

I loved when she called me that silly title. My smile blossomed despite the crap my family was still flinging. I hadn't realized how much had changed since meeting Nala last Wednesday. It was only the following Monday, not even an entire week had passed, and yet.

"Seong wasn't lying," I interrupted, "Nala Nightingale Williams is her name. She's from Bluffton, South Carolina. And I think you'll love her. She was a waitress like you—"

"A *waitress*?" My mother shrieked condescendingly. As though that wasn't what she was before my dads. Upholding double standards was her default. The surrounding patrons glared as Seong snorted obnoxiously through his blow hole. "She's not good enough for you, Yu-Jin!"

Thankfully, Father stilled her mid-rant with a palm to the shoulder. Giving Appa the opportunity to jump in, "Why would you tether after knowing someone for a week?"

If only he actually knew.

When Seong opened his maw to burst my bubble, I—*somehow*—managed to ward him into silence. It wasn't one of my prominent gifts, and

I rarely practiced… But took the win. My parents were still in various states of shock over the news. *Keep it moving, Jin.*

"Nala was easy to fall for. I've never met anyone like her. She's caring and hilarious. I didn't see any point in waiting. She hasn't been fearful or daunted." I lowered my voice to add, "Timoset is her second bonded, she's already cracked his shell too." Appa nearly fell out of his chair. He'd known the dragon his entire life and they worked closely for nearly a century.

"It's not all bad then," Dad chirped, his mirthful expression a mirror to Min's. "You'll get to wring his neck forever now, Hae." Mom harrumphed. Then the four fell into their mind-meld. Locking a still muted Seong and myself out.

What else is new, Jin? At least, Mom barely reacted. You got out easy.

Seong, though… I was already thinking through possible retribution.

Why couldn't we just have a normal happy family?

Nala had become more to me than these five ever were. *Maybe harsh.* But if I was honest with myself for once? My parents weren't as supportive as I made them seem. Refusing Hae wasn't worth the resulting drama, so I rarely did. It was a generational duty I felt pressured to upkeep. I don't know why I pretended otherwise around Nala…

Around *anyone*, actually. I'd been doing it for years, and years. It became habitual. *That's what happens when you crave for things to be true, you fucking invent them.* I didn't blame my parents for being slightly below average; I didn't have any cause to hold resentment, it just was.

Regardless, the idea of forcing myself through the remainder of this dinner was more than stifling, it was suffocating. And of course, my brother flaunted a shit eating grin as he basked in our parents muted roast. Silent, but still pestering. Min was the reasonable one who intervened on my behalf, but she was rarely around these days.

However, none of it was penetrating the happy haze from Nala's interruption. *Maybe you shouldn't have been so distraught.* She was the one. The first to appreciate me, the first to listen, to understand without explanation. We weren't perfect, but it was everything I'd ever wanted. Perfection was trite anyway.

Why are you sitting here? Just accepting this? I'd much rather be with Nala love. Her aura was healing, her laughs even more so. She knew how to yank me out of the deep end. And as much as I hated admitting it, I was looking forward to seeing Ryloh and Timoset. Her eyes always seemed to sparkle brighter when the three of us were near.

We'd formed-

"I've gotta run," I said, standing abruptly. "Use my tab. Safe travels next week. I'll coordinate a time for you to meet Nala when you're back."

"Jin," Father said, clambering to his feet. "We were only messing around. I'm sorry."

Mom followed suit, motioning for me to kiss her cheek, but I shook my head, backing toward the exit. Disbanding the warding around Seong, and tossing over my shoulder, "Talk soon." We weren't the 'I love you' kind of family.

And yeah, Mom was gonna raise the dead because of my dodging, but I was now a mated male. There was only one being getting anywhere near my lips. As I cut through the tightly packed tables, Seong's boisterous voice carried, "I think Nala's already replaced you." I didn't wait to hear her reply, rifting the instant my feet crossed the threshold.

🐟 🐟 🐟 🐟 *.°

Most didn't know I was responsible for inventing Homie, the home connectivity platform, since I'd sold it to a conglomerate while in university. Programming came easy and I exploited my skill for as long as I could. Machines didn't have emotions; bugs were easy to fix. Politics was more challenging and fulfilling. However, somehow, Nala's Homie and I had formed beef.

Probably because you basically moved in. My studio was the last place I wanted to be now. What I once considered a haven, felt like a dungeon. Plus, there wasn't enough room-

What the fuck's he doing here?

"Avexei?" I questioned, using his preferred name since he tended to use mine. My beast did *not* appreciate the sight of him pacing outside of Nala's, though. The male stilled, his hair shifting rapidly as I asked, "Why are you out here?" *In the middle of the fucking street like a stalker?*

"*Well-* I can explain..."

"*Oh-*kay," I drawled, crossing my arms. He didn't resemble his mother, the only thing they had in common was their hair. Whereas his sister, Aphrodite, was the opposite.

Avexei's dark eyes darted around for a few beats until he said, "I'm keeping watch."

"Isn't Timoset upstairs?" My eyes narrowed as his scattered. "Are you stalking Nala?"

He was shifting from sneaker to sneaker as he ran a hand through his hair. "No! I just stand out here sometimes. That's it!"

"Sometimes?"

"There's no need to growl! I'm just sitting outside her building, it's a three out of ten on the creepy scale —"

"Can you fucking hear yourself?"

"It's bad. I know." Avexei tugged on his hair until it stood on end, completely black. "I'll leave." He offered, and I heaved a sigh. It was diffi-cult to hold any resentment toward him. He didn't ask for any of this to happen to him. Or to Nala.

"You're just going to come back once I'm upstairs and we both know it," I tossed over my shoulder, jogging up the steps.

"You're letting me stay?" He croaked in disbelief.

"She might still trade Ryloh for you," I replied earnestly.

Avexei cracked one of his wide grins. "You shouldn't expect that to happen, pupling."

"Do you have to be condescending? I'm not bursting your bubble." I was done accepting the puffer shit from anyone. Parents. My brother. Weird godly acquaintances. *No more, Jin.*

"Sorry. I'm on edge. I felt her anger earlier and haven't settled since."

"Fuck." It felt as if he stabbed me in the gut. Despite how I *also* felt her. With a sigh, I admitted, "Her prestige is sometimes thicker than Timoset's. Just wait until you experience it."

"You've cooled, then?"

I nodded. "It's not my goal to keep Nala from you, but you need to understand I'm not letting her go. Regardless of whether or not you're bound. And I guess I also understand why you're out here. In your posi-tion, I probably would be, too." It was exhilarating to admit aloud. A smile even spread. I anticipated Nala piping up any minute now or clambering down the stairs...

Oddly, the mind-meld was muted.

"Thanks for leaving me out here frothing," Avexei grumbled with a two-finger salute.

Skipping up the stairwell, I realized there was a reflective warding catching the light in Nala's doorframe. *No wonder you couldn't hear her.* Stretching a hand with a preparatory grimace, it passed right through. I opened the door to find them gathered in the living room.

The matcha green dress Nala was wearing had a similar effect to porn during adolescence. It left nothing to the imagination from the way it dripped down her curved frame. The blood drained from my head as I rushed to join the other males on the sofa.

"Hi, babe," she greeted, "sorry I lost it earlier." The sentiment only added to the tenting of my trousers. *How is she so fucking stunning?* It was nearly distracting enough to overlook the somberness of her voice.

"I'm sorry to corner you like this, but we've gotta have a serious chit-chat, Jin," she started, pacing from one side of the living room to the other. My nerve-endings pulled taut as the hairs along the back of my neck prickled. "I've been thinking about this a lot."

Yeah, this really is the worst day of your life, Jin.

My heart sped. Palms sweat. Lungs deflated.

"It's our first night actually together, together. All of us," Nala sighed. Then giggled. Then frowned. "I don't know how we're supposed to have this conversation. I guess there are no rules. But I do have to clarify something first." She directed the final sentence toward me, sucking the ether from my lungs. I was blinking back tears when her face shifted into a sad smile.

Does she no longer want you?

"It's not that," Nala suddenly rushed over, gripping my hands and falling to the floor between my knees. "I just have to take something I don't wanna take from you and I'm truthfully daunted by your reaction."

"Don't be, love. Please." My voice cracked. I might've been trembling. It didn't matter. I couldn't unglue from Nala's warm eyes as she fought back tears too.

"You can't come first anymore, Jin," she whispered. My initial reaction was stun. Which was quickly replaced with fury.

I stood. Incapable of sitting…

Shit, Jin.

You're losing it.

"Please, just listen before you freak out."

She's right. Fuck.

Holding her gaze, I gulped down as much ether as possible.

Then managed to slowly lower to the couch with a nod.

"I'm not saying any of this to upset you. It's purely factual. If you would've lost control without these two there last night, you might've hurt me."

You're gonna pass out, yeah.

I'd never felt worse. There were a plethora of swelling emotions attaching to guilt. Compounding the ache. My beast was cowering and whining. He'd never, not once, felt similar remorse. But it was warranted, he was to blame. *As are you.*

You don't deserve her. The one being you were never meant to disappoint, and you nearly destroyed her. Fuck. Fucking. FUCK.

Nala's nails clawed into my palm, and I finally got enough of a grip to realize I wasn't listening. "You're allowed to slip, okay? I don't blame you," Nala said softly, realizing I hadn't been paying attention. "My point is this can't be the two of us anymore. I need Timoset and Ryloh, and last night you proved that *you* need them too. Maybe unintentionally, but you know it's true. I love you, Jin, but you're no longer the only one. There can't be any competition. I have to love each of you equally. Separately. Together. We have to trust each other for this to work."

"You trust me, spice?" Ryloh interjected as my organs reluctantly began unclenching.

Usually, I would've fumed at his intrusion, but was relieved in this instance. It stole the spotlight from me. Granting a moment of reprieve. *You can do this, Jin. Nala loves you. And... Unfortunately, she's right.*

Which I knew, but it sucked to acknowledge.

"I do trust you, Ry. Timos, too, but he already knows. What I'm trying to say is that I want them to be able to come and go from here as much as you do, Jin. They wanna move-in, too. You're allowed as much time as you need to process. Or space —"

"No space," I rushed out, pulling her off the floor and against my chest. As soon as her scent filled my nostrils I instantaneously relaxed. Her skin was so damn soft. I could never have enough. "I don't care about them living here, Nala. You're right."

She withdrew with a shy curl to her lip before facing the other two. "So, then you trust me with this? To love you separately? I'm not always gonna get it right, but I'm gonna try to be what you deserve."

"Duh," Ryloh muttered with an eye roll. I nearly whacked him. Timoset did in my stead.

There was a loud exchange of slaps happening as Nala turned back around to walk two of her fingers up my shirt buttons as she whispered in my ear, "Are you sure you're alright, Jin?"

The hopefulness on her gorgeous face urged me to nod. But I couldn't lie just to please her. Nala deserved more than that.

Are you fine? The weight on my chest from five minutes ago had dissipated. The only thing in its wake was a realization that maybe, just maybe, I was actually happy about this whole thing. When I eventually nodded, the grin she shared could've fucking replaced the sun.

I was nothing more than a melted marshmallow as she kissed me softly. "I love you so fucking much, Jin. That hasn't changed."

"I know," I murmured. "Thank you for telling me like this." She nodded, eyes sparkling.

"Can we talk through the fun stuff now?" Ryloh whined. "You promised."

"Alright," Nala relented. "So, onto the sex stuff. I don't wanna put any pressure on you. Whatever you're down for, I'm probably down for. At least to try once." My brows hit my hairline.

"I have n- no limits," Ryloh proclaimed, to absolutely no one's surprise.

Timos went next, "I do not believe I will have qualms with sharing, Naliti. As far as preferences, I have never explored but I am open."

Was this shit choreographed?

They all turned to me expectantly. "No idea," I replied. "We can try, but I don't know how it'll go. You've seen my beast, he's insane, but he heels for her, so I don't fucking know." I was staring at a spot on the wall, anticipating judgment when I finally mustered the courage to witness their reactions. But no disdain or disappointment reflected back at me.

"We have a plan," Nala explained. "Wednesday night after my last date, we can go stay at Timos' where he's got the fancy warding that can contain you if need be. I wanna accept those two and it just seemed right to wait so I don't accidentally fall into heat before then. But, Jin," she clawed into my shoulders, "you don't have to join. I don't want you to feel pressured." I didn't, though. The only pressure was in regard to missing out.

"It would be way worse not being there," I said with a scratch of my chin. "I don't hate the idea, especially after seeing how much it lights you up."

Ryloh made a sweeping motion with his arms, and she rolled her eyes. Timos smacked him again and her resounding laugh rattled my erection. Nala's ease with the three of us here was doing things to me. She was effortlessly sharing affection without even trying. My nature even remained quiet.

"What else did I miss?" I questioned. Alright, so you're still a little needy, so what?

"We were intimate yesterday," the dragon dropped with a smug grin.

"What?!" Ryloh and I erupted.

Nala barked a surprised laugh.

Timoset shrugged as he pushed up his glasses. "No more secrets."

"I love Timos too, by the way," she all but slapped the scowl onto my face. Ryloh's too.

Timoset, once no more than a statue, was giddy and giggling. It was as unsettling as it was frustrating. The fucking boogey-male had become a cheerleading captain.

"Th- This really isn't fair, spice," the fae grumbled. "You've hardly spent as much time with me as you have with them."

"So, let's fix that. Can you play hooky tomorrow?"

And although I'd *never* fucking admit it aloud, didn't hate the idea of her spending time with the barnacle. Nala was happier with all of us. And he wasn't entirely terrible to me. Not anymore…

Huh.

If you would've told Gale the snail a month ago that she'd be sleeping with *three* dudes in her bed and didn't have sex with any of them, she would've laughed in your face.

However, I actually had spent my night draped across their randomly moving bodies since my bed wasn't large enough. Ryloh lost rock, paper, scissors, landing himself in the middle. Timos' hands were tangled in my curls, which would've been cute if it wasn't yanking chunks repeatedly. At least his thigh made a chilly pillow, the other two cooked me alive.

"This place feels like a shoebox," I grumbled. Then yawned, stretching my arms above my head before hopping up. Homie's morning message went unnoticed as we came to life on this sunny Tuesday. Surprisingly, Jin and Ry were getting along. Neither complained about the sleeping arrangements once.

"I'm already searching for larger," Ryloh proclaimed before jogging down my spiral staircase. His voice carried to add, "Since my contract expires tomorrow, I figured I should house-hunt." Jin and Timos were equally confused.

"What contract?" I yelled. There wasn't any reply as I followed Jin into my closet, changing into a bikini and cover up. Ryloh and I planned on accompanying Timos to Gro while he aided his siblings with their warding training. Although it was deemed Ry day, they still felt as though my dragon should remain near.

Abandoning the closet, I found the fae clanking upstairs with a tray of static underneath four coffees. "Saturnians are forced to sign agreements with the leader of the planet they immigrate to. My six years with her Highness was the lone reason I ran for duke; it was one of her terms. With its expiration tomorrow, I'm free to do as I please and resign. At least, until the Council gets ahold of me again." I frowned, peeved by the last part.

"As of tomorrow, I'm jobless. My lease also will expire. It's the first I've ever had the opportunity to select a role for myself. Perhaps I'll become th- the caretaker of our harem. I don't mind cleaning or babes..." Ryloh trailed off. "I would never trust a stranger, or *any* of you for that matter, to clean properly. Bacteria can get ya."

"I would support you as the stay-at-home parent if it were your desire. Take any role you please," Timos replied, and Jin nodded thoughtfully. Meanwhile, my jaw unhinged. *How were they being so casual about this conversation?* Despite our progress last night, I was stunned, men didn't act like where I was from. Timos noticed my shock and supplicated, "You deemed us your family last night, Naliti. We are now a mated family."

"Mating mob," Ryloh corrected, and I clapped my approval. "He's right, we're well off enough financially between us. My role as duke was a ruse—"

"Is that why you've fucking copied everything I've done?" Jin thundered.

Ryloh's face split into a smirk before he shrugged a single tattooed shoulder.

"Why did you do it?" Jin's frustration peaked as he looped his tie through with a white knuckled grip.

"It's what pissed the Queen *and you* off most. So yes, I might've duplicated some of your legislation. What of it? I'd be happy to duel, pupling. Or have you come to your senses and remembered I top the list of assassins in our galaxy?" Ryloh taunted with a flash of his headlights and a wide grin.

Why are you so attracted to him being a complete asshat? The serial killing wasn't deflecting from my attraction after the fae's offer to play house daddy.

"The duke drama is in the past now though, right, Ry?" I questioned, stepping between them. He nodded, so I deflected, asking, "Are you searching in Thalla? It's kind of a bummer we have to move. This is such a pretty area."

"This is a rental. Otherwise, we could attempt to purchase and expand," Timos said before taking a sip of his coffee.

"Truthfully, haven't looked because the homes aren't as sizable as they are in Bahasa or Ookea," Ryloh explained. "Remaining in Th- Thalla would likely require the purchase of multiple units, then expansion and renovations. It's not impossible but would require more effort."

My face fell, I didn't wish to be a heavier burden. Not on any of them. Least of all, Ry, who I hadn't given my heart to yet. "Don't worry about staying in Thalla then, having more space is most important. I'm sure whatever you find will work, Ry. No pressure."

Instead of the relief I anticipated seeing, his frown transformed into a grimace. "Don't, Nala. If it's your preference then we're going to live in Th- Thalla."

Jin chuckled, saying, "She doesn't like us going out of our way to please her. That's the main reason she contested Timoset's tailing. It's not because we stole her freedom."

I gasped loudly in offense.

"It's true," Jin poked. "I'm in your head, love. Just admit it. You're the one who said no more secrets between us."

"He's got you there, spice," Ryloh said as Timos grunted in agreement. *Unbelievable, they've already unified against you!*

Gro's side of the island was heavily forested, and its beaches reflected that. There were at least a dozen snakes slithering through the shallows or sunbathing in the sand. They seemed to keep to themselves, but I still kept an eye on the anaconda sized few just to be safe. At least there were no tigers.

The trio of dragons, one copper and two blue, were flying over the distant wavy depths. Osri and Persis, who were fraternal twins, only remained in prima forma long enough for introductions. Their resemblance was uncanny, but unlike Timos, they possessed darker eyes and variously shaded blue locks. Osri's a bright azure, while Persis had moody teal curls against their taupe skin. Both were more stoic than Timoset, too. Especially Persis, she only shared a grunt in greeting.

Not that I was much better when meeting my sibling's spouses. *Probably karmic retribution.* Once they were out of earshot, Ry explained most gods were emotionless. And how these two were centuries older than Timos. Fun fact: you could gauge a first-generation Drago's age by the initial of their first name. Apparently, Mama and Papa alphabetized their horde.

Anyway, Ryloh and I were tanning on some oversized boulders as they did their thing. He was tapping away on his shell-phone while I attempted to read one of the romance books purchased with Gabs. *Attempted,* being the key word.

The silence was eating me alive. There were no distractions. It was the first taste of peace I'd gotten since the ball dropped and my rose-colored goggles cracked. Sure, it was my own fault, I'd forced the truth out. But that didn't make it any less than a punt to the stomach. The catch was more than a hook.

Transformation. Heats. Dick magic. Scientific testing.

It was suffocating.

I was hoping Ry wouldn't take note of my sudden pallor. Of the way my chest was quaking. Of how I hadn't stopped fidgeting.

The hypnotic glimmering of the ocean wasn't a worthy deflection. Shockingly, neither were the magnificent dragons cutting through the clouds. And breathing exercises only left me dizzied. None of my attempts broached the layer of unease I felt each time I thought of my incredibly vivid dream of the silvery he who must never be named. It wasn't just Timos' face in those headshots-

"Who the fuck is that?" I couldn't help but stand. My anxiety attack shifted into a full-bodied zizz at the sight of an enormous horned creature in the distant depths.

Ryloh shielded his eyes with a pale palm and breathed, "Feck this."

"What is it? Or who?" I demanded, readjusting my oversized hat for a better look. *Sea monster?* It was definitely serpent-like. At least, the part we could see poking a couple dozen feet above the waterline. It was difficult to decipher its color from our distance, but its scales seemed reflective. The dragons lowered, flying parallel to its stag-like horned head to... *Chit-chat? Interesting.* When I spun back towards Ryloh, he didn't look pleased.

"He shouldn't be here," was all he murmured in explanation. Then plucked our towels from the rock, shoving them into my bag with an inhuman speed. I didn't have a chance to argue before we rifted back to the loft.

When I raised a brow, Ryloh sighed, tossing my tote to the floor. It only took several seconds for him to regret that and pick it up to hang from the back of a stool. "Ryloh!" I couldn't withhold my frustration as he avoided my gaze.

"Th- That was an Uktena," he muttered. Then raised his voice to normal as he strolled into the kitchen to ask, "Are you hungry? It's a bit l- late for l- lunch..." He clamped his mouth shut.

"An Uktena?"

"It's an enormous zoatalan snake with antlers," Ryloh said with his head tucked into the fridge as he rifled around. When he clocked my exasperation, he shrugged, tacking on, "Sorry, I th- thought it was obvious." He piled up the ingredients for wraps on the counter, humming to himself as if we weren't mid-freaking-conversation.

Why were there still omissions?

It was that moment, as inopportune as they come, when I remembered Gabs' tarot reading. How she'd all but predicted this. I shook my head as a giggle escaped, and Ryloh raised a brow before going back to lunch making.

After several more minutes of muted disbelief, the fragile leash around my compliance snapped. "We said no more secrets!" Ryloh's head canted in response, several messy inky locks falling into his face, a poor attempt at innocence. The realization of how well I knew the male already smacked me like a brick in the forehead. "It's not just you who can act as a lie detector, Ry. Spit it out."

"Y- You don't think I know you're also continuing to keep secrets? I felt your unease. You're spilling if I am." Ryloh disappeared, rifting to press his shirtless front to my nearly bare back. A warm fist decorated my neck, sending heat cascading down my spine. When my heart sped, I felt his following closely behind, our connection a physical thing.

Being skin to skin with Ryloh was adrenaline inducing. Dizzying when coupled with his stormy scent. "L- Let's make it a game," he purred. "Will you play nice, soulmate?"

My ego fought with a verbal response but couldn't keep my neck from bobbing.

"Good girl," he cooed, instantaneously leaving my skin gritty with goosebumps. Like sandpaper. "I think we should start with why you were panicked in Gro. If you answer honestly, I'll—"

"I want to touch you." We hadn't been playing fair, the current orgasm scoreboard was 7-0.

Ryloh chuckled into my ear. "Done. Go on then."

"Like this?" I squeaked, causing his grip around my throat to tighten. I became a wanton mess as my ass pressed against where he was stiff and ready.

"Don't pretend you aren't enjoying it just as much, Nala spice. Go on, the game's begun."

Swallowing the whimper at the tip of my tongue, I said lowly, "The catch is disconcerting."

"Heats?" he clarified. "Or the transformation?"

"All of it." My rapid breaths were no longer just from Ryloh's nearness. Panic ricocheted from every corner of my brain. It was there. On the tip of my tongue.

I had a big, biggie, BIG secret. One I'd been avoiding acknowledging at all costs. The instant I saw the beautiful male's dark gaze in his head-shot, awareness struck. *I knew him.* From his tanned skin to thick brows and that ancient nose. It might've only been a wet dream, but it felt so real. I still remembered how frigid his tongue was sliding against my skin.

The only difference between his photo and my recollection was the shade of his hair.

WD. Silvery he. Rainbow himbo.

Avexei.

It doesn't matter, you can't have him regardless. It was just a dream! Cut it out!

Ryloh's eyes narrowed as though he could sense the way I struggled to breathe. "T- Tell m- me. Right now, Nala."

I shook my head, his grip around my throat tightened. Instead of allowing a moan to flee, I accidentally allowed the worst of it out. "There was an eerily realistic sex dream before—*Shit.*"

Despite having caught myself, the damage was done. Ryloh spun me, his starry pupil sparking as he demanded, "Of who?" The fae wouldn't allow the shake of my head in refusal, gripping my chin he snarled, "N- No secrets."

Ugh. He's right. You gotta just...

"Avexei," I whispered shakily. It was the first time I'd said WD's name aloud. It tasted delicious on my lips. But there wasn't a chance to savor it, Ryloh didn't just release me, he staggered back a step. I spun to find his mouth gaping. Face paling. Sputtering. Limbs staticking here and there. He'd never looked more out of sorts. "You're scaring me, Ry."

"Wh- Wh- While on Earth?" He eventually rasped. I nodded, now frowning. He did a head shake, a cheek slap, then a knuckle *crack*. "That decides it then," he muttered before clearing his throat. Proclaiming at full volume as he closed the distance, "We aren't waiting until tomorrow, spice. N- No chance. The dragon and Uktena are better matched to duel for you than the pupling and I anywho."

"What are you talking about?" I tried, but he ignored me. The strings of my bikini were pulled as deft fingers unraveled my sloppy braid. "Are you saying what I think you're saying?" His answer was a bolt of static zapping my clit. That moan I held back earlier unleashed with a humiliatingly desperate vengeance.

"Th- The only question is how?" Ry muttered to himself, dropping his charcoal swim trunks. His pink pierced dick's bounce was equivalent to hypnosis. I couldn't even muster an ounce of embarrassment as he shared a pointed look.

"What the fuck is this? You agreed to wait until tomorrow!" We both spun, finding Jin. Home for lunch. Now growling.

Whoops.

It was such an inconvenience that I couldn't sense him.

I cackled and ran up the stairs as they started going at it. It was likely time to shower and start getting ready for the dinner with Zaire anyway.

"You never told me you worked as an assassin." We were heading to Ambrose, one of Zaire's many restaurants in Ookea. Ryloh matched my pace with an arm slung over my shoulders as we walked underneath the dragon's shadow. Admittedly, their attention felt less like babysitting today. *A lot more boyfriendy. Husband-y. Mate-y -nope, no, no. Scratch that.*

"It wasn't by choice initially; I was only eleven. The Council discovered that I uniquely excelled at both stealth and slaughtering. Th- They offered more than an orphan could dream. For a time, I prided myself in being the most sought-after executioner. I didn't remain on Saturn for long, constantly in transit from one hit to the next. My contractual release was six years back. Neptune is my first extended stay since childhood."

I frowned, unsure how to feel about the fact he was under contract to professionally *pew-pew. Or more accurately, zip-zap.* "So, you did that for two-hundred years?" He bobbed his head. "Was it out of obligation or pride? I can't tell from how you're talking."

"Th- That's because it was a bit of both by the time I retired," Ryloh explained. "I've been killing since I could walk, spice. My options were to either return to Saturn with nothing, or to travel the galaxy with more funds than I could spend. There were trainers and schooling I wouldn't have had access to otherwise. I don't regret it. The times have changed since though, it's become frowned upon for the Council to eliminate their foes."

For most, his nonchalance would've been a huge red flag. For me, though? I couldn't blame him. Not even a little bit. Between Ryloh's stutter and his unflinching transparency, I knew the male did whatever he had to do to survive. The blood wasn't on his hands, it was on the damned Council's.

Ry continued in his alien accent as I stewed on his younger behalf, "I was listless for most of it. I didn't believe there was a purpose to the random chaos of life for the overwhelming majority of mine. It was you who saved me, though, soulmate. I now look forward to my future. To our future. It's a sensation I was never acquainted with prior."

"I'm excited, too," I said, mirroring his swoony grin, despite discussing a macabre instance of child labor. This was typically how my conversations with him went. I'd already concluded Ryloh was the most morally grey of my mating mob. "So, magnificent master of murder, how many hits did you carry out?"

Ry chuckled and planted a peck on the top of my head. "I knew it wouldn't daunt you."

"Yeah, yeah, we share a lacking moral compass. Whatever." Waving a dismissive hand as the street we were on transitioned from burgundy shingled façades to the endless brick of Ookea. "I know you've counted. Tell me how many they forced you into slaying."

Ryloh let out a rumbly laugh before saying, "Three-thousand-thirty-three. The majority of whom deserved what they got."

Woof.

That's when I remembered who called the shots. "Timos' parents are responsible?"

"The Suprema more than the Supreme," Ryloh said. When he caught my furrowed brow, he explained, "Timoset's mother is known as the Suprema, his father as the Supreme, together the Supremae oversee the Council, our galaxy, everything. H- However, I never carried out a hit on his father's behalf, only his mother's. Her requests were admittedly sparse. There are thirteen Councilors, I was at each of their behest."

"So," I started, "you were their on-call murder puppet?" He nodded. "That's grim... Isn't Neptune's Queen also on the Council?"

Ryloh's entire demeanor changed with the mere mention of her. Which resurfaced a fresh wave of guilt in unknowingly calling him 'Lolly.' *Sheesh.* He clearly loathed her far more than Jin.

"Yes. However, I desired permanence on Neptune, and was forced to sign another contract in exchange... Sh- She has unfortunately d- delighted in wh- wholly owning m- me."

"What the fuck does that mean?" I snapped.

Gonna need to source a guide on how to murder a Titan.

"I- I..." Ryloh sighed. "I think you know," he finally replied with a full-bodied shudder. "I'd rather not discuss the specifics. It will ruin my appetite. I require an entire case of alcohol for th- that conversation with you."

Yep, she's deader than dead.

My heart squeezed painfully, with enough force to steal the air from my lungs. I snaked my arms around his middle and clung on despite the awkward walk it forced. "I'm so sorry, Ry, wish I could do something to fix it."

"Don't be. You have." A wicked grin pulled at his lips as he said, "Once your scent is smothering mine, I'll be permanently protected from unwanted advances. Lest they wish to deal with your wrath."

I didn't like that he was joking to deflect or the forced smile on his handsome face.

"I'm so lucky you're mine, Ry, even despite your beastie slip and the scuffling with Jin. I didn't anticipate caring for you this fast, but it feels right. Fuck fate, and the bond, I would've chosen you regardless. You've had my back when the others didn't."

Ryloh *tutted*, flicking my nose. "We have your back equally, the other two only have a worry-driven means of showing it. However, my superiority is obvious. Especially when compared with pupling. That I can agree with wholeheartedly."

I was tempted to share how he'd already grown on Jin from what I'd heard in the mind-meld, but said instead, "You'll be besties soon enough. I'm calling it now."

"Perhaps," Ryloh shrugged a shoulder, "if he sticks around."

Before I could ask what the Hell he was talking about, I caught sight of Min hunched over her phone outside a strip of brick businesses facing the ocean. "Doctor Min," I greeted, skipping over. Then I did the awkward, 'do we hug' dance. Settling on a one-armed tangle she reciprocated.

"Hey," she greeted wearing a white swishy midi-dress accentuating her lean frame. Her lavender hair was pulled back into an elaborate bun while her cheeks were dusted with a subtle daytime shimmer. My fresh face paired with black athleisure were a stark contrast. "You brought Cabbage and Drago, but where's Ji-Ji? I hoped I'd get to see him."

"Still at work dealing with the Gala drama," I explained, "he'll show if he can."

With a wave to the airborne dragon, we ambled through the heavy glass door, into what could only be described as Wonderland. Unlike Sirenuse's incredibly modern design, Ambrose could only be described as cottage-core. I didn't expect it from Zaire, not even a little bit.

The entire brick establishment was decked out in greenery. Tall grassy arched walls circled every table, each with an elaborately carved fountain at their center. While oversized trumpet vines covered the ceilings, their orange florals dangling overhead intertwined with twinkling fairy lights.

Despite the early dinner hour, we had to wait in line for the hostess. "You've wasted no time in accepting your tether," Min directed at Ryloh. "I hope you've at least better prepared her."

He frowned, but I squeezed his hand before rising to his defense. "Ry's been the most forthcoming. I don't think he's refused a single question of mine. You should save the scowl for your brother and the other. If they join us, that is. And again, Min, we haven't accepted yet," I said. She leaned over, taking an exaggerated whiff of my hair before frowning and shaking her head.

We were interrupted by a flustered and pimply teenage employee who led us to the outdoor patio overlooking endless teal waves. The tables still possessed their grassy walls and fountains, but the glittering ocean added another layer of beauty. Zaire, suited in all black, rose once he caught sight of me leading our party.

Then he fell right back down into his seat once sis came into view. The turnu was sputtering, clover eyes bugging out of his head. Min didn't skip a beat, cooing, "Surprise."

Ryloh sat closest to me, whereas Min and Zaire sat at our opposite, partially hidden by the fountain centerpiece. "You're not supposed to be here," the turnu finally rasped after we placed our drink orders with the whizzing robo-waiter.

"She's here because of me," I interjected. Zaire's shock transformed into confusion. "There's something fishy between you two. Since she's now my sister-in-mate, I offered her the opportunity to come in my place. We can grab another table if you'd rather have your privacy."

Min raised a lilac brow. "Do we require privacy, Z?"

"You shouldn't have fucking meddled," Zaire grumbled. Ryloh's static made a momentary appearance, until I discreetly kicked him under the table, effectively nullifying it.

"He's the one cursing at you. It's rude and unacceptable, you only had this twat's best in- interests i- in m- mind," Ryloh muttered in self-defense.

Zaire rolled his eyes while Min cackled. "He's got the most severe case of mating manacles I think I've ever seen!"

"As if you weren't insufferable enough before, Cabbage," Zaire said.

"Manacled I may be, but it's leagues above whatever tension-filled tangle you lot are currently trapped in," Ryloh replied. "For Nala to have noticed, I'm shocked your flirting didn't m- make the press."

Min's face fell, she heaved a sigh before revealing, "He's right. That's why I agreed to come. It's been too long since we'd last discussed our circumstances."

"There's nothing to discuss," Zaire all but growled back. Sending my brows to my hairline as Ryloh grabbed our drinks from the robot's tray. "You know it isn't wise to expose to strangers, especially not in such a public set—"

Ryloh threw up a warding bubble and our crowded surroundings went mute. Zaire's mood soured. He fidgeted with one of his locs as Min narrowed her gaze. "What's your next excuse? I don't care if they know," she clipped, and I had to withhold from snapping my fingers in support.

"Fine," Zaire growled, planting his elbows on the table. "You wish to reveal our secret? The one there's no solution for. Go ahead."

Too many cumbersome blinks were shared between the pair before I gave up on watching. I caught sight of the spiky amber dragon swimming in the distance in my peripheral and shared a wave. By the time I spun back toward the table, my lips were readied to break the muted tension.

"He's my amoroso," Min revealed. I shrieked, flicking my gaze between them. It was the last thing I expected, considering how rare the tethers supposedly were. Even Ryloh's maw fell agape. "Before Jin was born my mom was the Program guide to Zaire's, they became close, and were pregnant together. We've been around each other forever but the amoroso discovery came when Z turned sixteen." I couldn't help but wonder where the turnu's mom was abducted from on Earth, but it was an irrelevant question.

"Minny is thirteen years my senior, though. As you can imagine, it was as daunting as it was humiliating for her. My initial shift at five years was the result of us first coming into physical contact. Her hand brushed against mine accidentally and I turned into a Leviathan... Truthfully, I've always felt atypically drawn to her," Zaire revealed.

Min's cheeks were crimson as she said, "I didn't groom him, I swear. We've never even... Anyway, that was seventeen years ago. We've been dodging acceptance of our bond since."

"Fuck," I breathed.

"Th- The Council won't allow y- you to accept," Ryloh said before downing his drink and motioning for a passing bot to deliver another. Apparently the waiters could get through his ward. "Timoset could petition his father, but Mbombo's untethered when pissed. I doubt the Supreme would cross Zaire's whacked father, he's impossible to restrain once he gets into a tizzy."

Zaire nodded grimly. "I know, Dad's one of the many reasons we can't."

"The bonds are treasured aren't they? Wouldn't he understand?" I pressed.

"Mbombo and Zaire are the only pair of-age turnu. Only a human can g- guarantee another turnu child being born," Ryloh explained as a staring contest initiated between Romeo and Juliet. "Min's rarity adds further complexity. They could spawn a child more powerful than a Titan."

I rolled my eyes while taking a swig of my zon-von. *Screw the Council.*

Zaire pinched his dark brows. "Mbombo is one blocker. Likely the most severe, but there's also her career. Half of her podcast is of her own experiences dating humans. She'd lose her following after spending years —"

"I've told you I don't give a damn about abandoning the show! I still have enough private practice clients to cover my bills. I'd resign if you told me we could finally accept."

Zaire's demeanor chilled. "I could never hinder your success, Minny. It's one of the things I appreciate most about you... Besides, you still wouldn't be able to move here."

"I'd just be in Venus on weekdays! So what?" Min demanded.

I raised my hand to ask, "Why does Min seem more willing than you, Zaire?" It was needling me, honestly. She deserved a partner who would go to any lengths.

"I see no reason to pretend we can participate in more than we already do," Zaire snapped, his deep lilt rising several octaves.

Ryloh cackled. Once our collective gaze shifted, he explained, "If you're hooking up it's only tempting Min's heat. Tether acceptance or not, she holds far more prestige than you, Zaire Mensah. You're playing with fire." Min threw her hands up in an 'I told you so' towards her amoroso who shook his head in vehement denial.

"It would have already surfaced, we've been at it for over a decade," he argued.

"You barely held yourself back on Sunday," Min exclaimed, now seething. "It's not a fucking solution, Z. Please, I'm begging you. We have to figure this out."

Ryloh left the ward for the restroom, which surprisingly remained intact, abandoning me with the devastated pair. Their circumstances were difficult to digest. Not only the unrequited feelings and Min's dick-speration, but the Council's interference. "Maybe Timos could help," I offered. "He seems close to his dad."

"The Supreme and Suprema rule together," Min explained.

"They would not side with us," Zaire grumbled. "Mom told me the only solution is to mate with a pair of humans first, then perhaps we could petition the Council with the promise that we wouldn't have any of our own."

"You *told* her?" Min shrieked.

Zaire nodded grimly. "I had to. She found me in a state after your third date with Jared."

"Who's Jared?" I couldn't help but snoop.

"A human I got semi-serious with in the Program," Min replied with a sigh. "It didn't go anywhere. He wanted to mate with multiple femmes. It's not something I'm comfortable with."

"Is there artificial insemination? Because I couldn't even think about someone who wasn't one of mine. Like Zaire, no offense, but you're no more than a blob with locs. How do either of you intend to get juiced for anyone else?"

It seemed my question finally got through to Zaire, who groaned and threw his head back. "You're nothing more than a blob to me as well! The Council would have to consent to artificial insemination, which would force us to reveal the situation. They're obsessive when it comes to genetics."

"And Mbombo's on the Council. As soon as he finds out, he'll rampage. The damage from turnu frenzies are historically worse than vampires," Min supplicated.

"Let's involve my dragon," I said, searching the waves and coming up short.

As I spun back toward the table, I found Min standing behind me. Suddenly leaning over to stab the back of my hand with her fork. Naturally, I screamed.

Why are you constantly being sliced? The river of blood from my wounds tinted our fountain's waters red. She gave an apologetic shrug as Ryloh and Timos suddenly appeared. Both pissed as they stormed through the warding. Ryloh healed me since the suppressant was muting my magic, but their severe expressions remained.

"Sorry, I had to get your attention," Min said dismissively. Zaire's hackles rose in defense as my pair went apeshit. Smoke flurries filled the bubble as static bounced all over Ry.

"So, you harmed Nala?" Timos growled. I patted the empty seat beside mine and gripped his frigid hand once he was seated. *Probably not the best idea before asking for a favor, Min.*

<<*"Are you alright, love?"*>

"Great, my suppressant faded again," I muttered, firing off a mental reply to Jin. Ryloh and Timos exchanged a —*now*—weary glance. Ignoring their reaction, I explained, "Those two are fated and mated. Do you think there's any way they could accept their bond?"

Timos adjusted his spectacles as he shook his head. Min's shoulders fell and yanked mine along for the ride. "Not unless they swear to never procreate. Which would infuriate Mbombo, Zaire's father, who is deadly and impulsive enough without cause."

"Would the Council consider doing artificial insemination if your dad stepped in, Timos?"

"Perhaps. He could raise it to the other Councilors. He does have a weakness for amoroso tethers," Timos relented. "However, as I said, you both must be willing to forgo your own."

Min gave a pleading look to Zaire, who looked ten seconds from vomiting. "You can't do that for me, Minny. You're only one of two Leviathans."

"You sound like my dad, not my soulmate, Z," She rightfully clapped back. "I thought you felt the same. You claim to—"

"I have loved you for my entire existence, Minny! Of course, I feel the fucking same."

Min's gaze was on the fountain, lower lip trembling. It took her several blinks to leverage a seething lilt. "Then why are you refuting Timoset's offer? This is why I involved Nala, because you needed to hear how nonsensical your hesitation is from someone uninvolved."

Ryloh mumbled, "She's got y- you there."

"I'm worried about the repercussions," Zaire exclaimed. "How am I meant to be the male you deserve when sacrificing a career and family is a prerequisite?"

"I understand his hesitation," Timos said. "His father could eventually be placated with insemination, yes, but it would require decades of convincing. Even with Supremae backing. Mbombo has never possessed an amoroso, he lacks comprehension."

Min was losing her grip. I could see her struggle to keep from shifting as her french-manicure kept accidentally turning into black claws. "Every relationship requires sacrifice. It's my decision as to what's acceptable and what isn't," she hissed.

"*Period*," I said with a clap. "It's up to her, Zaire! Just say yes to the offer so you can bang already." Ryloh chuckled. Timos gave me a perplexed look, so I added, "They've been dancing around their tether for over a decade!"

After we placed our orders with a droid, there was a tense beat of silence. Min was glaring at the side of Zaire's face while he took a sip. Ryloh and Timos were ogling my cleavage so blatantly that I opened my mouth, at the ready to scold them.

Shockingly, Zaire interrupted the circus with, "Fine!"

Min lunged into his lap and kissed him with a squeal. When they withdrew, Zaire wasn't smiling though. "If you truly believe this is the best course of action then," he heaved a sigh, "I suppose Timoset should try."

As the duo started making out, I shifted my attention toward mine. "The Council seems like a bunch of fun suckers. Why are they obsessed with genetics? Is that how the PPP started abducting humans?"

"Most Titans are consumed with prestige, not genetics, Naliti. Magical superiority maintains the differentiation between Titans, gods, and the general population. There are rare outliers, such as Ryloh, who were coincidentally born with equivalent standing. However, the bulk were planned. Zaire is a relevant example. His father only procreated with mortals to ensure they were turnu."

"But what about gods, like you, with two classes? Your mom wasn't a dragon was she?"

Timos shook his head, readjusting his obsidian frames. "Demon. Three of my siblings are entirely demon, and there are a pair of us who are dual."

"You're half demon?!" I squawked, and he nodded as if it weren't a big deal. "Wait," I mused, "is that why you have a rose-gold tint to your eyes? And scales."

"I suppose," he replied.

Ryloh snorted. "You witnessed how peachy he was beside Osri and Persis, most dragons are—" Timos interrupted with a disapproving *cluck* of his tongue, the fae rolled his mismatched eyes before carrying on. "Anywho, the widespread mortal abducting began after the Queen molested one. She assaulted then slaughtered a human, and the resulting god she birthed was more prestigious than n- ninety-nine percent of the rest. Then the PPP was born and became all the rage."

"What crimes has this cunt *not* committed?" My voice was deadly. There would be no restraint if we ever met. Especially not once I had my powers.

"You mentioned the Queen's infatuation with you?" Timos raised as if they were discussing the weather. Ryloh gave a queasy nod, turning the dial on my fury to its maximum setting.

Zaire loudly cleared his throat. Once we spun toward them, he said, "She called us to her office after the Skerry. Jin was forced to tell her Nala was Timoset's and his to diffuse the situation. Seong's stirring the pot, I don't know why, but he suggested bringing Nala to the Palace for an interrogation."

Min growled, then picked up her phone with a scowl. *Hopefully giving her brother a hard time on our behalf.*

"What?" Timos demanded, suddenly furious.

Ryloh shook his head with a boisterous laugh. "The cunt is flailing because my contract ends at midnight."

Back at the loft, Timos rifted elsewhere to dial his father. While Jin was still on the clock. Ry and I were on the couch, my knees draped across his lap with a freshly popped bowl of corn, browsing the Holotube channels. When his phone vibrated, he answered with a smirk. "What's up?"

"We have a problem," a deep—*somehow*— incredibly familiar voice replied. "My fucking mother is downstairs." I knew Aphrodite was the daughter to her Horrific-ness, but a son? *Or they.* Whoever it was caused my heart to skip. More than once. *It's just your rumbly voice kink.*

"I've been screening her calls, so I'm n- not surprised. However, she can't get through the wards," Ryloh replied while harmless sparks zipped between us. "After midnight, her hold on me dissipates. Three more hours until my resignation letter is scheduled to send. As long as I remain within Timoset's protection, it should—"

"You're willing to risk Nala for three hours against the wrath of that psychopath?"

"N- No," Ryloh clipped. "Why can't *you* deal with her?"

"And say what?" The fae scrambled to shift the phone back to his ear. But I still caught, "That Nala's not just yours—"

What?!

Goosebumps slathered my skin. It felt like being embalmed. Not just the context, but the voice was driving me to madness. Not only did it feel inexplicably familiar, but my body was having a visceral reaction. *It's just a hot lilt, get your shit together!*

"Fine. I'll go down there and speak to her through the door, but I'm not leaving the wards," Ryloh eventually said before hanging up. "I must rid us of a Queen apparently, Na- Nala spice."

"I'm coming with." When he shook his head in refusal, I flung arms and legs around his middle, tossing popcorn everywhere in the process. Eliciting a curse from the clean freak, but he couldn't get rid of me now, I'd koala-ed with his ribs as my branch. "You're taking me with you. Please. If she can't break through Timos' fancy wards then what's the harm?"

Timoset reappeared by the entry wearing a grimace. "The cunt is downstairs."

I cackled, and even Ry cracked a smile. "C- C- Could you take Nala so I can get rid of her? I planned on remaining within the wards, don't worry," Ryloh said.

To my surprise, Timos shook his head. "Nala's presence will deter her. As will mine."

"Mine, too."

I peeked over Ry's shoulder, finding Jin home, looking a bit exhausted but otherwise fine. My heart swelled. We had a ways to go, but this progress was more than promising. Squeezing Ryloh around the middle, I said, "No more facing the bad without us, okay?"

Ryloh crashed his lips to mine for what could've been a sweltering kiss if Jin hadn't loudly cleared his throat. I climbed down, settling on a hand hold as Ry led the way down to the lobby. By the time our feet hit the landing, I wasn't sure which of us was strangling with more force.

The femme on the other end of my glassed entrance could've been a twin to my abductor. Their milky complexions, baby blues, and upturned noses were identical. The only discernible difference was the Queen had straight hair... Which was changing like a mood ring.

Each pin-straight strand shifted from a plethora of gloomy shades to a bright pink the instant her sparkly eyes landed on Ryloh. She made sure to reposition her nearly transparent gown to expose a shoulder, and by some fucking miracle, I managed to keep an innocent look on my face through the entire ordeal.

"So, you *have* tethered to this human then, Lolly?" *Ugh*. My stomach sank. And not just from how her voice tinkled like an eerie chime. Or the disgust on her face as she spat 'human.' The kicker was the nickname I accidentally used, that skewered me right through the gut.

"I have," Ry replied with a bored expression. It was times like these I wished we already shared the mind-meld. I would've been hootin' and hollerin' in his brain with pride. Settling on a squish of his hand felt mediocre.

I didn't know what this wench was responsible for yet. But my hatred seemed validated. Plus, she was undressing him with her eyes. Making my skin crawl.

Jealousy was not fun. Once strangers, we'd become well-acquainted since my arrival. I found it worse than normal anxiousness. It had created a festering pit in the bottom of my soul. Despite knowing Ryloh wanted less than nothing to do with her, my envy raged.

She swished up to the glass, causing Timos and Jin to step up to our sides. *Guard mode activated*. It was difficult to keep my composure as their hackles lifted.

The only tell the Queen was equally perturbed was the rapid shift of her hair. A chilling smile painted across her lips as she eyed me from head to toe. There wasn't much to see, I was in the same athletic set as earlier with my hair in its typical unbound ringlets, but the tyrant scrutinized as if I were the Mona Lisa.

The tension among my gang peaked. Smoke plumes danced as the air grew suffocatingly thicker with live static. Jin growled, eliciting a giggle from our uninvited guest. "Fated, *hmm*? Rare. If not impossible. Very well then, Lolly," she backed a step, wearing the same terrifying smile. "I look forward to seeing how she fares in testing."

"Are you idiotic enough to make threats in my presence, Imera?" Timoset demanded. That name didn't suit her. *She deserved to go by something awful… Like Molester*.

Molester's laugh was Tinkerbell reminiscent, it made her seem eviler. "Only stating the obvious, Timoset. Her prestige will garner special attention."

The panic I'd had at the beach resurfaced with a vengeance. My lone grip on reality was the warmth from Ryloh's hand. I was struggling to inflate my lungs when Jin took my free palm, it helped, but not by much.

When her eyes perused Ryloh's chest —*again*—, a growl burst from my chest.

Molester painted a saccharine grin. "No need to get attached to this one. It's doubtful a measly mortal like her will survive what's to come."

Snarls echoed.

I knew this creature was as old as literal dirt and could probably murder me with a thought. However, none of that logic deflated my emotional upheaval. I couldn't sit idly and allow the males to keep coming to my defense, either. *You're no princess. You're a fighter. Fucking act like it, Nala!*

It was just me and her as I stepped forward to taunt. "Honestly, I'm not sure what's more pathetic. The way you're standing out there desperately pining after *my* amoroso, or, how you aren't stacking up against a puny mortal! I can see why fate didn't find you worthy!"

Ryloh barked a laugh while Jin pulled me back from the window.

"How dare you, scum?" she shrieked, recoiling. My grin was immovable. As was Ry's.

"Leave, Imera," Timos commanded, his voice all dragon gravel. There was no need to peek, I assumed he pulled a half shift. "You are more fragile than Nala at present." *Welp. That proves she's not indestructible.*

"Y- Y- You heard him," Ryloh said, then slammed his eyes shut with a clench to his jaw. I squeezed his hand in support.

Jin gripped Timos' shoulder to keep him back as our suicidal guest slammed her palms against the glass door. Then dragged her nails down with a *screech*. "Stammering again, I see. How pathetic," the cunt taunted.

My initial shock spiraled into a tornado of rage. It wasn't just theirs either, this trash came to *my* house and threatened *my* fucking family. Insinuating my untimely demise?! Then making fun of my man?! The one she *wanted* to keep for herself?!

She asked for the bumpkin to surface.

"Don't you DARE call Ry pathetic, he's worth a million of you!"

The frustrated flush I'd developed became an inferno. Despite standing underneath a frigid blast of air con, I was sweating. *Shit, your skin is actually boiling.* Jin released me with a yelp. When my gaze flicked to where Ryloh and I were still intertwined, there were sparks.

Static.

It wasn't just our hands. I was covered in bolts. From elbows-to-fingertips and knees-to-toes, lightning swarmed. Instead of burning me as it once had, it was now no more than a tingle. Ryloh looked thrilled. The awe in his gaze palpable, and I couldn't help but mirror his grin.

"How?" Timos breathed.

A wretched cackle rattling the glass ripped us back to our present conundrum.

"Just wait until the Council hears!" The poison lacing her threat extinguished my static. Coupled with my trifecta's various looks of unease, I knew we'd unlocked a new catch. This one with a tangible fear factor.

The only positive was she rifted out shortly after blowing a kiss to Ryloh, who shuddered. We stomped back upstairs in complete silence. The worst part was that I didn't fully understand the severity. *And you're questioning whether they'll be truthful...*

Once the door clicked shut behind Jin, Ryloh's phone started buzzing. He didn't put it on speaker this time, hiding in my laundry closet. It was deflating because I needed him to unwrap the static transference. None of that made sense. I thought we had to accept our bond or whatever.

"So," I started, unsure how to best finagle answers. Although we agreed to no more secrets, there were lines this pair hadn't yet crossed. *Ry's definitely the most forthcoming.*

"She thinks Ryloh is more trustworthy than we are, Timoset," Jin tattled in a huff, crossing his suited arms. "Just ask what you want to ask, Nala," he clipped.

I gawked, cheeks heating. Forgetting the mind-meld's existence was a horrid habit I needed to break. Timos' coppery wings shook in agitation as the lines in his handsome face deepened. *You gotta come up with something, genius.*

"*Uhm,*" I fidgeted as my voice shook, "so, this seems pretty bad. Both the static and her threats."

"No shit," Jin muttered.

Timos' eyes were sunny slits as he clipped, "I hoped we could avoid her notice until your transformation settled." My shoulders fell. "She has likely already rung my mother, no doubt."

"Your mom wouldn't protect us?" I asked with a frown.

Ryloh finally emerged from the closet to interject, "Th- The Suprema doesn't play favorites. Not even to her own children, not since Dmitri betrayed her with Malice in the last war. The Council just joined the list of those we must shield you from." He turned toward Timos to ask, "H- Have you called your uncle for possible immunity?"

"Who's Dmitri?" I questioned.

"Timoset's older brother and Malice's amoroso. He's the only evil drag-on." *Interesting.* D meant he was fourth born.

"Uncle Olo is aware," Timos grumbled. "As is my father."

"Vex said the wench had Seong hiding in the neighbor's bush filming," Ryloh revealed on a sigh. "Th- They have evidence of Nala's static on video."

I gulped. My gaze ping-ponging from one handsome stressed expression to the next.

"Is there something you'd like to fucking share?" Jin snapped. "I caught them naked together at lunch—" My squeak of dismay was swallowed by Ryloh's howling laugh.

When Timos filled the room with a chorus of echoing growls, I shouted, "Nothing happened."

"How did you fucking manifest static then?" the dragon rightfully demanded. Ryloh and I both shrugged, eliciting a louder rattle from his chest.

"I'm just a freak," I cried. "The way that cunt was taunting us got my blood pumping, and I dunno, one second I felt hot. The next, I just sparked up!" Jin and Timos' gazes darted between Ryloh and I. The fae was looking mighty guilty so I emphasized, "*We haven't!*"

It was exhausting having to play defense when we needed to prioritize offense. This wasn't trust. Sure, we stood side by side downstairs, but these accusations took us ten paces backward. The chaos was surfacing my childhood trauma. Distrust was rampant among my siblings and me. Just as it was between Isaiah and me. Also, Andy… *Huh.*

Definite pattern there.

Taking a breath, I attempted to reset. *Prioritize, then conquer, Nala.*

Starting with Ryloh, I gave him a kiss on the cheek and a whispered, "I'm proud of how you stuck up for yourself, Ry." The genuine joy reflected back softened his sharp features. He snaked an arm around my middle, but it wasn't appropriate for the next part.

Backing a step, I raised my arms over my head in preparation for the chaos that would likely ensue. The males were staring back with varying degrees of perplexity. "I know I'm to blame for this mess, so I'll share my final secret first." Heaving a sigh, I revealed the topic I'd been avoiding most, "When I was on Earth, there was a dream. Maybe even more than one, I'm not totally sure, but it starred Avexei. Ryloh found out earlier and his reaction made me realize it was a bigger deal than I knew initially—"

"Are you fucking kidding me?" Timos roared, forcing Ryloh to push him back a step.

Jin was too devastated to string together a sentence, not only could I physically feel his disappointment, because of the lapse in suppressant, but he deflated instantly. Limbs falling onto the couch in an unnatural heap.

"So," Ryloh said, his eyes darting between their panic, "c- can I tell her now? She's right, we need to air out. We not only have Malice to contend with, but the Council."

"Would you like to remain tethered to Yu-Jin?" Timos snapped at me, and I recoiled. *Why would he even ask that?* I chewed on my lip as our eyes fell on my squishy boy scout.

<<*"Because you'll lose me if you have a tether with Avexei. We're not fated, love. We're breakable. You can't keep four of us, the Council will clip our bond."*> *Jin's dour mood suddenly made a lot more sense.*

That wasn't happening.

Fuck fate, Yu-Jin Rapax was mine. Nothing and no one would change that. Especially not a stranger. Even if I couldn't physically feel our tether, like with the others, we were *meant* to be. "Jin, we're a packaged deal, babe. You don't need to worry," I said firmly, holding his plum teary gaze and climbing into his lap. The tension in his broad shoulders waned when I pressed a peck to his lips. "Now, can you please calmly explain why you're edgy over a dream? You're acting as though this is worse than the static."

Ryloh and Timos mutely faced off until I huffed for them to get on with it.

"It's worse," Ryloh said, taking the seat nearest ours and gripping my ankle. "Destiny typically doesn't take our desires into account, Nala spice. Anything could happen in that regard."

Jin looked near collapse despite how I tightened my grip around his neck. "The thought of my life without you is unfathomable. I mean it." His chest heaved underneath me, a sigh leaving on exhalation before he painted a forced smile. At least he was himself, there were no Siarc tells rising to the surface. It was likely the best we'd get, so I spun toward

Timos raising our next pressing issue. "Are we safe here? What if she comes back with more Titan friends in tow?"

"Unlikely. Most despise her," Ryloh explained.

"We must remain through your date tomorrow," Timos tacked on. "Otherwise, I would suggest we temporarily relocate to Uru. At least until your transformation has settled."

Jin tugged on a curl, recapturing my attention to say, "You shouldn't fear her. Timoset will keep you safe. Neptune's still your home, Nala."

"No," shaking my head, I reasoned, "you three are my home. If we've gotta ditch and skip out of town, we should. I can't stomach the idea of her doing something to Ryloh again."

Timoset's rage resurfaced. "Again?" Ryloh gave a grim nod to the question. Eliciting a full-bodied shudder from all of us. "Perhaps we should consider permanent relocation," the dragon eventually replied with a scratch to the back of his neck. "Although it would arguably benefit to keep a close watch on Imera."

<<*"I would leave my role as duke if we had to leave Neptune."*>

Jin's position hadn't crossed my mind. --*"I wouldn't want you to."*-

"We can't leave," I grumbled, "Jin loves being duke and he's improved so many lives. We're just going to have to fight back. The Queen. The Council. The scientists or whatever." I waved dismissively. "However, to do that, we can't have any more omissions. So, what's left? What haven't you told me?"

"My father and uncle have been aware of your existence for some time, Naliti. That is why he sent Osri and Persis to take my position so quickly. Father is attempting to shield you from testing. However, it will be temporary. There is no escaping it."

Fan-fucking-tastic.

"I haven't purposely hidden anything else," Jin said, "but I did exaggerate the closeness to my family." The rest of us exchanged a weary glance because Zaire had asked us to keep their secret. But I didn't want to. This needed to be the final trust conversation. I was sick and tired of having them. Ryloh gave a nod in encouragement.

"Jin, you should know, Zaire and Min are together. They asked Timos to talk to his dad on their behalf." There, enough, but not everything. Min and Zaire could fill in the gaps.

"Fuck," he mumbled, staring at the painted brick wall behind me in a daze while his brain flitted through the evidence of their secret romance.

"My final omission is that if you inherit dragon fire, the target on our backs shall worsen in severity. It is highly unlikely, but it has haunted my thoughts," Timos added with a frown. "I do not wish to cause you more strife, Naliti."

I kept my expression aloof, but internally celebrated. Possessing those bleached icy flames seemed enticing. Regardless of the stipulations. *Bet you could take down Molester!*

Ryloh squeezed my ankle, taking the seat beside Jin on the sofa. "I'm best friends with Vex. Have been for nearly thirty-years now." Earning himself a pair of gasps from the others. "And," Ryloh drawled for dramatic effect, "I've dreamt of you since you were born, spice. It was only snippets here and there, but it's how I came to Neptune. The same goes for Vex. We were both reanimated, and it's common to have prophetic visions after death."

I sputtered in shock.

My mind unraveled like a spool on a sewing machine at full-speed.

Ryloh kept bobbing his head. As though it would help me digest the crazy. "It- It's the true cause behind my beast's slip when we met."

Thirty years? That's over ten-thousand dreams! Heavy spook spook.

He also included WD.

My breath caught and I hoped they wouldn't raise it.

Somehow, they didn't. Jin was lost to his sibling drama, mostly frustrations with his brother that I wholeheartedly mirrored. The others were equally lost to their thoughts.

The silence was thick as the moons glittered through my oversized windows. Jin's fingers were drawing circles on my hips while Ryloh massaged my feet, both seemingly quelled. Unlike the dragon who was continuing to pace from one end of the living room to the other. Wings spreading every now and then.

"I should have known after Avexei referred to you as 'Lo-Lo'," Timos broke our calm to accuse with a pointer.

My morning was decided prior to Molester's surprise appearance, and I was glad for it.

The males were suspicious when we went on a market spree after dinner last night, but eventually let it go. Since we had two reasons to celebrate, I rose with the sun, and thankfully no one stirred.

After the Queen drama settled, I battered the trio with questions regarding the Council. They were forthcoming, but every fresh piece of information was more unnerving than the last. The most prevalent take-away being we were facing a plethora of unknowns.

They didn't expand on what testing entailed, and I was too chicken shit to press.

Celebrating our wins became a requirement to counteract the scary, we needed the opportunity to breathe together. And with the dark cloud circling my final date tonight, I knew it would require forceful inter-vention.

Lucky for the Musketeers, they snagged a chef. Throwing ingredients together was one of my favorite distractions. Although the cooking experi-ence was lackluster without a playlist blasting, I made do. By 8:00am the spread filled the entire kitchen island; fresh biscuits and gravy, hashbrowns, shakshuka style eggs, etc. There were two separate cakes, one for Ry, the other for Timos, flavored like french toast and topped with fresh berries spelling out their names.

I was cleaning the mess when Homie proclaimed, "Your guests have awoken, Nala." Three sets of heavy-footed steps pounding on the iron before a collection of gasps.

My grin stretched longer than a bargepole as I spun to find them shirtless too. Except for Timos, but it was okay, we would work our way up to his comfort. "Where's *my* cake?" Jin interrupted, crestfallen. Instantaneously stealing my joy with his grimace.

"You didn't retire," I squeaked. "Didn't the banner make it obvious?" I spent an hour cutting out letters from printer paper to spell, 'Happy Retirement,' and strung them across the kitchen cabinets. But the pang of guilt was inescapable. Despite having spent hours and hours on this breakfast party, the regret for not making Jin a separate pity cake cleaved through my happiness. *You knew today would be extra tough on him.*

I, too, was emotionally fragile, though. More so than I'd ever admit aloud. Between the multidimensional catches and the grimness of our looming reality, it was going to be an overly sensitive day.

Ryloh pulled me in for a hug. Then Timos. I was near tears by the time the Siarc's salty scent hit my nostrils. "I'm so sorry, Jin," I murmured into his chest, "this wasn't to make you feel left out." When my voice cracked, Timos ripped me away.

"Hey!" Jin protested, but the dragon wasn't having it. He carried me over to the couch, gently plopping me down before kneeling at my feet so we were eye-to-coppery-eye.

"Are you alright, Naliti?" Timos tucked a stray curl behind my ear as his softened expression searched mine. I shrugged, incapable of voicing my overwhelm without a sob breaking free.

<<*"I love you, Nala. I didn't mean to give you a hard time, I'm so sorry."*>

Jin's disappointment was suffocating. The awareness of his intent was buried deep, beneath layers and layers of emotional turmoil. No matter what these males spewed from their lips, they couldn't hide their real feelings. Especially not Jin, the Cancer was the easiest to read, fated foo foo or not.

"Perhaps you should think before you speak, pupling," Ryloh jibed, piling a plate high.

Timos smashed me against his chest when my first tear fell.

"Fuck." The couch dipped as Jin landed beside us. "Please don't cry. I'm just stressed out. It was a stupid thing to blurt, I'm sorry, Nala. I don't need a cake. Please forgive me."

Timos was refraining from taking physical action, keeping me swallowed by his cool embrace, but I knew he was likely glowering. Ryloh abandoned his food to plant a kiss atop my head. Their care only instigated further weeps.

I felt bad for my behavior.

The tears poured like a waterfall after a storm. Before I knew it, my entire body was shaking as a wail tore through my chest. It wasn't my intent to upset Jin further, but no matter how many attempts I made to quit, the worse my cries became.

The Council was after me.

Because you're a freak. Always have been. Always will be.

The Queen was after Ryloh.

She traumatized him!

The transformation would be Hell.

Because nothing gained ever comes easy —

"Nala, please, love," Jin murmured, pulling my lower half into his lap as Timos clung onto my upper. "Didn't mean to upset you. I feel so fucking terrible. Please." His voice was little more than a croak, worsening my guilt.

"I swear to Karma, Y- Y- Yu-Jin, if you ever make her cry again, I'm going to fry you. What were you th- thinking?" Ryloh snapped. Eliciting a growl from Timos.

Of course, they're fighting now, just the cherry atop of this crap sundae.

"I didn't fucking mean to, it just slipped!"

Fifty paces backward. All progress lost. Will they ever get along?

Clamping my eyes tight, I attempted to slow my erratic breaths as the males erupted. *Space. You need a break, Nala. Away from them.*

It was vital.

I craved to disappear. To hide. The opportunity to quell without them breathing down my neck. This morning was *for them* because they've given up so much.

Yet, it became about me instead.

You're such a terrible partner. The cresting wave of self-loathing was inescapable. Why can't they just leave you alone to cry it out for ten minutes?

You were alone all morning, and that wasn't enough?

Maybe I wasn't made for relationships.

Jin attempted reaching me via our mind-meld, but it was too late, the hyper fixation rooted.

I just wanted to be alone.

It had been so long. After nearly a decade with unlimited privacy, I hadn't realized how much I'd taken peace and quiet for granted. How much sharing myself could hurt. There was an unshakeable desire to tear my heart from my chest. To scamper back into my too small shell.

A foreign sensation overcame my senses. There was a shift in the air. Timos' frigid chest was no longer pressed to my wet cheek. Jin's warm arms disappeared. The couch wasn't under my bum. I cracked an eye to find I'd made it to the bathroom. *AKA your official hidey hole.* Before processing the fact that I'd very much just rifted myself upstairs, I slammed and locked the door, sliding down to lay against the tiles in a heap.

They left me be.

Hours likely passed as I doled out self-loathing and punishment. Wallowing in my circumstances. In how I wished to actually disappear. Their spat dissipated forever ago, and I hadn't heard a peep since.

There was nothing left of me, I was empty.

The heavy ache of my limbs when finally plucking myself from the tiles was painful.

Quietly as possible, I peered into my bedroom with a prayer to the universe that no one would be there. By some miracle, they weren't. My next stop to somewhat recollect was the closet, but I barely made it when Jin's arms circled me around the middle and yanked me against his chest. He hadn't gone to work then.

Which tempted further weeps as he trembled while holding me tight. *You clearly destroyed Jin, you monster.*

However, my internal chiding went unnoticed, I was too spent to form a reaction. "Fuck, Nala. I hate myself for hurting you," he choked, planting sloppy tear filled kisses wherever he could reach. "I'm so fucking sorry."

It wasn't about Jin, not entirely, I didn't mean to incite his guilt. I didn't mean to worsen our mess. I wanted to scream it at the top of my lungs. To crack open my chest to show him the truth.

Not even a breath left my lips.

That was the thing about anxiety, depression, and stress, the combination rendered me a ghost. I never knew when an episode would rear its ugly head. It was a struggle to keep contained on Earth. A miracle I hadn't relapsed sooner. The others were stomping up the stairs, but I couldn't face them either. My eyes remained firmly planted on the rug as Jin continued his unrequited affection.

Which was smothering.

I loathed myself for feeling that way, too. Jin deserved better.

"N- Na- Nala," Ryloh used the gentlest tone I'd ever heard from him, "please talk to us. What do you need? How can we help fix this?"

I shook my head.

There's no fixing you.

<<*"There's nothing wrong with you, my love. I know this is a mess. Please forgive me."*>

My gaze remained glued to the rug.

Jin rasped with a sniffle, "I pushed her over the edge."

"Each of us are at fault. If we would have discussed the truth sooner, she would not have reacted so poorly. I apologize Naliti, it was a short-sighted attempt to protect you."

"I'm sorry too, N- Nala spice," Ryloh murmured.

Nothing. I felt nothing as I shook myself out of Jin's arms. Nothing but exhaustion as I shimmied out of my pajamas and into a dress I hardly looked at before sliding it over my head. Nothing as they peered into the closet with various expressions of concern. Thankfully, I didn't physically feel terrible anymore thanks to the lacking suppressant.

But mentally, I was still in shambles.

"Leave." It was the only thing I could voice. Even so, it was little more than a whisper. When they stared back in shock, I repeated myself. Three frowns returned. So, I tried again, and again. Until I was choking on fresh tears and swaying.

"We can't," Ryloh finally croaked. "At least, *I* can't l- l- leave you like this. You were in that bathroom for two hours, N- Nala. After spending Karma knows how long in the kitchen attempting to do something nice for us. I'm sorry to refuse your wishes, but I cannot fathom walking away from you."

"It's not up to you."

There was probably half-a-day left to fill with self-pity before I had to go on another stupid date. This one likely the- *You can't even broach that topic yet, Nala.* I'd been successfully avoiding it for weeks, what were a few more hours?

"Leave," I whisper-shouted as they exchanged a wordless blink. Jin looked the most devastated, but I was too hollow and overextended to comfort him.

"We'll be downstairs, alright?" Jin offered weakly and I nodded.

When they finally disappeared, I pulled my mess of hair back with a sniffle and began cleaning obsessively.

It wasn't my first breakdown, I was a veteran, but it was the worst in years.

By the time I'd finished scrubbing every inch of the loft, I'd almost returned to myself. Thankfully, my swelling faded quickly, eyes and vocals were restored when I mustered the courage to ring Jin at 2:55pm. Instead of answering, he rifted in, scaring me half to death. My phone landed in a corner with a *crack* as his body suffocated mine. "I'm so sorry, Nala," he said, tightening his hold.

"It's okay, I forgive you. It wasn't you, Jin," I said, hugging him back. "I didn't mean to escalate past the point of return. It just sorta happened."

Jin's heavy breaths turned to sobs as we clung on. "I love you so much," he sighed into my hair. "I didn't mean to, Nala. I really didn't even think before I said it —"

"*Shh*. It's alright, Yu-Jin Rapax, I know. I'm sorry I made it worse," I said, clawing into his back. "I love you too, that hasn't changed."

The regret for my overreaction was tugging on my gut and souring my resolve. Tempting another freak out. Tempting another teary fit... Except, it didn't feel as tough to refrain this go around. Perhaps it was because I cried myself numb, but I knew the truth.

I needed them. Jin's warm embrace was reattaching my shattered pieces. Aloneness was no longer the answer. *You need to remember that for next time.*

<<*"That's why I didn't wish to leave your side, love. We're the same, remember? Your feelings are mine. You don't have to be alone anymore, not ever."*>

"Thank you for loving me when I'm a chaotic mess, Jin," I murmured into his chest. "For understanding enough to give me space despite knowing it wasn't the right move." He heaved a sigh against my cheek.

"Always."

I might've reverted to old habits, but I could still pick myself up and try again.

Or fake it till you make it.

"Bugger off, pupling," Ryloh grumbled. "It's m- my turn." I was yanked into a warmer pair of arms. "Please don't ever force us out of sight again, Nala spice. It was a nightmare keeping the dragon from coming up." A chuckle escaped.

Timos grunted from before I was passed to his frigid embrace next. "I worried you might attempt to run," he admitted.

My heart pinched as I met his teary copper gaze. "I wasn't going to run." *Where would you even run to?* The idea of living without them was ulcer inducing. As I met their varied blurred gazes, it dawned on me.

They were all I had. All that mattered. They were my purpose, fated fuckery or not.

"I could never live without you. Any of you. Not anymore," I breathed. The admission freed me from the last of the residual guilt.

You're allowed to fuck up and panic sometimes.

Motioning for them to sit on the couch, I intended to lay across their laps like Cleopatra would. It had to be a mood booster. However, Ryloh refused with a shake of his head to say, "Once you've eaten, we're heading out to practice y- your static."

"Really?!"

"You haven't left the house, depressed little mouse. Might as well train you while we're outside. I'd feel much better knowing you can defend yourself if need be," he replied mirroring my smile.

The training session was like therapy for the soul. Static only required focus and trust. It was initially difficult to believe in magic's simplicity but felt natural once I let go of those notions. After the first hour of basics, Ryloh's guidance shifted to taunting, which was my preferred learning style. Each time I'd successfully wield a three-dimensional object made of bolts; my worries shrank. At least they had *temporarily*.

Returning to the loft to get ready wiped that slate.

I'd successfully distracted myself from the looming date but couldn't any longer.

Since avoiding the suppressant, Jin's rampant stress was mine. Although I still couldn't sense his physical presence, like with Ryloh and Timoset, his emotional turmoil was unavoidable. Quelling him was futile, too. Especially once he glimpsed the pleather, skintight, midi dress Ry insisted I wear.

Leaving was an ordeal; I wanted to walk, but they refused for safety reasons. So, we rifted.

The Thallan restaurant was oddly named 'Nightingale's,' and nearby, if its lavender painted street had anything to say. Goodbyes took double the time and effort, Timos and Jin equally clinging. Eventually, an annoyed Ry tore me from the tenth hug, shoving me through the revolving doors.

If I picked a daily favorite, Ry would be today's winner. Not only did he know how to help me bounce back after the episode but remained cool as a cucumber. He was the lone reason I'd laughed since breakfast, and I was more than appreciative. Was it love yet? No, but our foundations were solid. Trust came easiest with Ryloh, and as much as I loathed to think it, Jin and Timos were lagging.

My heels echoed against the mosaic tile floors as I gawked at the interior of the fancy restaurant doubling as a library. Every inch was decorated in a Versailles reminiscent style, from the carved pillared columns to the domed tiled ceilings. Classical art decorated the walls, and unlike the lilac exterior, the interior was golden and cream. The center of the first floor was arranged for dining, whereas the second story was solely dedicated to reading with loungers and worktables; where many had noses tucked into books.

The blended scents of garlic and parchment swarmed as I ambled toward the bar. Since it was my final, first date *ever,* I arrived early to enjoy a drink alone. *You know, for a goodbye toast to singledom.* The halter dress wearing, attractive, bartender had gills painting each side of her neck like Aphrodite, but I still didn't have a clue as to which subspecies either were.

After ordering, my eyes darted back to ogling our gorgeous surroundings. It felt Earthly in here. *Recognizable, maybe? You have gone to Paris twice.*

While sipping on my zon-von, I caught a woman with a blonde bob glaring in my direction, she was perched at the other end of the bar. Her low-cut obsidian top was cute, but it seemed to be the only nice thing about her.

Initially, I thought her mean mugging was just a figment of my imagination, that perhaps she had a bad case of RBF. However, after ten minutes, her eyes were still boring with enough hatred to prickle my neck with unease.

I ignored her, though.

There already were too many neurons firing off in my noggin. *No vacancy for disgruntled strangers.* I couldn't show my cards at the loft, but here? Without my mob's presence? The wave of unease finally crested because I was drawn to Avexeidros. Avexei. *No, Vex.*

Just the name left my entire body shivering like I'd been tossed into an igloo naked.

I was fretting over my lacking self-control, despite the changes and progress I'd made thus far, this morning proved that old habits die hard. Then there was the destined droll, because I couldn't deny how it drew me to Ryloh, would the same happen with Vex?

Two of my existing were closely tied to this male, and Jin also admitted to not having any grievances. It wasn't them preventing a fourth, it was the Council. The idea that a bunch of old farts were calling the shots was sparking a rebellious craving.

But it wasn't in the cards. If I gave in, it would only lead to suffering. No matter how many scenarios I voiced last night, the males made it crystal clear: me + four = impossible. Only a handful of Titans possessed four or more tethers, and all of them were fated, and thus, irreversible.

What if you lose Jin?

The thought left me struggling for air. Yu-Jin Rapax was my first love. I couldn't let him go. He was an emotional hurricane sometimes, but so was I. *You can do this, Nala. You can be nice without flirting.*

In theory, sure…

In practice, not so sure. Not when the wet dream of Vex's silvery head between my legs remained at the tip of my consciousness. How I could feel the press of his tongue. Now, absolutely certain, that I hadn't imagined his cooler temperature when recollections struck.

I was swimming in musings when the sour blonde stood in my peripheral. Her glowering in my direction was still going strong. There was no familiarity whatsoever.

However, when she made her way over drink in hand, and proceeded to tilt, then dump, said glass onto my lap, I knew the hatred was intentional. Thankfully, the liquid slipped right off my pleather dress as I stood. Clearly, fate struck again with Ry and his forced fashion.

Bob gal tilted her head, meeting my taller gaze to sneer, "You're nothing more than a mediocre slut. I can't believe you stole Chadwick from me!"

Oh-ho-ho, no! I was *not* expecting that. Laughter struck, a full body twist and shout. *She can't be serious! Oh, my tits. Really?*

"I don't even know who you are, hon! You know nothing about me either, given I have less than zero interest in that sucker, he's all yours," I exclaimed with a giggle as the bartender started sounding alarms to the hostess standing behind Miss unhinged.

"*As if* you don't know who I am," she shrieked in accusation, and I shrugged. Engaging with the mentally insane wasn't on my bingo card today and I didn't wish to egg her nonsense on. "I'm the only one who didn't tether from our group!"

Then it clicked: *Dayna*.

But I thought she was sent home?

"Lakshmi chose Vepar? Good for her! I wonder if I could visit them in Hell, I'm curious as to what it's like. If there's actually fire and brimstone, you know?" I said offhandedly, hoping my deflection would diffuse her.

"Don't try to distract me, you fugly cunt," she clipped. I guffawed. Solid burn, considering it came from a Chad licker. "You know I'm Dayna. You also know that Chadwick doesn't want me anymore thanks to you. *It's all your fucking fault!*"

"He isn't on my roster anymore." I hadn't texted Aphrodite yet, with everything else going on, but I doubted Chad would try for a second date.

"That's not true, I'm going to *murder* you!" Dayna lunged with her long black nails extended, and I side stepped to the left. Sending her crashing into the bar. There was no withholding my chuckle as she let out a raging scream.

However, taunting her was a mistake, she immediately went for my face with those claws. *They're growing!* Her nails stretched into obsidian bony salad fingers the same moment her canines lengthened. The ocean blue of her eyes was replaced with Darth Maul red.

Vampire!

The bartender cupped her palms around her mouth, thundering, "LEECH!" Pandemonium struck. Momentarily distracting me as patrons rushed for the exit. Until the clacking of Dayna's oversized maw stole my attention back. *Defend yourself!*

The blade on my phone was useless. My heels would've made a worthy makeshift weapon, but Dayna lunged before I could take advantage, forcing me to settle on physical strength. The dick magic had improved my stamina as we held each other at arm's length, but she was rabid. Snapping her fanged jaws and clawing. Likely suffering from bloodlust.

When one of her sharp daggered chompers mauled my forearm, the pain brought static to the surface of my skin. Effectively burning her mouth. As her hands flew to her face and she wailed, I ducked behind the bar, giving my gash a chance to mend.

Once healed, I grabbed everything in reach, throwing glass after staticky glass at my assailant. Then moved onto liquor bottles. The shattering crashes echoing in between her furious grunts. Dayna, unfortunately, ducked and dodged most of the attacks. The bloodsucker was quick. She was also disturbingly licking my DNA and moaning ever so often.

"What *the*—" A familiar deep voice interrupted my focus. I peered behind the vampire to find my date. And nearly fell over. I stumbled from the bar to get some distance, but my eyes never left him. They couldn't.

Vex was huge, Timoset's height, but leaner. I couldn't help but stare at his dusky lips as my core clenched. Heat eviscerated my lower half. I couldn't stop reminiscing the way his perfect mouth felt against my — *That was just a dream, you psychopath!*

I hadn't seen another Neptunian resemble a human more, which was probably thanks to the Nike Air Jordan's paired with his black suit. Instead of a tie, the first few buttons of his white shirt were unbuttoned, exposing a tantalizing sliver of his deeply tanned chest. *He's really hot, yeah. You can admit it, but that doesn't mean you have to act on it.*

Avexei was *disturbingly* beautiful, from his endless obsidian gaze to his imperfect-but-somehow-still-perfect nose. His dark features and clay undertones along with the sharp planes of his face screamed indigenous adjacent descent, which created a weird combination with his mother's hair, but it worked somehow.

I'm not gonna lie, when I initially saw his rainbow highlights in the headshot, I thought it was on the clown-y side. But in the flesh, Vex's rapidly shifting hues added to his appeal. I craved the knowledge of which emotion each color attached to. He was so prismatic that I couldn't look away. *Actually, everything around became greyscale.*

I was full-on gawking. Frozen. Unblinking.

As was he.

Oh no… He smells of a fresh cotton scented candle. Kryptonite!

My brain went lights out as he neared.

Which was why I missed the Louis Vuitton carryall swinging in my direction. Dayna hit her mark, the right side of my skull. I went down, *hard*. Falling right into a mess of glass shards. *Did she have fucking bricks in there?*

Before I could process, Avexei rifted behind the vampire looming over-head wearing a triumphant smirk. She lunged, her jaw spreading to an inhuman width, at the ready to chow down.

Until a pair of veiny hands gripped each side of her blonde bob. And twisted. There was a loud *crack* as her face transfigured into a silent scream. He didn't stop there. I was suddenly blinded by a fire hydrant's spray of black ichor. A chorus of squelching sounds echoing through the now empty cavernous space.

He literally just ripped her fucking head off.

With his bare hands.

Oh, maaah gaaah!

My palms flew to my face, to wipe the gunk, but they didn't do much before Avexei was on me. In the puddle of Dayna's DNA. On the filthy floors. His heavy frame pressing mine horizontally.

Lips first.

Wish I could say I didn't kiss him back.

But of course, I motherfucking did.

Jin always kissed me soft and sweet. Whereas Timos kissed me like the world might end at any moment. Ry's were rough and demanding. However, Vex was something else entirely. For someone who dove on top of me his mouth was playful and teasing.

Mine wasn't. I needed him like air in my lungs, my tongue forcing past his lips with abandon. The feeling of his fingers tangling through my hair after he used those hands to kill left me frantic. The foul taste of blood did nothing to detract from how desperate our kiss became. I was leading, my hands untethered in their exploration of every inch I could reach.

His tongue was forked too, and longer than normal. Which only spurred me on.

Then a buzzing interrupted the sounds of our make out, yanking me back to reality.

What's going on in your chest now?

I was vibrating. My body ignited, tingles breaking out across my skin as a rattle-like noise emitted from the right side of my ribs. *What the fuck?!*

Vex didn't care that I'd stopped moving, his tongue ravenous as his drenched hands tangled in my hair. When he moaned into my mouth, I toppled back into the trance of him. Completely bewitched. There was no withdrawing.

Whatever was going on internally didn't matter.

I was two seconds from lifting my dress and riding him in the middle of this bloodied mess. *Why's that so fucking hot?!*

The thought made the weird thing in my chest worsen. A thing which was far more difficult to ignore than the ice cube from Timos. Or the tug from Ryloh on my heart.

Which could only mean…

Shit. Shit. Shit.

THREE YEARS EARLIER

Where the fuck is Nala? It was going on four minutes past. My gaze hadn't stopped flicking between my iPhone and the hotel doors. Three whiskeys hadn't diffused the edge.

Calm down, Vex, she's coming. Nala was always late here. She'll show.

She also won't remember a lick of you, so prepare yourself for the blow. Blinking away the tears brought on by that delightful reminder, I shoved the phone in my pocket to keep from checking the time. *This is humiliating, even for you.*

It wasn't just me *this* was destroying. *This* being my traveling to Earth and accompanying my soulmate on her vacations. It began out of valid safety concerns, she was flitting around alone, and I had over a decade of witnessing how unworthy mortal men leered everywhere she went. She could take care of herself. Logically, I knew that, but still couldn't stomach the possibility of an accident.

She nearly got herself killed a few years back. All because I refused to intervene while she was with someone else. I thought it would be crossing a line…

Look at you now, boyo.

I had covertly woven myself into her life, sneaking funds into her account to instigate further travel, so we could see each other. *Harmless, no biggie.* We were both suffering in our existing realities, and I was weak as fuck.

I had to confirm she was okay. I had to lift her spirits. I had to be her person, if only temporarily. She was constantly dancing with depression since her friend's betrayal. I fucking *hated* him… *And fuck her shitty family, too.*

Nala was alone, and it hurt me as much as it did her. Honestly, it was tempting to stay until the time came. But Olorun specifically told me not to, that it could alter destiny, *blah, blah. Don't even tempt yourself with thinking it.*

Heaving a sigh, I ran a palm through my spelled hair. My appearance was almost the same, only shorter and with tresses like Lo-Lo's. Although there were humans over seven feet, they were sparse. Even at my current six-foot-five, a ruler less than the norm, there was far more ogling than I appreciated. Nala's eyes were the only pair with permission.

Despite loathing my mother enough to avoid using any of our shared gifts throughout the bulk of my life, I was forced to leverage one for this to work. Although the Neptunian Queen's mental command gene skipped me, I could still erase recent memories without causing damage.

So, Nala never remembered. She recollected the trips, but I was always subtracted. I wiped her memory when leaving her at the airport. As stalk-erish as my behavior was, I hoped when she finally learned the truth, it wouldn't matter. I could even restore her memories if she wanted—

Shit!

Nightingale sighting! Finally! Fuck, how is she so fucking stunning?

The sway of her hips drew me in. I became a moth to her flame as she scurried over in a white top and jeans. She always looked so tired here. *Another reason you're doing this, Vex, she's always beaming and well-rested by the time you're saying a teary goodbye.* I couldn't even wait for her to cross the lobby, meeting her halfway.

"Hi Aleksi, I'm Nala," she said nervously, extending a shaky palm. Pathetic, I know, but it was close enough to pretend she was saying my real name. "You're so tall," she gushed.

And my cock wept.

Again.

It was a near replica of our other 'first' introductions for the last three years. I'd create a profile on a dating app to entice her with initially. Then we'd spend days in each other's company, running around cities, eating incredible foods, laughing every other sentence. Falling in fucking one-sided love…

In a day, you'll find your tongue tucked between her delicious legs like clockwork.

Again.

I'd never take it any further. Not yet. It wasn't time. That restraint was the easy part though.

"Hey Nala," I all but yelled, incapable of refraining from swatting her outreached hand and picking her off the ground for a hug. The instant her jasmine scent hit my nostrils was pure bliss. *Don't even get started on her body against yours.*

You always do this, Vex. Quit touching her without permission. She thinks you're a stranger! "Nice to meet you," I tacked on once her feet hit the tiles, and she gulped. Her deep coffee eyes drinking me in.

Again.

Like they always did.

I could fucking rip Olorun to shreds, *this* was all his fucking fault!

PRESENT

You just fucking kissed her without permission!

Forget that, look at this fucking crime scene. Dayna was everywhere. Bits and droplets scattered like confetti. The restaurant I built for Nala was gonna require a dozen cleaning spells. At least. *Do you think she noticed this was a copy of the library in Paris you took her to?*

Shit, you're doing it again. Deal with your mess, Vex!

I knew my sister had shipped this shrew back to Earth on Monday, it was concerning that Malice spliced and returned Dayna through the wards unnoticed. However, we all knew the tyrant was growing bolder. My soulmate was the current priority.

Nala looks terrified. But actually… Truthfully, she was just dazed. Our bond in her chest was purring from our closeness, and I couldn't restrain my grin.

Mine. Mine. Mine.

I *knew* she was mine.

My emotions no longer fit my current form. *Hell, they were probably swelling past the ozone layer.* I'd been awaiting this fucking moment for thirty-two-years. I had zero intentions of giving her up to Jin. To anyone, really. *None whatsoever.* It wasn't as if they could stop me anyway, I controlled the sun. I'd never been gladder of that fact than in this current moment.

Nala was still in a state of shock, with one hand over where she buzzed incessantly. *Fuck.* Seeing her in human form didn't come close to experiencing her immortality. She was resplendent. Even drenched head to toe in viscera. Possibly even more so because of it.

I loved her like this. Pupils blown. Tits rising and falling rapidly. Her pouty lips split just wide enough to peep her delicious tongue.

You forced her into that kiss, just like you used to force those creepy hugs.

Except. She kissed back. No hesitation. No preamble. Nothing. Nala didn't even give a fuck about the blood. My dick was still dancing in my pants over it. I could kiss every author responsible for warping her sense of self-preservation.

"Let's get you somewhat cleaned up," I murmured, plucking her up from the macabre puddle, and striding towards the washrooms. *At least you cleared the place.* There wasn't a single being to witness. It was only a matter of time before Mo, or one of the two blues showed for damage control, though. Hopefully my sister would keep her distance, I didn't need her tattling.

"Are you okay?" I questioned, placing Nala onto the edge of the sink. She nodded, gulping and batting her long lashes. I felt possessed as I fell to my knees to pluck the glass from her heels. Karma help me, even touching her pretty feet was giving me a thrill.

She probably finds you unhinged.

I mean, I *was* unhinged. A blink felt like an insurmountable distance between us, so I hadn't blinked once since she arrived. *Uktena perks.*

"Vex." Just hearing my preferred name on her lips caused a wave of hysteria to settle over my shoulders, it was bonkers. "I have to ask you something, but I don't know how. Are you—" She stopped herself with a bite to her lip, averting her dark eyes.

"Am I what?" I breathed as Nala's blown pupils returned to mine. I still awkwardly had her ankle in my palm mid ether. Despite the fact I'd removed the shards from her shoe. I *couldn't* let fucking go. Wish I could blame it on my beast, the Uktena *was* a bastard, but I was fully in control. He was sated enough by her presence to observe without comment.

"Have we met before?" She questioned, and I shook my head. It was best to lie. It was a tiny omission. I couldn't tell her yet. "It's just…"

"What?" I pressed.

Nala fidgeted, whispering, "I'm gonna sound crazy but I have to say it." I waited as she became more and more flustered with each passing blink. Her gaze darted around the washroom before finally landing on where I held her ankle four inches away from my raging erection.

She cleared her throat before her gaze finally landed on mine. "I've dreamed of you."

That aided me in releasing her foot, but nothing else.

"I think you're…" Nala tried again. I didn't know what to do as the most incredible creature I'd ever known attempted to collect her thoughts. How to speak. How to fucking breathe.

"You're mine, aren't you?" She asked, and I swayed. It took her clawing her long nails into my shoulders to keep upright. I nodded as her fingers trailed up my neck and into my hair.

"I dreamed of you too," I rasped as she scratched my scalp.

Nala grinned, then frowned. "How?"

"Does it matter?" I replied. She shook her head, sending gore splattering further.

"I can feel you here," Nala said, removing one of her hands from my hair to tap the opposite side of her heart. "It's more intense than…"

"What?"

"It's—Your hair. It's the same as it was in my dream." I peered over her shoulder into the mirror, finding a silvery hue I hadn't ever seen on myself before. *Weird.* "Sorry, irrelevant. I was trying to say that whatever this is, it's way more intense than what I feel with Timos."

Mo.

The reminder of my brother resurfaced the logic my beast attempted to override. Nala had to know the truth. She deserved a choice. I hadn't considered how much I would crave pleasing her. It was more overwhelming than the urge to keep her. It took several heavy sighs to muster the courage. "As much as I'd love to bask in that statement, we can't be together, Nala. Not if you want to continue being tethered to Jin."

"Christ on a crumbled shitty cracker, I forgot," she breathed, eyes wide. When she took her lower lip between her teeth, I had to battle the urge to kiss her again.

We held eye contact, both grimacing.

Nala struggled before eventually shaking her head. "I can't lose my Jin."

"No," I muttered. The confirmation was as devastating as it was relieving. I had whiplash.

As imperative as it was to keep her, disappointing her outranked it. I refused to be the cause of grief. Refused to be her complication. And my Uktena was no longer quiet, he raged against the mentally constructed bars of his cage, refusing to comply with my decision.

"I don't want to lose you either, Vex. I know it's absurd. I don't even know you yet, but—" She stilled, catching my tear, one I couldn't stop from falling with her finger. When her warm palm cradled my cheek, a purr rattled my chest, louder than a tank. "I can't let you go. Any of you. You're mine."

It wasn't what I anticipated she'd say. It would've been easier to walk away. *But who are you to refuse your kontrolii?*

"Fate always fucks me over," I revealed with a sigh.

"No. Not this time. I'm glad fate gave me you before the others," Nala whispered with a sad, but beautiful, smile. "I haven't been able to stop thinking of you since that dream."

Before I could reply, the bathroom door swung open to reveal my favorite dragon. "Did you have to rip her fucking head off?" Mo questioned with a scowl.

"She harmed Nala," I couldn't withhold my shout in reply. Which left the femme in question, grinning from ear-to-ear. *She's tantalizingly twisted.*

Mo grimaced as he scrutinized us. "You are tethered then?" We nodded. "Olo has a potential solution. We must travel to Uru, but it could work." The furrow in Mo's brows told me everything I needed to know. The odds in my favor were slim at best.

It was time to part ways. Nala was better off without me. I was the most damaged of the lot, the only one to have failed a prior mate and child. I'd lost one family, I didn't deserve a chance at another. I didn't even deserve Mo or Ryloh's friendship, let alone Nala's.

You can't forget how you spent four years on Earth erasing her memories and didn't tell her. She deserves better. With tears blurring my gaze, I conceded.

"Nala, you should leave with Mo. Your first week's dates are technically finished, the Program's curse won't send you back to Earth. I shouldn't—"

"No," she interrupted, flinging her arms around my neck. "He just said there's a solution." My hands fisted by my sides as I attempted to keep the wall of my resolve intact. It was difficult with her breasts pressed against my face. Her jasmine scent left me in a constant state of arousal.

"I would release him, Naliti. You are tempting his nature with your touch," Mo chided. It was true, but I still scowled in his direction. It was tempting to claim Nala, right this second, ideally in the puddle that was once Dayna.

"I can't," she cried, before inhaling my hair. My heart nearly combust as my breath hitched. "You don't get it, Timos." When Nala withdrew and we caught sight of her shifted eyes, Mo fell to his knees beside me. Those were... *Fuck. Fuck. Fuck.*

It shouldn't be possible.

Her eyes were... *Draconic?*

Nala's gaze had transformed into a rainbow behind slitted pupils. *Those eyes match your fucking scales!* I'd never witnessed anything like it. Nothing nearly as beautiful. I couldn't keep my grin from spreading despite the severity of the steaming pile of shit we'd just plunged into.

"What's wrong with me?" she questioned, canting her head. Eyes blinking wildly.

"Fuck," Mo croaked to my right.

Nala frowned and searched both our faces. "Why's my vision all weird? You're both sparkly and everything else is like... *Blurry*? One of you better fess up!"

"I'll explain. Don't panic, Nala. Please. You'll send our beasts into frenzy," I said.

"Impossible," Mo whispered. Since he was barely coherent, I decided to play the voice of reason. It wasn't my typical role, but one of us had to step up.

"We've gotta leave. Where do we take her? What if she—"

"What if I *what*?" Nala demanded. "I'm so fucking sick and tired of all of you hiding things from me." Her final sentence left her lips in an inhuman growl before she threw her hands into the air and screeched at the ceiling.

"We take her to mine. It's been dragon fire proofed," Mo said, managing to recollect himself. I grabbed them both without hesitation and rifted us to the cave he'd called home for the last two thousand years.

"Naliti, please, you must remain calm," Mo begged, rising to his feet and dragging her with him to the leather sofa. I didn't know how he managed to stand when her lure was prodding me with hatred. Nala was rightfully fuming and pushed him back a step, before stomping with her fists clenched at her sides. The fervor of her anger had cast lures.

Lures were anything but pleasant.

It was time for another tactic, so I revealed, "You can shift, Nala." Mo shook his head as if we could've hidden it from her. I nearly gave into my Uktena's craving to swallow him whole. "It shouldn't be possible, but your eyes have already. That pretty much proves you can. And why your vision is weird. Your nature exposes what she wishes for you to see."

Nala stilled, blinking rapidly a few times, her slitted gaze flicking between us. She finally crossed her arms and pointed a hip. "Explain." I turned to find Mo's eyes shifted along with mine. Just from the lure woven into Nala's command. My tongue lengthened in my throat, and I had to wonder if his had too.

She was fucking overflowing with prestige, overwhelming the ether with it.

"It's his fault, you took on his nature when you two fucked," I blurted, unceremoniously.

"We haven't yet!"

Denial struck and I spun toward Mo who nodded in confirmation, rendering me speechless.

"Neither of you know how this happened?" Nala demanded, and we both shook our heads. "What did my eyes shift into? Can you tell?"

"Your eyes are dragon right now, little lioness. Without question." The term of endearment slipped, but she thankfully didn't seem to notice. Her gasp had to have been about the dragon bit.

Nala spun towards where Mo was muttering incoherently to himself. "Has this ever happened to other dragon's mates before?" He shook his head. "Has it ever happened to another human before?" We both shook our heads and she groaned. "Why can't I be normal? Why do I always have to be such a fucking freak?!"

Despite her scream shredding my eardrums, I smiled. They both shared confounded looks in response, so I explained, "If you weren't such a freak, then you wouldn't have been fated to the four of us. Mo's the second—"

"Third," he corrected, like he always did. Although with less fervor than usual.

I ignored him. "He's the most powerful child of the Supreme rulers of our universe, Nala. Then you have Ryloh, who's the only fae to possess a dua forma. Jin is only one of two Siarcs alive. And Mo and I are two out of ten gods born with dual classifications. I'm the only one to have a homo sapien sire. We're *all* freaks."

When her grin mirrored mine, I felt as though I was caught in another dream. But I wasn't, I'd never seen this conversation. Honestly, I'd never glimpsed her this out of sorts.

"I love that," Nala whispered, her eyes becoming glassier by the blink. "Can I cry normally with these peepers?" She asked, and I bobbed my head. "Good."

"What else would you like to know?" I could see her wheels turning.

She sniffled, asking, "How are you half human? You're humungous."

"I've never been human. I'm zoatalan and seraph, that's how I can take both the forms of Uktena and Siren. My father was a class of homo sapien that predated yours. A larger and more developed species than current humankind."

She scrunched her nose adorably. "How old are you?"

"Over six thousand, Mo and I are only a few months apart. His parents raised me."

She spun towards the dragon, her eyes narrowing. "Timos, why do you look so...?"

"I am unwell," he croaked.

"We've gotta get you cleaned up," I said, plucking her off the floor again. There was no stopping the Uktena's insistence to care for her. "I'm gonna take her down to the springs, Mo."

"Not without my oversight," he clipped, stomping ahead.

"Why's he so upset?" Nala whispered. "I know none of this is ideal, but why's he acting like the world just ended? I didn't ask for my eyes to shift or to feel as though I've known you forever."

The pressure in my chest grew with every step. *You've gotta tell her.*

But I couldn't do it, I couldn't fucking muster the damn truth. I was a snake, through and through. A fact I once reveled in. No longer. The idea of risking her kept my lips sealed tightly.

Instead, focusing on Mo, I said, "One of us will be left out of this, Nala. I thought you'd already bound yourself to him and Ryloh, since you haven't, you could just as easily lose them." She shook her head against my chest in denial. "It's true." She remained in contemplative silence as I carried her down to the lowest level of the caverns.

Mo had frozen the walls in the main living areas to keep his plethora of plants alive. Down here was nothing but quartz because of the six springs' variously heated waters. Nala loved her showers boiling, so my feet stopped before the steamiest pool. When I placed her back onto the ground, she shook her head, clawing into my shoulders. "I need you near me," she breathed, so softly that I hoped Mo didn't hear.

A futile wish, dragons had exceptional hearing.

"What the fuck?" he erupted. Nala had unzipped and tossed aside her dress, leaving her in a lace bra and thong, but that— *somehow* - didn't divert from the frustration with my oldest friend.

"Don't snap at her," I hissed. "None of this is her fault, calm down or leave. Get your shit together." Nala's warm arms flung around my neck, eliciting another grumble from the dragon.

When she jumped to wrap her legs around my— *now* - painfully erect dick, I couldn't help but groan. Just a little. Unfortunately, Mo's wings shot from his shoulders in response.

"Vex, please," Nala rasped, her nails clawing into the back of my neck. "I need to know what's going on. They haven't been as forthcoming." Mo's rumble echoed around us. She ignored him, questioning, "Why do you think my eyes shifted?"

"Do not tell her," Mo snarled, earning an incredulous look from Nala.

Hypocritical as it was, I found myself saying, "You can't shield her from any of this. I don't know why you're even trying to." Our beasts were in an overprotective state. Nala was our purpose. Our kontrolü. But I couldn't be more furious with him. However, his flaws weren't a priority at present. Focusing on the soft curves pressed against me, I lowered us into the spring.

Nala's full-bodied shudder and sigh against my neck, left me weak in the fucking knees.

"We don't know why your eyes shifted before acceptance," I

murmured, trying to ignore how my cock was hardening painfully from her nearness. "It's abnormal, but I think you already knew that." She harrumphed as I lowered us deeper into the pool, so it came to our shoulders. We were both incredibly filthy still, but I couldn't muster the control to release her and grab a sponge. It felt too right having us pressed chest to chest. "What else do you wanna know?" I rasped in attempted distraction.

"How is your lingo Earthlier than theirs?"

Fuck. I was so damn tempted to form the words. They sat on the tip of my tongue. However, Mo surprisingly butted in with, "I told you he was obsessed with your customs, Naliti." She chewed on that, eventually seeming satisfied.

"Who's your favorite person?" she asked next, this time with a shy smile.

"You," I said. Mo scoffed in the background.

"Not Ryloh? He said you were his. Or Timos? Didn't you grow up together," she rambled, and I shook my head. "What about your least favorite person?"

"My mother."

Nala gave a grim nod. "I despise her too. What'd she do to you?"

"Murdered my mate and child, Jules and Phillippe." When she gasped, I explained, "It happened a long, long, long time ago. Back when Titans were able to do whatever they wanted. She didn't appreciate that I'd settled down with a lesser demon. I miss them but it was four thousand years ago. The memories feel more like figments of my imagination at this point."

"I'm so sorry, Vex. She's unbelievably horrible," Nala whispered, her fingers tucking several strands of my hair behind my ears. Sending my entire body aflame as she vibrated against me. My dick was still celebrating. Honestly hadn't stopped since she came into view.

Untangling her from my middle, and grabbing a nearby sponge, my hands washed away every bit of Dayna I could find. From her toes to the top of her hair. "Why were you in the Program if you dreamed of me?" Nala asked as I rinsed her hair, her coffee eyes narrowed in rightful suspicion.

"To keep my mother off my back," I explained. "My compliance in her science project predated my dreams of you. And I knew we'd meet through the PPP, so there wasn't a viable excuse to withdraw until your arrival. I didn't take any of it seriously, which is why I never matched."

At least my admissions seemed to quell her, the angry lure had dissipated.

"We should call Olorun," Timos muttered. A faraway *ring* sounded as Nala and I dove into another staring contest. I couldn't stop my hands from touching her. *Her hands also haven't left you once.*

"Yellow Mo-Mo," the joyful timbre of our uncle echoed. "Her eyes shifted then?" Olorun asked, and I huffed. *Of course, he fucking knew.*

"Yes," Timos replied with a resigned sigh. "When should we depart for Uru?"

Nala raised a brow, so I mouthed, "I'll explain."

"A transporter will arrive at dawn. And Mo-Mo, make sure to bring Vex."

"Why?" he demanded, clearly having planned on leaving me behind.

There was a loud cackle before Uncle Olo asked, "Has she released him yet?"

"No," Mo snarled.

"Therein lies your answer, my boy. See you tomorrow, ta-ta!" The call ended and Timos scowled at our tangle. "Avexei, you are only torturing yourself."

"Fuck off, dude. Like you would move if she was in your arms," I clipped.

Nala interrupted us with a wave of her arms, "Is Uru short for Uranus?"

"No," I said, "it's a planet too, but those you knew back home aren't real."

When Nala's mouth opened for another question, Mo interrupted, "Naliti, we must inform Yu-Jin and Ryloh of the impending travel—"

"So, call them," she replied breezily.

You've gotta let her go. She wants to keep Jin. You can't interfere. Even if it kills you. "We should probably separate," I relented.

Nala nodded with a pout. Neither of us moved. Not even a millimeter.

Lo-Lo rifted in, there was a humid shift in the caverns; however, neither of us budged. There wasn't even a battle about trying. Not for Nala either. I could feel her ease.

"Have her eyes changed or is m- my jealousy causing hallucinations?"
Ryloh sneered.

Mo grabbed him, huddling in a faraway crevice, and Nala's face fell.
"They're always keeping secrets," she whined.

"Get your asses back over here and tell us what you're saying," I
barked. There was no helping it. Ryloh winked his starry pupil as he
paraded towards us, all but dragging Mo behind him. Nala's grip on me
tightened as her lips spread conspiratorially.

When she leaned in and whispered, "You're my favorite today."

An explosion of joy erupted under my skin.

I nearly shifted.

I nearly stole the sun from our galaxy as it momentarily flickered under
my skin.

Light exploded in the caves. Nala was glowing too. "You're beautiful,"
she murmured with a wide grin as her fingers tangled in my damp hair.

I nearly died.

"So, y- you're tethered then?" Ryloh loudly interjected, squashing our
moment, from where he stood at the edge of the pool. "Y- Yu-Jin is
going to —"

He didn't have the opportunity to finish because the pupling himself
arrived. Raging, I might add. "What the fuck is this, Nala?" She squirmed
in my embrace but wouldn't release me. Not even when I attempted to
force her off.

"You have not yet glimpsed her eyes, Yu-Jin. We have greater
concerns than her sudden attachment to Avexei," Mo said with a snap of
his fingers. That did the trick, Jin leaned over to get a closer look, then
began cursing. "The five of us must travel to Uru. Nala will require our
support through her transformation. We will not have to worry for the
Program or Council's prying while she adjusts. It could take days, it could
require a week, make the proper arrangements."

The other three fidgeted uncomfortably as Nala and I hid in the steam.

"Nothing's changed between us, Jin," Nala eventually interrupted the
silence. Maybe they were having a mental argument. "Vex isn't taking
anyone's place. He has his own." My grin was immovable. "I know y'all
have tried convincing me it's impossible to keep the four of you, but we
haven't even tried. I refuse to give up before we try."

Lo-Lo began undressing before joining us in the waters. "Y- You and I are bonding tonight, spice. As promised." My brows pulled together. *They planned on accepting tonight?*

Irrational as it was, because it wasn't my place to say a damn thing, I was pissed. Ryloh trying to rip Nala from me also didn't help. "I dunno that we should," Nala replied, clinging to me tightly. "Things have changed."

"You just said *nothing's changed*," Jin roared.

To make matters worse, Mo blurred our surroundings with pearly smoke.

Outrageous. I'd never seen him lose his composure quicker. I could feel the prestige surging. They were one thought away from frenzy. The lot of them, Lo-Lo included. His stubbled jaw was ticking as Nala yanked her slippery hand out of his grip. My defensive hackles rose.

"Nothing between us has changed, Jin. I was talking about the fated frou-frou with these —"

Mo and Lo-Lo growled, earning themselves an eye roll from Nala.

"She wants to keep him badly enough to withhold bonding with you two," Jin spat. As if it weren't obvious.

"If she wanted us hearing her thoughts, Nala would voice them," I hissed, and they had the audacity to bristle in response. "You realize you're upsetting Nala, right? Can't you feel it? How you're letting your own fucking egos get in the way of prioritizing her needs?!" I didn't voice it to earn myself brownie points, their reactions were genuinely infuriating. Sure, there was a lot of shit hitting the proverbial fan, but you didn't see me acting a fool. I wasn't even in her official starting line-up. "Have you been ganging up on her like this? Because it's completely unfair."

Nala had severe anxiety. Her acceptance of our world was stress-inducing enough without their frenzied flustering piling on. *They aren't fucking deserving.*

"Vex is right, you know," Nala said, intentionally pausing to share a glower with each of as she wrapped her legs around my waist. Thankfully, none but Ryloh could see under the water, but the male saw and oozed envy.

Don't you dare! Don't think about her closeness to your dick.

I was harder than a gargoyle. As still as one, too.

"This is exactly why I freaked out earlier. Your hearts are in the right place, but it hurts when you intentionally exclude me." Nala's revelation yanked me from the horny haze I'd fallen into. "You aren't thinking of my feelings and I'm an incredibly sensitive person. It may not seem that way all the time, but I am. I live in a state of never-ending turmoil."

At least the idiots looked forlorn. "It was not my intention," Mo said with a sigh.

Jin followed, "I'm sorry, Nala. It's tough keeping it together with you pawing all over him."

Her grip on me tightened and my heart burst.

I underestimated how much these idiots would fuck up.

She *needed* me.

But that didn't mean it would happen tonight like they planned. I required more notice. It mattered too much; Nala deserved more than some random night in a cave.

It's a divine fucking privilege to accept your tether.

They weren't going to continue dragging Nala down, not on my watch.

I couldn't see my surroundings, similar to being trapped in a house of mirrors. All my vision discerned were the males and the surface of the steaming waters, everything else was pitch. Which was fitting, considering the tension poisoning the air. At least my feet reached the bottom of the pool, so I didn't have to worry about drowning.

Jin was struggling to keep from shifting, his plum gaze oversized as he paced back and forth. He was understandably in the worst emotional state. While Vex was the opposite, his slitted eyes had a silvery backdrop mirroring the hue of his hair as he grinned, flaunting a dimple. Timos was deflating back to aloofness, and Ry was scowling, likely by default.

There was something severely wrong with me because I couldn't detach from Avexei.

Whereas Timos felt icy, Vex was only crisp, a slight chill I wanted to press every inch of myself against in this hot pool. The urge to keep him close was consuming. An out-of-body sensation kept circling, insisting I knew this complete stranger. Like an infuriating version of déjà vu. Everything about him felt familiar, from his thick coarse hair between my fingers to the way he devoured me with his gaze.

It was insane. I knew him for all of thirty freaking minutes. And could *not* consider losing Jin. I love, love, loved Yu-Jin Rapax. My decision had been made, set in stone.

However, I couldn't put an inch of distance between us. My body's reaction was significantly more intense around Vex. From the weird pulsing opposite my heart, a twin-beat that only came alive around him. To the way his chilly arms sent shudders up and down my spine. It was more than overwhelming.

I could fully believe he was a god. Typically, sitting this close, and with my upward facing angle I'd find imperfections like a booger, but no, Vex was disturbingly perfect. His only flaw being a slight bump in his nose, could've been from a breakage or hereditary. And honestly, that minuscule imperfection added to the overall appeal.

"You're tempting Nala into heat from your closeness," Jin's baritone sounded from the faraway distance. My head felt lighter, almost hazy. His voice was no louder than a fly buzzing nearby. Although I'd forgiven them for the ruined retirement party this morning, there was a lingering sourness between us.

Plus, Vex had doused our problems in gasoline then dropped a match.

It was understandable, the trio's concern, but there was a tiny petty piece of me that blamed them. A lingering distrust I struggled to shake, although it'd been the topic of conversation *for days*, I didn't feel stable. There were too many unknowns. We still hadn't even discussed the specifics of dick magic.

Which was what led me to spout, "I'll let go of Vex if you tell me what I'll be inheriting. Will my fingers be wands? None of you ever answered me about that."

"They seriously haven't told you yet?" Avexei rumbled, and I shook my head. Incoherent curses and sighs echoed around us. "Jin's physically stronger than most zoatala and has a better sense of smell. Lo-Lo's got improved healing and hearing. Mo's got elemental command, portaling, spirit speak, time control, and sixth sense—"

"Sixth sense?"

Timos piped in, "I can sense oncoming danger."

"And time control? Like backwards and forwards? I'll be a time machine?" I asked in awe.

"Solely within a five-minute span, give or take."

"What about you, Vex?" The others didn't appreciate my inclusion, but I didn't care.

Avexei's smile was radiant. "I have control over most light sources. Stars. The sun. Any natural light source is at my command. So, yeah, theoretically your fingers would be wands," he chuckled. Raising a palm, a prismatic beam shot forth, dancing like an inflatable man at a car dealership before he formed a fist and it disappeared.

Okay, reverse shadow-daddy.

"Vex could be the cause of your eyes shifting, Nala spice, your irises match his scales in both his dua forma," Ry tacked on.

"What color are your scales?"

Vex's cheeks reddened. "They shift, like my hair."

"My eyes are a rainbow?" Four heads bobbed while I gawked. "That's wild. Since none of us have boned yet, what could it mean?" Gazes began darting, so I used my scariest voice to shout, "Tell me!"

"Your prestige is through the fucking roof, it can't mean anything good," Vex said.

Of course he spoke first.

<<*"You better be glad I'm not repeating that."*>

"I'll say it aloud then, Jin!" The mental link wasn't a fair guilt tactic, especially when I rarely intercepted his thoughts, I'd been on auto-pilot, ignoring unless his emotions peaked. "Why is Vex the one openly telling me stuff?"

"He's attempting to slither his way into your heart, so you'll drop one of us instead, love," Jin griped, with Timos and Ryloh nodding along. *One clingy hug session and they're worried about abandonment?!*

I couldn't muster a response.

Avexei laughed, the motion pressing his hardness against my clit. I had to bite my lip to stifle any sort of reaction. "You aren't listening to her at all, are you?"

I gasped, my arousal peaking further. Vex was making control impossible.

"Nala's past the point of turning back, I think she deserves answers. You planned a sex-party before setting her expectations. Has she even heard about what happened to the last dragon's mate, besides your mother, who inherited dragon fire?" Vex pressed. Timos growled.

"What happened?"

"The Council killed her in testing. Purposely. My sister perished soon after because the only means to eliminate a dragon is their tether," Timos gritted out.

I choked on air.

"We aren't l- letting them anywhere near you, Nala. That's why we're going to Uru tomorrow," Ryloh said. "Technically, I shouldn't be roped into this nonsense. The only things I kept from you were in regard to the Uktena you're clinging to."

I tossed my head, groaning. "This conversation keeps circling and it's driving me insane. We've promised 'no secrets' and trusting each other both collectively and separately, yet it's still not happening…" My voice trailed off as I slogged through possible solutions.

"I have voiced my concern with revealing too much with your looming transformation. We are ill-equipped to ensure you experience little discomfort as possible. We must make it to morning," Timos said. *Whoops, forgot about the whole transfiguration thing.*

"I'm fucking trying!" Jin echoed.

Ryloh crossed his arms, splashing me in the process. *Likely on purpose.* "When did y- your eyes shift, Nala?"

"When I attempted to separate her from Avexei," Timos replied. "Their tether is sounding in her chest like a song. Have you ever heard of similar?" All the males shook their heads. "I feared as much," he conceded softly, repositioning his glasses.

They'd given me access to their phones last night to cuttlefish my heart out, so their sour expressions were anticipated. There wasn't much on the topic of mortals turned immortal because it was disgustingly exclusive. Also, recent, having only become popular within the last century. Not every planet's Pairing Programs followed the exclusionary facets of Neptune's, but reading the specifics was a scratchy pill to swallow. And I only saw the *public* knowledge, who knew how much worse reality was.

The most discouraging facet being the Neptunian support in gender binaries and forced heterosexual relationships despite the existence of artificial insemination as well as multiple subspecies who could reproduce with any gender. At the Queen's behest. Of course.

"Olorun is our best hope for answers," Timos eventually said, his back straightening. "Your polyamorous nature is highly unusual. Eke your kontrolü status."

"Do you still believe you dragon cursed me?" Timos shook his head, the stress left his eyes slitted, and my sternum iced with the need to have him near. I motioned for him to come closer.

Which only compounded *someone's* emotions. He began spinning like a top, again. "Jin, please don't freak out, I wouldn't have been able to tether to any of them without you. You've said it yourself." He nodded, then slapped his cheek.

"Why doesn't everyone hop in with us?" The physical distance sucked. *You're also not helping with that.* I finally gathered the resolve to push from Avexei, ignoring his frown. Despite not being able to see anything but them, it was a pleasant swimming experience. The water was salty but just the right toastiness. *And thanks to your new skills, no pruning.*

However, despite Jin and Timos hopping in, there was still a chasm between us.

Ironic, considering they're the only pair you're in love with.

<<*"I have every right to be uncomfortable right now, Nala. If things don't go our way, I'm the one who gets booted. I don't want you to lose any of us either, but I'm the one who's fate hangs in the balance."*>

--*"I know, Jin, and you're right. I'll cut you some slack."*- Timos was only thinking of keeping Jin, too. Their hearts were in the right place. However, there was still the question of how to bridge the trust gap... *Hmm.*

This rollercoaster was about to get a whole lot worse for everyone involved. In more ways than one. Frenzies were on the horizon. *Maybe even yours.* Which was the moment I remembered Min explaining dominance through sex. Could it assist in us finally building trust? And to be fair, it hadn't been tried yet. *Maybe it could work?* A chaotic plan quickly formed.

They're going to hate this, Nala.

It didn't stop me. Mind made, I dog-paddled to the edge of the pool and pulled myself to a sitting position. Ignoring their leering was second nature, but that didn't mean their eyes weren't searing against my skin. When I reached back and unclipped my bra and slid off my thong, the grumblings were no longer in anger. The loud *slop* of my soaked lingerie against the rock was pretty gruesome, but it didn't dissipate the tension.

Once naked, I lifted my strange gaze to find all of them gawking. "So, here's what's going to happen," I said, rising to my feet. "Since Jin is struggling, he's going to fuck me while I suck Ryloh's cock." The fae chuckled, while Jin looked stunned. Vex's mouth hung agape as Timos repositioned his glasses with a frown. "While they're busy, you two are gonna stop being at each other's throats. Maybe you'll get a turn after if you can play nice."

It was, quite possibly, my most enticing fantasy come to life. My body was humming from the sheer anticipation as their hooded gazes collided with mine.

When none jumped into action, I stood, then bent over. My ass was apparently a beacon because Jin and Ryloh wasted no further time in rifting over. Hands gripped my waist and hair, sending a thrill down my spine. "You're sure about this?" Jin questioned. His voice low as he pressed down on my clit. "Fuck," he whispered when I gushed onto his hand with a whine.

I licked my lips, nodding as Ryloh's piercings came into view. "She's sure," Ryloh said, gripping my hair into his fist as I gripped his thick tattooed thighs for balance. Feeling their four hands roam locked me in a dream-like state.

Jin plunged home, causing my jaw to fall open, which Ry took as his cue. Static zinged along his piercings as I ran my tongue along the length of him. He tasted like the saltiness of the pools with the zing of pop-rocks from his static. "Shit," Ryloh muttered, his eyes rolling back. It was a bit daunting, considering how the piercings could chip a tooth, but he seemed to know how to angle his hips.

Their mirrored groans sent a thrill zipping through every inch of my being, and I forgot all concerns. Jin withdrew with a slowness that left my knees wobbling. While Ryloh became rougher with each thrust into the back of my throat. Even without a gag reflex, I was choking, tears streaming. The suffocation compounded the euphoria in my core.

--*"You're doing so good, Jin."*- He didn't respond, focusing on grinding his hips against mine until my vision darkened, and he cursed. I was a sloppy mess, drooling, dripping, loving every instant. When I swallowed around Ry at the same time I clenched around Jin, they both shuddered.

I held the reins, and they knew it.

"Quit looking at me, you freak," Jin mumbled. It was surprising to hear his normal voice, I anticipated a visit from beastie, but he seemed in control despite having picked up the tempo. Ryloh huffed in response as he tightened his grip on my hair. I felt him thicken in my mouth and hollowed my cheeks to torture him further. It worked; he only lasted another two pumps before releasing into the back of my throat with a breathy moan.

When my mouth popped off his pink dick, and I swallowed, Ry cupped my cheek and wiped the tears that fell inadvertently. He crouched down, earning a growl from Jin who slammed into me. I was close but there hadn't been enough friction against my clit.

A bolt of static combined with Jin hitting just the right spot, sent me flying. Soaring. I momentarily blacked out with Ryloh's lips on mine as he tugged on my hair. Jin picked up the pace, finishing shortly after.

The Siarc didn't have a chance to withdraw before Ryloh ripped me away and teleported us into the waters. To where Avexei and Timos were both staring, mouths agape, fully agog.

"We made up," Vex whispered.

"No more omissions," Timos croaked.

//"I'm surrounded by fecking numbskulls."/

Jin and I gasped, our gazes wide.

<<"You heard him, too?">

Ryloh's jaw fell off its hinges.

"Hold up," I couldn't help but shout. "Ryloh, did you just call them numbskulls?" He nodded mutely. "Jin and I can hear you now? How?!"

Timos recoiled with a severe grimace, while Avexei scratched his stubbled chin. "Just fucking great," Jin mumbled as he plopped back into the pool, "another oddity to add to the list."

"At least you didn't frenzy, my love," I replied, swimming over to plant a kiss on his cheek. Then I turned towards the others to ask, "When Timos got a blowjob, this didn't happen, so why now?" Ryloh snorted while the others remained serious. My eyes were also still in their strangely focused state, making their ridiculously handsome faces glow against the blackness.

"Avexei's nearness seems to have released your nature," Timos mused.

Great, now you've made another mess, Nala.

//"Don't be so hard on yourself, spice. You didn't mean for this to happen."/

I sighed, pinching my brow. Having two of them rifling around my thoughts was going to take some getting used to. I'd only just learned how to block Jin out, and Ry's maddening accent was a more intense distraction.

"Damn, you weren't kidding about the noise in her chest. What the fuck is that?" Jin demanded as I audibly trilled beside him. *If only he knew.* Although they could hear the link to Avexei, my heart was racing because of Ry, while my sternum frigidly pulsed thanks to Timos. All of it overwhelming. Especially because it was turning me on.

//*"We know it's turning you on, your lure is suffocating."*/

I gulped a few times. Then squeaked, "Is there any point in preventing our tethering? All of us? Don't give me that look, I'm serious. Didn't your uncle say he had a solution?" They were frowning, and my heart was speeding with panic.

"That depends whether or not you wish to remain on Neptune. Maintaining your bond to Yu-Jin would require distance from the Queen. She is the lone Titan who holds domain over bonds. We cannot escape the Council entirely, but we could likely remain tethered elsewhere in peace. The Councilors would require sacrifice; however, we could likely remain together," Timos explained.

Jin's face fell, dragging my gut along with it. It wasn't just his role. Neptune felt like home.

"Same," Ryloh agreed. "I think the decision is yours, spice. I'm willing to do whatever to keep you happy. Even if that list includes relocation. Timoset and I no longer have any ties to Neptune. The other pair do, though."

"The farm doesn't need me here. I haven't been there much lately anyway," Vex said. That was a slight relief, but it left one stone unturned.

"But you love your job?" I whispered, turning toward my devastated Siarc and clinging around his middle.

Once Jin caught my fearful expression he sighed, khaki shoulders falling. "Not as much as I love you, Nala. They're right, we can figure it out. I trust you to make this decision."

Trust. Such a basic concept and yet, we'd struggled so much to build it. Meeting each of their gazes, I couldn't help but ask, "Is there actually trust here?"

"Of course we trust y- you, it's everyone else we've been concerned with," Ryloh said.

"What about each other? Because we have to act as a team," I stressed.

//*"Do you still loathe me, pupling?"*/

<<*"Not as much, but that's all you're getting."*>

"You don't have to worry about that with us. Mo and I shared everything growing up. While Lo and I's relationship formed for you," Avexei said offhandedly. I looked towards Timos who gave a shy nod. "Jin and I are acquaintances, but I doubt we'd ever be in opposition. It's your decision."

<<*"And he's always called me Jin when everyone else refuses at Skerry meetings and such, I have no issue with Avexei either."*> *Jin's expression was as serious as theirs.*

"So, we're going to accept the other bonds then?" I pressed. Despite having just been railed mere minutes ago, my clit was pulsing, aching for more. I couldn't help it.

There was a terse beat of silence before Timos' chilly hands grabbed me around the waist and rifted us out of the pool. He crushed me against one of the rock walls, their uneven cool surface dug into my back as his lips slammed into mine. His shirt was soaking, and I wished we already had the mind-meld so I could mutely ask his comfort level. "Timos, is it okay if you…?" I broke apart to say with a pointed look at his drenched sleeved arms.

His pained expression changed my mind. Gripping his soft chestnut curls, I kissed him with more fervor. I loved Timoset Drago regardless. He was driving me insane with his icy fingers pulling at my nipples while he trailed kisses down my neck. "Avexei, get the fuck over here," he barked.

"I don't know if I should," echoed back softly, forcing me to shove out of Timos' arms with a frown. When I met the Siren's gaze, he explained. "Nala, I want to. Obviously, I fucking want to. But we shouldn't." Avexei's hair went obsidian as he shook his head and sighed. From an Earthly perspective, his hair should've been that shade; it matched his brows and deep eyes, but it didn't suit him.

Disappointment swallowed me whole. The vibration in my chest worsened. My gut sank, every inch of me went clammy. I could barely feel Timos' grip as the words formed on my tongue, "Are you rejecting me?" *Woah, where'd that even come from?*

<<*"Your nature, love. She wants all of her amorosos to accept her."*>

//*"She's pissed and forcing the words out."*/

Oh-kay… Unsettling.

"You are infuriating her n- nature with your refusal," Ryloh said to Vex. "Can't you feel her?" I attempted to distract myself by leaning back against Timos, but it was no use. My excitement had been extinguished, and he registered that fact the same moment I did. Interlacing our hands I dragged him back towards the edge of the pool to sit with me.

"Maybe I should leave," Avexei mumbled, dodging my question and sending me spiraling further. Beastie or not, it was awkward now.

I squirmed, mostly in attempt to keep from spewing vitriol like my inner *nature thing* wanted. That crazy bitch was pumping me with rage. It was unreasonable, if Vex wasn't comfortable, I wasn't gonna force him or make him feel badly for his decision.

He was making it difficult to avoid an eruption, though. I could feel his discomfort. We'd gone a full ninety degrees in minutes. The others exchanged an unreadable look before shaking their heads. "Naliti's gaze shifted in your presence, it is unwise to refuse her," Timos chided, squeezing my hand.

"Why?"

"If he rejects y- you, there's no turning back on it. The bond between you would wither—"

"I didn't reject her," Vex hissed. "I just don't think it's wise to dive in right now. We just met an hour ago, Nala." Despite being entirely reasonable, the statement landed like a slap to the face. Timos' heavy arm fell around my shoulders before I emptied my lungs through my lips, as though he could sense my unease.

Maybe Vex is right though. I couldn't shake the thought once it solidified. Half due to the weird, destined intervention, half from how much his refusal stung. The adrenaline I'd been feeling since Dayna had dissolved into exhaustion. Rubbing my eyes as I yawned, there was a list of tasks piling up. A shower was necessity. *You also need to pack for Uru tomorrow—*

"I've already packed for you," Ryloh said. "Nala's tired, she wants a shower. We should l- likely remain here, Timoset. Just in case." Whatever that meant, I couldn't muster the energy to care.

As I reopened my eyes, my normal vision was restored, revealing our deep blue quartz surroundings. The cave pools were beautiful in a gloomy way.

Timos didn't give me the opportunity to take it all in before rifting me to a bathroom. Although the walls were also made of roughly carved navy quartz, they were covered in plants. It felt like being in a biodome. The amenities were modern and familiar, with an oversized shower stall and dual sinks. He shoved a fluffy towel in my arms before gripping the handle. "Take your time, I will keep the others at bay."

"Thank you, Timos. I'm sorry we didn't. It doesn't change how much I love you."

He didn't acknowledge my apology before rifting back to the others.

The shower was heavenly. Someone had also brought my stuff. The jasmine of my shampoo was a welcome comfort, as was the coconut of my curl cream. Timos left behind one of his long-sleeved t-shirts, which fit like a mumu. My tiredness was spiking, but there was another feeling I also couldn't shake.

I'd changed.

Believing it happened after meeting Ryloh was a mistake, that paled in comparison to feeling my *nature*. Beastie was the cause of the weirdness in my chest, there was no denying it. It was difficult to accept fate's intervention. My feelings no longer felt valid, they felt out of my control, forced. Like I wouldn't have a choice if I wanted one when it came to any of them.

Jin and Ryloh remained quiet while I showered, their sparse thoughts were regarding the looming travel. It was difficult to know what time it was because Timos' cave didn't have windows, the lone illumination as I trekked down a long hallway were the bioluminescent florals spiraling overhead. A shaggy runner cushioned my feet as I peered into the empty rooms in passing. There was a disheveled office littered with books. Then a laboratory, which was neatly organized with racks and shelves full of vari-

330

ously sized vessels. It wasn't until I reached the end of the long hall that I found them.

All on their phones in the open living area. Avexei leaning over the adjoining kitchen counter, chewing on something. While the other three lounged on the fire-engine-red leather couch. The expansive space was sparsely furnished, with more sharp lines and modernity than I expected from Timoset. Everything was in yellow, red, or blue in a neoplasticism style with pops of plants and potted trees. It paired well with the swirling blues of the cave walls.

"Feeling better?" Ryloh questioned, patting the seat beside him. I nodded, falling onto the sofa with a yawn. "It's just after eleven, we should probably get you to bed."

"Come, Naliti," Timos said, motioning for me to follow. "The guest rooms are arranged for the remainder of you." Someone immediately began pouting in our mind-meld, earning himself a zap from Ryloh.

Jin gasped, stilling Timos, and I spun to find him gawking at Ry. "Your static doesn't burn me anymore! What the fuck?!" Ryloh sent a barrage of static in his direction, and it seemingly dissipated into his khaki skin as he laughed.

"It doesn't hurt," Yu-Jin hollered in bewilderment, plum eyes wide.

"We're fucked," Avexei muttered, hair shifting rapidly as he stomped past and down the hall. I couldn't withhold my frown staring at his chiseled tan back. His refusal did nothing to diffuse my attraction. Or the way I was inexplicably drawn to him.

Unfortunately.

Timos gripped my hand, tugging me back to reality. "How do all of these plants survive without sunlight?" I asked in attempt to ignore the emotional upheaval. It worked. Timos' grin was radiant as he pushed aside some vines to palm the wall.

"Feel," he instructed. I found the rocky surface as frigid as his skin. But balmier, like it was melting. "It took some effort to manipulate their survival to rely on freshwater alone."

"And you're keeping these spelled with your magic, 24/7?" I questioned, and Timos nodded, repositioning his glasses before tugging me back in the direction of the bathroom. He trekked past the blue rounded door, and into a yellow version at the end of the passage.

It was a calming and peaceful space. The carved navy walls lacked the plants, showing off their natural swirly patterns. Similar to his office, there were books stacked high in several corners, some with their spines cracked. The bed was triple the size of mine, its white sheets a stark contrast to the deep blues. Once I caught sight of the gaping hole beyond the immediate sleeping space, a squeal escaped me.

There was a beach cove connected to his bedroom. Endless waves extended beyond the rocky terrain, glittering as they reflected the moons and scattered stars. "I knew you would appreciate this," Timos said, circling my waist to spin me around. His nervousness was palpable as his kaleidoscopic gaze searched mine. For what? I didn't know. "Glad you saw before we might abandon it."

"Are you sad to leave? You've lived here for so long," I said, guilt lacing my tone.

Timos shook his head with a slight curl to his lips. "I did not choose Neptune, Father did. It has been an age since I last traveled. We shall have planets and realms aplenty to explore."

"Realms too, *huh*?" I questioned, as his coppery eyes sparkled. "As long as there's an ocean I'll be happy. Swimming here on Neptune kind of freaks me out anyway. Once I cuttlefished the piranha overpopulation, it was game over," I babbled.

A muted staring contest settled between us. Timos' smile inched further from his ears until eventually disappearing. His voice was hardly above a whisper when he asked, "Do you no longer wish to—" I silenced him with my lips.

Understanding collided like a semi-truck. Why Timos didn't ask the others to sleep in here despite the humongous bed. Why he hadn't responded to my apology in the bathroom earlier. He had planned this alone time for us. Which was why I ripped right through his damp shirt as our tongues tangled. He groaned when I ran my fingers down his bare chest, wings erupting from his broad shoulders.

Then I was lifted and tossed onto the plush bed, my shirt somehow disappearing on its own accord. I didn't question it, too distracted by how enticing Timos' naked body was as he loomed over me. Every line was severe, from the scars to his stacked muscles. My grin was immovable as he dropped trou.

"On your back, legs spread," Timos commanded, sending a chill of anticipation down my spine. I obeyed by making a dance of it, extending each leg leisurely as his gaze iced against my skin. It was entirely unexpected when he lunged with an inhuman speed, caging me in, lips first. The first press of his icy hardness against my slickness left me moaning.

Timoset Drago was apparently just going for it.

"No foreplay?" I breathed as he licked up my throat and pressed his crown against my clit. The frigidness left me shuddering, legs tremoring, as he chuckled darkly.

"You have lured me for fucking *hours*, Naliti," Timos murmured into ear, slowly pressing into me. I'd concluded that luring just meant they were sensing my rampant horniness.

He stilled after stretching me an inch, breath catching, wings flying from his back. I whimpered as he nipped at my neck. "Fuck," he breathed. "Unfortunately, this will not last us long," he rasped, sliding in another few inches. I could no longer tell if my eyes were open, closed, or rolling into my head. My senses were hyper fixated on how a menthol-like tingle spread through every inch of my body.

Instead of numbness, it was pure icy bliss.

"Faster," I begged, "please. More. More. More." Timos pressed in another inch slower than dripping honey and I flung my legs around his hips, attempting to swallow him. The worries of him cleaving me in two flew out the window. I wasn't in pain and didn't know whether it was due to the lacking suppressant or the incredible temperature of his skin, but honestly didn't care.

Timos, finally, slid into my g-spot. I clamped around him, crying out from the fullness. That was apparently all it took because his leash slipped with a groan, and he slammed our hips flush. A scream tore from my throat as he dropped his weight onto my clit. My orgasm felt like being dunked into freezing waters.

I was a shivering goosebump covered mess. He smiled against my neck before pistoning his hips. A soft moan leaving him as he reacquainted with my cervix. "I love you," he whispered before withdrawing, my legs shook. Tingles started in my toes, inching upward, his next thrust dissolved the air in my lungs as my vision went black. Then he started pounding into my g spot like hammering a nail.

It was too much. I was too full. Too weightless.

My next orgasm was near painful.

Timos followed after with a roar, his cold cum filling me as his dick twitched.

Then I felt it, the icy intertwining, the magic swelling underneath my skin.

When my eyes finally cracked, I found Timos' gorgeous face grinning, with glasses adorably askew. We were caught in a windy bubble as vines circled our tangled limbs, but that didn't matter. Gripping his cheeks, I kissed him with fervor, teeth, tongues. He pulsed inside of me, and I released a whimper from the sensitivity.

[["Are you alright?"] Ohhh, me likey Timoset's brain voice.

I nodded.

There was a loud *pop* and several more voices flooded in.

<<"The better question is if you're finally going to let us in, you fucker!">

I chuckled into Timos' neck, guessing, "You warded them out?" He nodded sheepishly. "Well, let them in then." The door slammed open, and I peered over Timos' shoulder to find three disgruntled faces staring back. "This is kinda awkward with you inside me, Timoset," I started because he was still semi-hard, but the dragon shook his head.

"We are slumbering conjoined," he declared, earning groans from the others. Each of whom had already plopped down onto the mattress.

"Y- You aren't permitted to breed her without us present, Drago—"

I squealed, *"Breed* me?"

"Why else?" Avexei exclaimed. "It's a dragon thing, he's going to be insufferable for the next week. Especially with how much stronger your lures have gotten." *And here you thought the dragon's danger ranger-ing couldn't get worse.*

"Can you at least reposition to spooning? You're gonna crush me," I tried. Timos rifted as asked, his dick never leaving its place. Somehow I wasn't sore, it wasn't even unpleasant. Although, it should've probably been.

Ryloh fought his way to my free side, while Jin interlaced our fingers against the fae's bare chest. Avexei climbed in behind Timos, pulling one of my ankles from between the dragon's legs into his grip. There were a few sighs before the lights suddenly went out.

"We're really doing this?" I squeaked, because it was ridiculous.

"Yes. Go to fucking sleep, we can feel how tired you are."

Their clinginess reached fresh heights.
But you love it.

Today's the day, Uru we're heading for you.

Before leaving, Ryloh forced us into wearing matching sweats. The little shit knew exactly what he was doing. Their pants were the distracting kind, you know, the grey heathered ones. If I weren't so miserable I'd be drooling. However, I was too preoccupied with remaining upright instead.

The transformation started tickling under my skin the second I woke. There was a constant itching deep within the depths of my marrow, one I couldn't quite reach. It was also fever-adjacent in wooziness, and my ears trilled like a case of severe tinnitus. We couldn't get to our destination quick enough.

We were huddled atop a mountainous peak in Gro awaiting the transporter vessel. Apparently the distance wasn't rift-able for a variety of reasons they explained but I was too exhausted to follow. The sun had just begun its upward trek. We were surrounded by dense trees and foliage, the edge of the cliff acting as a window showcasing the rolling clouds shrouding the valleys of farms below.

"You have yet to release him. Why?" Timos asked as he eyed where Avexei and I's hands were locked together. I'd been grabby since his cool skin came within reach. It didn't matter that the Uktena was blatantly keeping his distance, he noticeably quelled some of my wiggling discomfort. I was too chicken to voice it. Especially after his refusal last night.

Plus, the tether in my chest was sounding like a vibrator from the early 1900's. As if the tension wasn't humiliating enough on its own. The only thing I could think to reply was, "I feel a pull, he's my amoroso." Hoping it was enough of a concession to placate.

[["Avexei's nearness soothes you?"]

Welp. Hiding from them was futile now. I bobbed my head under Timos' intense scrutiny, and he dragged a taupe palm down his face.

<<"At least he's making himself useful."> Jin's grumble was definitely an overshare as he tipped his head back and cursed.

--"Jin, stop. Yes, I feel less crappy when touching him. No idea why. Can y'all just let it go?"-

Our conversation was interrupted by a blaring *pop*. A flash of gold zipped through a hole in the branches, then suddenly grew. Expanded. We were cast in shadow, enveloped in a sickly-sweet smoke. *Holy macaroni, that's a real UFO!*

The enormous matte ship was disc-like, shockingly floating without disturbing a single leaf. LED's dotted the edges as sparkly mist billowed from its bottom half. It was everything you'd expect from an unidentified flying object. Except for the exterior panels, which were yellow.

A warm glow from the underside of the transporter cast onto us, so bright it blurred our forested surroundings. As I readied to question how we'd embark, we were sucked into its guts. I felt a pull, similar to a hook, yanking my center and shrieked like a banshee.

<<"This is to be expected."> *Jin insisted.*

We landed in a long empty passageway, lined with floor to ceiling striped lights. The interior panels matched the exterior, everything citrine in the chamfered space. It was also more minimal than anticipated, there weren't any buttons or labels, just eight tube-like pipes running the length of the roof overhead.

Timos started down the well-lit corridor with us on his heels. Avexei tucked me into his side, moving our tangled hands to hang over one of my shoulders. He leaned in, blanketing me in his cotton scent, and it took all my willpower to not flare my nostrils. "They're losing it because you shouldn't be this drawn to me," he whispered. "You should be clinging to them and nesting."

"Whatever. They know I'm anything but normal by this point," I replied dismissively. At full volume because they'd hear it anyway.

Ryloh slung an arm around my waist, saying, "I hope y- you're not including me in that, Nala spice. I'm not bothered by your *current* infatuation with Vex. Once you get him out of your system, I know who your most frequent favorite will be." I cracked a smile despite Jin's scoff.

Timos paused before the first aperture. The entrance was see-through, a thick plexiglass barrier, whirring open to reveal a lounge. There were two couches with a round low table stacked with square water bottles. The only décor was a long strip of glossy white cabinets in front of a dining table for six. *No view?*

"That's a window there, spice," Ry explained, walking towards a hexagonal panel, a less opaque wall than the others. He waved a pale palm, causing it to blink open, revealing a bird's eye view of Neptune's cloudy morning. Timos plopped down on one of the sofas, whipping out his conch phone. Ryloh settled at the table, and Jin explored the cabinets. "You'll want to be seated for take-off."

"Have all of you ridden one of these before?" I questioned, earning myself four nods as Avexei and I plopped down beside Timos. The couches were foam, we sank into the pleathery fabric. "How far away is Uru?"

"Far. It should only take three-hours traveling at light-speed, though."

"Olorun left you a present. The note says, 'welcome to the family.'" Jin said, taking my free side, extending a five-inch matte chrome disc with several square notches. "These are expensive, I don't even own one." It was lightweight and glossy, whatever it was. A bit smaller than a CD.

"Is that a *récepteur*?" Avexei exclaimed, and Jin nodded. "Damn, I'm jelly."

We were interrupted by a Simon Says-like *beep, boop, bleep*. "Preparing for departure. As a safety precaution, please remain seated. Departure in ten... Nine... Eight..."

"*Oh*-kay," I mumbled, inspecting the disc. "What does this thing do?"

"A récepteur can connect to the internet of any planet or realm in our galaxy."

"Are you telling me this will lemme download my books?!"

Before receiving a response, the countdown finished, and we were suddenly jerked upwards. Then aggressively to the left, my face smashed into Vex's shoulder as white light replaced the Neptunian sun's rainbow rays. We were ripped to the right, where my shoulder rammed into Jin's chest, and into darkness. Surprisingly, none of the furniture or water bottles moved. Unlike my belly, which flopped as we took another sharp ninety-degree turn.

The sensation faded as quickly as it came, transitioning to steady coasting. Darkness stretched beyond the window with random blurs of stars and planets that left me dizzied. It was surreal knowing we were zooming like a grain of salt in deep space. "Yeah, you should be able to access your library," Avexei interrupted my awe.

"One of you better connect this thing right fucking now," I hollered. Jin snatched the disc after gathering my phone and anticlimactically magnetized the back to the top right edge. The récepteur went from blankness to technicolor, revealing a circular screen with a list of selectable planets and an alphabetized... "What's 'R-A'?"

"Realm A. The R's are realms," Avexei explained.

I tapped Earth from the drop-down and my phone's screen transitioned from the lock screen of Jin's abs to a Google search tab in Chrome. A squeal escaped as Kindle's website loaded and I logged in. It didn't seem as though I could download the app, but web view was better than nothing. Everything else faded away as my favorites appeared.

There were a few conversations happening, but I didn't pay them any mind. It was thrilling to have access to my TBR again. The last I heard was, "I think we've lost her."

⚓ ⚓ ⚓ ⚓ ⋆.°

Beep, boop, bleep. "Preparing for arrival, please remain seated for landing. Arrival in ten... Nine... Eight..." The trip flew by, with Timos and I glued to our phones while the other three chit-chatted. I probably should've slept, as my eyes were drooping, but reading was engrossing.

I stretched my arms overhead and cracked my neck. "I'm excited to explore Uru," I said on a yawn. The males followed suit. Then my stomach growled angrily, and I bent over my knees from the sudden ache. "And for noms."

"Why didn't y- you mention you were hungry, spice? There were snacks in those cabinets," Ryloh chided. *Their relentless mother henning's getting annoying.*

"You just aren't used to it yet, love."

"No mind-speak," Avexei groaned with darkening strands. Until I relaced our hands, causing the others to grumble as we shared a coy smile. There was a sudden downward yank that buried me in the sofa, and I was mighty glad to not have eaten yet.

Bloop, bloop, beep.

"Welcome to Acidity, the local time is 7:07am, and we parked in Transporter Dock, Section G. Please gather your belongings and make your way towards the embarkment chamber. Thank you for trusting Hexos with your transport, we hope to see you again soon," the robotic lilt announced before we ambled back into the golden passageway.

As we neared a glowing rounded hexagonal panel on the floor, Timos stepped through, and disappeared. I gasped, realizing it was a hole, peering below to find my dragon smiling with extended arms. It was a ten-foot drop but felt like nothing as I jumped into his icy embrace. Someone tossed the luggage beside us before they joined.

We were in an enormous warehouse filled with a dozen parked sunny UFO's. There weren't any windows, just a big round dome that seemed to open for transporters in the ceiling. No one else was around, unless you counted the hundreds of droids flitting between the ships. They were three- or four-foot-tall headless robots with steampunk wings on their backs. Some were replacing parts, while others carried cleaning materials.

"Come on, let's get Nala fed." Jin's voice echoed as he started towards the only exit. "Where are we staying, Timoset?"

Upon approach, the doors whirred open, revealing a robed and faceless, but still humanoid, creature. Its head jiggled like Jello. Whatever it was didn't have hair or skin, it was more aqueous. They were almost effervescent and entirely aubergine, their only discernible feature being their glowing lilac orbs for eyes, no pupils or irises, just floating spheres.

//*"Before you panic, it's alright. It's just a Mor,"/ Ryloh explained. /"Mages possess the ability to create Mors as beings of servitude. They only live for a few decades depending on the spell cast. They shrink in size with each year until they inevitably disappear completely."/*

Unnerving on multiple fronts, especially given this one was only about three-feet tall.

"Welcome to Uru, Drago quintet. My name is Moralo, and I am to serve as your guide for the duration of your stay. Please follow me to your quarters." So, there was a mouth, but the slant remained invisible until use. I didn't see any teeth before Moralo spun, their robes swishing audibly. They floated down a blank well-lit corridor, which was when I noticed they lacked legs, and their hands only had three digits each. *Creepy.*

"When did we decide on us taking Drago?" Avexei asked. "And I'm not technically included." His hair transitioned from silver to slime-green.

"Yet," Ryloh snapped. "You will be soon en- enough."

Timos explained, "The granted surname is traditionally the most powerful in the mating group." *Huh. I certainly didn't mind the sound of Nala Drago.*

[["I fancy it myself, Naliti."]

"But Nala's the most prestigious," Vex interjected. "Technically, it's her choice."

"Am I allowed to make one up? Williams sucks. And I don't particularly want people knowing I'm related to Gabs or Seong, so I'll skip on Rapax. No offense, Jin babe."

"None taken," he replied.

I mused, "Ryloh's has negative connotations, and we all hate Avexei's mom. So, it's gotta be Drago or whatever my noggin conjures up. *Hmm.* Maybe we can go by the Loons—"

"Drago," they confirmed, in sync, like my very own boy band.

Jin scratched his chin. "It has its perks. You're galactically known."

"And feared." Ryloh winked.

We ambled after our friend down the windowless passage. The white corridor eventually led to an enclosed elevator, which was rose-gold instead of stainless-steel. "Moralo, where are we staying?" Jin questioned as the Mor pressed the lone triangular button.

"Master Olorun has made arrangements in personal residence." Timos and Vex seemed to have known, whereas the others lost their minds. Jin's plum eyes saucered while his lips gaped in awe, like a kid seeing their presents on Christmas morning. "It is quite the honor to remain in residence with The Sages," Moralo explained, seeing my confusion.

--"The Sages?"-

[["It is their surname. Olorun and his bonded are Uru's rulers."] Timos replied.

//"And the unofficial spokesbeings of mage-kind."/

We ambled into the box which lacked buttons. It was definitely a lift, but abnormal in that I felt it scanning my body as I stood in the corner.

There weren't any lasers, but a misty presence gliding down my frame from head-to-toe. Once the doors slid closed, a *ding* sounded, and Moralo placed their three-fingered palm against an invisible scanner. Then we were off, lurching not only upwards, but from side-to-side. Jostling us like maracas.

<<*"Olorun's mating group is one of the most accomplished in our galaxy. They're credited with nearly every invention since the Dawn."*> Jin explained as my stomach somersaulted.

--*"What's their Titan domains?"*-

Someone pinched my ass, *hard*. I yelped, and Ryloh chuckled before covering it with a cough. Despite the dizzying path we were on, I spun to find that Timos was—*shockingly*—the culprit! With a gorgeous guilty curl to his lips. Avexei shared a frustrated glance, but I shrugged. He only had himself to blame for not being a part of the brain gang.

[[*"That was a pinch of pride for remembering domains, Naliti. Olorun commands Invention and Destruction, Simargl commands Wisdom and Stupidity, and Yemaya commands Magic and Mortality."*]

--*"They're polyamorously bonded, too?"*-

//*"Yes, and Yemaya's also kontrolü."*/

[[*"Their bond is not quite like ours, Sima and Olo are also in a relationship separate from Yemaya.]* Timos explained.

Heat flooded my cheeks as scenarios danced through my brain. --*"I'm not opposed to that setup in case any of you are ever tempted."*-

Timos and Jin's eyes darted while Ry chuckled.

//*"Noted. All three of the Sages are powerful Seers, so they know what's to come and how we can best support you. That's why we're here."*/

"I thought all Titans were assholes, though?" I questioned, *accidentally,* aloud. Avexei huffed as Moralo shook their bald, earless head in disapproval.

[[*"You should no longer think in such absolutes, all have their positives and negatives, Titans are no different. Except for Malice, she is indeed an asshole. Similar to Chadwick."*]

The copper tube finally came to a halt, but my body didn't. Vertigo struck. I swayed off-kilter. Avexei swooped in, tucking me against his chest, with an arm under my knees.

<<*"He didn't even give me a chance to catch her, and she was falling in my direction."*>

//"Have you already forgotten how he's fecking helping? Or how Nala requested we drop the subject altogether? She's uncomfortable, Yu-Jin."/

[["We get it. You are on team Avexei, Ryloh."] Timos paired his grumbling with an eye roll as he readjusted his spectacles. Ryloh and Jin gawked.

I barked a surprised laugh before proclaiming, "Timos is my favorite today!" Leaving Dumb and Dumber in the dumps as we exited the lift.

Avexei carried me as we trekked down a lengthy skywalk with glossy floors and glass concave sides. We were surrounded by skyscrapers in every direction floating among the clouds. All golden in hue, some rectangular, others curvy or spherical. They were a stark contrast to the blue of the sun's rays. It wasn't just a backdrop here, the sun was literally shining in every shade of blue among the yellow buildings and green accents. Every facade, no matter whether it was curved or flat, was draped in plants. And no ground in sight.

I was prepared for glass enclosed structures, like this passageway, due to the toxicity in the air; but I wasn't prepared for greenery. Some balconies had vines, others had bushes, with a handful of scattered jungle trees popping up every now and again. Peering below only revealed thick and fluffy purple clouds which many of the buildings poked through. "How is this possible when the ether is poisonous?"

"That was a century-long pet project of Olo's. He acclimated the fauna to the atmosphere. They are merely for vanity, but mages have a wide-spread appreciation for aesthetics," Timos said.

Ryloh's phone *chimed*. He tapped around, brows furrowing, before exclaiming, "Gabriela is at the l- loft. She l- let herself in."

I rolled my eyes. "She has no boundaries whatsoever." Then my phone began vibrating. "What is it, Gabs?"

"Where are you?" she pressed. Ryloh showed me the video feed, where she dug through my closet, making a mess, tossing shit over her shoulder. *What's she hunting for?*

"Not home, why?" I replied, consumed with curiosity. We'd decided not to mention our travels since they were in violation of the PPP contract.

There was a pause on her end, and I watched as she made a face at her shell. "I came over to celebrate the last of your dates. Aren't you gonna report back to Aphrodite soon?" All four of the males shook their heads vehemently as we continued down the passageway.

"Ah, sorry I'm staying at Timos'."

"You aren't planning on having your mating ceremony this week?" she questioned.

<<*"Tell her you're trying to keep Ryloh away from The Queen, so we aren't reporting anytime soon. She'll know of the visit because of Seong."*>

"The Queen's been weird about Ry and me, so we're holding off until it blows over," the lie flew from my lips easily. "Didn't Seong tell you she's obsessed with him?"

Thankfully, my deflection worked. Gabs started rambling about this and that while continuing to tear my place apart as we watched. We'd made it down several more glassed passages, with the males growling when Gabs would cross a boundary, like sniffing a towel. I laughed though, because it was *so* weird.

When we finally hung up, she started discussing my whereabouts with Homie. Ryloh had a transcript appear on screen as we watched her violate my privacy. "Why do you think she's doing all this?"

"Gabs is the nosiest femme I've ever met," Jin replied. "Min can't stand her because of it."

"It's l- likely harmless," Ryloh replied. "She's cleaning her mess now." We followed Moralo from a distance as Ry held up his phone for us to watch.

When Gabs finished putting everything back in its place, she reached into her bag and withdrew her tarot deck. I sighed, saying, "You can put it away now. You're probably right."

"Aren't you worried she's got another prerogative?" Vex frowned, and I shook my head.

My stomach growled again, louder this time. The males exchanged a glance before linking arms. With a snap of Timos' fingers, we rifted from the skywalk to a minimal, expansive, and futuristic living room. The walls and floors were nearly the same ashy oak shade, while the furniture was in cream or bleached tones. The three curved-back sofas were arranged around a triangular table before a wall of windows. The cyan beams casting through painted shadows of palms onto the floors.

Avexei gingerly placed me down, as the males continued their conversation about food, I skipped through the oversized archway into another cavernous room. This one with a circular bed large enough to sleep ten with several loungers scattered around it. There was an equally minimal washroom with three sinks decorated in concrete tones, two urinals, and one normal toilet tucked in a water closet.

The view from the bedroom was spectacular. Glass reflective passageways crisscrossed between the towering structures like glittering spider webs. I could see crowds gathering in a large dome a few stories down with a swimming pool.

"One bed, really?" Vex grumbled. I spun to find him grimacing, his hair matching Ryloh's.

"Take a couch then," I snapped, incapable of hiding how much his reaction peeved. "If you're planning on rejecting me again, I'd rather you didn't sleep in here either."

Initially, I was proud for sticking up for myself, but it only lasted a few moments. Until Avexei's onyx eyes narrowed, his tongue lengthening as he spat, "That's because you *chose* Jin over me." He'd never weaponized that, and I recoiled with a wince.

Vex bent so our faces were parallel, his hair shifting like a moody flag as his cheek ticked. "I've been *waiting* for you for thirty-two years. *Pining* after you. *Obsessing* over you. For fuck's sake, I changed my entire vocabulary for you!" His forked tongue was slipping out more than usual, adding lengthened hisses to his words.

Cowardly as it was, my feet backed a step on instinct. But Vex closed the distance, remaining in my orbit as he growled, "I'm not gonna take this shit from you, Nala. *You chose him.* Not me. And what have I done in return? Tortured myself! You think I wanted to refuse you last night?! You think it didn't hurt me too?! I'm sorry that I care enough to—"

I kissed him.

He'd voiced all I wanted.

Vex immediately withdrew, wiping his mouth with disgust. I cringed. "Don't you fucking dare! I don't know why I even tagged along. Mo was right!" That was all he said before disappearing.

Leaving me stewing in the barren room with my heart cracked. What he said was the painful truth. It was all my fault and kissing him was selfish. When Ryloh's head peeked through to check on me, the tears started falling. My self-loathing spiked when the fae's expression crumbled. "Don't you dare feel pity for me, I deserve his disdain."

"N- No, you don't," Ryloh said with a sigh, pulling me into his stormy embrace. "He shouldn't have rubbed y- your face in it. It was un- unfair." I opened my mouth, argument on the tip of my tongue, but he barreled on. "Y- You only followed your heart. It wasn't as if you kn- knew fate's plans."

I shook my head, shoulders falling. "Yeah, but—"

"No. Let's get you fed, there's several trays worth of breakfast," Ryloh chided as he pushed me by the shoulders back into the living room. Leading into an enormous dining room with a round table for twelve in the center. Similar to the remaining decor, it was minimally modern, with light walls and a plethora of arched windows.

There were chrome trays piled high with every possible breakfast. Bacon. Bagels. Beans. Cheeses. Eggs. Ham. Hashbrowns. Roasted peppers and potatoes. Sausage. Steak. Toast. It was distracting enough to push aside the Avexei drama. *At least, temporarily.*

Timos and Jin were chuckling about something until they caught sight of me wiping my cheeks. I raised my arms in surrender, saying, "I'd rather not get into it. Vex left."

"Alright," Timos said with a frown. "Eat. Olorun awaits us in the lazaretto."

My brows furrowed. "What's that?"

"A healing room of sorts," Jin explained. "There's an apparatus they designed specifically for your transformation. He said it should counteract the itch."

"Thank fuck for that."

Avexei still hadn't shown. The trifecta wasn't concerned with his disappearance, but I couldn't refrain from mentally plotting my apology. I still hadn't come up with an ideal approach. It was distracting. So much so, that I hardly paid attention to the expansive futuristic golden passageways we trekked through.

Timos knew his way around the residence, acting as our guide. Mostly for Jin, who was *ooh*-ing and *ahh*-ing at the entrances of every lab we passed. And there were many. It was definitely a nerd's dream mansion. When we approached a large spiral staircase at the end of a hallway, he stomped his way up, motioning for us to follow. I was the last in line, so I heard Jin's peal before seeing for myself.

When my feet crossed into the concrete room, my jaw unhinged. It was a stunningly gorgeous skydeck, with cubed windows lining the walls and a strip of the ceiling, to reveal just the right amount of sunlight to sparkle like sapphires against a rectangular swimming pool's surface. There were six minimal and modern white loungers on one side, while the other side had a rounded egg-shaped machine the males were circling.

"What's that?"

"This is what they have invented for you. It is a machine which should —" I didn't allow Timoset to finish, pressing the triangular lavender button at the center of its face. A *click* sounded, and mist spread as the top of the shell opened slowly. Revealing an iridescent interior with a seat in the center, it reminded me of a massage chair back on Earth, but fancier.

"Damn," Jin breathed as I climbed in, too desperate for relief from the transformation to wait.

The seat began to dimly glow as it hid my males while repositioning me in zero-gravity mode. "Welcome to your personalized wellness pod, Nala," a robotic voice greeted as the dome sealed. A spherical, holographic, screen appeared in the sparse air between my head and the lid. It was claustrophobic, for sure, but I ignored my panic. As soon as three options appeared on the screen, I chose the one that touted, 'relief.'

A rainstorm suddenly crashed through the speakers. Then came the droplets against my skin. Chilly globules slid down my scalp, face, shoulders, then legs and feet. Except, I wasn't actually getting wet. It was just a replication of the sensation over my clothes.

"Intravenous hydration will be inserted in three… Two… One." *Ouch!* My right wrist was pricked. Whatever fluid they pumped me with had an instantaneous effect as it spread up my arm, soothing most of the itch.

[["*Are you alright, Naliti?*"]

--"*Yeah, fine!*"- I spent five minutes attempting to figure out how the rain was happening to no freaking avail. After which I realized my discomfort was completely gone. With a sigh, I settled deeper into the foamy chair, noticing rollers lightly shiatsu-ing my back.

"Would you prefer meditation or reading?" the voice probed. *Call me impressed.*

"Reading," I replied. Just like magic—*or science, whatever*—the page I'd left off on the transporter appeared on the round holographic screen. In the same dark-mode settings as my e-reader. *Gaaah, they're gonna have to drag me outta here.*

You'll put a target on her back.

You're a threat to her life.

You can't go back and apologize.

No matter how bad you want to, Vex.

You'll be the death of her spirit.

You. Can't.

Cannot.

"You are wandering into dangerous territory." My gaze lifted to find none other than the male responsible for this fucking mess. For my decades-long emotional distress. He was the reason I didn't pass into the afterlife when I should've.

Olorun Sage. *The* Titan Seer. My uncle.

"We both know I am essentially your father… *Mmm*, technically, I suppose Atha and I shared the role. I would rather not take full responsibility for your behavior at present."

"Don't fucking joke right now," I hissed as he approached. "You knew! You fucking knew and you allowed this to go on without ever saying—"

He muted me with his mind-command.

The controlling prick.

"We both know blame is merely the shell which the truth hides within the confines of," he said. I narrowed my eyes as he paused. It wasn't like I could do much more. Not that I wanted to give him the satisfaction either. "Why are you operating in fear, my son?"

I felt my vocals return but refused to speak.

My *so-called* father *tutted*. "I did not grant you access to Nala so you could hoard the secret and allow the guilt to swallow you whole. It was meant to bring you closer. Restore her memories."

"That's the opposite of what's best for her!"

Nala would fall in love with me. She wasn't safe loving me. She wouldn't be happy with me, despite what she may think. We led to destruction. I saw it in my sparse and unsettled few hours of sleep after refusing her last night.

The second my weary eyes closed; nightmares swarmed.

Except they weren't ordinary terrors. These could actualize and come to fruition.

Every prestige obsessed player in our galaxy would be after her if we accepted.

I couldn't allow it.

Should I have snapped instead of sharing the truth with her? *Probably not.*

It felt easier to deal with her hatred.

You're a coward.

"Agreed. It is Nala's decision, not yours," Uncle Olorun murmured, wearing perturbance. His comment fell upon deaf ears because I could spare her. Save her. *I* wasn't worth the hassle. I wasn't worth her being in danger for the rest of her years.

Uncle sighed, shaking his umber head. "Have it your way then." His steps began fading, echoing through the gym I was holed up in. When he lifted a leg over the threshold, I panicked.

Anxiety swelled. The male had *seen* almost everything. Likely this, too.

"Wait." The word left my lips without consent.

My uncle spun and raised a plum brow expectantly. *Fuck.*

Olorun's knowing gaze peered into my soul as my resolve crumpled. "She won't be able to live a normal life with me," I rasped, voice trembling. "How do you expect me to live with that? To live with myself knowing I'm the reason she's so fucking prestigious. Not Mo. *Me.*"

"It is Nala's life, and her choice. Not yours. She will learn the truth whether or not you continue this foolishness."

With that fucking nail in the proverbial coffin, he rifted.

Maybe he's right.

No, don't start.

Nala chose Jin. That was the right choice

You aren't.

Light burst from my skin. I was so out of sorts it was difficult to know where it was siphoning from. The longer I remained unsettled, the more control waned.

Hours hadn't deflated me. I was definitely too riled up for meditation or yoga. There was one form of exercise and self-expression that usually helped more than weights or cardio. But…

Huh.

I doubt she'd forgive me, an immortal wouldn't…

The males wouldn't let her, especially not Mo. *Two birds, one stone.*

When the IV withdrew, I didn't know how much time had passed. The lid cracked, revealing three handsome faces peering back. "I don't know if I wanna get out yet. I love this thing," I pouted.

"You've been in there for twelve hours," Ryloh said on a chuckle. "Olorun assured your vitals were stable enough to skip lunch. Are you hungry?" I shrugged.

"What were y'all doing during?" I questioned as Jin helped me out of the egg. Unfortunately, the aches resurfaced. With a vengeance. The males' joy was quickly replaced with concern as I stumbled. Jin bent over and motioned for me to hop on his back.

As we trekked down the spiral staircase, Timos explained, "Yu-Jin spent the day with Simargl while Ryloh and I practiced our newly blended abilities."

"And Vex?"

"We haven't seen him since," Ryloh revealed with a frown. "I texted him but I'm n- not sure if he'll show." I heaved a sigh, squeezing Jin tighter. We made it back to our rooms in silence. The others were equally unsettled, although I wasn't listening in on their thoughts, I could still feel their unease.

When they put me down in the humongous circle bed to discover trays floating within perfect reach, I hummed in delight. Especially when noting the seafood selection. "Thank you for this," I said, snatching up a peeled shrimp and dipping it into a nearby sauce.

Ryloh kneeled by my feet and began unlacing my sneakers while I chewed. Timos was calling someone in the corner by the windows. "How are you feeling, my love?" Jin asked.

"Okay, I guess. Not as good as I felt in the pod, obviously, but fine."

Timos low voice interrupted the momentary silence as we chowed down. "Where are you?" We couldn't hear the reply, but I felt the dragon's annoyance spring in response to whatever was said. "So, we should not expect your return then?" I stilled mid bite, causing Ryloh and Jin to scowl. "I am not your fucking handler," Timos clipped before hanging up.

"Are you alright, Timos babe?"

He shook his head, stomping over to grab a finger sandwich from a neatly arranged stack. "Avexei is dispirited at the moment," he said. I wasn't sure if mine or the fae's cringe was more severe. "Perhaps Ryloh could placate him, but I cannot muster the patience."

"Did you find out what the possible solution from Olorun was?"

"Not yet," Timos replied. "He intends to join us for breakfast."

Ryloh stood and started toward the washroom, tossing over his shoulder, "I- I'll fetch him." Timos nodded and shot a message before joining Jin and me on the mattress.

"What?" I quizzed the dragon who was avoiding my eyes. "What is it?" I turned to Jin who was scratching the back of his neck uncomfortably. Since neither were replying, I turned inward, and attempted to listen in mentally... But they weren't there. Inaccessible.

"Olorun placed a temporary block on our mind-meld from whatever he injected you with in that pod. He said it would ease your transformation," Jin explained.

"*Oh*-kay," I drawled as they dodged my gaze.

When Ry left the bathroom, he said, "I'm off to find him th- then." My appetite vanished. The idea of Vex brooding somewhere bothered me to no end. I had to help.

"I'm coming with."

The guys were radio silent and tense as we rifted outside of a barren passage filled with oversized black doors. Unlike most of Uru I'd seen, this hallway was windowless. I stared at the neon 'Church' sign above the entrance with perplexity. Wherever we were, they weren't happy about it. Jin and Timos refused to stay behind, so it became a family affair. I was acting as Jin's backpack as we scurried inside the dimly lit space.

A partition hid the establishment from view, with a lingerie-clad hostess standing before it. Her ears were rounded, so she was probably mage. "Hi, can I help you?" The brunette greeted, eyeing us suspiciously. We were still wearing our matching grey sweats, and I snorted at the realization.

"Is there an entrance fee?" Timos asked. When she nodded, he passed his shell. She handed it back wordlessly, then waved an arm to raise the partition. A gasp escaped as a brothel slash strip club was revealed. They were blasting 90's R&B hits, and I couldn't keep my head from bobbing to the retro Usher as Jin stomped inside.

The name tracked as it was modeled after a dated Christian church, with vaulted wood beamed ceilings, stained glass windows, and chained pendant lights strung between them. Unlike a typical place of worship, the stage had a golden stripper pole dead center, and every inch was cast in deep red lights. The pews were remade into lounge-like seating with areas for drinks and other poisons while patrons were serviced in various stages of undress.

The employees were discernible by the iridescent subtle shimmer covering their skin. The club was admittedly cleaner and more luxurious than any I'd been to, but that didn't lessen the blow. Avexeidros has been here... *For how long?*

Wait, does it even matter?

No, it doesn't. He's not yours!

I bit my lip as my eyes scanned, checking each pew. Ryloh and Timos were a few paces ahead, arguing in hushed whispers. It was a relief when none of the rutting couples revealed Vex. "Why the fuck would he come here?" Jin spat, voicing my thoughts as we ambled into the madness.

"It cannot signify anything positive," Timos grumbled, readjusting his spectacles. The severity of my males' scowls deterred anyone from approaching.

Suddenly, the lights went from red to blue, eliciting a few squeals and claps from the unoccupied crowd. Then a blinding white beam cast onto the golden stripper pole atop the dais. "Take your seats," a passing nude glittery femme instructed.

Jin plopped down beside me, and Timos took my other side, hand in his; while Ryloh remained standing behind us, both palms on my shoulders. I could feel him raging most, with the dragon trailing closely behind.

When a waiter came to take our drink orders, waving his sparkly boner in Jin's face, I couldn't even crack a smile. In differing circumstances, I would've probably cackled, but anxiety was holding me hostage. *What if he hooked up with someone else?*

No, no, no. You aren't allowed to be upset.

You aren't technically together.

"It's Raining Men" started blasting and I cracked, smiling behind my palm. The others were really dampening the vibe. I would've probably felt less paranoia if they weren't suffocating me in their overreactions.

"I swear to all th- that is holy, if he betrayed you in any way, shape, or form, I will n- never speak to him again," Ryloh mumbled before clenching his stubbled jaw.

There wasn't an opportunity for me to react before Avexei strutted out onto stage nearly naked, glistening from head-to-toe. His tanned skin completely flawless, more defined and sculpted than the sexiest DaVinci. *At least his butt is covered.*

Ooop, nevermind. His black speedo had a thong back, he mooned the audience as he took a spin around the pole. I was too stunned to function. Lightheaded, as the male started dancing like a scene from *Magic Mike*. Vex had the most incredible body and moves.

Is this fucking real?

Muscles flexing, abs shimmering. Even his bare feet were enticing. I was drooling. As was everyone else. Each spin around the golden pole sent the onlookers into hysterics. Vex's face remained completely aloof, though. I couldn't even begin to guess what he was thinking.

My god. The cushion underneath me was likely soaked through. I hadn't even realized my mouth fell open until Timos closed it for me with the press of his icy finger.

"He's betraying you, why are you *aroused?*" Jin demanded, clearly peeved. I shrugged, incapable of averting my gaze from where Vex bent backwards and spun down to the stage. "Is he that…?"

"No," Timos clipped, earning a chortle from Ry.

"Vex is an attractive male. Not as much as me, though... Or probably you, Timoset. Maybe not even you, pupling," Ryloh taunted. I huffed, but the show was too distracting to intervene on their nonsense.

The crowd was going wild. A clique gathered around the stage to toss glitter as Vex neared. When he did a floor humping move, I might've squeaked. Timos snarled.

I couldn't decide whether I was more turned on or pissed off by the femmes and theys attempting to flirt with *my* man— *Shit. He's not, Nala.*

The only consolation was Avexei's inky hair, signifying his displeasure with their attention. It was a maddening ordeal. "This is unacceptable," Timos sneered. I shook my head, eyes still clamped onto the show. I couldn't stop myself from wishing *I* was that pole, honestly.

"Agreed," Ryloh said, cracking his knuckles.

Suddenly, a pair of the rowdy femmes jumped on the stage. Groping and grabbing at Vex. Despite him immediately shoving them back, my skin prickled with rage. It wasn't a normal bout of jealousy; this was something else entirely.

The edges of my vision darkened, it could've been from the transformation, or it could've been from my fury. Regardless, a growl clawed up my throat and fled. A clamorous one. Loud enough to finally capture the performer's attention.

"Shit," Vex mouthed. Freezing center stage. Face paling. A deer caught in the headlights.

The audience scattered in fright.

Of me.

Their reactions were validating. Static rose to the surface of my skin, sending a few surrounding patrons screaming. The establishment was emptying as I stormed the stage.

Avexei looked humiliated or terrified. Which was ridiculous, he was talented as shit. I couldn't help the slight curl to my lips, slithering my arms around his neck, whispering in his ear, "I was enjoying that until the end there." He was still unblinking, now shivering. "Vex?" I tried. Receiving nothing in return. The male could've been carved from glittery stone.

I heard the others nearing, bickering in hushed tones as their fury peaked, but they weren't my concern. "Did I do something wrong?" I pressed, deflating with every breath. *Quit touching him, you don't own him.*

"I'm so sorry," I breathed, arms tucking back to my sides, heart thumping erratically like it was trapped in the clothes dryer. I backed a step. All my prior arousal and excitement wiped when his dark brows fell.

"What the fuck is wrong with you?!" Timos shouted, shoving Vex's chest. His expression finally morphed. Dread seeped through my veins as Avexei's eyes narrowed in my direction. I didn't want to fight anymore. The constant bickering was exhausting.

"What are you doing here?" he rasped. As if that were a worthy question.

Ryloh lunged, punching a staticky fist into Vex's nose with a *crunch*. "How could you be so daft?"

Vex feigned a laugh, wiping the spewing blood with nonchalance, as if I weren't sensing his rampant discontent. "No one touched me, and even if they had, it doesn't matter! Nala's not mine!" I recoiled, walloped by the venom in his voice. Timos shrouded us in bleached smoke. The urge to scream 'but you're mine' clawed up my throat, but Ry interrupted.

"You're pathetic," Ryloh spat. "L- L- Likely th- the weakest being in this wretched place!"

"No, you are! You're the one who's whipped by someone who doesn't even love you back," Vex seethed as our surroundings were cast from red to white.

Harsh. I took Ry's hand, shaking my head in disapproval, it was an awfully cruel thing to say. Leaning into the fae's pointy ear, I whispered, "The most wounded creatures hit back the hardest." He nodded, but his lower lip wobbled.

This was getting out of hand.

"At least I'm attempting to im- im- improve my standing. Un- Unlike you, who's doing what right now exactly?" Ryloh groused. The Uktena hissed and they exchanged a shove.

"I was trying to free myself of *her*," Vex shouted.

Fucking Hell.

That hurt.

Far more than it should've. The thing in my chest was fuming. Stealing the air from my lungs.

I attempted to conceal my overreaction, but Timos slung an arm over my shoulder, likely sensing it. The music came to a screeching halt the second the room cleared. Surprisingly, no one bothered us or approached. But that was the least of my worries.

"She might not be angry with you, but we are," Jin grumbled. Ryloh clapped a palm to his shoulder in solidarity and my jaw unhinged from surprise. *Really?*

This is what it takes to unify them?

Avexei's obsidian eyes were avoiding mine. Pretending as if I weren't present. *It shouldn't bother you; he's made his intentions clear.*

After the refusal last night, he claimed it wasn't a rejection, but it sure felt like one now. Fitting that it took place in a church, one of the settings I've dreaded most throughout my life.

"Can you take me back?" I murmured to Timos. Thankfully, he immediately obliged.

Thank Karma, Timoset removed Nala.

The fecking bagnio, really?

<<*"I can't believe he came here, either."*>

I was fuming. Vex not only broke his trust with her, but with me. Mated immortals do not seductively dance for an audience. No loin sharing with strangers!

"Wh- What were you thinking?"

The feigned angry mask fell from Vex's face, stealing some of my frustration with it. Not all though. With Nala spice now gone, the male shattered. Piece by piece, Yu-Jin and I witnessed as reality settled over his shoulders.

He fell to the disgusting sparkly stage in a heap of limbs, thong wearing ass up. *For Karma's sake.* I softly kicked his side with my sneaker, forcing his arse out of direct view. "I've been losing it. I couldn't take it anymore. The way Nala looks at me like I'm- I can't believe I was idiotic enough to think I could try to… FUCK," he broke.

Yu-Jin aggressively dipped his chin, in a 'say something to stop him,' conveyance. I sighed, pinching my brow. This was calamity and I lacked the patience to cushion my words. "Y- You've made a mess, Nala spice left near tears."

359

My comment didn't land well.

Avexeidros was now, distastefully, weeping. Paired with the glitter coating his skin, he looked doubly ridiculous. Yu-Jin gave him a sympathetic look, but I refused. His actions were astoundingly moronic. Distastefully basic. Even his dancing was off beat and horrid, as though his limbs weren't in agreement with his decisions.

Nala might've been impressed, but I wasn't.

The male had spent the last thirty years in love with her. The last two weeks stalking her incessantly. Enthralled by her whereabouts. By her habits. He went from the most bewitched among us, to the scoundrel. It hardly added up.

The lone reason Vex supposedly refused to accept their tethering was to save her from harm. To give Nala the opportunity to become further acquainted with him. *And yet...* "Y- You could've just accepted last night instead of this, you know," I clipped, incapable of reining myself in despite the fecking stammer. His blubbering worsened alongside my sputtering. Which was infuriating.

<<*"Give him a break, he's wrecked."*>

I rolled my eyes in response, gripping both males before rifting us back to the residence. From our closeness, I could now sense Nala's unease. I lifted my pointer to my lips as Avexei's wailing echoed through the living room. Jin forced him onto the couch as I peered into the bedroom, finding Timoset pacing outside the bathroom door.

Snapping my fingers, I motioned for him to follow, then warded the four of us in an attempt to remain out of earshot in the den. The dragon took one look at Vex and rolled his eyes. "She is devastated because of the way you spoke to her," he raged, falling onto the sofa.

"I wanted her to hate me," Avexei sniffled.

Mirroring my sentiment, the dragon lost it. Flipping over the coffee table before fisting Vex around the neck. "Why?"

Timoset loosened the hold enough for the Uktena to rasp, "I lost all sense after our spat. The brothel wasn't the first place I went, okay? My frustration grew as time went on. I was desperate. It was a misguided attempt to repel her! No one touched me, but the intent was there... I'm sorry. I owe each of you an apology."

Yu-Jin grimaced. "He's clearly regretful, Nala will probably forgive him. You should release him, Timoset."

There was another facet they weren't aware of, but the Siarc was correct.

Avexei's head bowed as more tears cut down his cheeks. "I'm sorry, Mo. And to you too, Lo and Jin. I just—" he heaved a sigh, wiping his errant tears. "I just felt as though she would be better off without me. And wanted to see if I could get by without her… See if I could get hard."

I covered my laugh with a cough. *What a twat.* "And you couldn't get it up?" Yu-Jin clarified with a raised brow.

"No," Vex replied with a shake of his obsidian tresses. "What I did was inexcusable though. I know that. I want her forgiveness. Obviously. Even if I don't deserve it." When Timoset growled, and Avexei rushed out, "I'll do whatever she desires. Whether it's to bond—"

"No!" Timoset's unbidden growl left my ears trilling.

There was no withholding my sigh as I revealed the crux. "Although I vehemently agree with you, Timoset, unfortunately for us, what Avexei did wouldn't be considered as cheating on Earth."

"It would not?" Timoset validated with a frown, and I nodded. "But his ass was out for dozens to see?"

"N- No one touched him, touching is cheating. Not looking, as it is here. Even despite the way in which he exposed himself," I explained.

Nala chose that cursed moment to join us.

She'd done well in disguising her weariness, but her darting eyes gave the discomfort away. "Are y'all hollerin' in here?" I nodded, causing her to heave a sigh. She fell back onto the sofa, tucking her legs underneath her, ordering, "Jin, come sit by me." The Siarc obliged, all but sprinting over. "No offense, but the rest of you need lessons on emotional regulation. He's the only calm one here," Nala murmured, leaning into his side. Yu-Jin was now grinning from ear-to-fecking-ear.

She was right, though. A thousand times over. *Why are you so out of sorts over this, Cabbage? Vex's betrayal isn't your cursed problem, that incredible femme is.* Regulating my breath and straightening my back, I took Nala's other side, pulling her hand in mine. She attempted a weak smile, painfully forced. Yu-Jin and I shot scowls in Vex's direction at the opposite end of the sofa.

[["Avexei is unfortunately immune to dragon fire, otherwise I could have solved this."] Damn Timos for being so hilarious today. I broke, barking a momentary laugh, before regaining control. Until Yu-Jin and I locked eyes, causing a mirrored chortle to flee.

Yeah, Jin's not so bad.

"Why are you two crackin' up?" Nala demanded, her twang revealing her exhaustion. She loathed her accent as much as I loved it. *Especially when she says 'y'all.'*

<<*"Fuck, I love that, too."*>

Unfortunately, I could no longer find many faults with the pupling… *Unlike, Vex.*

"Timos has been on a roll today," I explained.

Nala's plush lips formed an O in shock. "Since when do you call him Timos?" she demanded, strangling my hand.

"Since today," I replied with a shrug. "Our friendship status is irrelevant. Why are we sitting out here while you're half asleep, N- Nala spice?" She gripped my hand with more force. I knew it was in support, but truthfully, no longer cared as much about stumbling in her presence.

"I've been in that chair all day, and I'm pretty sure I dozed off for a while. It's fine. I need to hear why this one was humpin' a pole instead of me. There's no way I'll be able to sleep without knowing."

[["She forgot to mention the fucking sparkles he doused himself in."]

That was it. Our trio *howled*. Nala couldn't help but chuckle along as we struggled to breathe. I couldn't risk a glance at the snake, not while he was glittering.

"It's not fair you're having a blast when I'm not in the brain gang," she pouted. "I've had a tough day, I wanna laugh too." We exchanged a glance, which only resulted in another giggle fit.

"You claim none touched you, so how did you get the sparkles?" Timos choked out, causing Avexei to frown as his hair darkened. Jin and I's shoulders shook as we attempted to rein it in.

Nala pouted, saying, "That's actually a very good question."

Our yowls broke free.

"It was a spell," Vex exclaimed. "Is that why you're laughing? *Oh*, grow up." I guffawed. "Dancing helps me relax! When I'm on stage with the lights and yelling the overstimulation soothes. I'm not gonna be ashamed."

"You shouldn't be," Nala insisted. "I would rather them tease you than hate you. Laughs over yells."

"He looked ridiculous," Timos exclaimed, and I felt the couch cushions dipping in sync with Jin's shaking shoulders.

Nala sighed, pinching her brow between her fingers. "Timos, I know you're ancient, babe, but no one should be embarrassed by their self-expression. Vex is really talented."

"He was exposing himself in a brothel!"

"Don't shame sex work," she chided with a deep-set scowl. Timos looked as though he might spontaneously combust from her reaction.

//"*She's not going to give in, dragon. I already told you this isn't a betrayal for her.*"/

My soulmate was so fecking forgiving and I loved her for it. When Nala revealed the strength she saw in my stammering stumbles, it tilted my view by several degrees, but tonight? She'd flipped the axis.

This former human understood each of us so thoroughly already.

Jin somehow managed to level his tone. "We aren't finished discussing how you ended up like this, Avexei. Help us understand."

"I second that," Nala said, crossing her arms.

With a heavy sigh and his head tilted towards the ceiling, Vex said, "After our fight, I was furious. At first, I went down to the gym, but it didn't quell. So, I started walking the streets. Just stewing over how angry I was with fate. Then with you." He said, dark eyes boring a hole into the rounded ceilings. "I know it's not your fault, Nala, but it was easy to blame you. Humiliating as it is to voice now, I spent hours convincing myself I hated you…" He trailed off as though there was more to it and Nala's face crumpled.

There was a terse beat of silence, and I kept my eyes on my sneakers to avoid an inopportune outburst. Our amoroso's emotions were stewing. Anger was typically a more fervent lure than arousal, but anguish seemed to cut the deepest. I felt her nature's sadness as though it was slicing my own black heart.

[["*He must suffer for upsetting her.*"]

//"*Tomorrow, Timos. They're both too fecking distraught tonight.*"/ *A puff of bleached smoke left the dragon's lips in aggravation.*

When a tear cut down Nala's cheek. It was likely her nature's reaction, however, Timos still roared. Sending an array of vines to wrap around the Uktena's neck.

<<"*We might have to restrain him.*">

Fabulous. Just what we needed, a frenzied fecking dragon.

"Timos, release him please," I said in exasperation, and surprisingly, he obliged. My attention was consumed by Vex, I needed to understand, craved it, couldn't pay attention to anything else. Including the rage circling the room. "So, you were trying to for- forget about me?" I grimaced after the broken whisper left my lips. *That sounded far more pathetic than intended.*

I actually enjoyed most of the show. *So, why are you upset, Dodo bird? Hmm...*

Beastie, probably. It was true, she was far more tormented than I was. And who was she to take control over my emotions like that? With my resolve in place, I wiped the stupid tears, and schooled my expression.

Avexei nodded, Timos released another blast of smoke, and Ryloh sighed. Jin was the only one who seemed to not be in a state, so I gripped him tighter. Sighing before asking, "And did your distraction work?"

"No. I never stopped thinking of you," Vex confirmed, his hair shifting to blues and greens. He held my gaze as his obsidian eyes shone with tears. Eventually breaking our silence to rasp, "I fucked up, Nala. I'm so sorry."

Ryloh supplicated, "He couldn't get an erection." As if that made any difference...

Did it though? Fuck if I knew.

Avexei's chin fell to his bare shimmery chest as he said, "It was a mistake, I knew it immediately. I was seconds from losing my shit when you growled. You should despise me for it, Nala. More than Mo currently does. He's probably gonna kill me, so I might as well admit it didn't work. Not even a little bit. What I feel for you is beyond modern language's comprehension."

He technically didn't do anything wrong, and you were turned on watching him, too. However, instead of sifting through the growing mess of my emotions, I prompted, "Why are you fuming, Timoset?"

He stilled. "Avexei blatantly betrayed you. The rest of us would never consider nearing a burlesque, let alone a brothel. There is no excuse." Similar disappointment was reflected in each of their faces, including Vex's. I knew Timoset and Yu-Jin loved me, without question. But Ryloh was barely looking at Avexei without devastation crossing his striking face.

Does he love you too? Damn.

I required confirmation. "You're all *this* upset on my behalf?"

"Obviously," Ryloh chided. Rendering me speechless. "It's a betrayal here, Nala spice."

My heart might've cracked. This unified front was... *They do love you. Clingers to infinity and beyond.*

"My issue is that Vex got snippy with Ry and me. The show was hot. Am I happy that he was trying to forget me? No." I sighed when several more growls slipped. "But," I drawled, "he's sorry. We've all been under a lot of pressure. Jin broke. Ry broke. I broke. Timos, what Vex did tonight is the same thing. He regrets it."

My dragon wasn't having it, he kept shaking his chestnut coils out of place.

"This is incredibly childish." The comment didn't come from one of mine. "And loud."

I spun, discovering an enormous Black male in the doorway. *Olorun.* Had to be. He was wearing a regal and futuristic robe, shifting in shade with his every step. Many of his features were similar to Timos, although with far deeper skin and a purple cloud of hair, there was a resemblance.

"Your assumptions are correct, Nala. I am Mo-Mo's father's twin. It is a pleasure to finally meet you," he said in a booming lilt that rendered the rest of the dumbasses silent. "Must I separate the remainder of you, or can you behave? Mo-Mo, you especially, take a seat before you topple into frenzy." Timos immediately did as told. His wings tucked away, too.

The Titan's prestige was evident. Weirdly, I could *feel* it. The power seemed to stifle the air flow.

"It's nice to meet you too," I said, when finally remembering my manners. "I'm so sorry we disturbed you. I'll try to keep them quiet."

Olorun shared a kind smile. "You are not to blame, Nala dear. I hoped we might wait till morning for introductions but arranged for an in-between, just in case. Follow me," he motioned over his shoulder, heading out the entrance. We scrambled after, with me at the lead.

"Where are we going?" I questioned.

"Dining hall," he replied before taking a left, where an automatic door *whirred* open. Revealing an expansive and brightly lit whimsical space. The arched roof comprised of levered glass, casting a light glow that made it feel like early morning, despite being the middle of the night. There were cartoonish statues towering overhead composed entirely of florals and fruits.

As I opened my mouth to inquire their purpose, Olorun said, "Those are to entertain Echo and Willa, our younglings, while they dine." There were dozens of installations scattered between round arranged tables.

With a snap of Olorun's fingers, a slew of Mors scurried in, each carrying a golden lidded tray. Garlic. Oregano. Rosemary. The scents were divine, and my stomach growled in turn. "Right on cue," Olorun said as he made his way towards the largest table.

I took a seat between Timos and Ryloh, across from the Titan who was already chewing away, while Avexei and Jin sandwiched his sides. Mors darted around us, delivering drinks, all different. Mine seemed to be filled with orange juice, while Ry's smelled like vodka, and Timos' had sparkling water. There was a blend of breakfast, lunch, dinner, and dessert gathered. All of my forking favorites. In every category. Olorun shared a wink as he chewed on some kimchi.

Afterward, cleared his throat to proclaim, "Vex's forgiveness is Nala's decision."

"I don't deserve her forgiveness," Avexei insisted.

"It's not your decision," Olorun chided over the rim of his glass. He took a measured sip under our scrutiny. "The lot of you should be grateful to possess such a relaxed and understanding kontrolü. My Yemaya would have castrated you, bond acceptance or not."

I giggled as the remainder of the table winced. "I hope I'll get to meet her before we leave."

"You shall," the Titan replied before taking another bite. I shoved one down my own throat without looking, just to break from staring agog at my new uncle. "She will delight in the fellow pack leader in you."

"But that's only the nature which chose Nala," Jin said with a frown.

"Untrue," Olorun replied, "the reason a kontrolü nature chose Nala was for her grit." A smile teased my lips as I shoved another forkful down my trap.

We fell into a comfortable silence with the cutlery scrapes as background music. "*Well*, five minutes have passed. I am surprised none of you have begun the inquisition yet," Olorun eventually interrupted.

My males shifted uncomfortably. There was an awkward pause where no one touched their food. "Are we just allowed to ask away?" I broke the silence, like a doofus. Olorun shared a coy smile in return. So, I pushed my luck and questioned, "Will I keep all four of them?"

"That is entirely up to you, my dear," he said.

Timos tried, "You must have *seen* —"

"Of course, I have been shown plenty. However, I have not yet *seen* a set path. Not with this particular facet. Each of Nala's actions could have lasting implications." *How very comforting.*

"You never saw me with her once?" Jin asked and Olorun shook his head, leaving him frowning. "She does make the decisions then."

Ryloh *tutted*. "Destiny is presenting Nala th- the options."

"Correct, fate is not fixed. Timoset was the lone male I saw mated to Nala initially, sometime around his birth. Several millennia passed before I glimpsed her with Ryloh or Vex. Both of your visions were never prophetic, unlike the dozen I have *seen* of her and Mo-Mo."

"Are y- you hinting he's the only m- m- male who sticks?" Ryloh demanded, fuming.

Olorun shrugged. "Not necessarily. As I have said, it is Nala who decides your fates."

Avexei grimaced, directing his question toward Uncle, "Did you know what I'd do tonight?"

The Titan nodded, expression declining, and I felt my gut sinking. Maybe it was the way he was so intentionally gentle despite his all-knowing ancient-ness, but I had a visceral reaction from his frown. "I hoped for the best, Vex. Although I knew your mistake was a risk, there were unfortunately more pressing motives for requiring your presence…"

Olorun's eyes suddenly began glowing, transforming from their hazel shade to blankness. He wasn't blinking anymore. It didn't even seem as though he was breathing. His expression softened as he stared behind my head.

"So…" I drawled.

"He's having a vision," Jin said.

"Yeah, I got that." I chewed on my lip until Timos' started snapping at me to speak my mind. "Listen, I know Uncle Olo's family and I do like him. He's cool. But do you really think this guy has solutions for us? He's being pretty evasive."

"I trust Uncle Olo with my life and yours. The reason for his bringing us here might not be immediately unveiled, but there is always a purpose behind his every word," Timos replied in his grumpy lump state.

"You spent half the day in an invention he made for you," Jin accused.

"Touché," I relented.

"It threw me for a loop when he joked about us questioning him. Uncle Olo usually despises being asked about what he's *seen*. No one else found that unsettling?" Avexei prompted.

"The n- numbskull has a point." Ryloh scratched his chin, adding, "I think we should—"

Uncle suddenly came to, interjecting, "The star shard." His yellowy hazel eyes returned along with the curl to his dark lips. "Nala must spend time with the star shard."

"What for?" Timos demanded.

Olorun shrugged as he sipped from his glass. "It has a message for her."

"What's the star shard?"

"The civilization of Stars was responsible for one beneficial contribution to our society prior to their demise. Since they were a population of Seers, they foresaw more of our galaxy's future than others. It is a crystalized artifact imbued with their remaining magic and visions which possesses its own consciousness.

"It was known as the star crystal prior to the Fall. However, after the Stars' demise, we voted to break it into pieces. There were thirteen shards divided between the most prestigious Titans. Majority were lost over time, some destroyed, others misplaced or concealed. Now, there are only two known remnants, one of which resides here," Olorun explained.

"It'll talk to me? Like warnings of the future?" I asked, and he nodded. "Can't you just share what it intends to say? Isn't that what you just saw?"

Olorun chuckled. "No, I only glimpsed the aftermath of your visit."

"Creepy," I mumbled as my quad turned green. "Should we go now?"

"No. You must first complete your transformation." Then Olorun stood, proclaiming, "I shall leave you to it. Please keep it down as Echo and Willa are slumbering. As a reminder, Avexei's forgiveness is Nala's decision alone. Ta-ta." And just like that, the Titan rifted out.

Knowing things likely couldn't get any worse, I broke our silence with, "Vex, you're sleeping on the couch with me tonight."

They erupted. *Again.* Not even the Uktena seemed pleased with my decision. "There are children sleeping," I whisper-shouted, and thankfully they shut up. "Uncle Olo told y'all this is up to me, and I want to have a conversation without you breathing down our necks."

Instead of responding, they eyed each other wearily.

"Please?" I tried. Unsurprisingly, Jin caved first with a nod. Then, came Ryloh. But the gods were holding firm. "Timos, you're supposed to be incapable of refusing me. What happened?" He grunted, avoiding my eyes. "Pretty please with a cherry on top? We won't bond. It's just to talk."

Ryloh scowled, snapping, "Shower first, Vex. You are filthy in m- more ways than I- I'm able to count."

"No one touched me!" Avexei's shoulders drooped. "Nala, our conversation can wait until tomorrow. You shouldn't overexert yourself. Sleeping on the couch can't be as restful."

"I'm your kontrolü, am I not?" Their heads bobbed. "Then I'll meet you on the couch, Vex. The rest of you are gonna share that nice bed and I don't wanna hear another peep. Are we clear?"

I gripped the two nearest shoulders and waited for them to rift us back. When no immediate action was taken, I growled, and they finally obliged. We reappeared in the residence.

While Avexei bathed, I decided to search the sparse cabinets along one of the dining room's walls for anything to take the edge off. Alcohol. Nicotine. Weed. It didn't matter. Defining feelings was pesky business. Unfortunately for me though, the storage was barren.

Which was why I paced. From one end of the dining room into the living room, then circling back. Again, and again. *Round and round the table we go.* My noggin was blank for once. Emotions continued ravaging my psyche, of course, but in eerie thoughtless silence.

I felt him once he mutely stepped into the room. The thing in my chest wasn't buzzing, no, we weren't close enough for that. It wasn't his fresh cotton scent, either. I'd been struggling to claim it because it hardly made sense. Our very tangible connection. It was more than a feeling. Greater. *Like atomic entwinement.*

Avexei's deep gravel repeating, *'beyond modern language's comprehension,'* rang through my brain unbidden as the only valid description. "Nala, I'm so fucking sorry. I don't know what else to say. There's no discussion to be had. You should go to bed —"

I interrupted him with a zap of static before turning around. Avexei was shirtless and incredibly distracting, slightly dripping as he ran a tan hand through his damp tresses to brush them back. Drool worthy even without the body shimmer. Washboard abs. Rib tattoos in a script I couldn't discern from our distance. "You shouldn't be using your gifts right now," he groused, and I rolled my eyes, motioning for him to sit. "I truly am so fucking sorry," he rushed out as the buzzing in my chest cranked up.

"I've told you I'm not mad, so what are you apologizing for exactly?" I questioned, taking the cushion at his opposite, tucking my knees underneath me.

He lifted a brow as his locks went from gloomy blues to a fiery red. "You might fool the others with your bullshit, Nala, but you can't lie to me." His dark eyes narrowed as his voice rose an octave. "You think I didn't see how much I fucking hurt you?"

"I don't need you to validate me, Vex! I, however, *do* need you to stop driving yourself to the point of insanity. We both know if you would've given into the bonding, this wouldn't have happened. It was more devastating being rejected by you than it was seeing your ass shaking around on stage. I liked the show, that wasn't an exaggeration," I snarked.

He tilted his head towards the high ceilings to sigh. "I don't know how to apologize to you properly. Or maybe I shouldn't —"

"Action, Vex. I need you to shut the fuck up and act," I snapped.

"What do you need? I'll do anything. I'd sacrifice myself if you asked. I don't care."

I rolled my eyes. *These four and their freaking extremes.* However, it was a valid question. As I stared into his imploring eyes, Ryloh's comment resurfaced. "Take your pants off," I demanded. It was mostly from curiosity.

Avexei sputtered as his head went through an entire rainbow and eventually landed on magenta. We exchanged a few wordless blinks.

"What?" he breathed.

Apparently I needed to spell it out. "You said you couldn't get hard." As expected, he shook his head. "Weren't you insinuating you could only get hard for me?" He nodded, his Adam's apple bobbing. "Then prove it," I said, crossing my arms.

"I don't know if I can with you looking at me like that," he murmured, onyx eyes wide.

"*Now.*"

Avexei jumped, throwing his sweatpants to the floor, sitting back down with both hands cupping the goods. He raised a brow as I canted my head. He audibly gulped. "Nala, you're being weird. Why are you looking at me like that? You told the others we wouldn't bond."

I barked a condescending laugh. He bristled, standing up again, hands still hiding his junk. "Are you scared of me seeing your limp dick?"

"*No*," Vex shouted, falling right into my trap. His big hands flew toward the ceiling in exasperation or proof. Either way, I got more than an eyeful. I died and was transported to wiener heaven. Times four because they were all equivalently impressive.

And he was hard.

Throbbing, actually.

He gave me 'are you fucking happy now' look as I bit my lip. My mouth dried, so it took a few tries to rasp, "You aren't having any issues." He looked down for a blink, then back to me, donning a smirk as he shrugged. Arms still raised as if he was surrendering. Making those ridiculous stacked muscles of his stretch and —

"What the fuck is this?!" Timos.

We both turned to find, not one, but all three Musketeers peering through the archway. Someone yelped the same second I went sideways from laughter. Tears were streaming as the dragon tackled Avexei. "No scuffling!" I managed to choke through my howls. "I forced him to get naked!"

"Wh- Why?" Ryloh demanded.

Their reactions hit harder. It took a while before I settled for long enough to explain. "It was to prove a point. He wasn't flashing me."

"Why the erection then?" Jin demanded. *Boner police, officer, sir.* I cackled.

Avexei shrugged, then revealed, "I'm always hard around her."

Jin and Ryloh both were shaking their heads staring at the floor. While Timos was struggling to keep from strangling the disgruntled Avexei standing beside him. Who was also, very much, still naked. And erect.

Timos released a puff of aggravation. "Quit staring at his cock!"

"I thought we agreed to y'all going to bed?" I replied.

"You're still staring, N- Nala," Ryloh clipped.

What did they expect with a giant standing there with his dick and general godorosity on display? Avexei was the only one grinning as I raised my eyes to shrug a singular shoulder.

"Have you forgiven him?" Jin questioned.

"That depends on whether or not he's gonna refuse me again," I offered.

We all turned toward Vex, who confirmed, "I won't. I swear, whatever you want, Nala."

"He's forgiven then," I proclaimed. Earning myself a growl from Timos. "That doesn't mean we're gonna bond anytime soon. Calm down."

Jin sighed. "What if we agree to allow Avexei into the bed?" When Ry and Timos opened their mouths to argue, he tacked on, "At our feet tonight in punishment."

"Done," I said in my best grumpy fae reenactment. Who didn't appreciate it one bit. Ryloh was scowling as I roughed up his hair and jumped to ride on his tattooed back to the bedroom. Shouting over my shoulder, "Vex's gotta sleep naked, though."

They didn't appreciate my joke.

Due to the worse wiggling and worming underneath my skin, Timos was forced to carry me to the lazaretto the next morning. The walk was a blur. I fell into a deeper slumber once locked into the pod. Until it emitted a, "*bloop, bloop,*" startling me awake. Oddly, it reminded me of a TiVo remote. "Transformation complete, removing intravenous hydration." The IV removal was less noticeable than the injection. I was yawning when the lid cracked.

To reveal a beautiful Black woman staring back. Her natural hair was decorated in an array of delicate chains, as were her hands, wrists, and bare feet, accentuating her luminescent skin and sleeveless futuristic robes. "I don't mean you any harm," she said. Her accent was odd, a blend of far too many to decipher, revealing who she had to be.

"I know. You're Aunt Yemaya, right?" I guessed with an awkward smile, and she nodded, remaining aloof. "Nice to meet you." She extended an adorned hand to help me climb out of the egg, her palm boiling. Once upright, I noticed she only had a few inches on me.

Then my eyes darted around the empty space. "Where are my goons?" I questioned, stretching my arms overhead and realizing the worming had cleared. *Thank you, Uncle Olorun.*

"They are confined to the residence. All fine. Irritating, though. I found the four cumbersome, far more than I remember either of mine being. Do they struggle with following orders?" I snorted in response, and she scowled. "I wished to spend some alone time with you. Perhaps a topic of discussion should be how they require a heavier hand." *Fair enough.*

I nodded, incapable of more as her sunflower-shaped eyes scrutinized me from head to toe. Yemaya's pupils were the seeded centers while her irises were the orange and yellow petals. *Neat-o!*

"You are fearless for a former mortal," Yemaya said over her shoulder as I followed down the staircase. "Most cower upon noticing the flames in my gaze." *Gross, that's gotta be triggering.* "Do you not fear me?" she grilled with a raised brow.

"Not really," I said, my nervousness was from wishing to impress.

Yemaya only hummed in response.

Once we made it to a glassed skywalk, I gathered enough courage to say, "It's gotta be tough being as old as time. I'm sure it's a nuisance being a Titan."

Yemaya chuckled as her elaborately layered chains *jingled* against the shiny floors with each step. "It is not always negative. Nor positive. Although I can confirm my visions of our kinship were correct. Not only are you rare in spirit, but prestige. I came to offer you my guidance, Nala. As a fellow kontrolü, and I am also one of the lone Titans who concern themselves with mortals. Your unique perspective is of personal interest," she said.

"I'll take as much help as you're willing to give."

"I suspected as much… They have been sheltering you, I see."

My brows furrowed. "Pardon?" *How's she seeing that?*

"I possess mind-command. You know little to nothing of what to anticipate." *Great, another in my noggin. At least this one was being helpful.*

"Really? They answered my questions. Eventually. It took a while. But I thought we had finally gotten to a trustworthy—"

Yemaya *tutted*. "My comment has nothing to do with trust, they are besotted. You failed to ask the correct questions."

"That's probably true," I relented.

Seemingly accepting, she shifted her gaze forward. "Being femme, especially one with above average prestige, is a battle. You will terrify and wonder most in equal measure. It is exhausting. Infuriating. Yet also rewarding, because you will disarm most." *Damn, you should be taking notes.* "As such, you will require a peaceful home. To circle back to the bickering males, you cannot cushion your feelings to spare them. Define boundaries. Otherwise, they shall remain incorrigible."

"We call that people pleasing on Earth and I'll admit, it's a bad habit of mine," I said.

"I understand. However, you cannot please everyone, Nala. It does not mean you should be intentionally hurtful. Emotions require validation. Besides, if you do not voice your desires, how can they fulfill them? Why have you not voiced how their bickering is reminiscent of those you willfully abandoned?"

I chewed on my lower lip, knowing she was right. *You're not alone and single anymore.*

"No longer," Yemaya confirmed, admitting she was listening in again. It didn't feel creepy or like an overstep, despite her blank expression, I knew she was trying to help. She tapped the top of my head, interrupting my musing, to ask, "Why have you hidden in the washroom when you possess invisibility? It seems far less dramatic to—"

"From who?!" My outburst couldn't be helped.

She frowned and replied, "Vex. You were unaware?"

I groaned. "We haven't gotten there yet. It's gonna be awhile longer, too."

"He cheated then," Yemaya snarled, the yellows in her eyes flickering like a pyre.

"Not technically. At least, not to me. I just question whether or not it's real, you know? Like, do I feel this way for Vex because he's playing hard to get, or is it fate? I question whether our connection's *really* real. It's not something I pondered with Ryloh or Timos either, there's something different with him. It feels out of my control."

Yemaya sighed and stopped in the middle of the walkway, gripping both my shoulders in her overheated palms. My skin adjusted suddenly, cooling to counteract her. The dick magic noticeably more potent. "Nala, does it truly matter?" She pressed, and I nodded. "The cause is irrelevant," she insisted.

"I don't think I can accept that. Olorun preached how it's my decision. It did feel like it was in the beginning with Jin, then Timos, sorta with Ry.

But with Vex I have no choice. We're connected so deeply, I can literally feel him without looking, it's spooky."

"Tethers, unfortunately, have remained a mystery since the Dawn. Yours do not behave as they should which only adds complications. My recommendation is to follow your feelings and dismiss causation entirely."

"I appreciate your transparency, but that's gonna drive me insane," I rebuked.

"If it may be comforting, Olo would claim it was fate. Whereas Sima would claim it was your nature. The other Titans would be equally split between the two."

"What do *you* think?" I had to know. Auntie had managed to earn my trust in record time. I valued her opinion. Probably more than Min's. She was in my brain, so how could I not?

Yemaya shared a pained curl of her lips, so feigned it was more of a grimace. "I believe you are the source. Just as I believe it is me who creates my own fate and controls my nature. The rest is irrelevant. It is your life, Nala. You decide which sensations and signs to heed. We are unfortunately one in the same. I fretted over the meanings behind why I was chosen for this role for millennia. Allow me to prevent similar disappointment, save your passion for that which holds the most significance."

"Why the sad smile then?"

"You will suffer."

Suffer?!

It was probably the most ominous thing anyone had ever said to me. The taste and smell of ash overwhelmed my senses. My breath hitched as panic swarmed. It took me awhile to recover the ability to speak. "Couldn't you pick a less aggressive term?" I rasped.

"It was not my intention to daunt you, Nala. Our world is more difficult for kontrolü. Not only will the Council subject you to harsher testing despite your connections to both Olorun and the Supremae, but you shall face many trials. None too great to overcome, but still, you will suffer often. Suffering is the singular facet all beings share. You should attempt to thrive instead of surviving when faced with the unfortunate."

It wasn't much of a comfort, but it was enough to inflate my lungs again. When the oxygen returned to my noggin, I decided suffering wasn't foreign. At least I now had a family who would ensure I reached the highest highs when not in the dumps.

"Yes, you possess a solid support system. The males are fiercely loyal, including Vex. As much as I loathed witnessing his path, the male has been 'scared straight,' as you mortals say." Yemaya said with a grimace, and I couldn't withhold my chortle.

"I think you're my favorite Auntie, Yemaya."

"I know," she replied simply, turning down a skywalk that gave a closer view to the swimming dome a few floors down. It was just as packed as it had been when I saw it yesterday.

"Are there any natural water sources on Uru?" I wondered aloud, and she shook her chains into a *tinkling* 'no.' "How do you manage? I couldn't live without having an ocean nearby."

Yemaya shrugged. "Uru has benefits which outweigh its lacking natural environment. We possess the most equated and intertwined community of any planet. You learn to overlook the negatives. I would know, we have spent significant time throughout the galaxy. Each must find the environment best suited for their needs and natures. For us, with two small children, it is incomparable."

"How old are Echo and Willa?" I quizzed.

Her face softened as she grinned to share, "One and two years."

I nearly yelled, *'so young,'* but tamped down the impulse. They probably had their reasons for waiting to begin their family, and who was I to pry into their ancient lifespans. Instead, saying, "They must be adorable." We passed the swimming dome in silence, heading down another hall.

Yemaya's mention of having seen every planet sparked interest. We were still planning on returning to Neptune, but that could easily change. "What's your favorite place besides Uru?"

"I am not one to select favorites."

"Well, I've heard Venus is nicer than Neptune," I shared.

She *tutted* again. "Neptune is for those who prefer an aquatic humid environment. As for its negatives, it is modern and lacks historical charm. It is also lacking in natural features besides its oceans. Whereas Venus is the opposite, it was the first planet inhabited; its buildings are ancient, and it possesses variable climates and landscapes. Although it does lack night and moons." *Interesting.* Especially considering I found Neptune's architecture incredibly dated.

A transporter flew past, its matte golden shell reflecting a blue beam into our eyes as it went, reminding me of Hades and the Underworld. "What about Hell?"

"Very similar to Venus, it was the second planet inhabited," Yemaya explained. "Hell has similar historical charm and a high population. However, they lack sunlight."

"I hope I'll get to see both," I said wistfully.

Yemaya nodded with a smile, "You shall."

"You've *seen* it?"

She turned down a cream hallway lined with holographic floating screens on each side. Some showed video feeds of what I assumed were rooms in residence, while others were set to control panels. "Yes. Just as on Earth, you will travel frequently. Not only for your own reasons, but the Council will require it of you."

As I went to open my mouth to ask why, we turned down a familiar passage. Yemaya had walked me back to our rooms. She paused in front of the closed archway to proclaim, "You require training."

The abrupt turn in conversation wasn't what I expected. "Alright," I chirped.

"Given your tangled emotional state, only Vex should accompany you." The Titan snapped her fingers, and a startled Avexei manifested beside us. He was in another casual set, wearing the same damn sweats, just black this time. "Training, Vex. Nala requires it now that her transformation has completed. You are best suited for the task. You know where to go."

Avexei's hair was shifting from shade to shade as he clarified, "The roof?"

"Yes. Apologies for my bluntness, Nala, but I have surpassed my daily limit for social interaction. I shall see you both prior to your departure." *You need to take notes on personal boundaries from her.* Yemaya disappeared with a wave.

Vex was fidgeting uncomfortably and avoiding my gaze as I greeted with a soft, "Hi." We hadn't spoken since last night's fiasco and his scent was driving me nuts. As was the stupid buzz in my chest.

"Are you sure you want me to help with this?" he grumbled, staring at the floors.

My heart panged unhappily. "Yemaya insisted it should be you."

Vex finally met my gaze. The tension between us pulled taut as his dark bottomless eyes searched mine. A few blinks passed before a boyish grin replaced his discomfort. "Your ears, Nala," he crooned, extending a digit to poke my right ear-tip.

"What?"

"Your transformation gave you Ry's ears," Avexei replied with a wide grin. "They suit you." I couldn't muster a response to his flirting. As much as I wanted to breeze past everything that'd happened, the destiny forced magnetism was holding me back.

So, I pulled a U-turn on the conversation. "I remember y'all saying no one questions Olorun, but I think Yemaya's the one actually running this ship."

Avexei chuckled. "No one gets a word in with Aunt Maya. She had us locked in all morning without any explanation." He offered his palm. When my skin felt the nippiness of his, the bond in my chest started blaring, effectively yanking on the strain between us. And then we rifted.

We reappeared in a barren concrete room with rounded corners. There wasn't a door or any windows. The lone illumination was a strip of skylights where a bright teal beam cast through. "What is this place? Are we still in their residence?"

Vex nodded. "Uncle Olo created this level for Mo and me to practice when we were kids. We spent most of our summers here, beating the ever-loving shit out of each other." There was a fleeting smile before it was replaced with a frown, as if the memories pained him. I hated it.

It was my fault. Timos was shoved into reclusion because Avexei became closer to Ryloh. Now with the Church nonsense the chasm between them had widened. Sure, Avexei made the mess, but it was all *because of me*. "I'm sorry." I said, squirming, shifting from foot-to-foot.

Vex's frown worsened, and my gut twisted. "Fuck that, Nala. I'm the one who's to blame. Can you please stop?"

"Stop what?" I bristled.

He gave me a once over before heaving a sigh. "Yemaya's right. I can already sense how much stronger you are. We should focus on you expelling as much as possible. It will help you maintain control."

"Ryloh's static is all I've been taught to use."

Avexei scowled. "Seriously?" I nodded, and his frustration worsened. "We'll start with static then, release what you can."

My gaze darted around the barren space as I asked, "Where should I aim it though? It'll bounce off these walls, won't it?"

"Hit me."

I shook. He nodded. We kept going back and forth until I shouted a vehement, "No."

Vex closed the distance to snarl, "Hit me. I fucking deserve it." His chest bumping against mine. Admittedly, there was a chaotic part reveling in the opportunity to dole punishment.

However, there'd already been enough drama. I backed a step. "I can't hurt you, Vex."

The next thing I knew, I was flat. My head hitting the concrete with a *smack*. The pain didn't last long, thanks to my faster healing, but still. *He shoved you to the freaking ground!*

"Fight back," Vex ordered, leering overhead as I rose to my elbows.

"You could've cracked my skull open," I snapped, my annoyance rising a notch.

He taunted me with a smirk. "And what are you going to do about it, baby?" *Ugh! Baby's a stupidly average and unbelievably mediocre term of endearment.* I wasn't sure whether I hated the word itself, or the way my body reacted to his rumbly lilt saying it, more.

"Don't call me that," I groused, hopping to my feet.

"Apologies, it slips, little lioness." *No! Even worse.* It was a far cuter nickname. From the smug look on his godly face, the male knew it too. His hair was also the perfect silver pigment that made the bronzed shade of his skin glow. It was annoying.

All of it.

"Why are you goading me?"

Avexei shrugged. "You seem to be struggling with directions. I'm the one in charge. At least, in here I am." My eyes narrowed as agitation peaked.

Something inside of me protested the validity of that.

Sparked.

Roared.

A shudder racked my limbs as the vibration turned to thrashing in my chest.

Woah.

Something felt different. Actually, *I* felt different.

I couldn't help the bolts of static that exploded forth, covering my frame in a suit of lightning. Jin's t-shirt was slowly burning off, so I attempted to rein it in like Ryloh taught me with deep breaths. But it wouldn't recede. Only worsening. At least my sports bra and leggings seemed to be static proof. *Probably Ryloh's doing.*

The sparks around my eyes blurred our concrete surroundings, forcing me to clamp them tight. I took several deep breaths. But it didn't quell the swarming sensation.

Avexei wasn't wearing the same fierce expression when I reopened my eyes. He was gawking as he extended a palm toward my electrified cheek. "So beautiful," he breathed.

Oh, ho, ho, no. Coming from the male who spent hours attempting to erase you last night? Absolutely not.

Now furious, I zapped him back a step.

It couldn't be helped. Nor could the way my chest rose and fell as I sent another barrage of bolts in his direction. None of which he dodged. Avexei took every hit with a grunt. His grimace didn't counteract how good it felt to finally release.

Fear. Overwhelm. Sadness. Self-pity. Rage… You name it, I let it go.

Eventually, Avexei began glowing, in what I assumed to be a ward.

I didn't know how much time had passed.

None of the static waned, if anything, it was strengthening the less I paid attention.

The force circling in my chest demanded I continue.

Zip, zap, inhale. Zappy, zippy, exhale. Again, and again.

I didn't realize I was screaming at the top of my lungs until the room went white. It didn't matter, I closed my eyes and reveled in how good it felt to let it go. This was exactly what I needed after the worming transition these past few days.

Relief.

"Nala!"

The minty air climbing up my throat and leaving my lips felt too soothing to ease.

"Fucking stop it, Nala!"

I didn't want to, though.

"NALA!"

I cracked an eye to find all of my males staring back. Along with Olorun and a terrifyingly furious Yemaya. *Whoops.*

My mouth clamped shut. The surrounding brightness faded a tad. But not entirely.

Which was when I took note of the fire.

Iridescent bleached flames in every direction.

The room was completely destroyed. Concrete crumbled. Particles dancing in the air. I spread a sheepish smile as my cheeks heated. Unsure of what to say. Someone was holding a bubble around us to keep out the poisonous air, but I couldn't tell you who.

"Dragon fire," Olorun broke the silence with a chuckle. Timos sputtered, then swayed, and almost fell to the floor but Avexei caught, then righted him. The others were equivalently stunned.

"You knew?" Yemaya growled at her soulmate. "And you still allowed me to send them here to train?!" Olorun's grin spread. She punched him, and he howled, hunching over and heaving from the force of his glee.

Vex recovered first. "Why the fuck have none of you been training Nala? This wouldn't have happened if she'd practiced *anything* prior." They grumped back in various states of displeasure. I was still too shocked to speak.

"I taught Nala spice how to leverage static. She's quite talented with it," Ryloh corrected. "T- Timoset is obviously to blame, he's been avoiding showing her the draconic gifts, hoping she wouldn't inherit them... And look what good it did. We will obviously pay for these damages, Yemaya." She growled in response, still glowering at her partner.

"I was attempting to protect her," Timos rasped.

"The star shard," Olorun interjected, straightening to his full enormity. "It is time for Nala to converse with the shard."

The tension during our walk to the star shard was thick enough to slice with a butter knife. I didn't know how to process. Initially, it seemed pretty freaking rad to have dragon fire. But it was impossible to hold onto that excitement when the males I wanted to celebrate with were panicking. I could feel the rampant discomfort stemming from every direction.

At least they weren't blasting me with their bummer thoughts. *Thank you, Uncle Olo.*

~~*"Now you understand the true cause for the suppressant."*~ *I didn't anticipate hearing Uncle's reply so clearly in my noggin, but after the chat with Yemaya, I wasn't overtly startled.* ~*"Your males have your best interests in mind, Nala. However, they do not process new information well. I wished to spare you while they adjusted."*~

++*"They are buffoons. You should spell her additional suppressant before their departure to give her temporary relief from their idiocy."*+ *Yemaya grumbled next.*

I was grateful for that after another glance at the gang. Jin was muttering to himself. Beside him, Ryloh stole worried glances when he thought I wasn't looking. Ahead of them Avexei was just staring at me, a mix of awe and fear in his dark eyes. And on my tail, Timos was experiencing a full-on conniption, he'd somehow shrunk since the fire discovery.

Shoulders hunched as his fingers fidgeted. Yemaya still looked peeved but insisted she should be present for the rock's reveal. The lone smiler was Olorun as we approached the first entrance to appear in the last ten minutes.

"Nala must enter alone," Uncle announced when we were a few paces away from the futuristic doors. When the males went to argue, he snapped his fingers… Rendering them mute. Their four mouths were in motion, but none uttered a peep.

"Yes, I silenced them," Olorun confirmed as he raised a hand and pressed it against a glowing neon triangle decorating the center of where the doors met. The white glossy shells parted with a *whizz*, revealing an expansive bright space.

With a nod to a confident Olorun and a tentative Yemaya, I stepped through, shielding with a palm as my eyes adjusted to the brightness. When they said, 'star crystal,' my mind went to Quartz Beach, to what Gabs shoved in my hands on my second day. I expected a broken, sharded chunk of gravel in a display case.

I didn't anticipate an enormous, spiky monstrosity filling the stadium arena of a space. The surface of the shard was glassy and transparent, while its hues constantly shifted, each point a different color from its base. Its shape was similar to an interconnected web of sweet-gum tree burrs. Some stretching from the shiny white floors to the expansive vaulted ceiling.

The creepiest part wasn't the size, shape, or shifting colors though, it was the way in which it was pulsing. Unlike a heart's steady beat, each section had its own rhythm, echoing in a terrifying chorus. *"Hellooo,* sinister," I muttered, recoiling as one of the nearby spikes flashed, like it was aware of my tip-toeing past.

"No, Nala Nightingale Williams Drago, I am not sinister." *Holy cannoli.*

I changed my mind. The whispered voice was *definitely* the most bone curdling part. "Sorry, I just didn't expect you to be so huge. No offense," I babbled. "When Olorun described you as a shard, I thought you would be one piece. Not all this."

The *entire thing* went red, sending me back a step. "I need not explain the importance of companionship to you."

"Fair," I croaked as its surface shifted back to its rendition of Mario

Kart's Rainbow Road. It was at least easier on the eyes, albeit distracting. "What did you want to discuss with me?"

"Balance," the shard said in a harsher rasp. The colors reversed their direction as it tacked on, "Did you know the galactic Council refused to consider naming mortals as their own classification?" I frowned, shaking my head. The spikes apparently registered the action, replying, "Yes. There are mortals present on nearly every planet, and yet..."

I didn't know what to reply, settling on, "Sure."

"Vampires were not granted until the Council conceded during the last war—"

"The intergalactic war was over whether or not vamps should be classified?" I couldn't stop myself from interrupting. The war took place three-thousand years ago, so I hadn't spent much time looking into specifics.

"Yes. Vampires have been considered no better than mortals since the Dawn. The two classifications, mortal and vampire, have always been ostracized."

I frowned. The perspective on mortality wasn't any surprise, but the bigotry toward the blood suckers was. Considering the majority were spliced against their will, why would they be outcast anymore than they already were? They were contained to two planets and could only travel for a few hours at a time whereas, oddly, demons could move freely—*Wait, wait, wait, Nala.*

You're drifting off-topic, this haunted boulder has news.

"Besides being ex-mortal, what does that have to do with me?"

The colors flashed. "The imbalance caused your creation." The pace in which the shades were shifting sped as the shard whispered, "Primordial of Balance."

Wrinkling my nose, I rebuked, "I don't know what that is."

"You shall be the first of former mortals to shift. The primary of your kind. You are responsible for regaining the balance, Nala Nightingale Williams Drago." Although shifting was an anticipated factoid, hearing it from this weird spiky all-knowing space crystal caused a visceral reaction. The fact no longer felt exciting. Not in here.

It felt stifling, the air in my lungs turned to stone as my stomach took a dive. However, I fought it, needing to know, and rasping, "What am I?"

"Guess," it demanded in a harsh tone.

"Fae?" I started with the obvious, feeling the point at the end of my ears.

The shard went red again, starling me into a gasp. "No," it replied.

"But I have the ears," I exclaimed.

"Only partially," the shard whispered. My face fell. Vex hadn't said, and they didn't feel any less pointy than Ry's. *When are you not a freak though, Nala?* It was a valid question, abnormality seemed to favor me. "Guess," it urged.

I didn't think it was possible but voiced it anyhow, "Dragon?"

"Not dragon," the shard replied as its color extravaganza restarted.

"Zoatala of some sort, maybe Siarc because of Yu-Jin?" I tried and the room went violently blood red again. Except this time, it flashed with each separate beat, and the resulting dizziness made me cover my eyes to keep from vomiting.

"Not Siarc. Nor mage. Nor turnu. Nor vampire," it replied.

What the fuck am I then? Which was when I realized it hadn't answered my guess. "So, I *am* zoatala?"

The colors stilled. "Not entirely," the shard replied.

How friggin' helpful. "I give up, just tell me!"

The voice was not nearly as terrifying as the chuckle the rock emitted, reminiscent of claws scratching against stone. Once settled, it said, "You are nothing yet. The ability to shift cannot manifest until you have accepted your final tether."

"*Ugh,*" I groaned in frustration, and it released another raspy chuckle. "But Ryloh and I haven't accepted yet, either!"

"His gifts embedded themselves. The Uktena's have not. If you go without, your soul shall shatter," it explained nonchalantly.

"My soul's holding together because of them?" I squeaked.

"Yes. Haven't you always felt hollow? As though you couldn't feel the same joy as others? As though you were missing something but did not know where to look for it?"

I was too gobsmacked to reply.

The shard kept going despite my rapidly heaving chest and saucered eyes. "Once you accept, you must refrain from shifting your entire form. Your first attempt must take place in a life-or-death circumstance. For yourself, not your bonded. Otherwise, you shall perish, Nala Nightingale Williams Drago."

That knocked me down a peg.

Shaking my head, I explained, "I can't die. I'm tethered to Timoset, he's indestructible!"

"You can and you will in two cases. One, if you do not soon accept the Uktena. Two, if you attempt to shift before the appropriate circumstance arises." The pigment of its glassy surface went back to rainbow waves as it said, "Then and only then may you restore the balance and find peace."

They're gonna go berserk.

"I don't like the sound of any of that," I mumbled. Although Timos would be mighty relieved I wasn't dragon. Which caused me to voice, "How did I get dragon fire and slitted eyes if I'm not a dragon?"

"The fire is from your dragon, but your eyes are not draconic." As I opened my mouth for further clarification it interrupted. "Your eyes may shift without consequence. However, the remainder of you shall not."

No shifting until I nearly die, got it. Cool. Cool. Cool.

"What about Yu-Jin, will I keep him although we aren't fated?" I tried.

"Too soon to tell," the shard whispered. "His destiny lies in your hands. As does his tethering." *Great. How absolutely useless.*

The colors suddenly froze, and I drawled, "Anything else I should know?"

"I agree with the mistrust you approach most beings with. However, you must *always trust yourself*. You create your reality. Beware of those who wish to betray you."

I heaved a sigh. "Is that all?"

"Olorun shall facilitate our future conversations. Accept the males. Fulfill your destiny. Remain vigilant, Primordial of Balance."

Then, like the thing was never there, the room emptied in my next blink.

"Hello?" My voice echoed.

Alrighty then.

I spun, sprinting through the double doors, and slamming into Vex's chest in the golden hallway. My lungs expanded happily as I finally choked down a full breath.

"Why's she always doing that with him?" Jin grumbled.

Olorun *tsked*. "There are higher forces at play, Yu-Jin. Their binding is abnormal."

"You knew?!" Avexei hissed.

Yemaya sighed and pinched her brow, pointing her hip with a no nonsense look. "You must reveal why you panicked yesterday, Vex. It is time."

"What are they talking about?" I questioned.

Avexei looked queasy. "I had a dream that night at Mo's, and our tethering won't just guarantee you the ability to shift—"

"Alright," Timos clapped his taupe hands, "crisis averted. You two shall never bond."

"What else, Vex?" I asked, pointedly ignoring the rest.

He heaved a sad sigh before untangling my arms and giving me a push towards Ryloh. "You'll become too prestigious, little lioness. You'll have a target on your back from not only the Council but every power hungry being in our galaxy. Mo's right, we can't bond. That's why I panicked. I knew we couldn't without major consequence." The fae's warm arms circled as Olorun shook his head in dismay.

"Do not be daft, nothing worthwhile comes without consequence," Olorun snapped. It was the first instance I'd seen him losing his cool. They all gawked, while Ryloh's arms tightened around my middle. Auntie and Uncle gave me a pointed 'spill the beans' look. But I was still processing, running a palm down my face as I attempted to muster the courage.

"There were rumors, I could never confirm as their extinction came unexpectedly, but it was thought the tainted mortals had more powerful bonds than the Titans. It was the reason behind why Avexei's tyrant mother chose his father," Yemaya mused.

Vex frowned. "Tainted mortals? That's what my dad's class was called?"

"Yes. Several Titans granted pieces of their prestige to a dozen of mortals on Earth as an experiment over six-thousand turns ago. They were not quite homo sapiens, nor quite mages, somewhere in between. Your father was thought to be the most prestigious of the tainted—"

"Until my mother raped, then murdered him," Avexei interrupted, seething. My own anger peaked. *Fuck that damned tyrant.*

~~*"I concur, Imera is the worst of us."*~

"We are drifting off topic. That buzz from his nearness confirms why he cannot refute her nearness, and why she, in turn, cannot refrain. They are bound uniquely. Likely due to the mortality they share... I would venture to guess it is how Vex also drew out Nala's prestige within minutes."

Jin cleared his throat, then said, "But I'm half of the same homo sapien —"

"No," Olorun shook his head, "your mother was turned prior to your conception, you are solely zoatalan, Yu-Jin." The lines in the Siarc's handsome face became more severe.

"You know far more than you let on last night, Uncle." Timos grumbled, his emotional state was the heaviest. Feeling his turmoil was making me dizzy. I spun in Ryloh's embrace to hide in his chest for comfort.

Olorun cleared his throat, then softly explained, "Nala's prestige is already unnaturally potent, far more than a typical dragon's amoroso, I did not wish to worry you further."

Yemaya rolled her eyes and said, "Once Nala has renascence after the final bonding, your communal prestige shall double —" I loudly gasped in interrupted, along with everyone but Uncle Olo.

Timos scoffed. "Impossible."

"Impossibility is a false construct. All is possible," Olorun replied with a sad smile.

There was a terse beat of silence. One in which I could no longer hide from, nor stand for. I stepped out of Ryloh's warmth to voice the cataclysm. "I'm not a dragon. I also didn't wanna panic you, but... The star shard explained that I'll die if I don't bond with Vex."

I braced myself for the inevitable chaos, clamping my eyes tight, but none came.

"This was, unfortunately, necessary," Olorun said, while Yemaya chuckled. I cracked an eye to find my trifecta trapped in glass tubes. There were circular patterns on the floors I hadn't noticed prior, ones which transparent cylinders popped out of, effectively caging each of the overreactors.

All except for one, who's hair was oddly the same shade of purple as Olorun's at the moment. "And Vex?"

"He was not in distress. They were. The barriers were designed to remain intact until they settle. I have *seen* it taking hours."

"So... Now what?"

Yemaya prohibited further training before shooing us into Acidity's streets. There was a vague exchange between Olorun and Vex, over something called 'manifest' which neither deigned expand upon. So now, I was following down the skywalk leading toward the Zone.

My shifty haired tour guide hadn't peeked over his shoulder to see whether I was following, clearly unsettled from the few paces he strode ahead. I didn't know how to broach the awkwardness, so I scampered mutely, focusing on our golden surroundings.

The community Yemaya mentioned was evident. Many of the resident's windows were left transparent, especially those with children, who waved at strangers like it was their favorite game. Their population seemed more social than Neptune's. Not only were beings constantly greeting with smiles as they passed in the domed halls, but hardly any wandered alone.

I knew we'd made it to what had to be Acidity's Times Square, the Zone, when the glassed passage opened to a congested, multileveled, rotunda. The ceiling was similar to Olorun's dining room, with concave rectangular frames around the opaque cream-colored glass panels. At the center, there was a fast-paced escalator connecting the seven levels with advertising holograms chasing patrons. Instead of storefront windows, like an American mall, there were only neon signs hanging over the various entrances occupying the floors.

The only thing I couldn't figure out were raised daises on each level which many were constantly rifting in and out of. "What's that?"

"Landing pads. Unlike Neptune, beings aren't permitted to just rift wherever they want on Uru. They have to use the closest landing pad to prevent jump scaring other citizens."

"*Woah*," I said, observing a horde of children appear. The dozen munchkins ran screaming toward the nearest set of doors behind them, which whirred open to reveal a playroom. Their babysitter, a blue skinned fae, was flustered as they attempted to count and keep track of their shrieking heads.

"This way," Avexei interrupted. We passed an array of businesses, behind the escalators, ambling toward the largest establishment hiding in a shadowy corner. 'Manifest' flashed above the lavender double doors, which rolled open, revealing… *A library?*

"What is this place?" I asked as Vex handed his phone to a robotic floating host.

The droid shared a nod, before Avexei turned to me to explain, "Most Uruans believe in fate, similarly to Uncle Olo. They see wish collecting as a way to petition destiny's favor. This is their manifestation moor, where they essentially keep tabs on what they've requested over the years."

He led through the dimly lit space lined with towering black shelves. Each row was stuffed with books, all of their spines uniformly white with ascending numbers in a block font. As my gaze traced the upward trajectory, I realized they spiraled the higher they went. There were iridescent, seemingly endless, winding staircases tucked between them, glittering despite the darkness.

"It's dreamy," I breathed, incapable of looking anywhere but up. The lone lighting was a teensy star shaped orb dancing above our heads.

"Olo drags us here once a year without fail," Vex griped. He suddenly turned left, between a pair of shelves listing the six-thousands. "So, to give you context, our other uncle, Lio, was the fun one. He was my favorite adult because he was so hilarious, and anyway, we didn't know what classification I would be. Fae are the only immortals born with their gifts and every class has a different timeline."

"Not even Olorun knew?" I asked.

Avexei crouched on the mirrored floors to search a bottom shelf. "No," his gaze narrowed as he searched the spines. "Well, maybe, but Olo never said. Anyway, Uncle Lio is a Sphinx. Do you know what those are?" He found what he was looking for in time to catch my nod.

When Vex opened the shiny shell of the container, it no longer resembled a book. It looked more like a rectangular jewelry box with a holographic screen where its mirror should be.

It softly dinged before saying, "Please submit your fingerprint, Avexeidros Valtameri."

Once unlocked, he swiped past the first few pages, knowing what he was looking for. "Here," Avexei's tresses were an olive that I now knew to associate with queasiness as he double tapped on a list of numbers. The screen went from a flat panel to a three-dimensional bust. The Vex staring back at us was no older than ten, he was so freaking adorable I couldn't withhold my grin. His hair was the same shoulder length it was now, but his dark heavily lashed eyes were enormously oversized for his chubby face.

"I am Vex, not Avexeidros, and I turn eight in four days." The voice was so squeaky that my heart pinched. "This year I only want one thing for my future. Well, besides becoming a lion." Baby Avexei paused, his hair settling on a shade of bleached magenta. "This year, the only thing I want for my future is a lioness."

My jaw unhooked and fell to the floor, gaze darting to the adult version, whose cheeks were burgundy as he held his breath. He motioned with his stubbled chin toward the hologram. To where I caught his younger self scratching his smooth chin in thought. Then he raised tiny fingers to itemize, "She has to be as fierce as me. Also, get along with Mo. Maybe we could share her, like Uncle Olo and Sima. Funny. I want to have the most hilarious amoroso since the Dawn. She does not have to be large. She can be a little lioness… Yeah, that is all." The hologram disappeared and my eyes *burned*. The need to release a sob, painful.

Fuck. Fuck. Fuck.

Breathing became a burden. My gaze aimlessly danced around the darkness as I attempted to unpack it all. *What're the odds?* He said he was eight years old… That made this video six-thousand-plus. *Shit.*

Vex's deep voice interrupted the thickening silence, "Nothing is coincidence. That's the one thing I've learned after all these years. Even the most minute occurrences are interconnected."

My mouth opened to reply, but nothing came out. Which was when the wave of denial crested. *This doesn't prove compatibility, it's just coincidental spook spook!*

Pivot, Nala!

Ignoring the pang in my chest, I changed the subject. "How disappointed were you when you didn't turn out to be a Sphinx?"

Avexei barked a laugh. "Total devastation. My gifts crested only two or three years after this was taken. I was inconsolable for weeks. Do I need to show you more of these, because there's at least a hundred that would fit."

I gulped. "No, no," then rushed out, "no need. Where to next?"

Scaredy cat. Obviously, I couldn't claim coincidence after more proof. However, it didn't debunk the issue of destiny calling the shots between us. Vex extended his palm and I had to battle with the memories of him rising to the surface proving otherwise.

Like that kiss after he ripped Dayna's head clean off…

Yeah, we're gonna ignore the full body zizz from that, you homicidal ho.

"I've dreamt this. At least, I have thus far. Aunt Yemaya will text the next location." Avexei nervously babbled, as I took his hand. The instant my skin registered the briskness of his, the surroundings brightened. Our eyes locked as the *thump-thump* of our hearts overwhelmed the buzz in my chest. *It's fate's doing, quit falling for it!*

I ripped my gaze away to stare at the floor. Just as he muttered, "Right on cue," when his phone buzzed in his pocket. Then there was a snort when he scanned the message. Then he led me by the hand back toward the landing pad.

"Doesn't it bother you that fate essentially plotted everything between us?" I probed. Avexei shook his silvery head before we rifted to a higher floor's pad. He pulled our intertwined hands toward a door with a neon purple 'Jinx' sign floating overhead.

It was a bar. A steampunk themed one with a conveyor belt distributing drinks from the robot slinging alcohol. It was Friday, so the crowding made sense. Although I didn't expect to see the plethora of non mages. Uru wasn't quite as intermixed as Neptune, but at least one-third of the throng weren't mages. The ceiling, walls, and floors were coated in a neon pattern of purples, pinks, and yellows. There was a row of connected screens cutting through the center of the square room's walls, showing a slideshow of black and white photos…

Of patrons kissing? *Strange.*

Avexei led me towards the only empty pair of barstools which happened to be right in front of the dozen armed bartender. I questioned why others avoided the seats to stand until the robot rattled five shakers in our faces at once.

"My prophetic dreams have made you feel like déjà vu," Vex said, continuing our discussion. "But the majority of our conversations didn't make sense in those dreams. I saw hundreds of snippets which were impossible to decipher. I know all of my actions are mine."

"How are you so sure?"

"How are you not?" His piercing onyx eyes narrowed as red highlights formed in his hair.

Unfortunately, a drink order screen interrupted, appearing in our faces the same moment, I grumbled, "We barely know each other." None of the drink names were correlating so I made a random selection and turned back toward Avexei who was already staring.

"What do you wanna know? I'm an open book, ask away."

I wasn't prepared, so I rattled off what came to me first: "What's your Earthly star sign?"

"Gemini." That tracked. Especially when considering his flip-flopping.

"You're the fun one then." My eyes were drawn towards the reel of photographs ceaselessly circling. It was far easier to look at, his dreaminess was too distracting.

"Ryloh would take offense to that." Just as Avexei said it, a photo of what could've been the pair smooching circled on the screens. Black messy locks and highlighted messy locks… *But it couldn't be, right? What're the odds?*

My heart was sprinting just from the mere idea of Ryloh and Avexei making out, though. The robot handed over a reddish drink in a highball glass, momentarily distracting me.

"Yeah, that's real," Vex said with a smirk, causing me to choke on my first sip.

"*What?*"

"Ryloh and I have kissed," He confirmed, causing me to nearly topple from my stool. "If you repeat the same thing as anyone in your group, the robo-tender forces you to kiss, and adds your photo to the reel. That's why it's called, 'Jinx.' Olorun set us up on our first soulmate date here, two years into us dreaming about you.

"Except he didn't explain, he only said we would have plenty in common. Anyway, the truth slipped from Ry. Then everything we'd both seen of you. There's a lot of photos, I know that's why Olo planned it, the fucker. We'd already seen us sharing you in more ways than one, so it didn't seem like a big deal," Vex explained.

My spit turned to sand.

As if on cue, another photo circled. This one more obvious than the last. Also, far more tempting. My petunia was pulsing. *Cut it out, Nala, it's just a peck.*

I guzzled my drink, which seemed to just be watermelon juice and rum to wet my tongue, before rasping, "What else have you gotten up to without me?"

Avexei spread a grin as he said, "We have slept in the same bed five times now."

He chuckled as my eyes saucered.

"We fell asleep talking about you, Nala. There has been nothing but you in thirty years." *Oof.* It was an alluring admission… Until remembering.

Bet his dead wife and child would feel real stoked hearing that.

A macabre thought, but somehow, it did nothing to dampen his overwhelming appeal. Or any of the urges to lunge at him. All of which worsened the alarms blaring in my brain.

"I just worry this isn't…," there wasn't another word for it, "*real.* Between us, I mean."

Avexei painted a determined look before squeezing my hand. I startled in my seat; having forgotten we were intertwined. "Let me prove it," he said, and I nodded, uncertain of how else to respond. There was an awkward pause, an exchanging of googly eyes.

"Olorun gifted me access to your library as a stalkerish birthday present of sorts," he blurted, totally flustered. His hair went lime in uncertainty or shame. I wasn't sure. "It's how I knew you wouldn't freak out about my killing Dayna. Or shifting. Or any of the kinky shit I'm sure Ryloh has already leveraged despite the pact we made to wait."

It required more than a few blinks to recover from that one.

I croaked, "Even the objectophilia novellas?" He nodded. "Even the balloon animal smut?!"

"I couldn't believe we read that, but yeah. No judgment by the way, it's been incredibly entertaining, if anything." Yeah, it was creepy, but... I couldn't help but match his grin. My unhinged library wasn't anything I ever anticipated sharing with another. It never even crossed my mind as possibility. *Was this fate's doing?*

Or the better question: do you even care?

"What's been your favorite read so far?" I couldn't help myself, I had to know.

He took a thoughtfully long swig of his water. Eventually replying, "Skeleton Society, the chapter headers were hilarious. Also, the stache."

"Holy shit, you've actually read my stuff," I bellowed, my hands clapping over my mouth. He nodded as if it was nothing. "Ry has, too?"

"We had a book club."

A screech left my lips.

Is this what experiencing an aneurysm feels like?

After the bed comment, my brain fell into naked nighttime tales. Fae on one end, Uktena on the other. With me sandwiched in the middle. It was a fetish I didn't know existed before then.

He interrupted, tacking on, "We also do yoga twice a week. There wasn't anyone on Neptune who knew what it was, so we had to train instructors and fund the first studio. It exploded in popularity and there's dozens of them now. It's been great, I'm addicted, probably only two or three weeks from balancing on my head without the use of magic."

I barked a stunned laugh. "No way!" There was a zero percent chance of putting kitty back in her cage. Imagining those abs in a yoga class was sweltering. He was... I bit my lip.

Avexei must've misread my reaction. "I'm serious," he said lowly, near hiss. "But the hobbies I've taken on from tailing you aren't all we have in common," he suddenly stood, quickly swiping his phone past one of the screens, before tugging me out of the crowded bar and back into the even busier Zone. "I should've forced you into watching more of those recordings," he muttered as we took an upward escalator.

Shrugging, I offered, "It was a lot." When a hologram of a standing femme with a bouquet of flowers appeared, Avexei waved a palm, and she faded to pixels, then nothingness. Advertisements were apparently that easy to skip on Uru.

"Well, this is gonna be even more intense. So, strap in." His mirrored eyes were narrowed as they met mine.

"Why do you seem frustrated?"

Vex tilted his head towards the roof, grumbling, "I need you to see it, Nala. It's more than fate's intervention. You and me, we're fucking real. If anything, we match *too* well."

I bristled, snapping, "Then why'd you reject me?"

"That was before learning it could lead to your fucking death," he volleyed, lowering into my personal orbit with a fierce determination. "It was to protect you. I was putting you first. Not only would you never lose Jin, but to prevent your shifting." He lowered his voice to add, "And the resulting chaos I've already glimpsed bits of."

"What have you seen?"

He grimaced, hesitating. *A first.*

I loathed it. My heart cracked. Vex's unfiltered explanations differentiated him. "Please don't keep secrets. Not after you've been answering so freely," I intoned. It felt as though he prioritized me. The others couldn't seem to cling to sanity when shit hit the fan. Jin had gone from squish to perma stressed. Timos had gone from my calm to flitting mother hen. Ryloh, thankfully, remained stable. However, his norm was a bloody and grey area in general.

Avexei's face softened. "The worst players, the absolute scum of our galaxy... Well, they may take you from us, little lioness. Mo and I are the only pair capable of keeping you safe. Even despite the other two inheriting our gifts, they didn't grow up training like we had. Don't get me wrong, I trust Ryloh completely, but he couldn't..." Avexei trailed off and I flung myself around his middle in thanks. The resulting grin as his hair transitioned to silver was painstaking to resist.

We stepped off the escalator on the top floor. There were only three doors on this equally spacious level. All, ominously, lacking signs overhead. He tugged our clasped hands towards the largest set of the three, explaining, "This floor is only accessible by the Sages and family. Titans have lived for so long they were forced to record their histories to keep track. That habit passed down to us over time, and now most have their own personal museum of sorts. This is where mine and Mo's are stored."

"You were quite close to Olorun, Yemaya, and Simargl, weren't you?"

"Yeah," he nodded, "especially me, because I didn't quite belong with the Dragos. Technically, neither did Mo. He's the quietest while I was the loudest in that madhouse. We were the odd ones out, mostly because of our abnormal prestige among his similarly aged siblings. Dmitri and Asmodeus were the only pair with equivalent power, and they were fourth and first born, ages and ages older. Rarely around. We used to unsettle the other kids, so, Mo's parents frequently shipped us to Uru. It was probably for the best."

Vex pushed through the bronze elaborately carved doors, revealing every hoarder's dream. Piles reached towards the windowed roof, while the brightly lit grid floors were a mess of antique objects. Similar to A Space Odyssey set, but dystopian. My eyes struggled to focus on any one particular thing as he tugged me past stack after stack. "This isn't what I was envisioning," I said, hopping over a rusty sword.

"This front room is where they store artifacts they don't know what to do with yet," he explained. As though it were normal to just toss valuables into piles. "We're heading to the database."

We crossed through an arched doorway into an even more expansive room, this one near barren. A war landscape decorated the length of an entire wall, but that was it. It was empty, like an art museum. Releasing Avexei's hand, I neared for a closer look. Realizing it wasn't a painting, as initially assumed, but a real freaking photograph. Of an ancient and unbelievably gory battle scene set against a sandy desert.

"This was the Titan's first skirmish among themselves. None were mortally wounded," he explained. As I leisurely walked the length, inspecting each life-sized dua forma in awe, my eyes found the silvery white dragon flying overhead first. Eventually stilling on a Medusa laughing maniacally, drenched in blood, running a sword through a scorpion-tailed male. There were two snakes on her head, parted right down the middle, and similar to boa constrictors in size as they protected her back. "That's Aunt Zuzu. Zusicia Drago. Mo's mom," Avexei said from, surprisingly, directly behind me. His cool breath sent my skin for a bumpy ride. "She's the Suprema, the most prestigious femme to ever exist."

"She's badass," I whispered.

"Zusicia's the Titan of Peace and War, so it kinda comes with the territory."

Then I caught sight of a black wolf with sunflower-shaped eyes. "Is that—"

"Yeah, it's Yemaya in dua forma. She and Olorun are Wolven." Which was when I noticed the purple slightly larger wolf biting someone's arm behind her.

"What's Simargl?" I asked, looking for another wolf. Although I hadn't met the male yet, I figured he'd be near his bonded.

Vex's big chilly palms gripped each of my hips, pushing me a few steps. My heart stilled when one of his tan veiny arms came into my peripheral, while he pointed at a humongous creepy as Hell raven. "Sima's a Rook."

There was a wash of color which stole my attention, to where a Sphinx was carrying a shifted Siren over his head. Her rainbow tail seemed inappropriate for the setting and situation. Gasping when I took a closer look at her features. I'd never forget the cretin's face. "Mother's useless in battle without abilities. They purposely muted gifts for this particular skirmish. But she refused to sit on the sidelines. That's Uncle Lio carrying her," Vex said.

My gaze flicked back to the ruddy lion's head atop a tanned and muscular male's body. His only resemblance to Egyptian Sphinx portrayals were his golden feathered wings.

It quickly tabulated. "Lio's her mate?" I questioned, and Avexei nodded.

"Both have separate mating groups and flit in and out of favor too often to keep up with. I didn't learn of their tether until after meeting her in my teenage years. Lio is Zusicia's twin."

My face fell. "You didn't know your mom's soulmate was your favorite uncle?" I questioned and Vex shook his head. "That's so grim. I'm sorry."

"Lio didn't want me knowing the specifics of her abandonment. He was a decent father figure, but incapable of raising me alone. At least, back then. They had a son later, my half-brother, Xerxes, who's two millennia younger."

Avexei started walking again, beckoning me to follow. "That photo isn't even the wildest one I've seen. It was taken before they knew how to fight." He flipped a switch once we crossed through the next room, this one circular. Once the light was on, I realized this was a crossroads of sorts, with eight hallways. Each leading into a differently arched and colored passage.

"They called it the Barbaric Age, the two centuries before the planets were claimed. The Titans were basically the only beings left after Uncle Atha, Mo's dad, took down the Stars," Avexei explained as we went down the fourth narrow passageway.

"It's so wild to have everything I've ever believed turned upside down. I could probably spend days going through the history in here, *huh*?"

"More like weeks," Vex corrected. "I'd be happy to join you. Explain what I can… If you wanted me to. That is." The tentativeness in his tone struck a cord.

Avexei might've believed the thing between us was real. How I could literally die if we didn't bang. Which was insanity, nearly as yoo-hoo as what supposedly came after. But he didn't seem certain of my choosing him. Which led me to asking, "Do you think I'm gonna bone then ditch you?"

He didn't reply, quickening his pace as we continued down the gratingly orange path, his head almost knocking into the low ceilings. His ignoring led to my festering. To questioning whether or not he'd *seen* me leaving him. Whether that could've been the real reasoning behind the rejections. After a minute of terse silence, I was fed up.

"Do you think I'm gonna abandon you?"

Avexei finally stopped, turning to share a glower. "No, of course not," he clipped. "You've been distant today. I get it. You're processing, but I have no clue what you're thinking… Outside of how this is *fake* between us."

"Not fake, *forced* by fate's manipulative fingers. It feels like we don't have a choice. And we just —*coincidentally*— learned we don't in fact have a choice!" My voice rose another octave as I let go and spewed the rest. "I'll admit, we're breezy together. We flow. Conversations with you are effortless. You're also incredibly, and I mean unfairly, just *unbelievably* attractive. If we would've met first, sans buzz, we wouldn't be having this argument. But *now*? Can you blame me? I turn into a human vibrator around you, it's anything but natural!"

Avexei smirked, closing the distance. "You're no longer human, little lioness."

"Whatever!"

"You don't think we would've connected without the tether?" he raised a dark brow.

Tossing up my arms, I groaned, "I don't know, that's the crux!"

"You're letting me show you, remember?" He spun on his heel, leaving me stewing in the wind of his maddening clean laundry scent. "Let's see how you feel after this." The orange walls thankfully didn't last for long, we were released into another blank room with brightly lit flooring with rows and rows of transparent shelves. *At least it's organized.* Then crossed another threshold, into a duplicative room.

"How big is this place?" I pressed after entering the *fifth* duplicative storage room.

Avexei shrugged as his hair went plum. "Tough to say. I know Uncle Sima had to spell an expansion a few years back, or maybe decades, I can't keep track. We're nearly there." *Purple equated to confusion then, interesting.*

There were another two similarly empty rooms. Until finally, Vex paused at a set of double doors with a triangle at their center. He unlocked with a palm unveiling a dark grid lasered room. *You're in the Matrix!*

"Database, could you recover some memories?" Avexei instructed as soon as the doors closed behind us. "The photographs from Phillipe's first birthday, I forget the date."

"Of course, Avexeidros Valtameri. Shall I initiate a slideshow?"

"Sure," he replied, crossing his arms. I squeaked when the green lines were replaced with a theater-sized family photo at our opposite. I hardly looked at the gorgeous femme, or the adorable chubby baby, it was difficult to avert from Vex's unsettled expressions as the photos flicked past. Dozens. So many pictures. I even glimpsed Timos in several wearing dated frames. But it was Vex who held my full attention.

His hair was obsidian in every fucking shot. When he didn't know he was being photographed, even if he was in the background, he was grimacing. Painfully so.

"Why were you *so*...?" I wanted to say miserable, but it didn't feel right to voice. I worried I was wrong. That perhaps I'd invented his unease as a means to deflect from his beautiful murdered family.

"Database, could you show the day of Philippe's birth?" Avexei instructed instead of responding.

Maybe three or four images passed of him with more dark haired discomfort before I turned my stare to the male, demanding, "Tell me why you look even unhappier here."

"We called Jules my soulmate. She wasn't, though. But I was less lonely than Mo. Anyway, her pregnancy was unexpected. I was doing the right thing. Until they died. It wasn't like I wished for their terrible fates. It took me millennia to admit that I was just getting by when they were alive. I grew to love Jules, and obviously, I loved Phili, but it wasn't—" his deep voice cracked.

Then he cleared his throat. "Database, please show photos of Ryloh and I's first overnight."

I swayed, nearly falling to the floor.

The darkness was gone. Vanished. Both physically and metaphorically.

Avexei and Ryloh were hunched over and laughing over something in the first picture. In the next, it was just Vex with his handsome head tilted back in glee, who clearly pranked Ryloh, given his grumpy scowl. Frame after frame, it was blaringly loud and clear.

Tears filled my eyes as I croaked. "You don't even look like the same person."

"Because I wasn't, Nala," Vex brushed away the first tear cutting down my cheek. It was more than overwhelming. "There's something you may never forgive me for, but I think it's time. I have to show you." Gripping my shoulder, he closed his dark eyes and scrunched his face in concentration.

The screen room vanished momentarily as my vision went blank. I blinked, and suddenly, it felt like water had been poured over my head. My fingers found my ringlets completely dry, though.

Avexei's hair was over a hundred hues as I cracked a lid.

There was a foreign sensation in my mind.

And then, like being hit by a bus, I *remembered*.

My Earthly travels. He was there. Always as Aleksi.

Minutes turned to hours together. Days. Weeks. Months.

Fuck, he was there for *years*.

Uhm. He also ate me out at least eighty times without reciprocation.

I didn't know how to feel as he observed in abject horror. On the one hand it was an overstep. There was the stalking. The catfishing. The trips he was funding. The hook ups. *He also wiped your memories!*

But on the other hand? I was *relieved*, because this wasn't just fated fuckery.

It finally makes sense! I had multiple photos on my phone in different locations where there was a big veiny hand in the corner. One I obsessively thought about for months. *Possibly years.* Anyway, Vex added the snippets of his memories when he erased mine crying after deleting the photos from my phone… *No wonder he completely lost his shit.*

I was weeping too, if you were wondering.

"I had to, Nala. I'm so damn sorry. I know its fucked up—"

Wiping my tears, I demanded, "Why?"

Vex's hair turned silver as he caught my gaze. "Half because I'm selfish. The other half because I couldn't watch you wither. You were alone. Listless. Always so fucking tired. I just—" he groaned. "You needed love, and this was the only way I knew to give it without messing up our future—"

I shut him up with a kiss.

It was just a peck, but now that I knew why he was so familiar it felt right. Like coming home. There were thousands of memories I couldn't wait to go through later.

"Olorun gave you access to my phone?" I guessed.

"He did… Do you believe me now?"

I bobbed my head with a pained smile.

"Database, please show the day we attached the plow to Mo's dua forma."

My weepiness had never cleared quicker. Nothing compared to witnessing a pissed off dragon plowing a field with his huge spiky tailed butt. I keeled over.

When eventually settled, Vex said with a grin, "Just wait until you see the farm."

"Can't wait, I love animals."

"I know."

"Wish there were dogs on Neptune, though."

Vex frowned, saying, "They can't rest their paws on the cobbles anywhere within the city limits from the heat." I grimaced, never having considered the logistics. "That's why there's serpents, skunks, and squirrels; they climb."

There was an awkward pause, where I stared at the images flitting past. "How were these photos taken and stored here?" I had to know.

"Olorun spelled them, kind of similar to a satellite. It keeps tabs on when our emotions spike." He raised his voice to order, "Database, could you please show my emotional meter from the last fifty years. Remove this past week from view." The screen shifted, showing a line chart against a black backdrop. Vex pointed to the lone towering peak, explaining, "That's the first night I dreamt of you."

My heart skittered. "What about this one?" I asked, seeing the second highest peak came two years later.

Vex's grin sliced wider. "When Lo-Lo and I met at Jinx."

"Fuck," I breathed. The male took that as his cue to walk me through every single peak. Each of which pertained to me. *He's lucky you're not an egomaniac.*

"Database, can you show my entire lifetime, please?" The chart zoomed out, conveying how the only peaks were primarily grouped in the years we'd already been looking at. "Do you see now, little lioness?" I nodded wordlessly as my heart sounded like a war drum in my chest.

Walking the length of the graph, I realized the tallest spike was a few days ago.

"Yeah, that's when we met on Neptune," Vex murmured softly.

I felt raw. Not in a negative sense. More like emotional upheaval. Because my heart had quadrupled, each version happily suctioned to the most incredible souls I'd ever met. They were mine. I was theirs.

In the not-so-dated past, I thought giving myself to another would be terrifying. The end of freedom. Of peace. The irony was how I'd never felt freer.

I'd lived more in the last few days than ever before, and it was strange to consider how much actually happened. But I couldn't worry about it at present. Avexei had his head canted as the stupid thing in my chest wheezed. *He knows you better than the others, that's why it's felt so atomic.* "I'm grateful you showed me, Vex. I forgive you for the stalking and memory wiping. Even for the strip tease last night. However, in penance, I do demand a personal show."

Avexei's smile was everything. "It's always been you, Nala. *Always.* Just you. Only you." He heaved a relieved sigh. "I'm so grateful you're willing to give me another shot —"

"Screw this. I thought y- you would've climbed him by n- now, but this is unbelievably boring," Ryloh's voice sounded from a shadowy corner. Where he was apparently hiding with Jin.

"Where's Timos?" I pressed as Ryloh's arm slung over my shoulder.

"Probably still caged. The dragon's been having a time."

"Why haven't you two bonded yet?" Jin questioned with a frown.

"You're no longer worried about being traded?!"

Jin ripped me from Ry's arms to shake my shoulders. "You're not dying over it, Nala!"

Ryloh crossed his arms, saying, "I concur with Jin."

"Since when have you called him *Jin*?"

They exchanged a shrug, in unison, and my brain exploded. There were too many images stored away of Ryloh with Vex already. Now add Jin to the mix? *Toodleloo, coherence.*

"No. We aren't voting on this, it's Nala's decision," Avexei interjected. Earning another point in his favor. I fully intended on voicing as much but didn't have a chance.

"We are being dismissed. Willa's gifts surfaced, it's madness at the residence. They require privacy as they aid in her transformation," Timos interrupted.

I gawked. "How'd you rift in here?! I thought you had to use the landing pads?"

"That does not pertain to the private archives," he explained with a reposition of his glasses. "There is no time to waste. We have a transporter to catch in twenty minutes."

Our transporter ride was uneventful. They were glued to their phones while I pretended to read from mine. When in actuality, I was reliving each of the memories Vex restored. Most of our conversations were duplicative, given I didn't remember him, but he had a knack at breaking down my barriers and piecing me back together again in no time.

Avexei might've erased himself, but he still became more assertive and possessive as the trips wore on. By the time I'd recollected my most recent travel to Cairo, he was growling when another would look at me. Despite taking notice, I didn't bat an eye.

I was in love with Vex. Then. Now. Probably always would be. He put his own emotional well-being on the line for mine. I didn't know how he managed to withstand the damage and persist. I'm not sure I could've done the same.

Thank my lucky tits for Uncle Olo and his stronger suppressant, because the others would go berserk if they knew. Thankfully, there hadn't been any further discussion of the revelations, either. I knew addressing the maelstrom was on the horizon but wasn't going to raise it myself. Not yet.

We landed mid-morning Saturday. As much as the clashing purples of the loft perturbed, I had missed them. Homie, too. Who was so thrilled by our arrival they didn't squabble with any of my males for once.

Ryloh left to clear out his old office since he didn't have the chance prior, similarly, Jin had to run a handful of errands. Which left me in godly company, with the pair who still hadn't settled their differences.

We were sharing an afternoon breakfast from a nearby café, seated in the stools at my kitchen island. Despite the sparse physical distance between us, there was a noticeable chasm. "Y'all are gonna have to move on," I ordered before stuffing a hashbrown into my trap.

Avexei was the first to break, whining, "He's the problem. I apologized. You forgave. He didn't. Despite the fact you'll *die* without me."

"What do you wish for me to say?" Timos snapped.

"You're gonna have to forgive him. I know that Vex broke your trust —" I attempted.

"It was *you* he disappointed. Avexei has been an imbecile since we were hatchlings, his betrayal was of no surprise to me," Timos snarled, his voice with a hint of dragon. I winced before patting the frowning Uktena's shoulder. The dragon didn't appreciate my placation though, growling, "Do not pity him. He does not deserve it."

"What's it gonna take for you to forgive?" Avexei's voice rose, revealing his own agitation.

Timos only growled louder in reply.

I couldn't take another second; they were ruining the noms. "Forgive him," I demanded. "We might not accept our tethering anytime soon, but you have to cut it out. Please. Isn't there enough drama without you beefing?"

"I cannot pardon his mistakes. Even if I could —"

I cut Timos off with an exaggerated sigh.

"You're refusing our kontrolü and upsetting her, dumbass," Vex hissed.

Both pushed away their stools to glare nose-to-nose. "Because you have been so reasonable, Avexei." I shoved my way between their chests, forcing each back a step with a scowl. Thankfully, my intervention seemed to have diffused them slightly. Timos was just grimacing, while Vex only looked green.

"You're right! I'm fucking unreasonable, Mo. All of this has been unreasonable. From our dreams, to Nala binding herself to Jin, to the target on her back. Are you saying you're fine?"

The dragon shook his head, he was still discontented, but the agreement was progress. He tilted down to me to say, "I apologize for how this distresses you, Naliti but I require time. Avexei must make amends prior to my forgiveness. I accept the pair of you must tether, as much as it pains me to admit. However, it is impossible for me to feign amnesty."

"That's fair," I relented. "Can you please stop glowering at him, though? Vex feels terrible enough without you giving him a hard time."

Timos grunted, but I knew it was the best we were gonna get.

Vex hung around until I wished to visit the shelter, which left him missing the farm. He and Timos hadn't bickered again, shockingly. Although it was still awkward, their outward aggression had ceased. I was celebrating that minute progress while walking the balmy Thallan streets cast in my dragon's shadow.

This was what I'd been missing. The beautifully architected buildings. The scents of fresh fruits wafting from the trees. The way everyone minded their business. Neptune might not've been as friendly as Uru, but it changed my life, and I loved it. Especially Thalla. Its rainbow painted streets always brought a smile to my face without fail.

Timos didn't follow me into the shelter, I figured he'd rather fly after the last few days without shifting. Pushing through the green door, into the contrasting stainless steel lobby, I found Penney behind the front desk clicking away on her laptop. She didn't lift her head to say, "Hi, can I help you?"

"Hey, Penney," I greeted. She raised her gaze to share a kind smile.
"Nala! You're back?"

Our cover story was that went to Earth. Mustering my best deceptive grin, I explained, "I'm here to volunteer if you'll have me for a few hours."

"Great! Go ahead. I won't keep you, there's food inventory to tabulate," she waved me off with a peach freckled hand as I pushed through the double doors.

I lost track of time. The lacking mental commentary made the hours

feel shorter. The suppressant Uncle Olo created was far superior to whatever Jin was pumping me with. It only stifled the mind-meld too, I could
still rift and call upon static, which was a plus.

Timos hadn't come to check on me. Neither had Penney. When I finally
peeked at my phone, it read 3:23pm. The lights suddenly began flickering
overhead. I'd never experienced an electrical glitch on Neptune.

But it had to be normal, right? I started texting our group chat.

However, my typing was interrupted by the animals going wild. There
was unified hissing and screeching as the lights continued flashing. The
squirrels and skunks rendered my sharper hearing useless with their
panicked wails and scratching. Even the serpents readied their fangs as
they repositioned to strike. *Freaky deaky.*

I pinged the guys, chewing my lip with hackles raised. It was difficult
to keep from obsessively checking my scallop's screen with every blink.
Something felt off.

Then the electricity went out.

A high-pitched scream cut through the ruckus.

You're not in a horror movie. It's just someone who's scared of the dark. That's all.

I stood completely frozen for several painstakingly long seconds,
continuing to peek at my phone. No response. No typing bubbles surfaced.
My heart raced as my palms slickened. A keening wail sounded outside,
overwhelming the surrounding petrified chorus.

From the way the critters' desperation went up a notch, I knew I
wasn't just imagining it.

"No! Please! *NO!*" Penney.

Since my eyes were adjusted to the darkness, I quietly crept toward the
partitioned window for the lobby… The pane of glass was splattered in
bright red. Blood. And it was fresh from the metallic earthy scent filling my
nostrils.

Shit. Shit. Shit.

Backing against the cages, I mentally ran through my options. *There's
nowhere to hide in here, Nala.* The front was also the sole exit. *Unless you rift…*

When the double doors slammed open, my desperation peaked.
However, no matter how much I focused, nothing happened. *C'mon, flee!*

I couldn't.

That was when I took in the appearance of my visitor.

Vampire!

I hollered to high heaven. With enough fervor my own eardrums *popped* in the aftermath. It worked in distracting the grey skinned Nosferatu-esque male as I sprinted past and out the exit. Nearly slipping in the mess of blood as I went.

That's Penney you slid through.

RIP.

FIVE MINUTES EARLIER

"Persis believes she found a means to disband the—"

"Wait, Osri. Another call is coming through," I interrupted, furrowing my brow at the blocked number on screen. Curiosity peaked as I hung up with my brother. "Hello?"

The galactic off planet fizzle was unmistakable, they were not calling from Neptune. As was the wicked raspy chuckle which preceded a greeting. A chill ran down my spine as I fought against the urge to smash the device to bits. "Hello, timid Timoset."

"Dmitrios," I growled. As if his call were not enough of a bad omen, the back of my neck prickled with unease. *Fuck*.

My sixth sense had yet to fail in alerting me of oncoming danger.
Nala.

She was unguarded. I had shifted to prima form to chat with my siblings and ventured a block, or so, from the shelter. Having anticipated her remaining within the wards.

However, the swelling unease confirmed that was a mistake.

Which was less than ideal.

"I knew you would identify me from voice alone," my evil kin taunted.

The memories of when the male spent weeks maiming me were rising to the surface of my consciousness, threatening to rope me in. I fought back. Naliti was my priority. *You must fly to her. Quit wasting time.*

Nothing came.

A groan fled from the realization.

I could no longer assume dragon form.

What the fuck did he do?

Then screams circled.

"She's in danger!"

I sprinted.

As if on cue, the torturer's laugh crackled. "Something wrong?"

"What did you do?!"

My wings were inaccessible. As was our mind-meld. My gifts, muted.

All sense of sanity fled.

"You know, fate really did us a favor," Dmitrios replied nonchalantly.

Turning a corner, ichor splattered across my path. *Vampire.* I was forced to slow, to save an innocent from a blood sucking bat. Chiropteras were the worst looking subspecies, their translucent leathery wings distastefully perturbing.

Which was why I shattered the appendages first, snapping through the tendon and spindly bones. Then I beheaded her. One handed, because I still held the phone to my ear in case the idiot spilled anything of use. He struggled with control, especially with his mouth.

Another leech flapped down from a nearby roof, circling a screaming teenager.

Unbelievable.

"Your femme is in peril, dragon."

My vision was blurred by ebony viscera, but I kept forward.

"Since you have likely come to terms with your conundrum, allow me to give you a taste of what's to come," Dmitrios said, his grating voice casting over the circling shouts.

Each shredded threat was replaced by another. I would have frenzied by now. *If you were not separated from your dragon.*

"What's your pretty little human's name, again? Remind me."

A roar escaped as I ripped a jaw apart at the seam.

There were too many. Majority splicing others. Dozens of Chiroptera's surrounded. My siblings were nowhere to be found. However, I could no longer delay.

So, I ran.

You are failing again.

If only Naliti had tethered to Avexei.

You should have forgiven him.

She might perish.

You fucking abandoned her.

"Alright. Her name does not matter. You would be surprised by the list of suitors we have lined up to breed her. You, Avexeidros, and Cabbage have so many enemies, timid Timoset."

No.

I stumbled.

Dmitrios laugh broke through the poor connection.

Ice licked up my throat on a bellow.

Dragon fire engulfed the street.

I lost control of the lone gift at my disposal.

There was a choral keening before the vampires crumbled to ash.

You likely struck several bystanders.

For the first time, I did not care.

Nala. Nala. Nala.

"Faster, Timoset!"

They could not fucking steal her from us.

I turned the corner for the shelter, shattering my phone to bits as I slammed it against the double doors. Nearly losing my footing in the process.

Blood.

The entire establishment was painted in blood. I swiped a hand, finding it warm. The scent was not Naliti's though. *Thank fuck.*

You must find her.

Springing out through the doors, I attempted to pick up her trail.

Then the sun disappeared, and Thalla was swallowed by darkness.

TEN MINUTES EARLIER

The tightly packed stucco streets were once my favorite part of visiting the shelter. No more. Now they were nothing short of a nightmare. Most of the green Moroccan-reminiscent buildings were splattered in gore. There was a crowd of vampires draining pleading innocents in every direction. None of which resembled the long and pointy-nosed and -eared vampire on my tail, they resembled other immortals. *Just add dripping fangs and batty wings.*

I didn't waste another second, sprinting up the narrowed alleyway as though my life depended on it. *Faster, faster, giddy up, Gale!*

Unfortunately, the scariest gray skinned guy was on my heels.

--*"SOS! VAMPIRE! HELP, HELP, HELP!"*-

No matter how I tried to reach my magic, it felt muted. Not even static was coming to the surface of my skin. --*"Vamp! Vamp! VAMP!"*-

Nothing. They weren't accessible. All I had at my disposal were my too lazy legs. Despite the immortal boost, my stamina was still complete and utter shit. Plus, the loaded hashbrowns smothered in delicious I'd eaten earlier were taking their toll.

My assailant had stopped to snack on two more bystanders since

415

Penney. I paused to catch some of the disturbing feeding session. It was incredibly stupid, I knew that, but exhaustion was catching up to me. He'd trailed me for two blocks. And lazily.

We'd already neared the yellow painted section of Thalla.

The creep's long black hooded robes weren't sparking enough panic among the masses. Neither were my hoarse screams of warning. These fools were far too trusting!

When I skidded around a sharp corner and nearly crashed into an oncoming bicyclist, the vamp lunged for me. At the last second, I side-stepped to the left. Which meant he unfortunately got a hold of the rider. I sent the innocent a silent prayer of gratitude before taking advantage of the distraction and propelling myself faster.

I didn't know what to do. Where to go. Whether or not it would be safer taking shelter.

Why in the love of Gandalf had you not discussed protocols with your dragon?!

Hang on. Where in the tarnation was Timos? He wasn't flying overhead like he usually was. Despite the mass slaughter, there weren't any dragons in sight.

When a bystander finally took notice of my terror filled rasps, they began dialing some kind of emergency services on their conch. However, I also caught how the vampire's sharp claws ripped through them when glimpsing over my shoulder.

I kept trucking, cursing my useless feet when I stumbled.

"Run faster, lamb!" The bloodsucker called from far too close. A fresh burst of adrenaline shot through my veins as I pushed myself forward. His disturbing lilt rose and fell, sounding like a chainsaw. "Oh, how I love the hunt!"

My hair fell from its tie from how quickly I was gunning it, arms pumping, ankles pulsing with each *thump* against the cobbles. Grateful for whatever higher power convinced me into wearing sneakers with this t-shirt dress.

The distant ocean came into view, and I attempted to keep my lungs inflating.

When I peeked and discovered Mister flappy nose smiling maniacally with those horrifying bloodstained fangs, a squawk of terror left me. The fear was dizzying. It was worse than any haunted house. Than any horror flick. I suspected my death was imminent. He wanted me as his dessert after the dinner show.

My trembling legs kept going. I didn't know how but didn't question it. When I turned down a butter hued street with my hair trailing like a cape, his salad fingers snatched a fistful and tore a chunk from my scalp. My vision darkened as my neck snapped back.

The next thing I knew, he was dragging me as I fought from the concrete.

I didn't want to give up. I didn't want to stop moving. I didn't want to die when I had just…

I was *finally* happy. A demented giggle of acceptance left me because it was just my luck that it took thirty-two years to find it.

The leech dragged me into an abandoned alley, his claws left my hair to slice through my forearm, yanking me close. I had no hope in fighting him off without lethal damage. His breathy chuckle blanketed me in the stench of death. My own so fucking close that I could taste it.

I mentally ejected as he *clacked* his bloodied fangs a few inches from my face.

Disassociated.

Memories filled my final moments. With Jin. Timos. Ry. Vex. They were all I could see. All I could hear. They were the lone reason I continued breathing.

My heart could've easily given out from how it thrashed against my ribs like a suicidal bird. My vision was already spotty and darkening. But I forced lucidity, slowing my breaths, just to enjoy their faces in the recesses of my mind. Their laughter, their touch in my last moments. I had to get my final fill.

Yu-Jin's love.

Timoset's Naliti.

Ryloh's spice.

Avexei's little lioness. Fuck, you shouldn't have waited with Vex. I loved him and Ry, yet they would never know it. That cut deeper than the rest.

A keening sob tore through my chest as a final wave of acceptance crashed.

"How prettily you cry, sweet lamb!"

This bastard was going to steal everything away. *It'd only take him milliseconds, too!*

Suddenly, I was spittin' mad.

"I'm not a lamb, you blood suckin' scrote," I screeched.

The action revived the last bit of my strength, and I managed to get a solid kick into his balls. He grunted and loosened his grip. However, I almost tore my own arm off to get free, like ripping from a bear trap. Tendon and bone were visible as I whimpered and shakily managed to drag myself a few feet from his ichor drenched robes. It wasn't much, but it was something.

The monster laughed maniacally before straightening and towering over where I was crumpled pathetically beside a dumpster.

Clamping my eyes shut, I cradled my destroyed arm against my chest. Bathing in my blood.

As acceptance swarmed, my skin grew hot.

I was boiling.

When my arm's numbness was replaced by a searing bliss, I gasped.

Heat.

I was having my first heat! *Now? It chose right now?!*

There was an exquisite wave of discomfort sparking underneath my skin.

When I cracked an eye, my captor was leering, taunting with a lick of his lips. Slap my ass and call me crazy, because I went limp and rode the heat wave. Locking my gaze tight to pretend there wasn't a seven-foot-five scary murderer clawing into my shoulder. Instead of screaming, a moan left my lips.

"Little lioness, we've been looking everywhere! What the —"

Darkness struck.

Endless.

Black.

Nothingness.

The sun was gone.

It went pitch and no matter how often I blinked, there was no change.

Are you dead?

A chorus of shrieks echoed from every corner of Thalla as a blast of light brighter than Timos' flames engulfed my vision. The claws in my shoulder disappeared instantaneously.

As did my wounds.

Then I was plucked from the cobbles and cradled into a familiar embrace. "I've got you, it's alright," Avexei whispered shakily as his chest rose and fell against my trembling cheek. The macabre scent of blood interchanged with his soothing cotton. "You're safe, Nala. I've got you." No touch had ever felt more euphoric. Not ever. I was sobbing from how overwhelming it was as he kissed the top of my head.

"You saved me," I whispered. Vex was close to squeezing me to death. But I didn't care. I never wanted to let him go, couldn't, and wouldn't. *Never again.* My voice tremored like the earth quaked beneath us, but I had to get the words out. "I couldn't stop thinking of how I should've told you how much I love you."

"I love you, too. Whatever comes next doesn't matter, even if it kills me, I have to have you for as long as I'm able," Vex murmured.

I flung my arms around his neck. There were tongues, teeth, I didn't know where he began, and I ended. Nothing else mattered as he groaned in my mouth, and my heat demanded more.

<<*"NALA!"*>

//*"She's not at the shelter! The streets are filled with carnage, Jin!"*/

"It is about time you earned my forgiveness, Avexei." Timoset. *[["I found them. We are near Citrine Circle."]*

Vex gingerly placed me on my feet. Then I was yanked and passed around. My eyes were sticky and struggling to remain open. I couldn't believe my survival. Couldn't accept it. It felt like I might've actually died and conjured it all.

Trapped myself in a warped, alternate reality.

//*"She's in shock."*/ Ryloh said, "H- How did a Revenant get through the wards?"

[["I was nullified and could no longer shift. It was planned."]

<<*"No wonder we couldn't fucking sense her!"*>

"You're going to have to call an emergency Skerry, Mo," Avexei said. "Lo and I will take her back to mine. Go deal with the aftermath."

"Your mother will expect you," Timos replied with a sigh.

"Fuck her, I'm not leaving Nala's side."

Timos kept his grip on my forearm as we arrived outside the Palace's keep. I raised a brow as his wave of panic crashed into me. "Malice *knows* of our predicament, Jin. We can no longer remain here," he said in explanation. I sighed, tossing my head back as that processed.

You nearly lost Nala. The last twenty minutes hadn't clicked into place yet. It was darting around my brain as I struggled to catch up. My fists were clenching to keep from shaking, but otherwise, I felt decently calm.

All things considered.

"Whatever we have to do, Timos. I don't care about staying here anymore. Not after she could've died today," I assured, and his shoulders fell a sliver. My brows drew together as I voiced my suspicion. "There's gotta be a traitor in our midst. First Dayna waiting for Nala, now the Revenant. We can't ignore it, there's been a pattern."

Timos gasped, eyes bulging as his freezing grip tightened. "Do you remember when Naliti was roaming around Bahasa after her date with Ryloh?" I nodded. That morning was impossible for me to forget, her avoidance stung. It was also still firmly ranked as the worst day of my life. "There were a pair of undetected breaches nearby! The first I caught was less than one-hundred meters from her," he shouted. Then released me to pace while palming his chin.

"Fuck, I forgot about the vamps that day," I groaned, rubbing the numbness from my arm.

"Someone in the fucking Command Centre is the source. They must be," he mused. Rightfully, so. No one else on the island had the access to bypass the wards.

"How do we find out who, though?"

The dragon stilled, a grin spreading across his lips. "I might have an idea."

꧂ ꧂ ꧂ ꧁ *.°

Timoset and I were waiting and watching as the Skerry meeting dragged on. The Code Indigo was packed to the brim, with his dad, the Supreme, stretching across the big screen in virtual attendance. Several Councilors rifted in after we explained the reasoning behind the sun's momentary disappearance. It was my first session warranting the dukes from Below's attendance. Also, the first time I'd been around a more prestigious Titan than the Queen.

All four were hidden behind matching deep-hooded robes. They were fucking terrifying. Especially Timos' mother. Hae couldn't hold a torch to the Suprema's rage spoiling the ether. There were a pair of rosy orbs locked onto her son, visible despite her face remaining concealed.

"And where is the civilian Avexei *supposedly* rescued now?" Imera drawled from her platinum throne, recapturing my attention.

"Yes, we should bring her in. A first-hand account may piece together what went wrong with the wards," Seong emphasized. When he caught sight of my scowl, a smirk lifted his lips. Murmurs erupted between the Councilors, while the Below dukes sloshed in their portable aquariums.

Timos all but growled, and I was forced to prod him mentally until he stopped. Using the most saccharine voice I could muster, I explained, "Avexeidros took her to a healer. That's why he isn't present. As you can imagine, facing a Revenant head-on didn't leave her unscathed."

My focus was glued to Seong as the remaining audience reacted. *Why's he stirring the pot?*

"The streets were painted in blood," Timos supplicated. "I was also forced to leverage dragon fire. The spliced were spreading too quickly."

"Chiropteras?" Suprema questioned, and Timos nodded. "None of you felt any of these beings cross the wards?" Grunts and shaken heads followed. Osri and Persis, our Protectorates, were completely distraught. Heads bowed.

Seong was the lone smirker in our midst and my hatred reached new heights.

"Then there must be a renegade in presence," the Suprema hissed. It was terrifying, but Timos and I held a mental celebration all the same. "I wish to speak to each of you separately prior to taking your leave. This meeting is now adjourned, you may talk amongst your—"

"Hey," Imera shouted, "this is *my* Court, Zu-zu! Not yours!" I recoiled along with the majority of the crowd. Clearly, Queen cunt had a death wish. She seemed to have realized her own mistake, her tresses shifting to gloomier shades.

<<*"She's fucking unbearable."*>

[[*"Unfortunately, I have witnessed worse from her."*]

The Medusa pulled her hood back, freeing the pair of burgundy snapping serpents extending from her scalp. "No. You have failed your constituents, Imera. This is not the first occasion, either. I have every intention of uncovering who is responsible. As Suprema, it is my duty, and mine alone."

The Queen, still somehow emboldened, grabbed her Hand and rifted out wordlessly.

"Now, who shall go first?" Zusicia pressed, crossing her robed arms before striding toward the door. She'd warded the rest of us in, so there wasn't any escape. However, this was exactly what we wanted. What we *needed* to happen. It was our plan all along.

Being a soul eating demon, the Suprema could distinguish malintent with ease. Our souls apparently darkened from selfishness according to Timos. She'd uncover the culprit far quicker than we ever could.

The room filled with audible gulps and hushed whisperings. "Timoset and Yu-Jin then," she called when none openly volunteered. We exchanged a shrug before ambling toward the entrance. When I remained in the room after Timos, a clawed scaly hand dragged me into the hall with them.

[["She likely knows all."]

"Why did you not tell me you have found her?" she demanded of her son. Timos feigned unawareness to his mother's question. I kept my face nonplussed as the Medusa's slitted gaze narrowed in my direction. "You are her fourth then, and unfated at that," she hissed. *Shit.*

The dragon's palm landed on my shoulder in solidarity or comfort. Regardless, I was grateful. He nodded before I had the chance to. Zusicia sighed as her snakes coiled around her frame. "Atha and I shall attempt to shield Nala from the Councilor's interest, but do not take severe action without your father and I knowing," she commanded.

Relief blanketed me in its warm embrace. Suprema was clearly going to help. We needed all we could get to survive this.

"Why?" Timos asked, his expression far more perplexed than mine. "You rarely interfere."

"This is not the same," she replied. "Nala has been through enough. Hurry back to her. Ensure Vex gives me a ring as well. We shall keep the rest at bay."

THIRTY MINUTES EARLIER

Avexei and Ryloh rifted us from the scene. We didn't return to the loft though. Or to Timos'. We landed in an otherworldly forest. The leaves on the towering trees matched the PPP lobby. Magenta leaves and petals in all directions.

I couldn't discern whether they were a twist of reality or not.

"We're in the woods outside the farm." Avexei's voice blared, and I jolted. Still suffering from the trauma of the last thirty minutes, or however long it'd been. I was too out of it to protest how the pair were carrying me like a log. It wasn't until my feet were dunked into a freezing pool that my eyes focused enough to discern a nearby waterfall, not having registered the sound prior.

"It's alright, Nala. Take your time," Ryloh murmured as I was lowered to my knees, yelping when the chill hit my thighs. It was admittedly soothing the heat's effects, but jarring.

"Is this alright? We thought it might help," Avexei rumbled.

--_"Too much."_- Even my mental voice was strained.

They plucked me from the waters. It took several breaths to register that I was horizontal and resting against a pillowy surface. "Bugs," I mumbled, worried about critters crawling in my hair.

"Nala, have you seen a single fly since your arrival?" Ry's voice had a taunting edge.

"No, but—"

"They don't exist on Neptune. The plants mostly pollinate themselves," Avexei explained. "Titans chose what species went where."

Despite my struggle, I exclaimed, "Even on Earth?"

"Yeah, I dunno why Zeus thought mosquitos were a brilliant idea, but he's long gone, so we'll never know," Vex replied.

I let the breath I'd been holding in free and relaxed. When I cracked an eye, the pinks of the treetops were dizzying. My upside-down view of the males was also kinda hilarious.

You're delirious.

The acknowledgement did nothing to contain my sudden burst of giggles.

Both frowned. "Wh- What's with you, spice?"

"You look like a Chase, definitely not a Cabbage," I said with a grin. "And you, Vex, you're more of an Ahanu. Your names are all wrong. Timos would be… Malik. Jin babe would be Kai. I think it means water in Japanese. He's Korean, though. Is that offensive?" I knew I was babbling like a brook, but it was consoling. Further proof I was alive. "At least names don't matter. Not really. Mine doesn't fit either, does it?"

They exchanged a frown.

"Lo-Lo, would you grab some rumpai leaves?"

"N- Now is not the time for y- you to have a smoke," Ryloh chided.

Avexei scoffed. "Not for me! For Nala, obviously. We need to get her heartrate down."

The crunching leaves blared like a microphone's static, and I groaned. However, clamping my eyes shut only worsened the spins. I couldn't tell whether it was the heat or the near-death adrenaline fleeing my system, but it was more uncomfortable than the transformation. "Hate this," I muttered. "Totally, woah-tally, woefully, despise it."

"What can I do, Nala baby?" Avexei said in a hushed voice.

"Quit calling me that," I snapped.

"Just checking your coherence. Are you feeling okay, little lioness?"

If I could've rolled my eyes without vomiting, I would've. Instead, settling on, "Shut up."

A chorus of breaking twigs circled, signifying Ryloh's return. "H-Here," he said in his alien accent before pulling my head into his lap. I groaned when he scratched my scalp. It felt better than it should've. "Are you hungry, Nala? I could instruct the others to bring food."

"Ask them regardless," Avexei said. "Can you sit upright, Nala? I think smoking will help."

"Is it weed?" I asked, crawling to a seated position with Ryloh's assistance. Marijuana was my most prevalently used drug besides sleeping pills and the occasional pain killer. Lifting my head caused a fresh wave of disorientation. The pair were doubled in my vision, dancing against the bright forested backdrop.

"It's more intense than weed, but I think you'll like it," the doppelgängers of Vex explained. "It should help." Ryloh used static to light the end of the rosy joint in Avexei's mouth. The scent filling the air was less robust, more floral. When they pressed an end to my lips and I inhaled, it filled my mouth with the taste of honeysuckles. *Fuck, that's delightful.*

I motioned for another puff, earning a grin from the four versions of Vex.

My vision slowed from Tilt-a-Whirl to carousel speed. Since the smoke had an instantaneous effect, I motioned for another hit. "Slow down," Ryloh chided.

"It's helping," I croaked. *Sort of.* There were still multiple sets of each male. Plus, the effects of the heat, which could only be described as drowning in a volcano's lava. One of them stole the rumpai from my lips, refusing to allow a fourth puff.

They held a silent conversation with their eyebrows. "Are you two gonna make out again?" I pressed. They burst into yowls. Which felt unfair. It wasn't that funny, was it?

"L- Let's try the ice-bath again," Ryloh said. I cringed in anticipation. Which was warranted since he rifted us in. Waist deep. A screech tore from my throat.

Avexei *tutted* before following, but I couldn't pay him any attention as my teeth chattered. "Go under, Nala. You're no coward," Ry urged. With a scowl, I dipped, allowing the frigid waters to engulf my shoulders. The shivering soon became more euphoric than shocking. It took a few breaths for courage, but I dunked. A bubbled sigh left my lips as the cold caressed my scalp. *//"You can breathe under there now."/*

No shit. I'd forgotten Timos' aquatic command. It took a while to gather the courage to inhale, but I could. Normally. *You're breathing in water!* My vision was still a blurred mess so I couldn't see the boulders under my feet, but the ice replacing the oxygen in my lungs was distracting enough to keep my gaze clamped tight.

When I eventually resurfaced, feeling a bit more lucid, the pair were mid-discussion. "Th- They will rage if we accept without their knowledge," Ryloh said.

The topic went straight to my clit. *Has to be the heat's fault.* My want quickly morphed to necessity.

"Nala could've died! Are you willing to risk her again? Because I'm fucking not," Avexei argued. "What if Malice sends multiple Revenants? What if she actually had a chance to take her—"

"F- F- Fine," Ryloh relented. There were no longer duplicative versions of them at least.

Although my mind still felt like a mashed potato, I knew they were discussing taking away my choice. It didn't sit right with me, despite the horniness. "What happened to tethering being my decision?"

"The Revenant happened," Avexei hissed, obsidian eyes narrowing to slits as he took a step to tower closer. "You have no idea how dangerous those fuckers actually are, Nala. They're the most difficult vampires to kill."

I scrunched my nose, then scratched a resulting itch, which caused a moan. *Whoops.* Every sensation was amplified. Their closeness was also causing my chest to play like a tambourine.

They were now gawking. Ryloh's pupils had overtaken his irises, there wasn't even a sliver of chrome left. Whereas Vex's tongue lengthened, the forked end peeking through his pouty lips. They were making it impossible to focus, but I managed to choke out, "I thought Wraiths were the most dangerous?"

"Wraiths cannot nullify your magic, unlike Revenants," Ryloh explained. "Al- Although Wraiths can dole equivalent damage, Revenants are far more difficult to destroy. They're also rarer. Their splicing requires a piece of Malice's prestige. As you can imagine, she doesn't just grant it freely."

"But Vex killed it in seconds," I argued, eliciting a dark chuckle from said male.

"I stole the sun, little lioness," Avexei replied. "That sort of exertion is impossible for most. I'm sure the Council's deciding my punishment as we speak."

My limbs were in motion before registering the action, arms flinging around Vex's neck and squeezing. "They can try to take you from me," I murmured into his drenched shirt. "But I'll rage worse than Timos' dad." He hugged me back, planting a kiss on my head.

"You too, Ry," I said, meeting his mismatched gaze before diving into his warmer embrace next. "If anyone tries to take you from me, I'll fucking lose it."

"I know you would, spice," he replied with a grin. Ryloh was painfully handsome. The planes of his face sharper thanks to his stubble lengthening to scruff. My heart swelled as we kissed.

//"I love you, Nala,"/ his alien accent boomed through my mind as our tongues tangled.

Despite my disorientation, I knew with absolute certainty that I loved him, too. It had nothing to do with my near-death encounter, either. Ryloh had been so patient. He'd been my constant through everything. Gripping his cheeks, I said, "I love you, Ryloh Cabbage. I'm only sorry it took me so long to admit. You've been so understanding. I swear I'll make it up to you."

"Now," he replied. "You'll make it up to me now."

"*Wha—?*" I was silenced by his staticky lips. My heart went from a gallop to a hundred-meter sprint as Avexei's body pressed against my back. The bloodied dress was ripped off, then bra and boy-shorts, followed by frigid hands trailing up my sides. Our hearts were audibly drumming to the same tune.

Vex kissed down the side of my neck as his hands moved lower. I groaned into Ry's mouth as he bit down on my lower lip. A thrill barreled down my spine as Ryloh tugged on my peaked nipples. Desperation swallowed me whole from the four hands playing my body like an instrument.

A beg readied on my lips as my fingers fought with the buttons on Ryloh's shorts. Between my dizziness and the slickness of the water, it was a struggle. We rifted back onto land, leaves crunching underfoot. My skin peppered from the slight breeze as they stripped. Once they were sandwiching me within grabbing distance, I took a throbbing cock in each hand, languidly stroking them crown to base.

"Both. *Please*. I need you both," I whined.

A groan left Ryloh's chest as he gripped my chin, fingers bruising. "Use your words, Nala spice. How do you want us?" My brows furrowed with uncertainty. A plethora of positions skipped across my vision. Choice overload left me sputtering.

"Answer, Nala," Avexei hissed as I twisted his shaft in my fist.

Apparently I was taking too long, because I was suddenly knocked onto all fours. "I- I'll take her ass since you haven't tasted her," Ryloh offered. There wasn't any opportunity to correct how wrong he was before a staticky tongue pressed into my rear.

Vex rifted underneath me in a sixty-nine position. His throbbing dick twitching against his abs. When I reached to fist him again, he latched onto my clit, and I couldn't withhold my squeal from the contrasting feeling of their tongues. It quickly became a moan as Vex added a finger and curled against my g-spot. My vision was already spotting, less than a full minute in. Ryloh's tongue plunged deeper, making me cry out from the intensity.

Ecstasy crashed through every nerve, muscle, and bone as I climaxed. Neither relented. The sloppy sounds of their efforts overwhelmed the forest's song. As relaxed as I felt, my skin was heating. Feverish times one-thousand. Like being roasted from the inside out. The heat was worsening. "It's not enough," I breathed.

"I won't be able to control myself," Vex grumbled against my pussy. "I can't be gentle."

"M- Me either," Ryloh said. "P- Perhaps we should take separate turns." I didn't *want* that though.

They're probably right, you were nearly ripped to shreds today.

However, the words formed on my lips of their own accord. "No. Both of you. Now." *Probably beastie's doing, that horny bitch.*

Ryloh hopped to his feet, pulling me upright. "Use your venom," he directed.

"You aren't worried about her drifting off?" Vex questioned with a furrowed brow.

My impatience skyrocketed. "Now!"

Avexei spun me, and the next thing I knew, his brisk tongue slid through my cheeks. The longer forked version. Unlike with Ryloh's recent ministrations, there was no resistance whatsoever. Because venom was fucking bliss.

Similar to MDMA, but the sensation contained to where his tongue caressed. I shuddered from Ryloh tugging on my peaked nipples. Despite no longer needing to worry about the suppressant and the heat's haze, I was a bit fearful.

There had only been toys in my bum in the past and their joysticks were enormous.

"Don't think you can take it, spice?" Ryloh said, and I could hear the smile in his alien accent. The *thing* inside me didn't appreciate his taunting, though. Not one bit. However, she didn't have a chance to act before I was bent over.

Fingers replaced Avexei's tongue, multiple hands teasing.

A mewl left my lips as Vex plunged into my pussy with a slow glide. Our moans collided when he twitched against my cervix, and my gaze shuttered. I couldn't tell if the buzzing in my chest had worsened or if we were literally vibrating. The feeling of rightness as his cold hard dick languidly slid out of me could only be described as transcendental.

Vex took his time, torturing the pleasure from me, forcing whimpers from my lips as I felt every ridge. My knees wobbled when a finger pressed into my ass and he picked me up one-handed, leaving my legs dangling. The venom made it feel so euphoric that I came with a cry immediately, wetness slipping down to my ankles as Vex cursed.

//*"Her taking another cock shouldn't be this bewitching."*/

Cracking an eye, I found Ryloh's stare boring into me which only ignited every sensation. He fell to his knees at my feet, licking the slickness from ankle to knee, and I nearly orgasmed from just the sight. "Radiant," he rasped, pupils blown. "You're glowing."

"It's not me," Vex panted. "All her." I didn't know what they were talking about, nor did I care. Despite my current satisfaction, the heat wasn't sated. *Or your beastie.* Regardless, something possessed me to motion for Ry to join. He rose to his feet with bolts covering his carved perfection wearing the most rakish expression, ever.

I was distracted by Vex adding another finger in my ass. Then he withdrew leaving me empty and wanton, before notching his crown where I feared most. My eyes clamped shut on instinct, bracing myself for the ache. But it was unnecessary because the venom made it pure euphoria.

"Eyes open. On me, Nala spice," Ryloh commanded, gripping my chin as he grinned. My lashes fluttered as I felt the freezing tip of a piercing ball press into my clit. He pressed a chaste kiss to my lips before biting the side of my neck, hard enough to leave a mark.

"Hurry up," Vex panted from behind us, he hadn't moved an inch since filling me to the hilt. We were shuddering together, his chest flush against my back. I could hardly breathe as Ryloh's crown slipped past my drenched folds. "Fuck," Vex groaned.

My head fell to Ry's shoulder as he thrust home. The feeling was unbelievable. Our breaths synced before we were soon doused in static. Neither of them had to move, a climax barreled through my consciousness from the mere fullness. Every sensation was deeper, more intense, as though the rapture sprouted from my soul.

I was barely conscious when they started rutting, so stuffed I could combust from pleasure. Each time their hips thudded against mine felt like electrocution. My body pulsed and spasmed, I was probably drooling, but too high on the orgy to care.

Their thrusts became slight and twitchy while I whimpered from overwhelm as endorphins bounced around my brain. Ryloh's eyes were rolled into the back of his head while Vex's tongue lapped the crook of my shoulder. They were both hanging on by the thread of a spider's web.

I could sense it.

My toes pointed as I dangled in Vex's grip, thighs clamping around where Ry's cock sluiced into me. The friction threw me over the edge, sending a zip of ice through my nerve endings. This orgasm near painful. Vex hissed as I clamped around them, sending Ryloh into a slew of shouted curses. When they filled me up, a shudder ripped from my toes to the tip of my head.

I didn't know how long we remained like that, but the ecstasy filled daze felt bottomless. I'd never been so sated. Vex withdrew first, hissing as he did. My feet didn't hit the ground, though.

The temperature of my skin eased before I cracked an eye. To find Ryloh grinning from ear-to-pointy-ear, his long lashes kissing his high cheekbones as he fisted my asscheeks.

"What's the verdict on my bells and whistles then, spice?" he questioned with a grin, pushing his —*now hard*— dick right into my g-spot. I gasped as the fae chuckled into my ear. My clit pulsed like it had its own heartbeat. So sensitive that I couldn't stop shivering.

"I can't, Ry, please. No more."

::*"Fuck. You shouldn't be so rough with her after that, Lo."*:

Ry stilled. I gawked.

"What?" Avexei said.

--*"We heard you!"*-

Vex's eyes became saucers as his obsidian gaze darted between us.

"You couldn't wait for us to get back first? We were covering for you!" Yu-Jin.

Whoops.

My gaze flicked behind Vex, finding Jin and Timos. Both scowling with takeout bags from my favorite Thallan restaurant in tow.

//*"We're going to have to rain check our solo session unfortunately, spice."*/ Ryloh's withdrawal left me wincing before he swung me into his arms bridal style. I sighed against his chest. It wasn't just the aftermath of the orgasms; I could finally breathe having them near.

"Her heat has passed?" Timos' soft voice pressed. Which was when I did a bodily scan, realizing he was right. The boiling had eased.

"Yeah. Let's go back to the house," Vex said.

"Wait," I hollered before Ry could rift us. "Grab more leaves. I wanna smoke again!"

Now that I was feeling somewhat capable of calm, there were unknowns ruining it. They'd suckered on like a barnacle I couldn't shake. Was it safe to stay? Would there be another breach? Beyond our Neptunian mess, there was the question of what the Council would do with me. How they'd react to Avexei stealing the sun. *Don't even get yourself started with Queen Molester.*

However, there was one thing I could say with absolute certainty. Vex's house was the most beautiful place I'd ever been. Not only was the structure itself made from a dreamy, whitewashed rock that extended from its exterior to the interior, but it was waterfront. The back patio sat atop an inclined collection of naturally formed turquoise pools. Both sides flanked with bushes in a bougainvillea purply hue.

"I knew you'd love it." Vex grinned at my awe. I extended a foot to find the water of the closest pool warm. It was only a brief respite from the chaos though, lasting no more than a blink.

Ambling back inside, we took our seats at the kitchen table where the others were unpacking the food. Vex grabbed a bottle of red wine and corkscrew from the counter in passing. I demanded the first glass, guzzling it like water, and trying again. Unfortunately, it did nothing to take the edge off because I was sturdier now, freakishly so.

Our bonding had several immediate and sobering side effects, and I couldn't feign unawareness. For example, how I could now *hear* our hearts. Like a permanent in sync drumbeat behind my thoughts, conversations, etc. Then came the fact that magic was exploding from me constantly, refusing to remain caged any longer. Blooming and glowing vines crackling with static crawled up and down my limbs. While my body kept shifting from hot to cold as if it couldn't decide which it preferred. *Damn you, Libra moon.*

There were also the drastically improved senses. *Oh, and can't forget the ghosts.* There were about a dozen or so which kept slipping in and out of the walls silently. They were mostly transparent, all except for their eyeballs. Which was creepy enough to lessen my hunger.

As if all of that weren't enough, Jin's brain was rambling nervously, while Timos was eerily silent. The way they picked at their plates gave away their panic, I'd never seen either approach a meal with less enthusiasm. The Revenant meeting was a bummer.

Conversely, at their opposite, Ry and Vex were chipper. Their smiles unshakeable, even while munching on their meals.

// "Because I know whatever's wrong, we can work through it, Nala spice. Together."/ Vex shared a wink in unity.

"Alright," Timos said, readjusting his spectacles. "We should get on with it." He heaved a weighted sigh, pummeling me in the stomach with unease. "Nala, do you wish to remain on Neptune?" he asked gruffly. *Well, that was unexpected.*

My answer came easily as I admired the kitchen. It was like being in Architectural Digest, everything adorned in natural tans and creams with pops of ash wood against the white rock. "I mean, if we can live here, then yeah." Ryloh and Avexei shouted excitedly, sharing a high five. But I couldn't pay them any mind. "Why are you asking that, Timos? What happened? Start at the beginning. Please."

Jin paled as Timos' eyes shifted. *Dramatic, much?*

"It is not dramatic," my protector clipped. "The Revenant was fucking sent for you, Naliti." I shrugged, having suspected as much. *Why else would he have gone into the shelter?* "If Avexei had not found you when he had—"

I silenced him with a shake of my head. "We're past that. What happened at the meeting?"

Jin scratched the back of his neck, saying, "The Queen threw a fit. Then Timos' mom showed with several of the Councilors to hear everything firsthand." He tipped his shaved chin at Vex. "Suprema asked you to call her, Avexei. And anyway, Imera demanded an army of dragons. Which the Council, shockingly, approved. Then they declared war. The remainder of the galaxy against Chiron—"

"War?! But it was only one Revy?" I exclaimed, and Ryloh snorted.

"Revenants were extinct. Malice was banned from creating more in her surrender. They should've killed her instead, though. She's not worth the hassle."

Timos nodded, adding, "Neither is Dmitrios. Yet they spared her solely for him."

"Your evil brother?" I questioned, and he gave a pained nod. The stab in his heart echoed in mine. Reaching across the table, I took his hand and squeezed.

"Dmitri's the one who tortured him for weeks during the last war," Vex said with a scowl. "Only dragons can scar each other. Uncle Atha didn't know it was possible for dragon skin to be marred until the fucktart got ahold of Mo."

Gasping, I rifted into Timos' lap. "Did you get him back?" Brushing the chestnut curls from his forehead, we locked eyes as his coppery gaze shifted into golden slits. A wave of fury crashed through my consciousness. Whether the emotion was mine or his was indiscernible. "We're going to get your revenge, Timoset," I swore as his arms slithered around my midsection. "That fucktart is gonna pay."

It wasn't much, but Timos nodded. While Ryloh and Vex clinked glasses in solidarity.

"Listen, there's more we have to tell you," Jin interrupted, looking green. "They're going to lock the cities down in three days. If we stay, we can't live in Gro because it'll be warded out. The Queen made the call to exclude them."

"But we fucking grow their food!" The force of Avexei's yell cracked his wineglass. He frowned at the fissure, and Jin shrugged; essentially conveying his Siarc prestige was the source. *Apparently we were all suffering from the effects of too much dick magic.* "She is so fucking insufferable," Vex muttered before rising to grab another glass. "I'm assuming none of you talked through evacuation plans for Gro?"

Jin and Timos both shook their heads and Vex sighed, pinching his brow between his fingers. "The press made the announcement while we were in the Skerry, and the population counting system in the Command Centre started dipping rapidly within minutes. Venus is encouraging refugees go there," Jin revealed with a devastated sigh.

--*"I'm so sorry, Jin babe. This doesn't discount any of the lives you've improved."*- *He shared a grim nod in return.*

Welp. There goes his job... Maybe there actually wasn't any reason to stay.

"I- I agree with you, spice. We could rent something in Acidity to not impose on the Sages. The war won't reach Uru. Olorun is one of the few who doesn't have qualms with Malice," Ryloh explained. "She would never cross him; we'll be safer there."

It sounded like a logical option, but I couldn't help voicing, "There's no water though."

"I need it, too. If that wasn't obvious," Vex offered. "Uru would be temporary. There aren't many options if we wanna avoid Malice. Hell could work, Dmitri's terrified of Asmodeus. Or Mercury—"

"Hell," I hollered. Accidentally shattering every single glass. My cheeks boiled as I mouthed an apology. Yemaya's description coupled with the Halloweentown pictures on Lakshmi's pamphlet left me with a hankering to see the so-called 'bad place.' I was more willing to give up the sun in exchange for the ocean. Moonlight was sexier anyway.

Vex shrugged, uncaring about the damage. Continuing on with our conversation, he said to Timos, "Can you text Asmodeus? You've probably talked to him more recently than I have."

Ryloh cleared his throat, we shifted our attention to find him smirking. "I have a place in Hallow. It was my residence when slaughtering for hire. It's our ideal option, and not solely because of how thrilled Nala spice is. We'd be untraceable there. Even to the Council. I have Moloch's favor."

"You're revealing this *now*?" Vex shouted. "We've been pals for years, you never said!"

The fae shrugged, his Cheshire cat grin expanding. "It never came up."

"How will we be hidden from the Council? I thought they were in everyone's business. You worked for them for centuries against your will."

"D- Demons unnerve most Titans due to their soul eating, and Hell is the most populated planet, chocked full. Although Moloch, their Overlord, refuses to acknowledge his Council seat, he's inflicted enough terror for the majority of non-demons to keep their distance," Ryloh explained. "Which was how we became close, our mutual loathing of the Council. He's got Hell locked up tight. Not even Timos' father could break through their barrier if he tried."

I swallowed thickly, having forgotten the whole soul eating bit, and rethinking whether this would be a good idea. *Then again, Timoset's half demon.* "Shouldn't we make nice with the Council before ghosting them? I don't want to live on the run forever and I'll eventually miss sunlight, Hell can't be permanent."

"We could write a letter," Vex suggested and I barked a disbelieving laugh. "I'm serious! Mo's parents and Olorun will keep them at a distance. You're right, we can't run forever, but we can at least buy you time for you to adjust to your prestige."

Timos created a piece of thick parchment with a snap of his fingers, and Jin pulled a pen from his pocket, playing secretary.

"We're going to have to offer something in exchange for Nala," Ryloh said with a scratch to his scruff. "P- Put sterilization down for me." I squeaked. Not entirely sure how to feel about that.

"Oh, me too," Vex said excitedly. When met with my confusion, he supplied, "We don't need to have a quad of kids to be happy, little lioness. There will probably be at least one baby anyway, it's not like they'd allow Mo to offer the same." I still hadn't come to any family related conclusions, there hadn't really been time for consideration or discussion. However, *one* did seem less daunting than *four.*

"I'll offer the same," Jin murmured.

"Give them a portion of my hoard in fines," Timos suggested. "My father can placate the worst with riches, they are easily bought." *Lovely.* It was difficult to associate Olorun and Yemaya in the same category the more I heard of the others.

There was a terse beat of silence, where the only sounds were of our hearts' drumbeat and the pen scratching against the thick parchment. Jin finished with a flourish, passing the pen to the others. When it got to Avexei he scribbled more than his name, explaining, "So I don't have to call Aunt Zuzu to discuss the sun before we go off grid." He finished and passed to me. I didn't read any of it, worried it might unsettle me further.

Signing my surname as Drago for the first time was fun, though.

"What about the PPP contract and me having to stay here until the mating ceremony?" I questioned. "We'll be in violation. Again."

"My father is keeping Aphrodite from taking action on our behalf," Timos explained.

"It wouldn't matter regardless," Ryloh butt in. "They won't be paying attention with the war. Your clone will remain intact through your fifth week —"

"WHAT?" My yell was probably heard for miles. "Clone?!"

"Yeah, the Program hired a mage to create a temporary copy of you," Jin explained "The clone hasn't been physically around your family, but it's there to keep up with your communications while you're here. It *believes* it's you."

"That's nutty," I muttered. "So, what happens when the five-weeks is up?"

"The doppelgänger turns to mist, which is when you're supposed to return, and placate your family," Ryloh said nonchalantly. "We have three weeks left. It should be enough time for you to settle into your prestige."

"And then we'll go to Earth together?" I questioned, and they nodded. Instead of beginning an entirely different war by voicing how they couldn't *all* meet my parents, I asked instead, "Where would we go after? Hell again? Uru? Here?"

They exchanged shrugs as Avexei said, "Does it matter? You'll have all of us together."

I shook my head, a grin tempting my lips. "Well, at least that's solved," Jin mumbled.

"So off to Hell it is," Timos proclaimed. "Shall I make a portal? It is unnecessary to delay for replaceables."

That deflated my excitement like a needle to a balloon.

"I haven't had a chance to explore Vex's house yet," I whined. "Plus, we just got back this morning. Can't we wait until tomorrow? You're right about our stuff, I don't care about belongings either. I need a moment to breathe. There's been too much change in such an unbelievably short span." Worried expressions peered back.

Apparently, you're asking for too much.

"Nala, I mean no offense by this, but look at you, love." Jin's gaze darted to where water had now joined the party, swirling around my vine and bolt covered hands. I sighed. *He's right.*

"Y- Your prestige is traceable on Neptune. It won't be in Hell. You're going to love the house, spice. It's set on a lush lake you can kayak on and there's an indoor pool," Ryloh gushed.

"Are there critters in this lake?" He shook his pretty head. *Oh-kay, that actually sounds ideal.* "You're all in agreement with us leaving this second?"

Avexei heaved a sigh, he was the lone member of my boyband shaking his head. "I have to help the residents get out of Gro. Or at the very least, ward their homes if they plan to stay. It won't take long, there's only a couple dozen families. If I had help," he said, canting his head towards Timos, "it would only take a few hours. We could leave right after."

"He's right. We should help them," Jin replied. "Ryloh and I can remain with Nala during. We can pack up the loft. I'll leave my resignation with Zaire."

"Are you sure about this, Jin? You love your role, I don't wanna take that from you."

He nodded, the slant of his brows severe, before leaning in to give me a kiss. << *"You matter more. Besides, I think this will be fun. I've never been to Hell. We're doing Earth and South Korea after. It'll be nice to have a break with you. With all of us."*> *I ruffled his navy strands in agreement.*

My gaze darted around the table, as I confirmed, "So, we're doing this?" Earning a quadrant of determined nods. Which was when my curiosity sparked. "Is Hallow a city or a town?"

"It's one of Hell's capital cities," Ryloh explained. "The manor is on the outskirts, so we'll have the best of both. There's plenty of space. You and the Siren will have m- multiple water sources. The geeks could build a laboratory if they desired. Although there's a supercomputer already onsite." Jin brightened from that revelation.

"There are stark cultural differences, Naliti. Although there are a variety of classifications in their population, the bulk possess fire and choose to don it," Timos explained. My eyes saucered as I attempted to picture an entire city dressed in flames. It seemed like a hazard.

Vex snickered. "It's fireproofed, every building in Hallow is made of granite."

"Are we gonna be running around wearing flames?" I had to know.

"When it's necessary to fit into a crowd, yes. Otherwise, no."

The males fell into comfortable chit-chat about Ryloh's, but exhaustion reared its ugly head and refused to allow my participation. My mind was a jumble.

You just arrived two weeks ago. Now you're a magic wielding badass. You'll live forever, hopefully with all four... FOUR. Gaaah, that's so insane. And you're moving to Hell. Of all places. My parents would probably stroke out if they knew. You can't worry about them; they have six other kids and a horde of grandchildren to deal with. Plus, they hardly thought of my feelings. So, why worry for theirs?

They've never been your people.

"Nala spice, are you listening?" Ryloh clipped, interrupting my internalizations. I shook my head with a sheepish smile. "Avexei said there's a film called, *The Lion King,* we should watch tonight. Would you enjoy that?" I squealed, hopping out of Timos' lap and into Vex's.

"Should we tell them how you know about that movie?"

The others pouted. "What's she talking about?" Jin questioned.

"I, *uhm,*" Avexei started, his cheeks darkening several shades as his hair went olive. "I was on Earth with Nala for a stint." I cackled as they were struck dumbfounded. Too stunned to react. Not even blink. Jin even sparked with bolts as he digested.

"Vex erased my memories but gave them back in Uru. That's how he speaks my lingo and knows so much about Earth."

There was a loud growl, followed by a whoosh of bleached smoke. "What the fuck?!"

"Y- Y- You lied to me!" Ryloh raged as the kitchen grew humid. "Y-You told me you were only keeping an eye from a distance," he accused with a pale pointer, a shot of water escaping and pelting Vex right in the face.

"I was keeping her safe," Avexei cried, hair shifting rapidly as he wiped the onslaught from his eyes.

It was a task to withhold my chuckle. "I'm not mad about it, so you can't be either," I declared. "Besides, you get to watch a cinematic masterpiece because of him. Do you have corn kernels?" Vex nodded, his hair shifting back to silver as he met my gaze. "Well, pop off then, *Aleksi.*"

He groaned.

Instead of sleeping peacefully, tucked in the embrace of my loves, my naked and restless butt snuck downstairs. Despite having a delightful evening laughing hard enough to cry, the scariness of change swarmed the second everything got quiet. Although my movements were reduced to the wiggling of my toes in the pools while sitting at the edge of Vex's patio, my anxiety rendered me light-headed. Unfocused.

I couldn't enjoy the moons and how their reflections danced in the pools. The comforting balminess of this summer night against my exposed skin.

"D- Did you really think you'd sneak down here unnoticed?" Ryloh *tsked* as he plopped down, a heavy bare arm draping over my shoulders. He nuzzled into my neck as if he was trying to claw under my skin and a sigh of relief escaped. My body went into autopilot, relaxing the moment we touched. It was his stormy scent. His nearness. Him. "W- Why aren't you upstairs?" he murmured into my hair.

"Couldn't sleep," I said on a sigh. His chrome gaze searched mine before he tucked me closer against his bare chest.

//"Karma, I could fecking eat her."/ Ryloh's thoughts were so... Him.

With a wide grin, I said, "I'm so glad you're in the mind-meld."

"Why?"

"Your musings are the easiest. I feel at home in your brain. You're never really weighed down with guilt or worrying..." I trailed off because it was too soon to comment on the last tether, we'd only been linked for a few hours.

"Or obsessing," Ryloh added, finishing my thought with a smirk.

I wrinkled my nose, not wanting to admit it. But he was right. Vex's brain was consumed with me. It was a lot to take in.

"I know you loathe secrets, so you should know. When Olorun locked them in the tubes, I didn't actually panic," he revealed with a slight frown. "H- He released me once you left and forced me to have a conversation with the shard."

I shuddered. That rock might've been creepier than the Revenant. Ry nodded with a grimace. "It didn't reveal much before emptying the room. However, it wasn't great, Nala spice. It confirmed I'm not entirely fae."

"Fuck," I muttered. "It said the same to me, blaming the tether with Vex. Did it say anything else?" I couldn't help but reach for my new ears, which were normal and fae, by the way.

"Only that you decide our fates," Ry answered. I rolled my eyes. "Y- You do," he insisted.

We fell into a comfortable quiet as I kicked my feet in the warm waters.

"I used to love traveling. It was my favorite activity for so long. When I wasn't jet setting, my life felt dull, but now, I know it's because Vex was there. My subconscious definitely made the connection," I forced out in a single breath. Ry's brows furrowed, so I explained, "All of that to say, traveling isn't the same. I feel at home here, on Neptune—" my voice cracked, the rawness of the warring emotions spilling over. "Why am I like this, Ry? Why am I so terrified of change when its only brought positives?"

"I- I..." He clenched his jaw, and I gave him a kiss on the cheek in conveyance to take his time. "I have a better question," he continued. "Why are you attempting to bottle up your feelings again? There were opportunities aplenty to mention your unease, and yet, you didn't utter a peep. Y- You waited until we fell asleep, then snuck downstairs to wallow alone." I gulped as Ryloh yanked my chin so I couldn't hide.

It took a few attempts to form the words under the intense scrutiny of his pretty mismatched eyes. "I didn't want to burden you, or them, further.

I'm enough of a hassle—" He interrupted me with a rumbly chuckle. "It's true," I tried.

"Th- That's crap and you know it. Do I need to wake the others to force the truth from you?"

I shook my head, feeling my cheeks burn. *He's right.* My voice shook pathetically as I whispered, "I'm *terrified*. Now. Earlier. The Revenant could've killed me a dozen times before heat struck. Timos would have a conniption if he knew. I don't want Jin to leave the job he loves more than anything and then potentially be ripped from us. I don't want to lose Vex either. I can't even begin to voice how the Queen and her obsession with you haunts me—"

Ryloh's lips silenced me. Similarly to our first time, I was shocked but fell right in. He tasted like the buttery popcorn from earlier, but when I tried to deepen the kiss, he annoyingly withdrew.

"I love you so much, you brat," he said, gripping my cheeks. I knew he did it to touch the tips of our new matching ears. "Qu- Quit worrying about me. Quit worrying for the others too, they'd go haggard if they knew. As for the vamps," his eyes darkened as a smirk crossed his lips, "you aren't defenseless, Nala spice. I'm not sure why you're acting as though you are. You breathe dragon fire. You could've likely broken the nullification from the Revenant if you knew how. We're going to teach you in Hell, that's why we're going."

It wasn't what I anticipated he'd say. I thought he'd say *he* would protect me. How no one could get past two gods, especially not Timoset Drago. Perhaps he'd placate me with some promise he couldn't keep. *Don't you know better though, Nala?*

Ryloh saw me for me. Always. Even when I couldn't seem to see myself clearly.

"Thank you." My view of his handsomeness blurred. Anxiety instantaneously replaced with overwhelming appreciation for him. "Thank you for believing in me when I didn't even consider it as an option. I love you, Ry." It'd been bothering me how I shared while Vex was there. "My love for you is so different. You know, I once thought you were the fun one, but I don't think that anymore."

"No?" he questioned, his thumbs wiping my tears as I clung to his middle.

I shook my head as much as his palms would allow. "I kinda think of you like the elements."

"Is that so?"

"Yeah, which is fitting that I control them all now. It's pretty rad," I said, smiling.

"Who's who?" He pondered, with an amused glint to his gaze.

"Jin is water, not only because he's a Cancer, but he's my emotional reflection. He's soft and easy going, but he can also flood and drown without much warning."

Ry *clucked* his tongue. "I should be the storm."

Shaking my head, I pressed forward, because Ryloh wouldn't want me to just speak about him as the others would. The Virgo needed confirmation of where he stood. "Timos is fire obviously. It's how passionate and protective he is."

"You mean possessive," he jibed.

"That too, and *potentially* destructive. Whereas Vex is my fresh air, he's easy to be around like breathing. And I literally bubble with happiness when he's smiling at me. I just—" My eyes blurred as I ran through what to say to the male who laid his heart at my feet for the last however long it's been. *Get it together!*

"You're my rock," I croaked.

His face fell, mismatched headlights narrowing. "It's t- terra."

"No, you're not earthy, Ryloh Cabbage. Stone is indestructible like your faith and understanding in me." The scowl was instantaneously replaced with a grin. Ry was far too attractive. It was sickening the way my entire lower half clenched as he gripped the back of my neck lovingly.

"Go on. Keep wooing me, Nala spice. Mention how my cock is as hard as stone, next."

"Yep, that too," I agreed, and he chuckled. "You're my unshakable foundation. It's you I need when something goes bad, Ry."

His eyes went boyishly wide, glistening as he took a hard swallow.

"You're crumbly, too. Sweet and funny at the same time. Plus, you make me fall to bits. I love you. So much that it scares me sometimes."

"The rock, Nala?" he feigned displeasure, but I *felt* his joy circling in the air.

"The rock, yeah. My constant. My strength. You never question what

I'm capable of. You've also never questioned my feelings for you even after I dragged you a bit. Which I'm sorry for, it wasn't my intent."

Our stupidly wide smiles mirrored as static buzzed at the surface of my skin.

"Thank you," I whispered. "Thank you for loving me so relentlessly, Ryloh."

He pulled me against his chest, saying, "I- I know my love isn't like the others, but at least I can properly care for you."

"I wouldn't trade you for anything. It's why you live directly in my heart, I think. What we share is more important than love. It's life."

"Mmm, I make you feel alive?" He murmured into my hair, and I nodded. "That's admittedly better than being a rock." I couldn't help but laugh.

When we pulled apart, and I glimpsed his eager silver eyes, a realization struck. Forcing words, I never thought would spew from my lips. "You're definitely going to make the best dad of the bunch. I don't think I'd even want a kid without you—"

Ryloh silenced me with another kiss. "Repeat it again, Nala spice. Right now."

"You're going to be the best dad," I emphasized. "That's not even something I would've ever said with glee before, you know."

"Am I your favorite today?" he questioned, that grin widening to a frightening extent.

There was no refusing him. Not like this. Not when his cheeks were flushed pink with happiness. It was the most carefree expression I'd ever witnessed on him. "Yes, Ry. You're my favorite today."

He didn't waste an instant, rifting us back to wake the others with the announcement.

Our final hours on Neptunian soil were slipping through my fingers like grains of sand. Timos and Vex were already long gone by the time we rose. Which left Jin and Ry with taking us back to their places to pack. Both only took minutes, not giving me any opportunity to snoop. Then we headed to the loft. There wasn't much to gather, my duffle only consisted of loungewear, hair- and skin-care. Jin downloaded my Homie onto a hard drive, so they could come with.

I was doing a final walk through when my scallop started vibrating. "What's up?" I said, answering Gabs' voice call.

"You're home! Would you wanna do lunch?" She questioned in a cheery tone. *How did she know?* My brows furrowed as Ryloh and Jin exchanged a perturbed glance.

//*"Seong does have a surveillance hobby."*/

I still required confirmation. "How'd you know I was back?"

"Seong led that meeting over the Revenant, *duh—*" I tuned Gabs' babbling out to shift my attention towards the others, both of whom were still frowning. --*"Why are y'all being weird? This is Gabs, my guide, sister-in-mate, superstitious pain in my ass, etc."*-

//" *We can never be too fecking cautious, spice."*/

--*"But it's Gabs? And after yesterday's fiasco I think we need some normalcy. It's also our last few hours on Neptune, it would be nice to enjoy them. We're done here anyway."*-

<<*"She's right, we're probably being too anal."*> *Jin relented with a brain sigh.*

I snorted, and the pair rolled their eyes.

"Are you there?" Gabs asked.

Scrambling, I replied, "Sure, we can have lunch."

"Yay! There's a new oceanfront place in Bahasa, I'll send you the address."

"Alright, see you around noon." Hanging up, I reminded them, "I know Timos and Vex are the big bad bodygods of our bunch, but y'all have gotta take a chill pill. We'll be fine going to lunch. I'm no longer killable—"

Ryloh scoffed. "There are worse experiences than death. We would rather you didn't validate the fact for yourself."

"I hoped after the Revenant you'd understand how dangerous our world is regardless of how prestigious you are," Jin said, whipping out his scallop. He started tapping away with his big khaki fingers. "I'm telling Timos and Avexei. Maybe they can get away for an hour—"

I smacked his phone out of his hands, and across the living room. Raising a pointer to scold, "No! Do not disturb them. They've dropped enough for me! They're helping innocents which is more important right now."

"If y- you feel as though our plans shouldn't be shared, th- th- then perhaps we shouldn't be going. I would rather not abandon the wards," Ryloh said with a serious expression. Rendering me speechless. *What the fuck's with the overprotectiveness today?*

"We're going," I commanded with a stomp of my foot. "The chances of another vamp attack are slim. You said it yourselves last night!" They grumbled, but eventually relented.

"I don't feel good about this," Jin said with a scratch to the back of his neck. We were walking through Bahasa's modern monochromatic streets, the restaurant was only five more minutes away, but they were continuing to panic. "Can I please just send Timos a text to let him know where we are?"

"Whatever," I relented. If the duo showed up now, at least they could join for the meal. Jin heaved a sigh in relief and texted the others with an inhuman speed.

Ryloh slung an arm over my shoulders and tucked me into his side, whispering, "You're being a brat again. Have you forgotten what happens when y- you're naughty? Do you require a reminder?" His taunting liquefied my insides as a delicious shudder coursed through my bones.

"Nala, maybe we shouldn't," Jin said, wearing a weary expression as his plum eyes pleaded. "Timos is pissed."

As if on cue, the dragon's growl filled our brains. [["I am fucking livid you abandoned the wards for something so trivial. Gabriela could have come to the apartment."]

"He's right, y- you kn- know," Ryloh chirped. "Perhaps we should make rearrangements."

"I needed out of the house. This is our last hurrah on Neptune. It's going to be fine. Everyone breathe. *Woo-sah*. We're relocating to safety in mere hours."

::"I'm sure it'll be fine, just don't stay long.": It was unsurprising that Vex gave in. I flung up my arms in a 'there you have it' motion as Jin and Ry rolled their eyes in sync.

As we approached the glass ocean front venue, Whakamutunga Canteen, several ominous clouds rolled in. It hadn't rained once since my arrival, which was why I asked the pair, "How often does it rain?"

"Almost never," Jin replied, his eyes narrowed at the purply clouds, as if they might attack us next.

We ambled through the modern entrance, finding minimal décor focused on the view. The hostess led to a patio which extended over the ocean, to where Gabs was already seated, eyes glued to her orange phone. I slid in beside her, while the others took our opposite.

When reaching for a hug, our typical greeting—

She bit my neck!

What in the—?

She withdrew with a yelp of horror and wide eyes.

I was pouring like a spout with my jaw hanging wide.

Jin had never moved faster, he had Gabs in a headlock as my blood dripped from her *fangs*. Ryloh and I gasped in unison. *She's a vamp! Holy shit!*

Thankfully, I healed in seconds, but still.

"I'm sorry," Gabs cried, her brown eyes now laser beam red. "You smelled so tempting since binding yourself to them!"

My tongue nearly fell out of my mouth from shock.

I rose from my chair, gripping onto Ryloh who clawed into my ribs as though I might disappear. "L- Let her go, Jin. We should get back. Screw this."

"You won't make it!" Gabs' yell was paired with her pointing out toward the waves. Where we found an entire fucking army closing in. Winged vamps. Floating drifting vamps. A huge ass black dragon, which might've been larger than Timos.

"I tried to warn you with the tarot reading, Nala! I'm so fucking sorry! I didn't have a choice!"

Proclaiming innocence? That's rich.

"Y- Y- You're telling us, you did not only just bite my soulmate, but y-you got us ambushed, Gabriela?" Ryloh roared, causing all the surrounding tables to empty. At least they had a chance to flee. Which was when I started yelling bloody murder in attempt to save as many innocents as I could. They were heeding since the Revenant appearance yesterday. *Fuck, that was yesterday—*

Nope! Worry about it later, Nala!

<<*"We have to get you out of here, love."*> Rifting wasn't an option. Even if we could. There would be too many losses. All of their deaths because of us. I couldn't live with it, shaking my head fiercely, I planted my feet firmly.

"We can't, there's too many innocents! We can't abandon them when they're only attacking because of me."

Jin growled in frustration, inadvertently shaking Gabs, who croaked, "I didn't have a choice, okay? It's not as if Nala can die!"

"Does Seong know you're fucking working for Malice?!"

Before Gabs could reply, the floating robes closed in. They were all wingless, but soaring overhead, circling. Too quickly to discern their features because of their hoods. Lightning struck the concrete a foot from where Ry and I stood, sending me shrieking.

Then rain pelted, in buckets, pouring over our heads as the waves became angrier.

When I tried accessing my gifts, they were gone. Including the male's voices. The three of us exchanged a worried glance. My panic from yesterday resurfaced with a vengeance because it wasn't just Revenants up there. There had to be Wraiths from how a handful slipped right through the wall of windows. They were more focused on the fleeing crowd than where we statued.

"I love you, Jin. I love you, Ry," I choked out, tears blurring my vision. It felt like the end.

'There are worse fates than death,' rang through my mind in Ry's voice unbidden.

"D- D- Don't you dare give up already," Ryloh clawed my shoulders with a scowl. Jin had released Gabs to furiously tap on his phone, and she —*somehow*— rifted to safety. *Go figure. The fucking traitor.*

You can worry about her payback later!

My eyes flicked back to the waves. Thankfully, Osri and Persis intercepted the darker dragon before it could catch up to the rest. The two smaller blues, tackling the enormous black into the gloomy depths. However, there were at least a hundred flappers with bat wings gaining on us.

"We have to fucking run!" Jin shoved us back into the restaurant, to where blood had exploded. The floors were flooded in red. Screams rattled my eardrums as we pushed through the packed entrance.

We didn't make it far.

There was a line of Revenants waiting in the street. Claws extended. Capes billowing in the rain. The surroundings were a chaotic slaughter. Red streaking the rainwaters. Shouts overwhelmed the booms of thunder.

It was definitely war.

It was like the surrounding scene was playing on fast forward as I attempted to process our options. Except...

There weren't any.

Ryloh was ripped away from me. He went limp in the Revenant's arms before a grin sliced its wicked, misshapen face and they rifted with my fae in tow. My scream tore through my vocal cords.

I couldn't react.

I couldn't breathe.

I couldn't *think*.

Then Jin was taken. Except, they apparently didn't have any use for him, his body was tossed over an enormous shoulder.

I was surrounded on all sides. Caged in. Which was coincidentally when my fury decided to join the party.

When have you ever given up without a fight?

Never.

As the monstrous Revenants snickered in haunting scratchy tones, thinking they'd already won, I managed to kick the pair clawing into my arms where their privates likely resided. Thankfully, my immortal strength was still intact, and they immediately crumpled.

I kicked and punched. Faces, thighs, necks. Whatever within reach. The growls leaving my lips from every exhalation were terrifyingly inhuman.

My efforts were futile, though.

They kept coming. Each time a Revenant went down, another appeared in its place. When the Wraiths joined the huddle, I was done for. Revenants were scary, sure, but cuddly when compared to a Wraith. Their features were rotted like red zombies.

Don't even get me started on the decaying stench of their breath.

"Get the fuck off," I cried, attempting to dodge the translucent clawed salad fingers reaching for me. "*Argh!*" They sliced right through. Skin. Muscle. Bone. Half of my wrist hung by a tendon.

The memory of Ryloh's limp form being taken filled my vision.

You're fucking weak.

Pathetic.

Useless.

It was my last thought before a glittery foul scented puff hit my face and rendered me unconscious.

To be continued…

WHAKAMUTUNGA CANTEEN, BAHASA
Hidden Recording Device Transcript
12:34PM

Drywall collapses.

Glass shatters.

Avexeidros Drago: "Finally! What the—"

Yu-Jin Drago: "They fucking took Nala!"

Roar.

Timoset Drago: "Who?! Malice?!"

Avexeidros Drago: "Is that why our mental link was muddled?"

Growl.

Timoset Drago: "How could you?!"

Avexeidros Drago: "Calm down, Mo. We knew Malice would try something. It's not Jin's fault."

Yu-Jin Drago: "It was Gabs! I can hardly believe it; she took a bite —"

Roar.

Avexeidros Drago: "Gabs is a fucking bloodsucker?!"

Yu-Jin Drago: "Apparently! It all seemed coordinated by her. She's been working for Malice. There was an entire army, your brother came, the black dragon. I can't believe they only came for Nala. They'd taken me out with death breath, I awoke as they rifted her to fuck knows where."

Hiss.

Avexeidros Drago: "We should've known that fucktart, Dmitrios, would show."

Timoset Drago: "Where is Ryloh? I can no longer sense him either."

Yu-Jin Drago: "They took him first."

Avexeidros Drago: "Did they splice him? Is he alive?"

Yu-Jin Drago: "I don't fucking know!"

Timoset Drago: "If Ryloh perishes, Nala will never forgive us."

Yu-Jin Drago: "Trust me, I'm well aware!"

Rock smashes.

Yu-Jin Drago: "I hoped this destruction would help."

Glass shatters.

Yu-Jin Drago: "But it hasn't. I won't feel sated until the galaxy's shredded."

Avexeidros Drago: "We're gonna get her back. It's just a question of how. Where do you think they took her? Chiron seems too on the nose."

Ring.

Avexeidros Drago: "Who are you calling?"

Ring.

Timoset Drago: "My father. He will have felt where they took her. Nala is far too prestigious to not be felt crossing between planets or realms."

Galactic fizzle.

Athanatos Drago: "Mo?"

Timoset Drago: "Father, did you feel Nala? Dmitrios and Malice ran off with her and Ryloh. Are they on Chiron or elsewhere?"

Galactic fizzle.

Athanatos Drago: "I hoped it was a fluke. Your mother and I only felt them for a second before the Realm was sealed by that damned tyrant."

Avexeidros Drago: "Where the fuck is she, Uncle Atha?!"

Galactic fizzle.

Athanatos Drago: "Realm X."

Timoset Drago: "Shit."

Avexeidros Drago: "That's where the Stardust mines are. She sealed it?"

Galactic fizzle.

Athanatos Drago: "The Council arranged for four of your siblings to break the seal, you may as well join. They depart within the hour."

Timoset Drago: "Alright, see you shortly."

Click.

Yu-Jin Drago: "You're going to have to go without me."

Timoset Drago: "Absolutely not!"

Yu-Jin Drago: "You have to. I have a ton of surveillance footage to hack into, then review. I'm more useful here. How else will we keep an eye on my brother and Gabs? Who's to say he didn't help orchestrate? He despises the Queen."

Avexeidros Drago: "*Mmm,* kinda. Seong backs a lot of her terrible ideas. They're frenemies."

Timoset Drago: "Frenemies?"

Avexeidros Drago: "Friends who remain close but squabble often. Seong is in league with her I think."

Yu-Jin Drago: "I know it was blood Gabs and Seong were concealing in their scent now. The pieces are falling into place. Not sure what that means for your mother, but…"

Avexeidros Drago: "Fuck, you think Seong's a leech, too?"

Yu-Jin Drago: "Maybe. Plus, I don't know how to use any of my new prestige. I haven't resigned from being duke yet. There's something bigger at play, how else will we figure it out?"

Timoset Drago: "I suppose this will test the limits of our mind-meld."

Heavy sigh.

Avexeidros Drago: "At least Nala won't die… Damnit, Lo-Lo. If he dies from splicing, I'll never forgive myself for insisting you go to this stupid fucking meal. I still can't believe it was a trap."

Yu-Jin Drago: "Imagine how I feel."

Timoset Drago: "Kindly shut the fuck up. Both of you. Now is not the time. Naliti and Ryloh require our focus, not tears. No goodbyes either. We shall soon reunite. All of us. I refuse to accept anything less."

Portal opening.

Avexeidros Drago: *"Sheesh*, Mo. Alright, give me a hug at least, Jin-Jin."

Yu-Jin Drago: "Get them back. Please fucking get them both back."

Timoset Drago: "We shall."

END OF TRANSCRIPT

ACKNOWLEDGMENTS

Thank you so much for giving this debut indie author a chance!

This book wouldn't have been possible without the many hands who helped create it...

- To Silvia, my illustrator, thank you for taking a chance on this baby author and bringing each of the characters to life so beautifully.
- To Annie, my editor, who ensured this story was the best it could possibly be. You're stuck with me for the next four incoming PPP series [and probably more]!
- To my army of betas, ARC, and sensitivity readers, thank you SO much for being a critical part of this journey.
- And last, but not least, to every single one of my lovely readers, I'm SO sorry for the cliff!

Book II, Splice and Sacrifice, is available to pre-order for May 2025, but might be coming sooner.

If you can't wait for what's next, there will be access to exclusive bonus chapters if you sign up for my newsletter.

<3 Until next time!